GRAND CENTRAL
PUBLISHING

LARGE PRINT

NICHOLAS SPARKS

THE WISH

GRAND CENTRAL
PUBLISHING

LARGE PRINT

Copyright © 2021 by Willow Holdings, Inc.

Cover design by Flag. Cover art by Tom Hallman. Cover photos: fireworks and background image © Getty Images.
Cover copyright © 2021 by Hachette Book Group, Inc.

Grand Central Publishing
Hachette Book Group
1290 Avenue of the Americas, New York, NY 10104
grandcentralpublishing.com
twitter.com/grandcentralpub

First Edition: September 2021

Grand Central Publishing is a division of Hachette Book Group, Inc. The Grand Central Publishing name and logo is a trademark of Hachette Book Group, Inc.

The publisher is not responsible for websites (or their content) that are not owned by the publisher.

The Hachette Speakers Bureau provides a wide range of authors for speaking events. To find out more, go to www.hachettespeakersbureau.com or call (866) 376-6591.

Library of Congress Cataloging-in-Publication Data

Names: Sparks, Nicholas, author.
Title: The wish / Nicholas Sparks.
Description: First edition. | New York : Grand Central Publishing, 2021.
Identifiers: LCCN 2021023037 | ISBN 9781538728628 (hardcover) |
ISBN 9781538706152 (large print) | ISBN 9781538728611 (ebook)
Classification: LCC PS3569.P363 W57 2021 | DDC 813/.54—dc23
LC record available at https://lccn.loc.gov/2021023037

ISBNs: 978-1-5387-2862-8 (hardcover), 978-1-5387-2861-1 (ebook),
978-1-5387-0615-2 (large print), 978-1-5387-0948-1 (signed hardcover),
978-1-5387-0949-8 (B&N signed hardcover), 978-1-5387-0883-5 (trade pbk. intl.)

Printed in the United States of America

LSC-C

Printing 1, 2021

For Pam Pope and Oscara Stevick

ACKNOWLEDGMENTS

This year marks my twenty-fifth anniversary as a published author—a milestone I certainly couldn't have imagined when I first held a copy of *The Notebook* in my hands. At the time, I honestly didn't know if I'd ever come up with a good story idea again, much less whether I would be able to support myself and my family on a writer's earnings.

The fact that I've been able to keep doing what I love for a quarter of a century is a testament to the brilliant and stalwart group of supporters who advise, celebrate, nag, comfort, strategize, and advocate on my behalf 24/7. Many of them have been by my side for decades. Take Theresa Park, for example: we met in our twenties, worked maniacally through our thirties and forties while raising families and making movies together, and are now trying to live wisely and productively in our fifties. We are friends, partners, and fellow travelers on the road of life, our relationship having weathered countless highs and lows in careers that have never, ever been dull.

I've known the entire team at Park & Fine for so long that I can hardly imagine publishing a book or marketing a film without them. They are without question the most knowledgeable, sophisticated, intrepid group of publishing representatives in the industry—Abigail Koons, Emily Sweet, Alexandra Greene, Andrea Mai, Pete Knapp, Ema Barnes, and Fiona Furnari bring excellence and expertise to everything they do on the fiction side; their colleagues who work in the world of nonfiction are every bit their equal. Celeste, I was thrilled to get to know you when you combined forces with Theresa—and could tell right away why you two were such a perfect fit!

Grand Central Publishing continues to be my home, all these years on. And although the faces have changed throughout the decades, the ethos of decency, kindness, and partnership with authors has been a constant. Michael Pietsch has led the company through countless evolutions and challenges with integrity and strategic foresight; publisher Ben Sevier has been a wonderful manager and architect of an evolving business; and editor in chief Karen Kosztolnyik has proven to be a gentle and encouraging champion of my work, rigorous and yet respectful with her editorial pen. Brian McLendon, your unflagging efforts to reinvent the look and messaging of my books, year after year, deserve an award—my team loves your irrepressible enthusiasm, which, along with the indefatigable Amanda Pritzker's efforts, keeps my books front of mind and perpetually ripe for discovery. Beth de Guzman, you are among the few people who have been with my publisher since the very first book, and your tireless work to keep my backlist fresh and appealing is one of the secrets to my success. Matthew Ballast is the Zen master of author publicity, soft-spoken and unflappable, and his colleague Staci Burt is the savvy, responsive publicist who fears neither COVID, unpredictable tour schedules, nor cranky authors. And to art director Albert Tang and my longtime cover designer Flag: you guys are geniuses, managing to surprise me with striking, beautiful covers year after year.

Catherine Olim deserves a medal of valor for all of the crises she's defused and the generous publicity she's garnered for my work— a plainspoken, fearless coach and warrior, she is never afraid to give me tips on my on-screen performances or protect me from unfair critics. LaQuishe "Q" Wright is the absolute star of the social media world, with instincts, relationships, and strategic savvy unparalleled in that mercurial and rapidly changing world. She loves her work, and her star-studded client roster benefits from her passion. Mollie Smith, is there a designer and fan outreach expert with a better feel for design AND audiences? You are the whole package and, together with Q, have always steered my public outreach with deft assurance.

My longtime Hollywood representative,

Howie Sanders of Anonymous Content, has been my wise advisor and deeply loyal friend for decades. I treasure his advice and admire his integrity; after everything we have been through together, my trust in him is complete. Scott Schwimer has been my relentless (yet charming!) advocate and negotiator for twenty-five years, and he's definitely seen it all—he knows me and the ins and outs of my career like few others, and he is an invaluable member of my close-knit brain trust.

In my personal life, I have been blessed with a circle of friends and family whose love and support I can rely on each and every day. In no particular order, I'd like to thank Pat and Bill Mills; the Thoene clan, which includes Mike, Parnell, Matt, Christie, Dan, Kira, Amanda, and Nick; the Sparks clan, including Dianne, Chuck, Monte, Gail, Sandy, Todd, Elizabeth, Sean, Adam, Nathan, and Josh; and finally Bob, Debbie, & Cody and Cole Lewis. I'd also like to acknowledge the following friends, all of whom mean so much to me: Victoria Vodar; Jonathan and Stephanie Arnold; Todd and Gretchen Lanman; Kim and Eric Belcher; Lee, Sandy, and Max Minshull; Adriana Lima; David and Morgan Shara; David Geffen; Jeannie and Pat Armentrout; Tia and Brandon Shaver; Christie Bonacci; Drew and Brittany Brees; Buddy and Wendy Stallings; John and Stephanie Zannis; Jeanine Kaspar; Joy Lenz; Dwight Carlbom; David Wang; Missy Blackerby; Ken Gray; John Hawkins and Michael Smith; the Van Wie family (Jeff, Torri, Ana, Audrey, and Ava); Jim Tyler; Chris Matteo; Rick Muench; Paul du Vair; Bob Jacob; Eric Collins; and last but not least, my wonderful children who mean the world to me. Miles, Ryan, Landon, Lexie, and Savannah—I love you all.

THE WISH

'TIS THE SEASON

Manhattan
December 2019

Whenever December rolled around, Manhattan transformed itself into a city that Maggie didn't always recognize. Tourists thronged the shows on Broadway and flooded the sidewalks outside department stores in Midtown, forming a slow-moving river of pedestrians. Boutiques and restaurants overflowed with shoppers clutching bags, Christmas music filtered from hidden speakers, and hotel lobbies sparkled with decorations. The Rockefeller Center Christmas tree was lit by multicolored bulbs and the flashes of thousands of iPhones, and crosstown traffic, never speedy in the best of times, became so jammed up that it was often quicker to walk than to take a cab. But walking had its own challenges; frigid wind frequently whipped between the buildings, necessitating thermal underwear, plentiful fleece, and jackets zipped to the collars.

Maggie Dawes, who considered herself a free spirit consumed by wanderlust, had always loved the *idea* of a New York Christmas, albeit in a *look how pretty* postcard kind of way. In reality, like a lot of New Yorkers, she did her best to avoid Midtown during the holidays. Instead, she either stayed close to her home in Chelsea or, more commonly, fled to warmer climes. As a travel photographer, she sometimes thought of herself less as a New Yorker and more as a nomad who happened to have a permanent address in the city. In a notebook she kept in the drawer of her nightstand, she'd compiled a list of more than a hundred places she still wanted to visit, some of them so obscure or remote that even reaching them would be a challenge.

Since dropping out of college twenty years ago, she'd been adding to the list, noting places that sparked her imagination for one reason or another even as her travels enabled her to cross out other destinations. With a camera slung over her shoulder, she'd visited every continent, more than eighty-two countries, and forty-three of the fifty states. She'd taken tens of thousands of photographs, from images of wildlife in the Okavango Delta in Botswana to shots of the aurora borealis in Lapland. There were photographs taken as she'd hiked the Inca Trail, others from the Skeleton Coast in Namibia, still more among the ruins of Timbuktu. Twelve years ago, she'd learned to scuba dive and had spent ten days documenting marine life in Raja Ampat; four years ago, she'd hiked to the famous Paro Taktsang, or Tiger's Nest, a Buddhist monastery built into a cliffside in Bhutan with panoramic views of the Himalayas.

Others had often marveled at her adventures, but she'd learned that *adventure* is a word with many connotations, not all of them good. A case in point was the adventure she was on now—that's how she sometimes described it to her Instagram followers and YouTube subscribers—the one that kept her largely confined to either her gallery or her small two-bedroom apartment on West Nine-teenth Street, instead of venturing to more exotic locales. The same adventure that led to occasional thoughts of suicide.

Oh, she'd never actually do it. The thought terrified her, and she'd admitted as much in one of the many videos she'd created for YouTube. For almost ten years, her videos had been rather ordinary as far as photographers' posts went; she'd described her decision-making process when taking pictures, offered numerous Photoshop tutorials, and reviewed new cameras and their many accessories, usually posting two or three times a month. Those YouTube videos, in addition to her Instagram posts and Facebook pages and the blog on her website, had always been popular with photography geeks while also burnishing her professional reputation.

Three and a half years ago, however, on a whim, she'd posted a video to her YouTube channel about her recent diagnosis, one that had nothing to do with photography. The video, a rambling, unfiltered description of the fear and uncertainty she suddenly felt when she learned she had stage IV melanoma, probably shouldn't have been posted at all. But what she imagined would be a lonely voice echoing back at her from the empty reaches of the internet somehow managed to catch the attention of others. She wasn't sure why or how, but that video—of all the ones she'd ever posted—had attracted a trickle, then a steady stream, and finally a deluge of views, comments, questions, and upvotes from people who had never heard of her or her work as a photographer. Feeling as though she had to respond to those who'd been moved by her plight, she'd posted another video regarding her diagnosis that became even more popular. Since then, about once a month, she'd continued to post videos in the same vein, mainly because she felt she had no choice but to continue. In the past three years, she'd discussed various treatments and how they'd made her feel, sometimes even displaying the scars from her surgery. She talked about radiation burns and nausea and hair loss and wondered openly about the meaning of life. She mused about her fear of dying and speculated on the possibility of an afterlife. They were serious issues, but maybe to stave off her own depression when discussing such a miserable subject, she did her best to keep the videos as light in tone as possible. She supposed that was part of the reason for their popularity, but who really knew? The only certainty was that somehow, almost reluctantly, she'd become the star of her own reality web series, one that had begun with hope but had slowly narrowed to focus on a single inevitable ending.

And—perhaps unsurprisingly—as the grand finale approached, her viewership exploded even more.

In the first *Cancer Video*—that's how she mentally referred to them, as opposed to her *Real Videos*—she stared into the camera with a wry grin and said, "Right off the bat, I hated it. Then it started growing on me."

She knew it was probably in poor taste to joke about her illness, but the whole thing struck her as absurd. *Why her?* At the time, she was thirty-six years old, she exercised regularly, and she followed a reasonably healthy diet. There was no history of cancer in her family. She'd grown up in cloudy Seattle and lived in Manhattan, which ruled out a history of sunbathing. She'd never visited a tanning salon. None of it made any sense, but that was the point about cancer, wasn't it? Cancer didn't discriminate; it just happened to the unlucky, and after a while she'd finally accepted that the better question was really *Why NOT her?* She wasn't special; to that point in her life, there'd been times when she considered herself interesting or intelligent or even pretty, but the word *special* had never entered her mind.

When she'd received her diagnosis, she would have sworn she was in perfect health. A month earlier, she'd visited Vaadhoo Island in the Maldives, on a photo shoot for Condé Nast. She'd traveled there hoping to capture the bioluminescence just offshore that made ocean waves glow like starlight, as if lit from within. Sea plankton was responsible for the spectral, spectacular light, and she'd allotted extra time to shoot some images for personal use, perhaps for eventual sale in her gallery.

She was scouting a mostly empty beach near her hotel in midafternoon with a camera in hand, trying to envision the shot she aimed to take once evening descended. She wanted to capture a hint of the shoreline—with perhaps a boulder in the foreground—the sky, and, of course, the waves just as they were cresting. She'd spent more than an hour taking different shots from different angles and various locations on the beach when a couple strolled past her, holding hands. Lost in her work, she barely registered their presence.

A few moments later, while scanning the line where the waves were breaking offshore through her viewfinder, she heard the woman's voice behind her. She spoke English, but with a distinctly German accent.

"Excuse me," the woman said. "I can see that you're busy and I am sorry to bother you."

Maggie lowered her camera. "Yes?"

"It's a little difficult to say this, but have you had that dark spot on the back of your shoulder examined?"

Maggie frowned, trying without success to see the spot between the straps of her bathing suit that the woman was referring to. "I didn't know I had a dark spot there..." She squinted at the woman in confusion. "And why are you so interested?"

The woman, fiftyish with short gray hair, nodded. "I should perhaps introduce myself. I'm Dr. Sabine Kessel," she said. "I'm a dermatologist in Munich. The spot looks abnormal."

Maggie blinked. "You mean like cancer?"

"I don't know," the woman said, her expression cautious. "But if I were you, I'd have it examined as soon as possible. It could be nothing, of course."

Or it could be serious, Dr. Kessel didn't have to add.

Though it took five nights to achieve what she wanted from the shoot, Maggie was pleased with the raw files. She would work on them extensively in digital postproduction— the real art in photography these days almost always emerged in post—but she already knew the results would be spectacular. In the meantime, and though she tried not to worry about it, she also made an appointment with Dr. Snehal Khatri, a dermatologist on the

Upper East Side, four days after her return to the city.

The spot was biopsied in early July 2016, and afterward she was sent for additional testing. She had MRI and PET scans done at Memorial Sloan Kettering hospital later that same month. After the results had come in, Dr. Khatri sat her down in the examination room, where he quietly and seriously informed her that she had stage IV melanoma. Later that day, she was introduced to an oncologist named Leslie Brodigan, who would oversee her care. In the aftermath of these meetings, Maggie did her own research on the internet. Though Dr. Brodigan had told her that general statistics meant very little when it came to predicting outcomes for a particular individual, Maggie couldn't help fixating on the numbers. The survival rate after five years for those diagnosed with stage IV melanoma, she learned, was less than fifteen percent.

In stunned disbelief, Maggie made her first *Cancer Video* the following day.

At her second appointment, Dr. Brodigan—
a vibrant blue-eyed blonde who seemed to
personify the term *good health*—explained
everything about her condition again, since
the whole process had been so overwhelming
that Maggie could remember only bits and
pieces of their first meeting. Essentially, having stage IV melanoma meant that the cancer
had metastasized not only to distant lymph
nodes but to some of her other organs as
well, in her case both her liver and her stomach. The MRI and PET scans had found the
cancerous growths invading healthier parts
of her body like an army of ants devouring
food laid out on a picnic table.

Long story short: The next three and a half
years were a blur of treatment and recovery,
with occasional flashes of hope illuminating
dark tunnels of anxiety. She had surgery to
remove her infected lymph nodes and the
metastases in her liver and stomach. The surgery was followed by radiation, which was
excruciating, turning her skin black in places

and leaving behind nasty scars to go with the ones she'd collected in the operating room. She also learned there were different kinds of melanoma, even for those with stage IV, which led to different treatment options. In her case, that meant immunotherapy, which seemed to work for a couple of years, until it finally didn't. Then, last April, she had begun chemotherapy and continued it for months, hating how it made her feel but convinced that it had to be effective. How could it not work, she wondered, since it seemed to be killing every other part of her? These days, she barely recognized herself in the mirror. Food nearly always tasted too bitter or too salty, which made it hard to eat, and she'd dropped more than twenty pounds from her already petite frame. Her oval-shaped brown eyes now appeared sunken and oversize above her protruding cheekbones, her face more like skin stretched over a skull. She was always cold and wore thick sweaters even in her overheated apartment. She'd lost all her dark brown hair, only to see it slowly grow back in patches, lighter in color and as fine as a baby's; she'd taken to wearing a kerchief or hat almost all the time. Her neck had become so spindly and fragile-looking that she wrapped it in a scarf to avoid glimpsing it in mirrors.

A little more than a month ago, at the beginning of November, she had undergone another round of CAT and PET scans, and in December, she'd met again with Dr. Brodigan. The doctor had been more subdued than usual, although her eyes brimmed with compassion. There, she'd told Maggie that while more than three years of treatment had slowed the disease at times, its progression had never quite stopped. When Maggie asked what other treatment options were available, the doctor had gently turned her attention to the quality of the life Maggie had remaining.

It was her way of telling Maggie that she was going to die.

Maggie had opened the gallery more than nine years ago with another artist named

Trinity, who used most of the space for his giant and eclectic sculptures. Trinity's real name was Fred Marshburn and they'd met at an opening for another artist's show, the kind of event Maggie seldom attended. Trinity was already wildly successful at that point and had long toyed with the idea of opening his own gallery; he didn't, however, have any desire to actually manage the gallery, nor did he want to spend any time there. Because they'd hit it off, and because her photographs in no way competed with his work, they'd eventually made a deal. In exchange for her managing the business of the gallery, she would earn a modest salary and could also display a selection of her own work. At the time, it was more about prestige—she could tell people she had her own gallery!—than it was about the money Trinity paid her. In the first year or two, she sold only a few prints of her own.

Because Maggie was still traveling extensively at the time—more than a hundred days a year, on average—the actual day-to-day running of the gallery fell to a woman named Luanne Sommers. When Maggie hired her,

Luanne was a wealthy divorcée with grown children. Her experience was limited to an amateur's passion for collecting and an expert's eye for finding bargains at Neiman Marcus. On the plus side, she dressed well; she was responsible, conscientious, and willing to learn; and she had no qualms about the fact that she'd earn little more than minimum wage. As she put it, her alimony was enough to allow her to retire in luxury, but there were only so many lunches a woman could do without going crazy.

Luanne turned out to be a natural at sales. In the beginning, Maggie had briefed her on the technical elements of all of her prints, as well as the story behind each particular shot, which was often as interesting to buyers as the image itself. Trinity's sculptures, which utilized assorted materials—canvas, metal, plastic, glue, and paint, in addition to items collected from junkyards, deer antlers, pickle jars, and cans—were original enough to inspire spirited discussion. He was already an established critical darling, and his pieces moved regularly despite their staggering prices. But the gallery didn't advertise or feature many guest artists, so the work itself was fairly low-key. There were days when only a handful of people entered the premises, and they were able to close the gallery the last three weeks of the year. It was—for Maggie, Trinity, and Luanne—an arrangement that worked well for a long time.

But two things happened to change all that. First, Maggie's *Cancer Videos* lured new people to the gallery. Not the usual seasoned contemporary art or photography enthusiasts, but tourists from places like Tennessee and Ohio, people who'd begun to follow Maggie on Instagram and YouTube because they felt a connection to her. Some of them had become actual fans of her photography, but a lot of them simply wanted to meet her or buy one of her signed prints as a keepsake. The phone began to ring off the hook with orders from random locations around the country, and additional orders poured in through the website. It was all Maggie and Luanne could do to keep up, and last year, they'd made the decision to keep the gallery open through the holidays because the crowds kept coming. Then Maggie learned she'd soon have to begin chemotherapy, which meant she wouldn't be able to help at the gallery for months. It was clear that they needed to hire an additional employee, and when Maggie broached the subject with Trinity, he agreed on the spot. As fate would have it, the following day, a young man named Mark Price walked into the gallery and asked to speak with her, an event that at the time struck her as almost too good to be true.

Mark Price was a recent college graduate who could have passed for a high schooler. Maggie initially assumed he was another "cancer groupie," but she was only partially correct. He admitted he had become familiar with her work through her popular online presence—he was especially fond of her videos, he volunteered—but he'd also come in with a résumé. He explained that he was looking for employment and the idea of working in the art world strongly appealed to him. Art and photography, he'd added, allowed for the communication of new ideas, often in ways that words did not.

Despite her misgivings about hiring a fan, Maggie sat down with him the same day, and it became clear that he'd done his homework. He knew a great deal about Trinity and his work; he mentioned a specific installation that was currently on display at MoMA and another at the New School, drawing comparisons to some of Robert Rauschenberg's later work in a knowledgeable but unpretentious way. Though it didn't surprise her, he also had a deep and impressive familiarity with her own body of work. And yet, though he'd answered all her questions satisfactorily, she remained a little uneasy; she couldn't quite figure out whether he was serious about his desire to work in a gallery, or just another person who wanted to witness her own tragedy up close.

As their meeting drew to a close, she told him that they weren't currently interviewing—though technically true, it was only a matter of time—to which he responded by asking politely whether she would nonetheless be willing to receive his résumé. It was, she thought in retrospect, the way he'd phrased his request that charmed her. *"Would you nonetheless be willing to receive my résumé?"* It struck her as old-fashioned and courtly and she couldn't help smiling as she held out her hand for the document.

Later that same week, Maggie had uploaded a job posting to some art-related industry sites and called several contacts at other galleries, letting them know she was hiring. Résumés and inquiries flooded the inbox and Luanne met with six candidates while Maggie, either nauseated or vomiting from her first infusion, recuperated at home. Only one candidate made it past the first interview, but when she didn't show up for the second, she was scratched as well. Frustrated, Luanne visited Maggie at home to update her. Maggie hadn't left her apartment in days and was lying on the couch, sipping the fruit-and-ice-cream smoothie Luanne had brought with her, one of the few things Maggie could still force down.

"It's hard to believe we can't find anyone

qualified to work in the gallery." Maggie shook her head.

"They have no experience and don't know anything about art," Luanne huffed.

Neither did you, Maggie could have pointed out, but she remained silent, fully aware that Luanne had turned out to be a treasure as both a friend and an employee, the luckiest of breaks. Warm and unflappable, Luanne had long ago ceased being a mere colleague.

"I trust your judgment, Luanne. We'll just start over."

"Are you sure there wasn't anyone else in the pool worth meeting?" Luanne's tone was plaintive.

For whatever reason, Maggie's mind flashed to Mark Price, inquiring ever so politely whether she would be willing to receive his résumé.

"You're smiling," Luanne said.

"No, I'm not."

"I know a smile when I see one. What were you just thinking about?"

Maggie took another sip of the smoothie, buying time, until finally deciding to come out with it. "A young man came in before we listed the position," she admitted, before proceeding to describe the meeting. "I'm still not sure about him," she concluded, "but his résumé is probably somewhere on my desk in the office." She shrugged. "I don't know if he's even available at this point."

When Luanne probed the origins of Mark's interest in the job, she frowned. Luanne understood the makeup of the gallery crowds better than anyone and recognized that people who'd seen Maggie's videos often viewed her as their confidante, someone who would both empathize and sympathize. They frequently longed to share their own stories, the suffering they had endured, and the losses. And as much as Maggie wanted to offer them comfort, it was often too much to support them emotionally when she felt like she was barely holding it together herself. Luanne did her best to shield her from the more aggressive contact seekers.

"Let me review his résumé and I'll speak with him," she said. "After that, we'll take it one step at a time."

Luanne contacted Mark the following

week. Their first conversation led to two more formal interviews, including one with Trinity. When she later spoke with Maggie, her praise for Mark was effusive, but Maggie insisted on meeting with him again, just to be certain. It took four more days before she had the energy to make it to the gallery. Mark Price was on time, dressed in a suit and holding a slim binder as he stepped into her office. She felt sick as a dog as she studied his résumé, noting that he was from Elkhart, Indiana, and when she saw his graduation date from Northwestern, she did a quick mental calculation.

"You're twenty-two years old?"

"Yes."

With his neatly parted hair, blue eyes, and baby face, he looked like a well-groomed teenager, ready for the prom. "And you majored in theology?"

"I did," he said.

"Why theology?"

"My father is a pastor," he said. "Eventually I want to get a master's in divinity as well. To follow in his footsteps."

As soon as he said it, she realized it didn't surprise her in the slightest. "Then why the interest in art if you intend to go into the ministry?"

He brought his fingertips together, as though wanting to choose his words with care. "I've always believed that art and faith have much in common. Both allow people to explore the subtlety of their own emotions and to find their own answers as to what the art represents to them. Your work and Trinity's always make me *think*, and more importantly, they make me *feel* in ways that often lead to a sense of wonder. Just like faith."

It was a good answer, but she nonetheless suspected that Mark was leaving something out. Setting those thoughts aside, Maggie continued with the interview, asking more standard questions about his work history and knowledge of photography and contemporary sculpture before finally leaning back in her chair.

"Why do you think you'd be a good fit for the gallery?"

He seemed unfazed by her grilling. "For starters, having met Ms. Sommers, I have the sense that she and I would work well together. With her permission, I spent some time in the gallery after our interview, and after a bit of additional research, I put together some of my thoughts about the work currently on display." He leaned forward, offering her the binder. "I've left a copy with Ms. Sommers as well."

Maggie thumbed through the binder. Stopping on a random page, she perused a couple of paragraphs he'd written concerning a photograph she'd taken in Djibouti in 2011, when the country was mired in one of the worst droughts in decades. In the foreground were the skeletal remains of a camel; in the background were three families dressed in brilliantly colorful garb, all of whom were laughing and smiling as they walked along a dried riverbed. Gathering storm clouds clotted a sky that had turned orange and red in the setting sun, a vivid contrast to the bleached bones of the skeleton and deep desiccation cracks that illustrated the lack of any recent rainfall.

Mark's comments showed a surprising technical sophistication and a mature appreciation for her artistic intentions; she'd been trying to show an improbable joy amid despair, to illustrate man's insignificance when faced with the capricious power of nature, and Mark had articulated those intentions well.

She closed the binder, knowing there was no need to look through the rest of it.

"You clearly prepared, and considering your age, you seem surprisingly well qualified. But those aren't my major concerns. I still want to know the real reason you want to work here."

His brow furrowed. "I think your photographs are extraordinary. As are Trinity's sculptures."

"Is that all?"

"I'm not sure what you mean."

"I'll be frank," Maggie said, exhaling. She was too tired and too sick, with too little time, to be anything but frank. "You brought in your résumé before we'd even posted that we were hiring, and you admitted you're a fan of my videos. Those things concern me because sometimes people who have watched my videos about my illness feel a false sense of intimacy with me. I can't have someone like that working here." She raised her eyebrows. "Are you imagining that we'll become friends and have deep and meaningful conversations? Because that's unlikely. I doubt I'll be spending much time at the gallery."

"I understand," he said, pleasant and unflustered. "If I were you, I'd likely feel the same way. All I can do is assure you that my intention is to be an excellent employee."

She didn't make her decision right away. Instead, she slept on it and conferred with Luanne and Trinity the following day. Despite Maggie's continuing uncertainty, they wanted to take a chance on him, and Mark started at the beginning of May.

Fortunately, since then, Mark had given Maggie no reason to second-guess herself. With chemotherapy continuing to wipe her out all summer, she'd spent only a few hours a week at the gallery, but in the rare moments when she was there, Mark had been the consummate professional. He greeted her cheerfully, smiled easily, and always referred to her as Ms. Dawes. He was never late for work, had never called in sick, and seldom disturbed her, knocking gently on her office door only when a bona fide buyer or collector had specifically asked for her and he deemed it important enough to intrude. Perhaps because he'd taken the interview to heart, he never referred to her recent video posts, nor did he ask her personal questions. Occasionally he expressed the hope that she was feeling well, but that was okay with her, because he didn't actually inquire about it, leaving it up to her to say anything more if she wanted to.

Moreover and most importantly, he excelled at the job. He treated customers with courtesy and charm, moved the cancer groupies gracefully toward the exits, and excelled at sales, probably because he wasn't pushy in the slightest. He answered the phone, usually by the second or third ring, and carefully wrapped the prints before shipping those ordered by mail. Usually, to complete all of his tasks, he would stay for an hour or more after the gallery had closed its doors. Luanne was so impressed by him that she had no worries about her monthlong holiday in Maui with her daughter and grandchildren in December, a trip she'd taken almost every year since she's started at the gallery.

None of that, Maggie realized, had been much of a surprise. What did surprise her was that in the last few months, her reservations about Mark had slowly given way to a growing sense of trust.

Maggie couldn't pinpoint exactly when that had happened. Like apartment neighbors regularly riding the same elevator, their cordial relationship settled into a comfortable familiarity. In September, once she began to feel better after her last infusion, she had started spending more time at work. Simple greetings with Mark gave way to small talk before segueing to more personal subjects. Sometimes those conversations took place in the small break room down the hall from her office, other times in the gallery when it was devoid of visitors. Mostly they occurred after the doors had been locked, while the three of them processed and packaged the prints that had been ordered by phone or through the website. Usually Luanne dominated the conversation, chattering about her ex-husband's poor dating choices or her kids and grandkids. Maggie and Mark were content to listen—Luanne *was* entertaining. Every now and then, one of them would roll their eyes at something Luanne had said (*"I'm sure my ex is paying for all the plastic surgery on that tacky gold-digger"*) and the other would smile slightly, a private communication meant just for the two of them.

Sometimes, though, Luanne had to leave immediately after closing. Mark and Maggie would work together alone, and little by little, Maggie came to learn quite a bit about Mark, even as he refrained from asking personal questions of her. He told her about his parents and his childhood, which often struck her as something akin to an upbringing imagined by Norman Rockwell, complete with bedtime stories, hockey and baseball games, and his parents' attendance at every school event he could remember. He also spoke frequently about his girlfriend, Abigail, who'd just started working toward a master's degree in economics at the University of Chicago. Like Mark, she'd grown up in a small town—in her case, Waterloo, Iowa—and he had countless photographs of the two of them on his iPhone. The photos showed a pretty young redhead with a sunny, midwestern affect, and Mark mentioned that he planned to propose after she received her degree. Maggie could remember laughing when he said it. *Why get married when you're still so young?* she'd asked. *Why not wait a few years?*

"Because," Mark had answered, "she's the one with whom I'd like to spend the rest of my life."

"How can you know that?"

"Sometimes you just know."

The more she learned about him, the more she came to believe that his parents had been as lucky with him as he'd been with them. He was an exemplary young man, responsible and kind—disproving the stereotype that millennials were lazy and entitled. Still, her growing fondness for him sometimes surprised her, if only because they shared so little in common. Her early life had been...*unusual*, at least for a time, and her relationship with her parents had often been strained. She herself had been nothing like Mark. While he'd been studious and had graduated with highest honors from a top university, she'd generally struggled in school and had finished less than three semesters at a community college. At his age, she had been content to live in the moment and figure things out on the fly, whereas he seemed to have a plan for everything. Had she met him when she was younger, she suspected that she wouldn't have given him the time of day; when she'd been in her twenties, she'd had a habit of choosing exactly the wrong kinds of men.

Nonetheless, he sometimes reminded her of someone she'd known long ago, someone who had once meant everything to her.

By the time Thanksgiving rolled around, Maggie considered Mark a definite member of the gallery family. She wasn't as close to him as she was to either Luanne or

Trinity—they'd spent years together, after all—but he'd become something akin to a friend nonetheless, and two days after that holiday, all four of them had stayed late in the gallery after closing. It was Saturday night, and because Luanne planned to fly to Maui the following morning while Trinity left for the Caribbean, they opened a bottle of wine to go with the cheese and fruit tray Luanne had ordered. Maggie accepted a glass, even though she couldn't fathom the thought of either drinking or eating anything.

They toasted the gallery—it had been far and away their most successful year ever—and settled into easy conversation for another hour. Toward the end, Luanne offered Maggie a card.

"There's a gift inside," Luanne said. "Open it after I'm gone."

"I haven't had a chance to get yours yet."

"That's fine," Luanne said. "Seeing you back to your old self these past few months has been more than enough gift for me. Just make sure you open it well before Christmas, though."

After Maggie assured her that she would, Luanne stepped toward the platter and grabbed a couple of strawberries. A few feet away, Trinity was speaking to Mark. Because he visited the gallery even less frequently than Maggie did, she heard Trinity asking the same kinds of personal questions that she had over the last few months.

"I didn't know you played hockey," Trinity offered. "I'm a huge Islanders fan, even if they haven't won the Stanley Cup in what seems like forever."

"It's a great sport. I played every year until I got to Northwestern."

"Don't they have a team?"

"I wasn't good enough to play at the collegiate level," Mark admitted. "Not that it seemed to matter to my parents. I don't think either of them ever missed a game."

"Will they come out to see you for Christmas?"

"No," Mark said. "My dad set up a tour of the Holy Land with a couple dozen members of our church for the holidays. Nazareth, Bethlehem, the whole works."

"And you didn't want to go?"

"It's their dream, not mine. Besides, I have to be here."

Maggie saw Trinity glance in her direction before he turned his attention back to Mark. He leaned in, whispering something, and though Maggie couldn't hear him, she knew exactly what Trinity had said, because he'd expressed his own concerns to her a few minutes earlier.

"Make sure you keep an eye on Maggie while Luanne and I are gone. We're both a little worried about her."

In response, Mark simply nodded.

Trinity was more prescient than he probably realized, but then again, both Trinity and Luanne had known that Maggie had another appointment with Dr. Brodigan scheduled on December 10. And sure enough, at that appointment, Dr. Brodigan had urged Maggie to focus on her quality of life.

Now it was December 18. More than a week had passed since that awful day and

Maggie still felt almost numb. Nor had she told anyone about her prognosis. Her parents had always believed that if they prayed hard enough, God would somehow heal her, and telling them the truth would take more energy than she could summon. Same thing in a different way with her sister; long story short, she didn't have the energy. Mark had texted a couple of times to check in on her, but saying anything about her situation via text struck her as absurd and she hadn't been ready to face anyone just yet. As for Luanne or even Trinity, she supposed she could call them, but what would be the point? Luanne deserved to enjoy the time she was spending with her own family without worrying about Maggie, and Trinity had his own life as well. Besides, there was nothing that either of them could really do.

Instead, dazed by her new reality, she'd spent much of the last eight days either in her apartment or on short, slow walks through her neighborhood. Sometimes she simply stared out the window, absently fondling the small pendant on the necklace she always wore; other times, she found herself people-watching. When she'd first moved to New York, she had been enthralled by the ceaseless activity around her, by seeing people rushing down into the subway or peering up into office towers at midnight with the knowledge that people were still at their desks. Following the hectic movements of pedestrians below her window brought back memories of her early adulthood in the city and the younger, healthier woman she once had been. It seemed like a lifetime had passed since then; it also felt as though the years had passed in the blink of an eye, and her inability to grasp that contradiction made her more self-reflective than usual. Time, she thought, would always be elusive.

She hadn't expected the miraculous—deep down, she'd always known a cure was out of the question—but wouldn't it have been great to learn that the chemotherapy had slowed the cancer a little and bought her an extra year or two? Or that some experimental treatment had become available? Would that have been too much to ask? To have been given one last intermission before the final act began?

That was the thing about battling cancer. The *waiting*. So much of the last few years had been about *waiting*. Waiting for the appointment with the doctor, waiting for treatment, waiting to feel better after the treatment, waiting to see whether the treatment had worked, waiting until she was well enough to try something new. Until her diagnosis, she'd viewed waiting for anything as an irritation, but waiting had slowly but surely become the defining reality of her life.

Even now, she suddenly thought. Here I am, *waiting* to die.

On the sidewalk, beyond the glass, she saw people bundled up in winter gear, their breath making clouds of steam as they hurried to unknown destinations; on the street, a long line of cars with glowing taillights crawled through narrow lanes lined by pretty brick town houses. They were people going about their daily lives, as though nothing out of the ordinary were happening. But nothing felt ordinary now, and she doubted things would ever feel ordinary again.

She envied them, these strangers she would never meet. They were living their lives without counting the days they had left, something she would never do again. And, as always, there were so many of them. She'd grown used to the fact that everything in the city was always crowded, no matter the time or the season, which added inconvenience to even the simplest things. If she needed ibuprofen from Duane Reade, there was a line to check out; if she was in the mood to see a movie, there was a line at the box office, too. When it came time to cross the street, she was inevitably surrounded by others, people rushing and jostling at the curb.

But why the rush? She wondered about that now, just as she wondered about so many things. Like everyone, she had regrets, and now that time was running out, she couldn't help dwelling on them. There were actions she'd taken that she wished she could undo; there were opportunities she'd missed and now would never have the time to do. She'd spoken honestly about some of her regrets in one of her videos, admitting to feeling unreconciled to them, and no closer to answers than when she'd initially been diagnosed.

Nor had she cried since her last meeting

with Dr. Brodigan. Instead, when she wasn't staring out the window or taking her walks, she'd focused on the mundane. She'd slept and slept—averaging fourteen hours a night—and had ordered Christmas gifts on-line. She'd recorded but hadn't yet posted another *Cancer Video* concerning her last appointment with Dr. Brodigan. She'd had smoothies delivered and tried to finish them as she sat in the living room. Recently she'd even tried to have lunch at Union Square Cafe. It had always been one of her favorite places to grab a delicious meal at the bar, but the visit ended up being a waste, since everything that crossed her lips still tasted wrong. Cancer, taking yet another joy from her life.

Now it was a week until Christmas, and with the afternoon sun beginning to wane, she felt the need to get out of the apartment. She dressed in multiple layers, assuming she would stroll aimlessly for a bit, but once she stepped outside, the mood to simply wander passed as quickly as it had come. Instead, she started toward the gallery. Though she wouldn't do much work, it would be comforting to know that all was in order.

The gallery was several blocks away and she moved slowly, trying to avoid anyone who might bump into her. The wind was icy and by the time she pushed through the doors of the gallery a half hour before closing, she was shivering. It was unusually crowded; she'd expected that the holidays would diminish the number of visitors, but clearly she'd been wrong about that. Luckily, Mark seemed to have things under control.

As always when she entered, heads turned in her direction and she noted dawning looks of recognition on some faces. *Sorry. Not today, folks*, she suddenly thought, offering a quick wave before hurrying to her office. She shut the door behind her. Inside, there was a desk and an office chair, and one of the walls featured built-in bookcases piled high with photography books and keepsakes from her far-flung travels. Across from the desk was a small gray love seat, just big enough to curl up on if she needed to lie down. In the corner stood an ornately carved rocker with flowered cushions that Luanne had brought from her country house, lending a touch of warmth to the modern office.

After piling her gloves, hat, and jacket on the desk, Maggie readjusted her kerchief and collapsed into her office chair. Turning on the computer, she automatically checked the weekly sales figures, noting the spike in volume, but realized she wasn't in the mood to study the numbers in detail. Instead, she opened another folder and began clicking through her favorite photos, finally pausing at a series of images she'd taken in Ulan Bator, Mongolia, last January. At the time she'd had no idea it would be the last international trip she would ever take. The temperature had been well below zero the entire time she was there, with biting winds that could freeze exposed skin in less than a minute; it had been an effort to keep her camera working because the components grew finicky in temperatures that low. She could remember repeatedly tucking the camera inside her jacket to warm it against her body, but the photographs were so important to her, she'd braved the elements for almost two hours.

She'd wanted to find ways to document

the poisonous levels of air pollution and its visible effects on the population. In a city of a million and a half people, nearly every home and business burned coal throughout the winter, darkening the sky even in brightest daylight. It was a health crisis as well as an environmental one, and she'd wanted her images to spur people to action. She'd logged countless photographs of children covered in grime as a result of stepping outside to play. She'd caught an amazing black-and-white image of filthy cloth that had been used as drapery for an open window, dramatizing what was happening inside otherwise healthy lungs. She'd also sought out a stark panorama of the city and finally nailed the image she wanted: a brilliant blue sky that suddenly, *immediately* gave way to a pale, almost sickly yellow haze, as though God himself had drawn a perfectly straight line, dividing the sky in two. The effect was utterly arresting, especially after the hours she'd spent refining it in post.

As she stared at the image in the solace of her office, she knew she would never be able to do something like that again. She would likely never travel for work again; she might never even leave Manhattan, unless she gave in to her parents and returned to Seattle. Nor had anything in Mongolia changed. In addition to the photo essay that she'd contributed to the *New Yorker*, a number of media outlets, including *Scientific American* and the *Atlantic*, had also tried to raise awareness regarding the dangerous levels of pollution in Ulan Bator, but the air, if anything, had grown even worse in the last eleven months. It was, she thought, yet another failure in her life, just like her battle with cancer.

The thoughts shouldn't have been connected, but in that instant, they were, and all at once she felt tears begin to form. She was dying, she was actually *dying*, and it dawned on her suddenly that she was about to experience her very last Christmas.

What should she be doing with these last precious weeks? And what did *quality of life* even mean when it came to the actuality of day-to-day living? She was already sleeping more than ever, but did quality mean getting more sleep to feel better, or less sleep so the days seemed longer? And what about her routines? Should she bother making an appointment to have her teeth cleaned? Should she pay off the minimum balance on her credit cards or go on a spending spree? Because what did it matter? What did anything really matter?

A hundred random thoughts and questions overran her; lost in all of it, she felt herself choke before letting go completely. She didn't know how long the outburst lasted; time slipped away. When she was finally spent, she stood and swiped at her eyes. Glancing through the one-way window above her desk, she noticed that the gallery floor was empty, and that the front door had been locked. Strangely, she didn't see Mark, even though the lights were still on. She wondered where he was until she heard a knock at the door. Even his knock was gentle.

She considered making an excuse until the evidence of her breakdown had subsided, but why bother? She'd long since stopped caring about her appearance; she knew she looked awful even at the best of times.

"Come on in," she said. Pulling a Kleenex

from the box on her desk, she blew her nose as Mark stepped through the door.

"Hey," he said, his voice quiet.

"Hi."

"Bad time?"

"It's all right."

"I thought you might like this," he said, holding out a to-go cup. "It's a banana-and-strawberry smoothie with vanilla ice cream. Maybe it'll help."

She recognized the label on the cup—the eatery was two doors down from the gallery—and wondered how he'd known how she was feeling. Perhaps he'd divined something when she'd made a beeline for her office, or maybe he'd simply remembered what Trinity had told him.

"Thank you," she said, taking it.

"Are you okay?"

"I've been better." She took a sip, thankful it was sweet enough to override her messed-up taste buds. "How was it today?"

"Busy, but not as bad as last Friday. We sold eight prints, including a number three of *Rush*."

Each of her photographs was limited to

twenty-five numbered prints; the lower the number, the higher the price. The photo Mark mentioned had been taken at rush hour in the Tokyo subway, the platform jammed with thousands of men dressed in what seemed to be identical black suits.

"Anything by Trinity?"

"Not today, but I think there's a good possibility of that in the near future. Jackie Bernstein came in with her consultant earlier."

Maggie nodded. Jackie had bought two other Trinity pieces in the past, and Trinity would be pleased to know she was interested in another.

"How about on the website and phone-ins?"

"Six confirmed, two people wanted more information. It shouldn't take long to get the sales ready for shipment. If you want to head on home, I can handle it."

As soon as he said it, her mind floated additional questions: *Do I truly want to go home? To an otherwise empty apartment? To wallow in solitude?*

"No, I'll stay," she demurred, shaking her head. "For a while, anyway."

She sensed his curiosity but knew he wouldn't ask more. Again, she understood the interviews had left a lingering mark.

"I'm sure you've been following my social posts and videos," she began, "so you probably have a general sense of what's going on with my illness."

"Not really. I haven't watched any of your videos since I began working here."

She hadn't expected that. Even Luanne watched her videos. "Why not?"

"I assumed you would prefer that I didn't. And when I considered your initial concerns about my working here, it seemed like the right thing to do."

"But you did know I underwent chemotherapy, right?"

"Luanne mentioned it, but I don't know the details. And, of course, in the rare times you were at the gallery, you looked…"

When he trailed off, she finished for him. "Like death?"

"I was going to say you looked a bit tired."

Sure I did. If gaunt, green, shrinking, and balding could be explained by waking up too early. But she knew he was trying to be kind.

"Do you have a few minutes? Before you start getting the shipments ready?"

"Of course. I don't have anything planned for tonight."

On an impulse, she moved to the rocker, motioning for him to get comfortable on the love seat. "No going out with friends?"

"It's kind of expensive," he said. "And going out usually means drinking, but I don't drink."

"Ever?"

"No."

"Wow," she said. "I don't think I've ever met a twenty-two-year-old who's never had a drink."

"Actually, I'm twenty-three now."

"You had a birthday?"

"It wasn't a big deal."

Probably not, she thought. "Did Luanne know? She didn't say anything to me."

"I didn't mention it to her."

She leaned forward and raised her cup. "Happy belated birthday, then."

"Thank you."

"Did you do anything fun? For your birthday, I mean?"

"Abigail flew out for the weekend and we saw *Hamilton*. Have you seen it?"

"A while ago." *But I won't ever see it again*, she didn't bother to add. Which was another reason not to be alone. So that thoughts like those didn't precipitate yet another breakdown. With Mark here, it was somehow easier to keep herself together.

"I'd never seen a show on Broadway before," Mark went on. "The music was amazing and I loved the historical element and the dancing and…everything about it. Abigail was electrified—she swore she'd never experienced anything like it."

"How is Abigail?"

"She's doing well. Her break just started, so she's probably on her way to Waterloo right now to see her family."

"She didn't want to come out here to see you?"

"It's sort of a mini family reunion. Unlike me, she has a big family. Five older brothers and sisters who live all over the country. Christmas is the only time of year they can all get together."

"And you didn't want to go out there?"

"I'm working. She understands that. Besides, she's coming out here on the twenty-eighth. We'll spend some time together, watch the ball drop on New Year's Eve, things like that."

"Will I get to meet her?"

"If you'd like."

"If you need time off, let me know. I'm sure I can manage on my own for a couple of days."

She wasn't sure she could, but it felt like she needed to offer.

"I'll let you know."

Maggie took another sip of her smoothie. "I don't know if I've mentioned it lately, but you're doing really well here."

"I enjoy it," he said. He waited, and she knew again that he'd made a choice not to ask personal questions. Which meant she would have to volunteer the information or keep it to herself.

"I met with my oncologist last week," she stated in what she hoped was an even voice. "She thinks another round of chemotherapy will do more harm than good."

His expression softened. "Can I ask what that means?"

"It means no more treatment and the clock is ticking."

He paled, registering what she hadn't said. "Oh...Ms. Dawes. That's terrible. I'm so sorry. I don't know what to say. Is there anything I can do?"

"I don't think there's anything anyone can do. But please, call me Maggie. I think you've worked here long enough for the two of us to use first names."

"Is the doctor certain?"

"The scans weren't good," she said. "Lots of spread, everywhere. Stomach. Pancreas. Kidneys. Lungs. And though you won't ask, I have less than six months. Most likely, it's somewhere around three to four, maybe even less."

Surprising her, his eyes began to well with tears. "Oh...Lord..." he said, his expression suddenly softening. "Would you mind if I pray for you? Not now, but when I get home, I mean."

She couldn't help smiling. Of course he would want to pray for her, future pastor that he was. She suspected he'd never uttered a profanity in his life. He was, she thought, a very sweet kid. Well, technically he was a young man, but...

"I'd like that."

For a few seconds, neither of them said anything. Then, with a soft shake of his head, he pressed his lips together. "It isn't fair," he said.

"When is life ever fair?"

"Can I ask how you're doing? I hope you'll forgive me if I'm overstepping..."

"It's okay," she said. "I guess I've been in a bit of a daze since I found out."

"It has to feel unbearable."

"At times it does. But then, other times, it doesn't. The strange thing is that physically, I feel better than I did earlier in the year, during the chemo. Back then, there were times when I was sure dying would be easier. But now..."

She let her gaze wander over the shelves, noting the trinkets she'd collected, each one imbued with memories of a trip she'd taken. To Greece and Egypt, Rwanda and Nova Scotia, Patagonia and Easter Island, Vietnam and the Ivory Coast. So many places, so many adventures.

"It's a strange thing to know the end is so imminent," she admitted. "It gives rise to a lot of questions. Makes a person wonder what it's all about. Sometimes I feel that I've led a charmed life, but then, in the next instant, I find myself obsessing over the things I missed out on."

"Like what?"

"Marriage, for starters," she said. "You know I've never been married, right?" When he nodded, she went on. "Growing up, I couldn't imagine that I'd still be single at my age. It just wasn't the way I was raised. My parents were very traditional and I assumed I'd end up like them." She felt her thoughts drifting to the past, memories bubbling to the surface. "Of course, I didn't make it easy for them. Not like you, anyway."

"I wasn't always a perfect child," he protested. "I got in trouble."

"For what? Anything serious? Was it because you didn't clean your room or because you were a minute late for your curfew? Oh, wait. You were never late for your curfew, right?"

He opened his mouth, but when no words came out, she knew she was right. He must have been the kind of teenager who made things harder for the rest of his generation, simply because he was wired to be *easy*.

"The point is, I've been wondering how things would have turned out had I chosen a different path. Not just marriage, though. What if I'd worked harder in school, or graduated from college, or had a job in an office, or moved to Miami or Los Angeles instead of New York? Things like that."

"You obviously didn't need college. Your career as a photographer has been remarkable, and your videos and posts about your illness have inspired a lot of people."

"That's very kind, but they don't really know me. And in the end, isn't that the most important thing in life? To be truly known and loved by someone you've chosen?"

"Maybe," he conceded. "But that doesn't negate what you've given people through your experience. It's a powerful act, even life-changing for some."

Perhaps it was his sincerity or his old-fashioned mannerisms, but she was struck again by how much he reminded her of someone she'd once known long ago. She hadn't thought about Bryce in years, not consciously anyway. For most of her adult life, she'd tried to keep her memories of him at a safe distance.

But there was no reason to do that any longer.

"Would you mind if I asked you a personal question?" she said, mirroring his curiously formal style of speech.

"Not at all."

"When did you first know that you were in love with Abigail?"

As soon as she said Abigail's name, a tenderness came over him. "Last year," he said, leaning back into the cushions of the love seat. "Not long after I graduated. We'd gone out four or five times, and she wanted me to meet her parents. Anyway, we were driving to Waterloo, just the two of us. We'd stopped for something to eat, and on the way out, she decided she wanted an ice cream cone. It was scorching outside and unfortunately, the air-conditioning in the car wasn't working that well, so of course it started to melt all over her. A lot of people might have been upset by that, but she just started giggling like it was the funniest thing ever as she tried to eat it faster than it could melt. There was ice cream everywhere—on her nose and fingers, in her lap, even in her hair—and I remember thinking that I wanted to be around someone like that forever. Someone who could laugh at the inconveniences of life and find joy in any occasion. That's when I knew she was the one."

"Did you tell her then?"

"Oh, no. I wasn't brave enough. It took me until last fall before I could finally work up the courage to tell her."

"Did she say that she loved you, too?"

"She did. That was a relief."

"She sounds like a wonderful person."

"She is. I'm very lucky."

Though he smiled, she knew he was still troubled.

"I wish there was something I could do for you," he said, his voice soft.

"Working here is enough. Well, that and staying late."

"I'm glad to be here. I wonder, though..."

"Go ahead," she said, gesturing with the smoothie. "You can ask whatever question you'd like. I've got nothing to hide anymore."

"Why didn't you ever get married? If you thought you would, I mean?"

"There were a lot of reasons. When I was just starting out in my career, I wanted to concentrate on that until I established a foothold. Then I started traveling a lot, and then came the gallery and...I guess I was just too busy."

"And you never met someone who made you question all that?"

In the silence that followed, she unconsciously reached for the necklace, feeling for the small shell-shaped pendant, making sure it was still there. "I thought I did. I know I loved him, but the timing wasn't right."

"Because of work?"

"No," she said. "It happened long before then. But I'm pretty sure I wouldn't have been good for him. Not back then, anyway."

"I can't believe that."

"You don't know who I used to be." She put down her cup and folded her hands in her lap. "Do you want to hear the story?"

"I'd be honored."

"It's kind of long."

"Those are usually the best kind of stories."

Maggie bent her head, feeling the images begin to surface at the edge of her mind. With the images, the words would eventually come, she knew.

"In 1995, when I was sixteen years old, I began to lead a secret life," she started.

MAROONED

Ocracoke
1995

Actually, when I'm being honest, my secret life really began when I was fifteen and my mom found me on the bathroom floor, green in the gills, with my arms wrapped around the toilet bowl. I'd been barfing every morning for the past week and a half, and my mom, more knowledgeable about such things than I was, raced to the drugstore and made me pee on a stick as soon as she got home. When the blue plus sign appeared, she stared at the stick for a long time without saying a single word, then retreated to the kitchen, where she cried on and off for the rest of the day.

That was in early October, and I was a

little more than nine weeks along by then. I probably cried as much as my mom that day. I stayed in my room clutching my favorite teddy bear—I'm not sure my mom even noticed that I hadn't gone to school—and stared out the window with swollen eyes, watching buckets of rain pour onto foggy streets. It was typical Seattle weather, and even now, I doubt there's a more depressing place to be in the entire world, especially when you're fifteen and pregnant and certain your life is over before it even had a chance to begin.

It went without saying that I had no idea what I was going to do. That's what I remember most of all. I mean, what did I know about being a parent? Or even being a grown-up? Oh, sure, there were times when I felt older than my age, like when Zeke Watkins—the star player of the varsity basketball team—spoke to me in the school parking lot, but part of me still felt like a kid. I loved Disney movies and celebrating with strawberry ice cream cake at the roller rink on my birthday; I always slept with a teddy bear and I couldn't even drive. Frankly, I wasn't even all that experienced when it came to the opposite sex. I'd only kissed four boys in my entire life, but one time, the kissing went too far, and a little more than three weeks after that awful barfing-and-tear-filled day, my parents shipped me off to Ocracoke in the Outer Banks of North Carolina, a place I didn't even know existed. It was supposedly a picturesque beach town adored by tourists. There, I would live with my aunt Linda Dawes, my father's much older sister, a woman I'd met only once in my life. They'd also made arrangements with my teachers so I wouldn't fall behind in my studies. My parents had a long discussion with the headmaster—and after the headmaster spoke to my aunt, he decided to trust her to proctor my exams, making sure I didn't cheat and that all my assignments were turned in. And just like that, I suddenly became the family secret.

My parents didn't come with me to North Carolina, which made leaving that much harder. Instead, we said our goodbyes at the airport on a chilly November morning, a few days after Halloween. I'd just turned sixteen, I was thirteen weeks along and terrified, but I didn't cry on the plane, thank God. Nor did

I cry when my aunt picked me up at a rinky-dink airport in the middle of nowhere, or even when we checked into a dumpy motel near the beach, since we had to wait to catch the ferry to Ocracoke the following morning. By then, I'd almost convinced myself that I wasn't going to cry at all.

Boy, was I ever wrong.

After we disembarked from the ferry, my aunt gave me a quick tour of the village before bringing me to her house, and to my dismay, Ocracoke was nothing like I'd imagined. I guess I'd been picturing pretty pastel cottages nestled in the sand dunes, with tropical views of the ocean stretching to the horizon; a boardwalk complete with burger joints and ice cream shops and crowded with teens, maybe even a Ferris wheel or a carousel. But Ocracoke was nothing like that. Once you got past the fishing boats in the tiny harbor where the ferry dropped us off, it looked...*ugly*. The houses were old and weather-beaten; there wasn't a beach, boardwalk, or palm tree in sight; and the village—that's what my aunt called it, a *village*—seemed utterly deserted. My aunt mentioned that Ocracoke was essentially a fishing village and that less than eight hundred people lived there year-round, but I could only wonder why anyone would want to live there at all.

Aunt Linda's place was right on the water, sandwiched between homes that were equally run-down. It was set on stilts with a view of the Pamlico Sound, with a compact front porch, and another larger porch off the living room that faced the water. It was also small—living room with a fireplace and a window near the front door, dining area and kitchen, two bedrooms, and a single bath. There wasn't a television in sight, which left me feeling suddenly panicked, though I don't think she realized it. She showed me around and eventually pointed out where I would be sleeping, across the hall from her room in what usually served as her reading room. My first thought was that it was nothing like my bedroom back home. It wasn't even like half my bedroom back home. There was a twin bed wedged beneath a window along with a padded rocking chair, a reading lamp, and a shelf crammed with books by Betty Friedan, Sylvia Plath, Ursula K. Le Guin, and Elizabeth Berg, in addition to tomes on Catholicism, Saint Thomas Aquinas, and Mother Teresa. Again, no television, but there was a radio, even if it looked a hundred years old, and an old-fashioned clock. The closet, if you could call it that, was barely a foot deep, and the only way I would be able to store my clothes was to fold and stack them in vertical piles on the floor. There was no nightstand or chest of drawers, all of which made me suddenly feel like I was visiting unexpectedly for a single night, rather than the six months intended.

"I love this room," my aunt said with a sigh, setting my suitcase on the floor. "It's so comfortable."

"It's nice," I forced out. After she left me alone to unpack, I plopped down on the bed, still in disbelief that I was actually here. At this *house*, in this *place*, with this *relative*. I stared out the window—noting the rust-colored wooden planking on the neighbor's house—wishing with every blink that I'd be able to see Puget Sound or the snow-capped Cascade Mountains, or even the rocky and rugged coast I'd known all my life. I thought about the Douglas fir and red cedar trees, and even the fog and rain. I thought about my family and friends who might as well have been on another planet, and the lump in my throat grew even bigger. I was pregnant and alone, marooned in a terrible place, and all I wanted was to turn back the clock and change what had happened. All of it— the *oops*, the barfing, the withdrawal from school, the trip here. I wanted to be a regular teenager again—hell, I would have taken being just a *kid* again instead of this—but I suddenly remembered the blue plus sign on the pregnancy test, and the pressure began to build behind my eyes. I may have been strong on the journey, and maybe even up until then, but when I squeezed my teddy bear to my chest and inhaled her familiar scent, the dam simply burst. It wasn't a pretty cry like you see in Hallmark movies; it was a raging sob, complete with snorts and wails and quivering shoulders, and it seemed to go on forever.

About my teddy bear: she was neither cute nor expensive, but I'd slept with her for as long as I could remember. The thin coffee-colored fur had worn away in patches, and Frankenstein stitches held one of her arms in place. I'd had my mom sew on a button when one of her eyes had popped off, but the damage made her seem even more special to me, because sometimes I felt damaged, too. In third grade, I'd used a Sharpie to write my name on the bottom of her foot, marking her as mine forever. When I was younger, I used to bring her with me everywhere, my own version of a security blanket. Once, I'd accidentally left her at Chuck E. Cheese when I'd gone to a friend's birthday party, and when I got home, I cried so hard I actually puked. My dad had to drive back across town to retrieve her, and I'm pretty sure I held on to her for almost a week straight after that.

Over the years, she had been dropped in mud, splashed with spaghetti sauce, and soaked with sleep drool; whenever my mom decided it was finally time to wash her, she'd throw her in the laundry along with my clothes. I'd sit on the floor, watching the washer and dryer, imagining her tumbling among the jeans and towels and hoping she wouldn't be destroyed in the process. But Maggie-bear—short for *Maggie's bear*—would eventually emerge clean and warm. My mom would hand her back to me and I'd suddenly feel complete again, like all was right in the world.

When I went to Ocracoke, Maggie-bear was the only thing I knew I couldn't leave behind.

Aunt Linda checked on me during my breakdown but didn't seem to know what to say or do, and apparently she decided it was probably best to let me sort through things on my own. I was glad about that, but kind of sad, too, because it made me feel even more isolated than I already did.

Somehow, I survived that first day, then the next. She showed me a bicycle she'd bought at a garage sale, which looked older than I was, with a cushy seat big enough for someone twice my size and a basket on the front hanging from massive handlebars. I hadn't ridden a bike in years.

"I had a young man in town fix it up, so it should work fine."

"Great" was all I could muster.

On the third day, my aunt went back to work and was out of the house long before I finally woke. On the table, she'd left a folder filled with my homework, and I realized that I was already falling behind. I hadn't been a great student even in the best of times—I was middle-of-the-pack and hated when my report cards came out—and if I hadn't cared much about acing my classes before, I was even more apathetic now. She'd also written me a note to remind me that I had two quizzes the following day. Even though I tried to study, I couldn't concentrate and already knew I was going to bomb them, which I promptly did.

Afterward, maybe because she was feeling even more sorry for me than usual, my aunt thought it might be a good idea to get me out of the house and drove me to her shop. It was a small eatery and coffee bar that offered a lot more than just food. It specialized in biscuits that were baked fresh every morning and served either with sausage gravy or as some sort of sandwich or dessert. Beyond breakfast, the shop also sold used books and rented out video cassettes; shipped UPS packages; had mailboxes for rent; offered faxes, scanning, and copies; and provided Western Union services. My aunt owned the place with her friend Gwen and it opened at five in the morning so the fishermen could grab a bite before heading out, which meant she was usually there by four to start baking. She introduced me to Gwen, who wore an apron over jeans and a flannel shirt and kept her graying blond hair in a messy ponytail. She seemed nice enough, and though I only spent about an hour in the shop, my impression was that they treated each other like an old married couple. They could communicate with a single glance, predicted each other's requests, and moved around each other behind the counter like dancers.

Business was steady but not booming, and I spent most of my time thumbing through the used books. There were Agatha Christie mysteries and westerns by Louis L'Amour, along with a good-sized selection of books by best-selling authors. There was also a donation box, and while I was there, a woman who'd come in for coffee and a biscuit dropped off a small crate of books, almost all of them romance novels. As I riffled through them, I thought to myself that if I'd had less romance in August, I wouldn't be in the mess I was in right now.

The shop closed at three during the week, and after Gwen and Aunt Linda locked the doors, my aunt took me on a longer, more extensive tour of the village. It took all of fifteen minutes and didn't change my initial impression in the slightest. After that, we went home, where I hid out in my room for the rest of the day. As weird as the room was, it was the only place I had some privacy when Aunt Linda was home. When I wasn't half-assing my way through my schoolwork, I could listen to music, brood, and spend way too much time contemplating death and my growing belief that the world—and especially my family—would be better off without me.

I wasn't quite sure what to make of my aunt either. She had short gray hair and warm hazel eyes, set in a face deeply lined with wrinkles. Her gait was always hurried. She'd never been married, never had children, and sometimes came across as a little bit bossy. She also used to be a nun, and even though she'd left the Sisters of Mercy almost ten years ago, she still believed in the whole "cleanliness is next to godliness" thing. I had to straighten up my room daily, do my own laundry, and clean the kitchen before she got home in midafternoon as well as after dinner. Fair enough, I suppose, since I was living there, but no matter how hard I tried, I never seemed to do it right. Our conversations about it were usually short, a statement followed by an apology. Like this:

The cups were still damp when you put them back in the cupboard.

Sorry.

There are still crumbs on the table.

Sorry.

You forgot to use 409 when you cleaned the stovetop.

Sorry.

You need to straighten the covers on your bed.

Sorry.

I must have said *sorry* a hundred times the first week I was there, and the second week was even worse. I bombed yet another test and grew bored by the view when I sat on the porch. I eventually came to believe that even if you stuck someone on a fabulous tropical island, the sight would get old after a while. I mean, the ocean never seems to change. Whenever you see it, the water is just *there*. Sure, the clouds might shift around, and right before sunset the sky might glow orange and red and yellow—but what fun is watching a sunset if there's no one to share it with? My aunt wasn't the kind of woman who seemed to appreciate such things.

And by the way? Pregnancy *sucks*. I was still sick every morning and sometimes it was hard to make it to the bathroom in time. I'd read that some women never got sick at all, but not me. I'd barfed forty-nine mornings in a row and I had the sense that my body seemed to be going for some kind of record.

If there was a plus side to the barfing, it

was that I hadn't gained much weight, maybe only a pound or two by mid-November. Frankly, I didn't want to get fat, but my mom had bought me the book *What to Expect When You're Expecting*, and as I reluctantly thumbed through it one evening, I learned that a lot of women put on only a pound or two in the first trimester, which made me nothing special. After that, though, the average weight gain was about a pound a week, right up until delivery. When I did the math—which would add twenty-seven more pounds to my smallish frame—I realized that my six-pack abs would probably be replaced by a keg. Not, of course, that I had six-pack abs in the first place.

Even worse than the barfing were the crazy hormones, which in my case meant acne. No matter how much I cleaned my face, pimples erupted on my cheeks and forehead like constellations in the nighttime sky. Morgan, my perfect older sister, never had a pimple in her life, and when I stared in the mirror, I thought that I could give her a dozen of mine and still have skin that looked worse than hers did. Even then, she'd probably still be beautiful, smart, and popular. We got along okay at home—we were closer when we were younger—but at school she kept her distance, preferring the company of her own friends. She got straight A's, played the violin, and had appeared in not one but *two* television commercials for a local department store. If you think it was easy being compared to her while I was growing up, think again. Toss in my pregnancy, and it was pretty clear why she was far and away my parents' favorite. Frankly, she would have been my favorite, too.

By the time Thanksgiving rolled around, I was officially depressed. That occurs in approximately seven percent of pregnancies, by the way. Between barfing, zits, and depression, I'd hit the trifecta. Lucky me, right? I was falling further behind in school and the music on my Walkman grew noticeably gloomier. Even Gwen tried and failed to cheer me up. I'd gotten to know her a little since our first introduction—she came to dinner twice a week—and she'd asked me whether I wanted to watch the Macy's Thanksgiving Day Parade. She'd brought over a small television and set it up in the kitchen, but even though I'd practically forgotten what a TV looked like by then, it wasn't enough to entice me from my room. Instead, I sat alone and tried not to cry while imagining my mom and Morgan making stuffing or baking pies in the kitchen and my dad in the recliner, enjoying a football game. Even though my aunt and Gwen served a meal similar to what my family usually had, it just wasn't the same, and I barely had any appetite.

I also thought a lot about my best friends, Madison and Jodie. I hadn't been allowed to tell them the truth about why I'd left; instead, my parents had told people—including Madison's and Jodie's parents—that I'd gone to live with my aunt in some remote place because of an *urgent medical situation*, with *limited telephone availability*. No doubt they'd made it sound like I'd volunteered to help Aunt Linda, being that I was such a responsible do-gooder. Lest the lie be discovered, however, I wasn't supposed to speak with my friends while I was gone. I had no cellular phone—few kids did back then—and when my aunt went to work, she would bring the cord from the home phone with her, which I guess made the *limited telephone availability* part as true as the *urgent medical situation* part. My parents, I realized, could be just as sneaky as I, which was a revelation of sorts.

It was around that time, I think, that my aunt began to worry about me, though she tried to downplay her concerns. As we were eating Thanksgiving leftovers, she casually mentioned that I hadn't seemed particularly chipper lately. That was the word she used: *chipper*. She'd also eased up a little on the tidiness thing—or maybe I was doing a better job of cleaning, but for whatever reason, she hadn't been complaining as much recently. I could tell she was making an effort to engage me in conversation.

"Are you taking your prenatal vitamin?"

"Yes," I answered. "It's yummy."

"In a couple of weeks, you'll see the OB-GYN in Morehead City. I set up the appointment this morning."

"Swell," I said. I moved the food around my plate, hoping she wouldn't notice that I wasn't really eating.

"The food has to actually go in your mouth," she said. "And then you have to swallow it."

I think she was trying to be funny, but I wasn't in the mood, so I simply shrugged.

"Can I make you something else?"

"I'm not that hungry."

She brought her lips together before scanning the room, as if searching for magic words that would make me *chipper* again. "Oh, I almost forgot to ask. Did you call your parents?"

"No. I was going to call them earlier, but you took the phone cord with you."

"You could call them after dinner."

"I guess."

She used her fork to cut a bite of turkey. "How are your studies going?" she asked. "You're behind in your homework and you haven't been doing that well on your quizzes lately."

"I'm trying," I answered, even though I really wasn't.

"How about math? Remember that you have some pretty big tests coming up before Christmas break."

"I hate math and geometry is stupid. Why does it matter whether I know how to measure the area of a trapezoid? It's not like I'm ever going to need to use that in my real life."

I heard her sigh. Watched her cast about again. "Did you write your history paper? I think that's also due next week."

"It's almost done," I lied. I'd been assigned to do a report on Thurgood Marshall, but I hadn't even started it.

I could feel her eyes on me, wondering whether to believe me.

Later that night, she tried again.

I was lying in bed with Maggie-bear. I'd retreated to my room after dinner, and she was standing in the doorway, dressed in her pajamas.

"Have you thought about getting some fresh air?" my aunt asked. "Like maybe going for a walk or bike ride before you start doing your homework tomorrow?"

"There isn't anywhere to go. Almost everything is closed for the winter."

"How about the beach? It's peaceful this time of year."

"It's too cold to go to the beach."

"How would you know? You haven't been outside in days."

"That's because I have too much homework and too many chores."

"Have you thought about trying to meet someone closer to your own age? Maybe make some friends?"

At first, I wasn't sure I'd heard her right. "Make friends?"

"Why not?"

"Because no one my age lives here."

"Of course they do," she said. "I showed you the school."

The village had a single school that served children from kindergarten through high school; we'd ridden past it during the tour of the island. It wasn't quite the single-room schoolhouse I'd seen in reruns of *Little House on the Prairie*, but it wasn't much more than that, either.

"I guess I could head to the boardwalk,

or maybe hit the clubs. Oh wait, Ocracoke doesn't have either of those things."

"I'm just saying that it might be good for you to talk to someone besides me or Gwen. It's not healthy to stay so isolated."

No doubt about it. But the simple fact was that I hadn't seen a single teenager in Ocracoke since I'd arrived, and—oh yeah—I was pregnant, which was supposed to be a secret, so what would be the point anyway?

"Being here isn't good for me, either, but no one seems to care about that."

She adjusted her pajamas, as though searching for words in the fabric, and decided to change the subject.

"I've been thinking that it might be a good idea to get you a tutor," she said. "Definitely for geometry, but maybe for your other classes, too. To review your paper, for instance."

"A tutor?"

"I believe I know someone who'd be perfect."

I suddenly had visions of sitting beside some ancient geezer who smelled of Old

Spice and mothballs and liked to talk about the *good old days.* "I don't want a tutor."

"Your finals are in January, and there are multiple exams in the next three weeks, including some big ones. I promised your parents that I'd do my best to make sure you don't have to repeat your sophomore year."

I hated when adults did the logic-and-guilt thing, so I retreated into the obvious. "Whatever."

She raised an eyebrow, remaining silent. Then, finally, "Don't forget that we have church on Sunday."

How could I forget that? "I remember," I finally muttered.

"Perhaps we could pick out a Christmas tree afterward."

"Super," I said, but all I really wanted was to pull the covers over my head in the hope of making her leave. But it wasn't necessary; Aunt Linda turned away. A moment later, I heard her bedroom door close, and I knew that I'd be alone the rest of the night, with only my own dark thoughts to keep me company.

As miserable as the rest of the week was, Sundays were the absolute worst. Back in Seattle, I didn't really mind going to church because there was a family there named the Taylors with four boys, all of them from one to a few years older than me. They were boy-band perfect, with white teeth and hair that always looked blow-dried. Like us, they sat in the front row—they were always on the left while we were on the right—and I'd sneak peeks at them even when I was supposed to be praying. I couldn't help it. I'd had a massive crush on one or the other pretty much as long as I could remember, even though I never actually spoke to any of them. Morgan had better luck; Danny Taylor, one of the middle ones, who at the time was also a pretty good soccer player, took her out for ice cream one Sunday after church. I was in eighth grade at the time and desperately jealous that he'd asked her, not me. I remember sitting in my room and star- ing at the clock, watching the minutes pass;

when Morgan finally got home, I begged her to tell me what Danny was like. Morgan, being Morgan, simply shrugged and said that he wasn't her type, which made me want to strangle her. Morgan had guys practically drooling if she so much as walked down the sidewalk or sipped a Diet Coke in the food court at the local mall.

The point is, back home there was something interesting to see at church—more specifically, four very cute somethings—and that made the hour pass quickly. Here, though, church was not only a chore but an all-day event. There was no Catholic church in Ocracoke; the nearest one was St. Egbert's in Morehead City, and that meant catching the ferry at seven in the morning. The ferry generally took two and a half hours to reach Cedar Island, and from there, it was another forty minutes to the church itself. The service was at eleven, which meant we had to wait yet another hour for it to begin, and the mass lasted until noon. If that wasn't bad enough, the ferry back to Ocracoke didn't leave until four in the afternoon, which meant killing even more time.

Oh, we'd have lunch with Gwen afterward, since she always came with us. Like my aunt, she also used to be a nun, and she considered attending services on Sundays the highlight of her week. She was nice and all, but ask any teenager how much they enjoy eating lunch with a couple of fifty-odd-year-old former nuns, and you can probably guess what it was like. After that, we'd go shopping, but it wasn't fun shopping like at the mall or the Seattle waterfront. Instead, they'd drag me to Wal-Mart for *supplies*— think flour, shortening, eggs, bacon, sausage, cheese, buttermilk, various flavored coffees, and other baking stuff in bulk—and after that, we'd visit garage sales, where they would search for inexpensive books by best-selling authors and movies on videocassette that they could rent to people on Ocracoke. Added to the late-afternoon ferry ride, all of that meant that we wouldn't get back to the house until almost seven, when the sun had long since set.

Twelve hours. Twelve *long* hours. Just so we could go to church.

There are, by the way, about a million better

ways to spend a Sunday, but lo and behold, as Sunday morning dawned, I found myself standing at the dock in a jacket zipped to my chin, stamping one foot and then the other while the frigid air made it appear as though I were smoking invisible cigarettes. Meanwhile, my aunt and Gwen were whispering to each other and laughing and looking happy, probably because they weren't slinging biscuits and serving coffee before the crack of dawn. When it was time, my aunt pulled her car onto the ferry, where it crammed alongside about a dozen others.

I wish I could say that the ride was either pleasant or interesting, but it wasn't, especially in winter. Unless you enjoyed staring at gray skies and even grayer water, there was nothing to see, and if the dock had been freezing, riding on the ferry was fifty times worse. The wind seemed to blow right through me and after less than five minutes outside, my nose started running and my ears turned bright red. There was, thank God, a large central cabin on the ferry where you could escape the weather, complete with a couple of vending machines offering snacks and places to sit, which was where Gwen and my aunt hung out. As for me, I crawled into the car and stretched out on the back seat, wishing I were anywhere else and thinking about the mess I'd gotten myself into.

The day after my mom had me pee on a stick, she brought me to see Dr. Bobbi, who was maybe ten years older than my mom, and the first nonpediatrician I'd ever seen. Dr. Bobbi's real name was Roberta, and she was an OB-GYN. She'd delivered both my sister and me, so she and my mom went way back, and I'm pretty sure my mom was mortified by the reason for our visit. After Dr. Bobbi confirmed the pregnancy, she set me up with an ultrasound, to make sure the baby was healthy. I pulled up my shirt, one of the technicians put some goop on my tummy, and I was able to hear the heartbeat. It was both cool and utterly terrifying, but what I remember most was how surreal it felt and how much I wished that all of it was just a bad dream.

But it wasn't a dream. Because I was Catholic, abortion wasn't even an option, and once we learned the baby was healthy, Dr. Bobbi gave us the *talk*. She assured both of us that I was more than mature enough physically to carry the baby to term, but emotions were a different story. She said I was going to need a lot of support, partly because the pregnancy was unexpected, but mainly because I was still a teenager. In addition to feeling depressed, I might feel angry and disappointed as well. Dr. Bobbi warned that I was also likely to feel alienated from friends, making everything harder. Had I been able to check in with Dr. Bobbi now, I would have told her, check, check, check, and check.

With the talk ringing in her ears, my mom brought me to a support group for pregnant teenagers in Portland, Oregon. I'm sure there were the same kinds of support groups in Seattle, but I didn't want anyone I knew to accidentally find out, and my parents didn't want that, either. So, after almost three hours in the car, I found myself in a back room at a YMCA, where I sat in one of the foldout chairs that had been arranged in a circle. There were nine other girls there, and some of them looked like they were attempting to smuggle watermelons by hiding them under their shirts. The lady in charge, Mrs. Walker, was a social worker, and one by one, we introduced ourselves. After that, we were all supposed to talk about our *feelings* and our *experiences*. What actually happened was that the other girls talked about their feelings and experiences, while I simply listened.

Really, it was just about the most depressing thing ever. One of the girls, who was even younger than me, talked about how bad her hemorrhoids had gotten, while another one droned on about how sore her nipples were before lifting her shirt to show us her stretch marks. Most but not all of them continued to attend their various high schools, and they talked about how embarrassed they were when they had to ask their teacher for a hall pass to go to the bathroom, sometimes two or three times during the same class period. All of them complained how their acne had gotten worse. Two of them had dropped out, and though both said they planned to go back to school, I'm not sure anyone believed them. All had lost friends, and another had been kicked out of her house and was living with her grandparents. Only one of them—

a pretty Mexican girl named Sereta—still spoke with the father of the child, and aside from her, none intended to marry. Except for me, all of them planned to raise their babies with the help of their parents.

When it was over, as we were walking toward the car, I told my mom that I never wanted to do something like that again. It was supposed to be helpful and make me feel less alone, but it left me feeling exactly the opposite. What I wanted was to simply get through this so I could return to the life I had before, which was the same thing my parents wanted. That, of course, led to them making the decision to send me here, and though they assured me that it was for my own good— not theirs—I wasn't sure I believed them.

After church, Aunt Linda and Gwen dragged me through the lunch/shop-for-supplies/ garage-sales routine before heading to a graveled lot near a hardware store, which held so many Christmas trees for sale that it resembled a miniature forest. My aunt and Gwen tried to make the experience fun for me and kept asking my opinion; for my part, I did a lot of shrugging and told them to pick whatever they wanted, since no one seemed to care what I thought anyway, at least when it came to decisions about my life.

Somewhere around the sixth or seventh tree, Aunt Linda stopped asking, and they eventually made the selection without me. Once it was paid for, I watched as two guys wearing overalls tied the tree to the roof of the car, and we climbed back in.

For whatever reason, the ride back to the ferry reminded me of the ride to the airport on my last morning in Seattle. Both my mom and my dad had seen me off, which was kind of a surprise, since my dad had barely been able to look at me since he'd learned I was pregnant. They walked me to the gate and waited with me until it was time to board. Both of them were really quiet, and I wasn't saying much, either. But as time inched forward toward the departure, I remember telling my mom that I was afraid. In truth, I was terrified to the point that my hands had begun to shake.

There were a lot of people around us and she must have noticed the trembling, because she took my hands and squeezed them. Then she led me to a less crowded gate, where we could have some privacy.

"I'm afraid, too."

"Why are you afraid?" I asked.

"Because you're my daughter. All I do is worry about you. And what happened is...unfortunate."

Unfortunate. She'd been using that word a lot lately. Next, she'd remind me that leaving was for my own good.

"I don't want to go," I said.

"We've talked about this," she said. "You know it's for your own good."

Bingo.

"I don't want to leave my friends." By that point, it was all I could do to choke out the words. "What if Aunt Linda hates me? What if I get sick and I have to go to the hospital? They don't even have a hospital there."

"Your friends will still be here when you

get back," she assured me. "And I know it seems like a long time, but May will come more quickly than you realize. As for Linda, she used to help pregnant girls just like you when she was at the convent. You remember when I told you that? She'll take care of you. I promise."

"I don't even know her."

"She has a good heart," my mom said, "or you wouldn't be going there. As for the hospital, she'll know what to do. But even in the worst-case scenario, her friend Gwen is a trained midwife. She's delivered lots of babies."

I wasn't sure that made me feel any better.

"What if I hate it there?"

"How bad can it be? It's right on the beach. And besides, you remember our discussion, right? That it might be easier in the short run if you stay, but in the long run, it will surely make things harder for you."

She meant gossip, not only about me but about my family as well. It might not be the 1950s, but there was still a stigma attached to unwed teenage pregnancies, and even I had to admit that sixteen was way too young to be a mom. If word got out, I would always be *that girl* to neighbors, other students at school, the people at church. To them, I'd always be *that girl* who got knocked up after her freshman year. I would have to endure their judgmental stares and condescension; I'd have to ignore their whispers as I walked past them in the hallways. The rumor mill would churn with questions about who adopted the baby, about whether I ever wanted to see the child again. Though they might not say it to me, they would wonder why I hadn't bothered to use birth control or insist that he wear a condom; I knew that many parents—including friends of the family—would use me as an example to their own children as *that girl*, the one who'd made poor decisions. And all this while waddling the school hallways and having to pee every ten minutes.

Oh yeah, my parents had spoken with me about all of it more than a few times. My mom could tell, though, that I didn't want to revisit it, so she changed the subject. She did that a lot when she didn't want to argue, especially when we were in public.

"Did you enjoy your birthday?"

"It was okay."

"Just okay?"

"I barfed all morning. It was kind of hard for me to get excited."

My mom brought her hands together. "I'm still glad you had a chance to visit with your friends."

Because it's the last time you'll see them for a long, long time, she didn't have to add. "I can't believe I'm not going to be home for Christmas."

"I'm sure Aunt Linda will make it special."

"It still won't be the same," I whined.

"No," my mom admitted. "It probably won't be. But we'll have a nice visit when I see you in January."

"Will Daddy come?"

She swallowed. "Maybe," she said.

Which also means maybe not, I thought. I'd heard them talking about it, but my dad hadn't committed to anything. If he could barely look at me now, how would he feel when I was doing my best to impersonate a female Buddha?

"I wish I didn't have to go."

"Me too," she said. "Do you want to visit with your dad for a while?"

Shouldn't you be asking him if he wants to visit with me? But again, I kept quiet. I mean, what was the point? "It's okay," I said. "I just…"

When I trailed off, my mom offered a sympathetic expression. And, strangely, despite the fact that she and my dad were shipping me off, I had the sense she actually felt bad about it.

"I know there's nothing easy about any of this," she whispered.

Surprising me, she reached into her purse and handed me an envelope. It was filled with cash, and I wondered whether my dad knew what she was doing. It's not as though my family had extra money lying around, but she didn't try to explain. Instead, we sat together for another few minutes until we heard the boarding announcement. When it was my turn, both my parents hugged me, but even then, my father glanced away.

That was almost a month ago, but it already felt like a different life entirely.

It wasn't nearly as cold on the ferry back as it had been in the morning, and the gray skies had given way to an almost shiny blue. I'd chosen to stay in the car for a while despite the fact that the supplies we'd picked up made stretching out on the back seat impossible. I was trying to play the martyr as neither Aunt Linda nor Gwen seemed to understand that Christmas tree shopping notwithstanding, Sundays were still the worst.

"Suit yourself," my aunt had said with a shrug after I'd declined their offer to join them in the cabin. She and Gwen had hopped out of the car, climbed the steps that led to the upper level, and quickly vanished from sight. Somehow, even though I was uncomfortable, I was able to fall asleep, finally waking after an hour. Turning on my Walkman, I listened to music for another hour until my batteries finally went dead and the sky turned to black, and after that, it wasn't long before I grew cramped and bored. Through the window, beneath the glowing ferry lights, I could see a few older men congregated outside their cars, looking exactly like the fishermen they probably were. Like my aunt and Gwen, they eventually made their way to the cabin.

I shifted in the seat and realized that nature was calling. Again. For the sixth or seventh time that day, even though I'd barely had anything to drink. I've forgotten to mention that my bladder had suddenly transformed from something I hardly ever thought about into a hypersensitive and highly inconvenient organ, one that made knowing exactly where to find a bathroom imperative at all times. Without warning, the cells in my bladder would suddenly start vibrating hysterically with the message *You've got to empty me right this very second or else!*, and I'd learned that I didn't have a choice in the matter. *Or else!* If Shakespeare had tried to describe the urgency of the situation, he probably would have written, *To pee or not to pee...that is NEVER the question.*

I scrambled out of the car, hurried up the steps and into the cabin, where I vaguely noticed my aunt and Gwen chatting with someone at one of the booths. I quickly found the bathroom—thankfully, it was unoccupied—and on my way back out, Aunt Linda motioned for me to join them. Instead, I ducked my head and exited the cabin. The last thing I wanted was another conversation with adults. My first instinct after descending the steps was to head back to the car. But the martyrdom wasn't working and the batteries in my Walkman had died, so what was the point? Instead, I decided to explore, thinking it would kill some time. I figured I had probably half an hour to go until the ferry docked—I could already see the lights of Ocracoke in the distance—but unfortunately, the tour wasn't much more interesting than the Pamlico Sound. There was the aforementioned cabin in the center, cars parked on the deck below, and what I guessed was the control room where the captain sat above the cabin, which was off-limits. I did notice, however, a few empty benches toward the front of the boat, and with nothing better to do I made my way there.

It didn't take long to figure out why they were empty. The air was icy, the wind felt like it was stabbing my skin with little needles, and even though I buried my hands in the pockets of my jacket, I could still feel them tingling. On either side, I noticed small breakers in the dark ocean water, little flashes that seemed to sparkle, but the sight of those tiny waves made me think about him, even though I didn't want to.

J. The boy who got me into this mess.

What can I tell you about him? He was a seventeen-year-old surfer from Southern California with beachy good looks, who'd spent the summer in Seattle with a cousin who happened to be a friend of one of my friends. I first saw him at a little get-together in late June, but don't start thinking it was one of those kinds of parties with absent parents and rivers of booze and marijuana smoke drifting from beneath bedroom doors. My parents would have killed me. It wasn't even at a house—it was at Lake Sammamish—and my friend Jodie was a friend of the cousin, who brought J along. Jodie convinced me to go, even though I wasn't sure I wanted to, but once I arrived, it took me all of about two seconds to notice him. He had longish blond hair, broad shoulders, and a deep tan, which was almost impossible for me to attain; my skin preferred to mimic a bright red apple when exposed to the sun. Even from a distance, I could see every single muscle in his stomach, like he was some sort of living human anatomy display.

He was also hanging out with Chloe, a senior from one of the public high schools I vaguely recognized but didn't know, who was equally gorgeous. It was clear they were together; Nancy Drew that I was, I couldn't help but notice, since they were making out and basically hanging all over each other. Even so, that didn't stop me from checking him out as I sat on my towel the rest of the afternoon, in much the same way I ogled the Taylor boys at church. I admit, I'd gone a little boy-crazy in recent years.

It should have ended there, but strangely, it didn't. Because of Jodie, I saw him on the Fourth of July—that one was a nighttime party because of the fireworks, but there were a lot of parents there—and then again a couple of weeks later at the mall. Each time, he was with Chloe and he didn't seem to notice me at all.

Then came Saturday, August 19.

What can I say? I'd just seen *Die Hard: With a Vengeance* with Jodie, even though I'd already seen it once before, and afterward, we went to her house. This time, her parents weren't home. The cousin was there, along with J, but Chloe wasn't. Somehow, J and I ended up talking on the back porch, and miraculously, he seemed interested in me. He was also friendlier than I'd expected. He told me about California, asked me about my life in Seattle, and he finally mentioned in passing that he and Chloe had broken up. Not long after that, he kissed me, and he was so gorgeous, things just got away from me. Long story short, I ended up in the back seat of his cousin's car. I didn't set out to have sex with him, but probably like everyone my age, I was curious about the whole thing, you know? I wanted to know what the big deal was. Nor did he force me. It just kind of happened, and the whole thing was over in less than five minutes.

Afterward, he was nice about it. When I had to leave to meet my eleven p.m. curfew, he walked me to the car and kissed me again. He promised to call me, but he didn't. Three days later I saw him with his arm around Chloe, and when they kissed, I turned around before he could see me, my throat feeling as though I'd just swallowed sandpaper.

Later, when I learned I was pregnant, I called him in California. Jodie got his number from the cousin, since J hadn't given it to me, and when I told him who I was, he didn't seem to remember me. It was only when I reminded him about what happened that he recalled our time together, but even then, I had the sense that he didn't have the slightest clue what we'd talked about or even what I looked like. He also asked why I was calling with a kind of irritated tone, and you didn't need a perfect SAT score to know he had no interest in me at all. Though I'd intended to tell him that I was pregnant, I hung up the phone before the words could come out, and I've never spoken to him again.

My parents know none of this, by the way. I refused to tell them anything about the father, or how nice he'd seemed at first or even that he'd forgotten me entirely. It wouldn't have changed anything, and by then I already knew I'd be giving the baby up for adoption.

You know what else I haven't told them?

That after that phone call with J, I felt stupid, and as disappointed and angry as my parents were with me, I felt even worse about myself.

While I was seated on the bench, with ears already red and my nose beginning to run, I saw a flash of movement from the corner of my eye. Turning, I spotted a dog trotting by with a Snickers wrapper in its mouth. It looked almost exactly like Sandy, my dog back home, only a little bit smaller.

Sandy was a cross between a golden and a Labrador retriever, with a tail that never seemed to stop wagging. Her eyes were a soft, dark caramel, full of expression; had Sandy tried to play poker, she would have lost all her money because she couldn't bluff. I could always tell exactly what she was feeling. If I praised her, her gentle eyes would shine with happiness; if I was upset, they were full of sympathy. She'd been in our family for nine years—we got her when I was in the first grade—and for most of her life she'd slept at the foot of my bed. Now she usually slept in the living room because her hips weren't so good and the stairs were hard for her. But even though she was getting white in the muzzle, her eyes hadn't changed at all. They were still as sweet as ever, especially when I cradled her furry head in my hands. I wondered if she would remember me when I moved back home. Silly, of course. There was no way that Sandy would forget me. She would always love me.

Right?

Right?

Homesickness made my eyes moisten and I swiped at them, but then my hormones surged again, insisting that *I MISSED SANDY SOOO MUCH!* Without thinking, I rose from the bench. I saw Imitation Sandy trotting toward a guy seated near the edge of the deck in a lawn chair, his legs stretched out in front of him. He wore an olive-green jacket and beside him, I noticed, was a camera mounted on a tripod.

I stopped. As much as I wanted to see— and yes, pet—the dog, I wasn't sure whether I wanted to engage in stilted conversation with the owner, especially once he noticed I'd been crying. I was about to turn away when the guy whispered something to the dog. I watched as the dog turned and trotted to a nearby garbage can, where it popped onto its rear legs and carefully deposited the Snickers wrapper.

I blinked, thinking, *Wow. That's kind of cool.*

The dog returned to the guy's side, settled, and was just about to close its eyes when the man dropped an empty paper cup onto the deck. The dog quickly rose, grabbed the cup, and put it into the garbage before returning. When another cup was dropped about a minute later, I couldn't help myself.

"What are you doing?" I finally asked.

The man turned in his seat and it was only then that I realized my mistake. He wasn't a man, but rather a teenager, maybe a year or two older than I was, with hair the color of chocolate and dark eyes flickering with amusement. His jacket, made out of olive-colored canvas with intricate stitching, was strangely stylish, especially for this part of the world. When he raised an eyebrow, I had the uneasy feeling that he'd been expecting me. In the silence, I felt a burst of surprise at the thought that my aunt had been right. There actually *was* someone my age around here, or at the very least, someone my age who was on his way to Ocracoke. The island wasn't entirely composed of fishermen and former nuns, or older women who ate biscuits and read romance novels.

The dog, too, seemed to evaluate me. Its ears perked up and it wagged its tail hard enough to thump the guy's leg, but unlike Sandy, who loved everyone immediately and intensely and would have trotted over to greet me, this dog turned its attention back to the cup, quickly repeating its earlier performance, once more putting it into the garbage can.

Meanwhile, the guy continued to watch

me. Even though he was seated, I could tell he was lean, muscular, and definitely cute, but my whole boy-crazy phase had pretty much died the moment Dr. Bobbi spread that goop on my tummy and I heard the heart-beat. I let my gaze fall, wishing that I'd just gone back to the car and regretting I'd said anything at all. I'd never been good at eye contact except at slumber parties when I was having a staring contest with my friends, and the last thing I needed was another boy in my life. Especially on a day like today; not only had I been crying, but I hadn't worn any makeup, and I was dressed in baggy jeans, Converse high-tops, and a down jacket that probably made me look like the Stay Puft Marshmallow Man.

"Hi," he finally ventured, breaking into my thoughts. "I'm just enjoying the fresh air."

I didn't answer. Instead, I continued to focus on the water, pretending that I hadn't heard him and hoping he wouldn't ask if I'd been crying.

"Are you okay? You look like you've been crying."

Great, I thought. Even though I didn't want

to talk to him, I didn't want him to think I was an emotional wreck, either.

"I'm fine," I asserted. "I was at the front of the boat and the wind made my eyes water."

I wasn't sure he believed me, but he was nice enough to act like he did. "It's pretty up there."

"There's not much to see once the sun goes down."

"You're right," he agreed. "The whole ride has been pretty quiet so far. No reason to even reach for the camera. I'm Bryce Trickett, by the way."

His voice was soft and melodic, not that I cared one way or the other. Meanwhile, the dog had begun to stare at me, its tail thumping. Which reminded me of the reason I'd spoken up in the first place.

"Did you train your dog to throw out garbage?"

"I'm trying to," he said before breaking into a smile, dimples flashing. "But she's young and still working on it. She ran off a few minutes ago, so we had to practice again."

My attention was fixed on those dimples and it took me a second to retrieve my train of thought. "Why?"

"Why what?"

"Why train your dog to throw out the garbage?"

"I don't like litter, and I didn't want any of it blowing into the ocean. It's not good for the environment."

"I meant why don't you just throw it out?"

"Because I was sitting down."

"That's mean."

"Sometimes the mean justifies the end, right?"

Ha ha, I thought. But actually, I'd walked right into the stupid pun, grudgingly acknowledging that it was kind of original as far as puns went.

"Besides, Daisy doesn't mind," he went on. "She thinks it's a game. Do you want to meet her?"

Even before I could respond, he said, "Break," and Daisy quickly rose to her feet. Walking over, she curled around my legs, whining, her tongue lapping at my fingers. Not only did she look like Sandy, she felt like her, and while I stroked her fur, I was transported back to a simpler, happier life in Seattle, before everything went sour.

But just as quickly, reality came rushing back and I realized that I had no desire to linger. I offered Daisy a couple of final pats and put my hands in my pockets while trying to think of an excuse to leave. Bryce was not deterred.

"I don't think I caught your name."

"I didn't tell you my name."

"That's true," he said. "But I can probably figure it out."

"You think you can guess my name?"

"I'm usually pretty good," he said. "I can read palms, too."

"Are you serious?"

"Would you like a demonstration?"

Before I could answer, he gracefully rose from his chair and started toward me. He was a little taller than I'd expected, and lanky, like a basketball player. Not a center or forward like Zeke Watkins, but maybe a shooting guard.

When he was close, I could see flecks of

hazel in his brown eyes, and again I noticed the trace of amusement in his expression that I'd seen earlier. He seemed to scan my face, and when he was satisfied, he motioned to my hands, which were still buried in my pockets. "Can I see your hands now? Just hold them faceup."

"It's cold."

"It won't take long."

This was weird and getting weirder, but whatever. After I showed him my palms, he leaned closer to them, concentrating. He held a finger up.

"Do you mind?" he asked.

"Go ahead."

He traced his finger lightly over the lines in my palms, one after the other. It struck me as strangely intimate, and I felt a little unsettled.

"You're definitely not from Ocracoke," he intoned.

"Wow," I said, trying to keep him from knowing how I felt. "Amazing. And your guess probably has nothing to do with the fact that you've never seen me around here before."

"I meant that you're not from North Carolina. You're not even from the South."

"You might have also noticed I don't have a Southern accent."

Nor did he, I suddenly realized, which was strange, since I thought everyone in the South was supposed to sound like Andy Griffith. He continued to trace for another few seconds before pulling his finger back. "Okay, I think I've got it now. You can put your hands back in your pockets."

I did. I waited but he said nothing. "And?"

"And what?"

"Do you have all your answers?"

"Not all of them. But enough. And I'm pretty sure I know your name."

"No, you don't."

"If you say so."

Whether he was cute or not, I was done with the game and it was time for me to go. "I think I'm going to go sit in the car for a while," I said. "It's getting cold. Nice meeting you." Turning around, I took a couple of steps before I heard him clear his throat.

"You're from the West Coast," he called

out. "But not California. I'm thinking...
Washington? Maybe Seattle?"

His words stopped me in my tracks and
when I turned, I knew I couldn't hide my
shock.

"I'm right, aren't I?"

"How did you know?"

"The same way I know you're sixteen and a
sophomore. You've also got an older sibling
and I'm guessing it's... a sister? And your
name starts with an *M*... not Molly or Mary
or Marie, but something even more formal.
Like... Margaret? Only you probably call
yourself Maggie or something like that."

I felt my jaw drop slightly, too stunned to
say anything at all.

"And you didn't move to Ocracoke perma-
nently. You're only staying a few months or
so, right?" He shook his head, breaking into
that smile again. "But enough. Like I said
earlier, I'm Bryce and it's nice to meet you,
Maggie."

It took a few seconds before I was finally
able to croak out, "You could tell all that
from looking at my face and my palms?"

"No. I learned most of it from Linda."

It took me a second to figure it out. "My aunt?"

"I visited with her for a little while when I was in the cabin. She pointed you out when you walked past our table and she told me a little about you. I'm the one who fixed your bike, by the way."

As I peered at him, I vaguely remembered my aunt and Gwen talking to someone in the booth.

"Then what was all that stuff about my face and my palms?"

"Nothing. Just having fun."

"That wasn't very nice."

"Maybe not. But you should have seen your expression. You're very pretty when you have no idea what to say."

I almost wasn't sure I'd heard him right. *Pretty? Did he just say that I'm very pretty?* Again, I reminded myself that it didn't matter one way or the other. "I could have done without the magic trick."

"You're right. It won't happen again."

"Why would my aunt tell you about me?" And, I wondered, what *else* had she told him?

"She wanted to know if I was interested in tutoring you. I do that sometimes."

You've got to be kidding me. "You're going to be my tutor?"

"I haven't committed to it. I wanted to meet you first."

"I don't need a tutor."

"My mistake, then."

"My aunt just worries a lot."

"I understand."

"Then why doesn't it sound like you believe me?"

"I have no idea. I was just going on what your aunt told me. But if you don't need a tutor, that's fine with me." His grin was relaxed, his dimples still in place. "How do you like it so far?"

"Like what?"

"Ocracoke," he said. "You've been here a few weeks now, right?"

"It's kind of small."

"For sure." He laughed. "It took me a while to get used to it, too."

"You weren't raised here?"

"No," he said. "Like you, I'm a dingbatter."

"What's a dingbatter?"

"Anyone who isn't originally from here."

"That's not a real thing."

"It is around here," he said. "My father and my brothers are dingbatters, too. Not my mom, though. She was born and raised here. We've only been back for a few years." He hooked a thumb over his shoulder toward an older-model truck with fading red paint and large wide tires. "I've got an extra chair in the car if you want to sit. It's a lot more comfortable than the benches."

"I should probably get going. I don't want to bother you."

"You're not bothering me at all. Until you showed up, the ride was fairly boring."

I couldn't exactly tell if he was flirting, but uncertain, I said nothing at all. Bryce seemed to take my lack of an answer as a yes and went on.

"Great," he said. "I'll get the chair."

Before I knew what was happening, the chair was angled toward the ocean beside his, and I watched as he took his seat. Suddenly feeling a bit trapped, I made my way toward the other chair and seated myself gingerly alongside him.

He stretched his legs out in front of him. "Better than the bench, right?"

I was still trying to digest how good-looking he was and that my aunt—the former nun—had set all this up. Or maybe not. The last thing my parents probably wanted was for me to meet anyone of the opposite sex ever again, and they'd probably told her that, too.

"I guess. It's still kind of cold."

As I spoke, Daisy moseyed over and lay down between us. I reached toward her, giving her a quick pat.

"Be careful," he said. "Once you start petting her, she can get kind of insistent that you never stop."

"It's okay. She reminds me of my dog. Back home, I mean."

"Yeah?"

"Sandy's older and a little bigger, though. I miss her. How old is Daisy?"

"She turned one in October. So I guess she's almost fourteen months now."

"She seems very well trained for being so young."

"She should be. I've been training her since she was a puppy."

"To throw garbage away?"

"And other things. Like not running off." He turned his attention to the dog, speaking in a more excited tone. "But she's still got a ways to go, don't you, good girl?"

Daisy whined, her tail thumping.

"If you're not from Ocracoke, how long have you lived there?"

"It'll be four years in April."

"What could have possibly brought your family to Ocracoke?"

"My dad was in the military and after he retired, my mom wanted to be closer to her parents. And because we'd had to move a lot for his job, my dad figured it was only fair to let my mom decide where to settle down for a while. He told us it would be an adventure."

"Has it been an adventure?"

"At times," he said. "In the summers it's a lot of fun. It can get pretty crowded on the island, especially around the Fourth of July. And the beach is really beautiful. Daisy loves to run out there."

"Can I ask what the camera is for?"

"Anything interesting, I guess. There wasn't much today, even before it got dark."

"Is there ever?"

"Last year, a fishing boat caught on fire. The ferry diverted to help rescue the crew since the Coast Guard hadn't arrived yet. It was very sad, but the crew was unharmed and I got some amazing photos. There are dolphins, too, and if they're breaching, I can sometimes get a nice shot. But today I really brought it for my project."

"What's your project?"

"To become an Eagle Scout. I'm training Daisy, and I wanted to get some good shots of her."

I frowned. "I don't get it. You can become an Eagle Scout for training a dog?"

"I'm getting her ready for more advanced training later," he said. "She's learning to be a mobility assistance dog." As if anticipating my next question, he explained, "For people in wheelchairs."

"You mean like a seeing-eye dog?"

"Sort of. She needs different skills, but it's the same principle."

"Like throwing out the garbage?"

"Exactly. Or retrieving the remote control or the telephone handset. Or opening drawers or cabinets or doors."

"How can she open doors?"

"You need a handle on the door, not a knob, of course. But she stands on her hind legs and uses her paws, then nudges the door the rest of the way open with her nose. She's pretty good at it. She can open drawers, too, as long as there's a cord on the handle. The main thing I have to work on is her concentration, but I think part of that is probably her age. I hope she's accepted into the official program, but I'm pretty sure she will be. She isn't required to have any advanced skills— that's what the formal trainers are for—but I wanted to give her a head start. And when she's ready, she'll go to her new home."

"You have to give her away?"

"In April."

"If it were me, I'd keep the dog and forget the Eagle Scout project."

"It's more about helping someone who needs it. But you're right. It's not going to be easy. We've been inseparable since I got her."

"Except when you're at school, you mean."

"Even then," he said. "I've already graduated, but I was homeschooled by my mom. My brothers are homeschooled, too."

Back in Seattle, I only knew one family who homeschooled their children, and they were religious fundamentalists. I didn't know them very well; all I knew was that the daughters had to wear long dresses all the time and the family put up a huge nativity scene in their front yard every Christmas.

"Did you like it? Being homeschooled, I mean?"

"Loved it," he said.

I thought about the social aspect of school, which was far and away my favorite part of it. I couldn't imagine not seeing my friends.

"Why?"

"Because I could learn at my own pace. My mom's a teacher and since we moved around so much, my parents thought we'd get a better education that way."

"Do you have desks in one of the spare rooms? With a chalkboard and a projector?"

"No," he said. "We work at the kitchen

table when we need a lesson. But we do a lot of studying on our own, too."

"And that works?" I couldn't keep the skepticism out of my voice.

"I think so," he said. "With my brothers, I know so. They're very smart. Scary smart, in fact. They're twins, by the way. Robert's into aeronautics and Richard's into computer programming. They'll probably start college when they're fifteen or sixteen, but academically, they're already prepared."

"How old are they?"

"They're only twelve. Before you get too impressed, they're also immature and do stupid things and they drive me crazy. And if you meet them, they'll drive you crazy, too. I feel I have to warn you about that in advance so you won't think poorly of me. Or them, so you know how smart they really are, even when they don't act like it."

For the first time since I'd spoken to him, I couldn't help smiling. Over his shoulder, Ocracoke was looming ever nearer. All around us, people had begun to wander back toward their cars.

"I'll keep that in mind. And you? Are you scary smart?"

"Not like they are. But that's one of the great things about being homeschooled. Usually you can get your work done in two or three hours, so you have time to learn about other things. They're into the sciences, but I like photography, so I had a lot of time to practice."

"And college?"

"I've already been accepted," he said. "I start next fall."

"You're eighteen?"

"Seventeen," he said. "I'll be eighteen in July."

I couldn't help thinking he seemed a lot older than I was and more mature than anyone at my high school. More confident, somehow, more comfortable with the world and his role in it. How that could happen in a place like Ocracoke was beyond me.

"Where are you going to college?"

"West Point," he said. "My dad went there, so it's kind of a family thing. But how about you? What's Washington like? I've never been there, but I've heard it's beautiful."

"It is. The mountains are amazing and there's a lot of great hiking, and Seattle is definitely fun. My friends and I see movies and hang out at the mall, things like that. My neighborhood is kind of quiet, though. A lot of older people live there."

"There are whales in the Puget Sound, right? Humpback whales?"

"Of course."

"Have you ever seen one?"

"Lots of times." I shrugged. "In sixth grade, my class took a field trip on a boat and we were able to get pretty close. It was cool."

"I've been hoping to see one before I leave for school. Supposedly they can be spotted off the coast here sometimes, but I've never been that lucky."

Two people walked past on either side of us; I heard a car door slam behind me. The boat engine groaned and I felt the ferry begin to slow.

"I guess we're almost there," I observed, thinking the trip seemed shorter than usual.

"That we are," he said. "I should probably get Daisy in the truck. And I think your aunt is looking for you."

When he waved behind me, I turned and saw my aunt approaching. I prayed that she wouldn't wave or make a scene, letting everyone on the ferry know that I'd met the guy she'd wanted to be my tutor.

She waved. "There you are!" she called out. I felt myself sink lower in my chair as she drew near. "I looked for you in the car but couldn't find you," she went on. "I see you've met Bryce."

"Hi, Ms. Dawes," Bryce said. He rose from his chair and folded it up. "Yeah, we had the chance to get to know each other a little."

"That's good to hear."

In the pause, I had the sense that both of them were waiting for me to say something. "Hi, Aunt Linda." I watched Bryce put his chair in the bed of his pickup, and I took it as my cue to stand. After folding mine, I handed it over, watching as Bryce placed it in the truck before lowering the tailgate.

"Hop up, Daisy," he said. Daisy rose and leaped into the back of the truck.

I could feel my aunt watching him, then me, then both of us at the same time, unsure what to do, before she must have remembered her pre-nun years, when she was probably closer to normal, with regular feelings. "I'll just wait in the car for you," she said. "Nice visiting with you, Bryce. I'm glad we had a chance to catch up."

"Take care," Bryce responded. "I'm sure I'll be in for more biscuits this week, by the way, so I'll see you then."

Aunt Linda eyed both of us before finally turning to leave. When she was out of hearing range, Bryce faced me again.

"I really like Linda and Gwen. Their biscuits are the best I've ever had, but I'm sure you already know that. I've been trying to get them to share their secret recipe, but no dice. My dad and grandfather grab a few every time they head to the boat."

"The boat?"

"My grandfather's a fisherman. When my dad isn't consulting with the DOD, he helps out my grandfather. Repairing the boat and equipment, or actually going out on the water with him."

"What's DOD?"

"Department of Defense."

"Oh," I said, unsure what else to add. It was hard to reconcile the idea that a consultant with the DOD actually chose to live in Ocracoke. By then, however, the ferry had stopped and I heard car doors slamming and engines rumbling to life. "I guess I should be going."

"Probably. But hey, it was great talking to you, Maggie. Usually there's no one even close to my age on the ferry, so you made the trip that much more enjoyable."

"Thanks," I said, trying not to stare at his dimples. I turned away and, surprising myself, I suddenly felt a strange mixture of relief and disappointment that our time together had come to an end.

I waited until the last minute before getting into the car because I didn't want to be confronted by questions, which was something I was used to from my mom and dad. *What did you talk about? Did you like him? Can you imagine him teaching you geometry and*

editing your papers if needed? Did I make the right choice?

My parents would have been all over me. On almost every school day right up until barf-day—or pee-on-a-stick day, whatever—they always asked me how school went, like attending classes was some sort of magical, mysterious production that everyone would find fascinating. No matter how many times I simply said that it was fine—which really meant *Stop asking me such a dumb question*—they continued to ask. And honestly, aside from *fine*, what was I supposed to say? They'd been to school. They knew what it was like. A teacher stood up front and taught stuff that I was supposed to learn in order to do well on tests, none of which were ever any fun.

Now lunch, that could sometimes be interesting. Or when I was younger, recess might have been something to talk about. But *school*? School was just…*school*.

Thankfully, my aunt and Gwen were chatting about the sermon we'd heard in church, which I barely remembered, and obviously, the ride took only a few minutes. We drove to the shop first, where I helped them unload their supplies, but instead of dropping Gwen off, we brought her with us to my aunt's house so she could help us haul the Christmas tree inside.

Despite my pregnancy, and despite them being older ladies, we were somehow able to muscle it up the steps and prop it in a stand that Aunt Linda retrieved from the back of the hall closet. By then, I was kind of tired and I think they were, too. Instead of decorating right away, my aunt and Gwen got busy in the kitchen. Aunt Linda made fresh biscuits while Gwen heated up yet more Thanksgiving leftovers.

I hadn't realized how hungry I was, and I cleared my plate for the first time in a while. And, maybe because Bryce had said something about them, I realized the biscuits were tastier than usual. As I reached for a second one, I saw Aunt Linda smile.

"What?" I asked.

"I'm just glad you're eating," my aunt said.

"What's in these biscuits?"

"The basics—flour, buttermilk, shortening."

"Anything secret in the recipe?"

If she wondered why I cared, she didn't let on. She cast a conspiratorial glance at Gwen before facing me again. "Of course."

"What is it?"

"It's a secret," she said with a wink.

We didn't talk more after that, and once I finished doing the dishes, I retreated to my room. Outside my window, the sky was filled with stars and I could see the moon hovering over the water, making the ocean glow almost silver. I slipped into my pajamas and was about to crawl in bed when I suddenly remembered that I still had to do the paper on Thurgood Marshall. Grabbing my notes—I'd at least gotten that far—I started the actual writing. I'd always been okay at writing—not great, but definitely better than I was at math—and had gotten through a page and a half when I heard a knock at the door. Glancing up, I saw Aunt Linda poke her head in. When she noticed I was doing homework, she lifted an eyebrow, but I'm sure she immediately thought it was better not to say anything lest my progress come to a screeching halt.

"The kitchen looks great," she said. "Thank you."

"You're welcome. Thanks for dinner."

"It was just leftovers." She shrugged. "Except for the biscuits. You should call your parents tonight. It's still early there."

I eyed the clock. "They're probably eating dinner. I'll call them in a little bit."

She quietly cleared her throat. "I wanted to let you know that when I spoke with Bryce, I didn't tell him about...well, your situation. I just said that my niece had come to stay with me for a few months and left it at that."

I hadn't known I'd been concerned about that but felt myself expel a breath of relief.

"Didn't he ask why?"

"He might have, but I stuck to the subject of whether he'd be willing to tutor you."

"But you told him about me."

"Only because he said he needed to know something about you."

"If I want him to be my tutor, you mean."

"Yes," she agreed. "And not that it matters, but he's the same young man who fixed your bicycle."

I already knew that, but I was still pondering the prospect of seeing him day after day. "What if I promised to catch up on my own? Without his help?"

"Can you? Because you know I can't help you. It's been a long time since I was in school."

I hesitated. "What should I say if he asks me why I'm here?"

She considered it. "It's important to remember that none of us is perfect. Everyone makes mistakes. All we can do is try to be the best version of ourselves as we move forward. In this case, if he asks, you can tell the truth, or you can lie. I suppose it comes down to the kind of person you want to see when you look in the mirror."

I winced, knowing I never should have asked a former nun a question that dealt with morality. With no possible comeback to that, I returned to the obvious. "I don't want anyone to know. Including him."

She offered a sad smile. "I know you don't. But bear in mind that pregnancy is a hard secret to keep, especially in a village like Ocracoke. And once you start showing..."

She didn't have to finish. I knew what she meant.

"What if I don't leave the house?"

Even as I said it, I knew how unrealistic that idea was. I rode the ferry with others from Ocracoke to go to church on Sundays; I would have to see a doctor in Morehead City, which meant yet more ferry rides. I'd been in my aunt's shop. People already knew I was on the island, and no doubt some of them were wondering about the reason. For all I knew, Bryce was doing the same thing. They might not be thinking pregnancy, but they would suspect that I was in some sort of trouble. With my family, with drugs, with the law, with...*something*. Why else would I have shown up out of the blue in the middle of winter?

"You think I should tell him, don't you?"

"I think," she said, drawing out the words, "that he's going to learn the truth, whether you want him to or not. It's just a matter of when, and who tells him. I think it would be best if it came from you."

I stared out the window, unseeing. "He's going to think I'm a terrible person."

"I doubt that."

I swallowed, hating this, hating all of it. My aunt remained silent, allowing me to think. In that way, I had to admit, she was way better than my parents.

"I guess Bryce can be my tutor."

"I'll let him know," she said, her voice quiet. Then, clearing her throat, she asked, "What are you working on?"

"I'm hoping to be done with the first draft of my paper tonight."

"I'm sure it'll be great. You're an intelligent young lady."

Tell my parents that, I thought. "Thanks."

"Is there anything you need before I turn in? A glass of milk, maybe? I have an early day tomorrow."

"I'm okay, thanks."

"Don't forget to call your parents."

"I won't."

She turned to leave before coming to a stop again. "Oh, another thing—I was thinking we could decorate the tree tomorrow night after dinner."

"Okay."

"Sleep well, Maggie. I love you."

"Love you, too," I said. The phrase came automatically, like it did with my friends, and later, when I was talking to my parents and they asked how I was getting along with Linda, I realized it was the first time we'd ever said the words to each other.

THE NUTCRACKER

Manhattan
December 2019

Mark was sitting with his fingertips pressed together when Maggie finally trailed off, his expression unreadable. He said nothing right away but finally shook his head, as though suddenly realizing it was his turn to speak.

"I'm sorry," he said. "I guess I'm still trying to absorb what you just told me."

"My story so far isn't quite what you expected, is it?"

"I'm not sure what I expected," he admitted. "What happened next?"

"I'm a bit too tired to go into the rest of it just now."

Mark raised a hand. "I get it. But still…
wow. When I was sixteen, I doubt I could
have handled a crisis like that."

"I didn't have a choice in the matter."

"Still…" He absently scratched an ear.
"Your aunt Linda seems interesting."

Maggie couldn't help smiling. "For sure."

"Do you still keep in touch?"

"We used to. She and Gwen visited me
in New York a few times and I saw her in
Ocracoke once, but mainly we wrote letters
and chatted on the phone. She passed away
six years ago."

"I'm sorry to hear that."

"I still miss her."

"Did you keep the letters?"

"Every single one."

He gazed off to the side before coming
back to Maggie. "Why did your aunt stop
being a nun? Did you ever ask?"

"Not back then. I would have been uncomfortable asking her, and besides, I was
too wrapped up in my own problems for
the question to have even crossed my mind.
It took me years to broach the subject, but
when I did, I didn't get an answer that

I really understood. I think I was hoping for more of a smoking gun or something."

"What did she say?"

"She said that life was about seasons, and that the season had changed."

"Huh. That is a bit mysterious."

"I'm guessing she got tired of dealing with all those pregnant teens. Speaking from experience, we can be a moody bunch."

He chuckled before growing contemplative. "Do convents still take in pregnant teenagers?"

"I have no idea, but I sort of doubt it. Times change. A few years ago, when I caught the 'I wonder' bug, I searched for the Sisters of Mercy on the internet and learned that they'd closed more than a decade earlier."

"Where was her convent? Before she left, I mean."

"Illinois, I think. Or maybe it was Ohio. Somewhere in the Midwest, anyway. And don't ask me how she ended up there in the first place. Like my dad, she was from the West Coast."

"How long was she a nun?"

"Twenty-five years or so? Maybe a little less or more, I'm not really sure. Gwen too. I think Gwen took her orders even before my aunt did."

"Do you think they were...?"

When he paused, Maggie lifted an eyebrow. "Lovers? I honestly don't know that either. As I got older, I sort of thought they might be, since they were always together, but I never saw them kiss or hold hands or anything like that. One thing I know for certain, though: they loved each other deeply. Gwen was at my aunt Linda's bedside when she passed away."

"Do you keep in touch with her, too?"

"I was closer to my aunt, of course, but after she passed, I made sure to call Gwen a few times a year. But not so much lately. She has Alzheimer's and I'm not sure she even remembers who I am anymore. She does remember my aunt, though, and that makes me happy."

"It's hard to believe that you've never told Luanne any of this."

"It's a habit. Even my parents still pretend that it never happened. Morgan too."

"Have you heard from Luanne? Since she left for Hawaii?"

"I haven't told her what the doctor said, if that's what you're asking."

He swallowed. "I hate that this is happening to you," he said. "I really do."

"You and me both. Do yourself a favor and never get cancer, especially when you're supposed to be in the prime of life."

He bowed his head and she knew he was at a loss for words. If joking about death helped her keep other, darker feelings at bay, the downside was that no one ever knew exactly how to respond. Finally, he looked up.

"I got a text from Luanne today. She said she'd texted you but that you didn't get back to her."

"I haven't checked my phone today. What did it say?"

"It said to remind you to open your card if you haven't already."

Oh yeah. Because there's a gift inside. "It's probably still on the desk somewhere if you want to help me find it."

He got up and started going through her inbox while Maggie rummaged in the top drawer of the desk. As she sorted, Mark pulled an envelope from a stack of invoices and handed it over.

"Is this it?"

"It is," she said, taking a second to examine it. "I hope she's not giving me a sexy Polaroid of herself."

Mark's eyes widened. "That doesn't sound like her..."

She laughed. "I'm teasing. I just wanted to see how you'd react." She opened the envelope; inside was an elegant card with a standard greeting, along with a short note from Luanne thanking Maggie for being a "pleasure with whom to work." Luanne was always a stickler when it came to correct grammar and verbiage. Enclosed were two tickets to the New York City Ballet's *Nutcracker* at Lincoln Center. The show was on Friday evening, two nights away.

She removed the tickets, showing them to Mark. "It's a good thing you reminded me. They're about to expire."

"What a great gift. Have you seen it?"

"I've always talked about going but never quite made it. How about you?"

"Can't say that I have."

"Would you like to join me?"

"Me?"

"Why not? It can be a reward since you've had to work late."

"I'd like that."

"Great."

"I also enjoyed your story, even if you left it with a cliff-hanger."

"What cliff-hanger?"

"About you, the rest of your pregnancy. The fact that you were beginning to forge a relationship with your aunt. Bryce. I know you agreed that he could be your tutor, but how did it go? Did he help? Or did he let you down?"

As soon as Mark said the name, she felt a stab of disbelief that nearly a quarter century had passed since the months she'd spent in Ocracoke.

"Are you really interested in the rest of it?"

"I am," he admitted.

"Why?"

"Because it helps me understand a bit more about you."

She took another drink of her melting

smoothie, and suddenly flashed on her most recent discussion with Dr. Brodigan. *One moment*, she observed cynically, *you're having a pleasant conversation with someone, and the next, all you can think about is the fact that you're dying*. She tried and failed to push the realization away before suddenly wondering if Mark was mirroring her thoughts. "I know you speak with Abigail every day. You're welcome to tell her about my prognosis."

"I wouldn't do that. That's...your business."

"Does she watch the videos?"

"Yes."

"Then she'll find out anyway. I was planning on posting about this latest development after I tell my parents and my sister."

"You haven't told them yet?"

"I've decided to wait until after Christmas."

"Why?"

"If I told them now, they'd probably either want me to immediately fly back to Seattle—which I don't want to do—or they'd insist on coming out here, and I don't want that, either. They'd stress and need to wrestle with their grief, and it would be harder for all of us. As an added bonus, it would ruin all their future Christmases. I'd rather not do that."

"It's going to be hard no matter when you tell them."

"I know. But my family and I have a...unique relationship."

"How so?"

"I haven't exactly lived the kind of life my parents anticipated. I always had the feeling that I was born into the wrong family somehow, and I learned a long time ago that our relationship works best when we maintain some distance between us. They haven't understood my choices. As for my sister, she's more like my parents. She did the whole marriage, kids, suburbs thing, and she's still as beautiful as ever. It's hard to compete with someone like that."

"But look at all you've done."

"In my family, I'm not sure that matters."

"I'm sorry to hear that." In the silence that followed, Maggie suddenly yawned and Mark cleared his throat. "Why don't you go ahead and take off if you're tired," he said. "I'll make sure everything is logged properly and handle all the shipments."

In the past, she would have insisted on staying. Now she knew it wouldn't serve any purpose. "Are you sure?"

"You're taking me to the ballet. It's the least I can do."

After she bundled up, Mark followed her to the door and pulled it open, ready to lock up behind her. The wind was harsh, biting her cheeks.

"Thanks again for the smoothie."

"Do you want me to get you an Uber or a cab? It's cold out there."

"It's not that far. I'll be fine."

"See you tomorrow?"

She didn't want to lie; who knew how she would feel? "Maybe," she said.

When he nodded, his lips a grim line, she could see he understood.

By the time she reached the corner, Maggie knew she'd made a mistake. It wasn't just biting outside; it felt arctic, and she was shivering hard even after entering her apartment.

Feeling as if a block of ice were lodged in her chest, she huddled on the couch beneath a blanket for nearly half an hour before she summoned the energy to move again.

In the kitchen, she made chamomile tea. She thought about taking a warm bath as well, but it was too much effort. Instead, she went to her bedroom, slipped into a pair of thick flannel pajamas, a sweatshirt, two pairs of socks, and a nightcap to keep her head warm, and crawled under the covers. After finishing half a cup of the tea, she dozed off and slept for sixteen hours.

She woke feeling *awful*, as though she'd just pulled an all-nighter. Worse, pain seemed to radiate from various organs, sharpening with every beat of her heart. Steeling herself, she was somehow able to rise from bed and make it to the bathroom, where she kept the painkillers Dr. Brodigan had prescribed.

She washed two of the pills down with water, then sat on the edge of the bed, still and concentrating, until she was sure she would keep them down. Only then was she ready to start her day.

Drawing a bath because showering now felt like being stabbed, she soaked in the warm, soapy water for nearly an hour. Afterward she texted Mark, letting him know that she wouldn't make it to the gallery today but would touch base tomorrow regarding the time and place to meet for the ballet.

After dressing in comfy clothing, she made breakfast, even though it was already afternoon. She forced down an egg and half a piece of toast, both of which tasted like salted cardboard, and then—as had become a habit in the last week and a half—she settled onto the couch to watch the world outside her window.

There were snow flurries, the tiny flakes flickering against the glass, the movements hypnotic. Catching a glimpse of poinsettias in an apartment window across the street, she recalled her first Christmas back in Seattle after she'd returned from Ocracoke. Though she'd wanted to be excited for the holiday, she'd spent much of December simply going through the motions. Even on Christmas morning, she remembered opening her gifts with feigned enthusiasm.

She knew that part of that had to do with getting older. Gone were the beliefs from her childhood, and she'd reached the stage where even smelling a cookie meant calculating calories. But it was more than that. Her months in Ocracoke had turned her into someone she no longer recognized, and there were times when Seattle no longer felt like home. In retrospect, she understood that even back then, she'd been counting the days until she could finally leave for good.

Then again, she'd been feeling that way for months by that point. Not long after returning to Seattle, once she began to feel vaguely back to normal, Madison and Jodie had been eager to pick up where they had left off. On the surface, not much had changed. Yet the more time she spent with them, the more she felt like she'd grown up while they'd stayed exactly the same. They had the same interests and insecurities they'd always had, the same sorts of crushes on boys, felt the same thrill at hanging out in the food court at the mall on

Saturday afternoons. They were familiar and comfortable, and yet, little by little, Maggie began to understand they would eventually drift from her life entirely, in the same way Maggie sometimes felt as though she were drifting through her own.

She'd also spent much of those first few months back at home thinking about Ocracoke and missing it more than she'd imagined. She'd thought about her aunt and the desolate, windswept beach, the ferry rides and garage sales. It amazed her when she reflected on all that had happened while she was there, so much so that even now it sometimes took her breath away.

Maggie watched a drama on Netflix—something starring Nicole Kidman, though she couldn't remember the title—took a late-afternoon nap, and then ordered two smoothies for delivery. She knew she wouldn't be able to finish both, but she felt bad ordering only one, since the check was so small.

And really, what did it matter if she threw one away?

She also debated whether to have a glass of wine. Not now, but later, maybe before bedtime. She hadn't had a drink in months, even counting the little get-together at the gallery in late November, when she'd pretty much simply held the glass for show. While she was undergoing chemotherapy, the thought of alcohol had been nauseating, and after that, she simply hadn't been in the mood. She knew there was a bottle in the refrigerator, something from Napa Valley she'd purchased on a whim, and though it sounded like a good idea now, she suspected that later, the desire would fade and all she'd want to do would be to sleep. Which might, she admitted, be for the best. Who knew how the wine would affect her? She was taking painkillers and ate so little that even a couple of sips might leave her either passed out or rushing to the bathroom to make an offering to the porcelain gods.

Call it a quirk, but Maggie never wanted anyone to see or hear her vomit, including the nurses who'd watched over her during chemotherapy. They would help her to the bathroom, where she'd shut the door and try to be as quiet as possible. Aside from the morning her mom had found her in the bathroom, as far as she could remember, there'd only been one other instance when someone had seen her throw up. That had been when she'd gotten seasick while photographing from a catamaran off Martinique. The nausea had come on fast, like a tidal wave; she'd felt her stomach immediately beginning to turn, and she barely made it to the railing in time. She retched nonstop for the next two hours. It was the most miserable experience she'd ever had while working, so over-the-top that she hadn't cared in the slightest whether anyone was watching. It had been all she could do to take any photographs that evening— only three out of more than a hundred were any good at all—and in between shots, she'd done her best to remain as still as possible. Morning sickness—hell, even chemotherapy sickness—couldn't compare, and she'd wondered why she'd whined so much back when she was sixteen.

Who had she really been back then?

She'd tried to re-create the story for Mark, especially how terrible those first weeks in Ocracoke had been for a lonely, pregnant sixteen-year-old. At the time, her exile had seemed eternal; in retrospect, all she could think was that her months there had passed too quickly.

Though she'd never said as much to her parents, she'd longed to return to Ocracoke. The feeling was especially strong in those first two months she was back in Seattle; in certain moments, the desire was almost overwhelming. While the passage of time diminished her longing, it never completely went away. Years ago, in the travel section of the *New York Times*, someone had written an account of their journeys in the Outer Banks. The writer had been hoping to see the islands' wild horses and had finally spotted them near Corolla, but it was her description of the austere beauty of those low-slung barrier islands that struck a chord in Maggie. The article summoned the smell of Aunt Linda and Gwen making biscuits for fishermen early in the mornings, and the quiet solitude of the village on blustery winter days. She remembered clipping the article and sending it to her aunt, along with a few prints of some recent photographs she'd taken. As always, Aunt Linda had responded by mail, thanking Maggie for the article and raving about the photographs. She ended the letter by telling Maggie how proud she was of her and how much she loved her.

She'd told Mark that she and Aunt Linda had grown closer over the years, but she hadn't elaborated fully. With her endless letters, Aunt Linda became a more constant presence in Maggie's life than the rest of Maggie's family combined. There was something comforting in the knowledge that someone out there loved and accepted her for the person she was; to Maggie it was the months they'd spent together that taught her the meaning of unconditional love.

A few months before Aunt Linda died, Maggie had confessed to her that she had always wanted to be more like her. It was on her first and only visit to Ocracoke since the day she'd departed as a teenager. The village hadn't changed much and her aunt's house triggered a flood of bittersweet memories.

The furniture was the same, the smells were the same, but the passage of time had slowly taken its toll. Everything was a bit more worn, faded, and tired, including Aunt Linda. By then, the lines on her face had deepened into wrinkles and her white hair had thinned to reveal her scalp in places. Only her eyes had remained the same, with that forever recognizable gleam. At the time, the two women were seated at the same kitchen table where Maggie had once done her homework.

"Why would you want to be more like me?" Aunt Linda had asked, taken aback.

"Because you're...wonderful."

"Oh, honey." Aunt Linda had reached over with a hand so birdlike and frail that it nearly broke Maggie's heart. She gently squeezed Maggie's fingers. "Don't you realize that I could say exactly the same thing about you?"

On Friday, after waking from her coma-like sleep and puttering around the apartment, Maggie swallowed some flavorless instant oatmeal while texting Mark her plans to meet him later at the gallery. She also made a reservation at the Atlantic Grill and arranged for a car pickup after dinner, since finding an Uber or cab in that neighborhood in the evening was often impossible. With all that accomplished, she went back to bed. Since a later-than-usual night was on tap, Maggie needed to be rested enough not to fall face-first into her dinner plate. She didn't set the alarm and slept another three hours. Only then did she start getting ready.

The thing is, Maggie thought, *when a face is as gaunt as a skeleton's, with skin as fragile as tissue paper, there's only so much you can do to appear presentable*. One glimpse of her baby-fuzz hair and anyone would know she was knocking at death's door. But she had to make an attempt, and after her bath, she took her time with her makeup, trying to add color (*life*) to her cheeks; next, she applied three different shades of lipstick before she found one that seemed remotely natural.

She had a choice about the hair—scarf or hat—and finally decided on a red wool beret. She thought about wearing a dress but knew she'd freeze, so she opted for pants with a thick, nubbly sweater that added substance to her frame. As always, her necklace was in place, and she donned a lovely bright cashmere scarf to keep her neck warm. When she stepped back to appraise herself in the mirror, she felt she looked almost as good as she had before chemotherapy started.

Collecting her purse, she took a couple more pills—the pain wasn't as bad as yesterday, but no reason to risk it—and called an Uber. Pulling up to the gallery a few minutes after closing time, she saw Mark through the window, discussing one of her photographs with a couple in their fifties. Mark offered the slightest of waves when Maggie stepped inside and hurried to her office. On her desk was a small stack of mail; she was quickly sorting through it when Mark suddenly tapped on her open door.

"Hey, sorry. I thought they'd make a decision before you arrived, but they had a lot of questions."

"And?"

"They bought two of your prints."

Amazing, she thought. Early in the life

of the gallery, weeks could go by without the sale of even a single print of hers. And while the sales did increase with the growth of her career, the real renown came with her *Cancer Videos*. Fame did indeed change everything, even if the fame was for a reason she wouldn't wish upon anyone. Mark walked into the office before suddenly pulling up short. "Wow," he said. "You look fantastic."

"I'm trying."

"How do you feel?"

"I've been more tired than usual, so I've been sleeping a lot."

"Are you sure you're still up for this?"

She could see the worry in his expression. "It's Luanne's gift, so I have to go. And besides, it'll help me get into the Christmas spirit."

"I've been looking forward to it ever since you invited me. Are you ready? Traffic is going to be terrible tonight, especially in this weather."

"I'm ready."

After turning out the lights and locking the door, they stepped into the frigid night. Mark raised a hand, flagging down a cab, and held Maggie's elbow as she crawled in.

On the ride to Midtown, Mark filled her in on the customers and let her know that Jackie Bernstein had returned to purchase the Trinity sculpture she'd been admiring. It was an expensive piece—and worth it, in Maggie's opinion, if only as an investment. In the past five years, the value of Trinity's art had skyrocketed. Nine of Maggie's photos had sold as well—including those last two—and Mark assured her that he had been able to get all the shipments out before she'd arrived.

"I was ducking into the back whenever I had a spare minute, but I wanted to make sure to get them out today. A lot of them are intended as gifts."

"What would I ever do without you?"

"Probably hire someone else."

"You don't give yourself enough credit. You forget that a lot of people applied for—and didn't get—the position."

"Did they?"

"You didn't know that?"

"How would I?"

He had a point, she realized. "I also

want to thank you for shouldering the whole load without Luanne, especially over the holidays."

"You're welcome. I enjoy talking with people about your work."

"And Trinity's work."

"Of course," he added. "But his are a little intimidating. I've learned that with them, it's usually better to listen more and speak less. People who are interested in his work generally know more than I do."

"You have a knack for it, though. Did you ever think about being a curator or running your own gallery? Maybe getting a master's degree in art history instead of divinity?"

"No," he said. His tone was good-natured but determined. "I know the path I'm supposed to take in life."

I'm sure you do, she thought. "When does that start? Your path, I mean?"

"Classes begin next September."

"Have you already been accepted?"

"Yes," he said. "I'll be attending the University of Chicago."

"With Abigail?"

"Of course."

"Good for you," she said. "Sometimes I wonder what the college experience would have been like."

"You went to community college."

"I mean a four-year school, with dorm life and parties and listening to music while playing Frisbee in the quad."

He lifted an eyebrow. "And going to classes and studying and writing papers."

"Oh yeah. That too." She grinned. "Did you tell Abigail we were going to the ballet tonight?"

"Yeah, and she's a little jealous about it. She made me promise to bring her one day."

"How's the family reunion going?"

"The house is chaotic and noisy all the time. But she loves it. One of her brothers is in the air force and he came in from Italy. She hasn't seen him since last year."

"I'll bet her parents are thrilled to have everyone around."

"They are. I guess they've been building a gingerbread house. A massive one. They do it every year."

"And had your boss not needed you, you could have helped them."

"It would definitely be a learning experience. I'm not very handy in the kitchen."

"And your parents? I heard you mention to Trinity that they're abroad now?"

"They're in Jerusalem today and tomorrow. They'll be in Bethlehem on Christmas Eve. They texted some pictures from the Church of the Holy Sepulchre." He pulled out his phone to show her. "This trip is something my parents have wanted to do for years, but they waited until I finished college. So that I'd be able to come home during school breaks." Mark put his phone back into his pocket. "Where did you go? The first time you left the country, I mean?"

"Vancouver, Canada," Maggie answered. "Mainly because it was driving distance. I spent a weekend taking photos in Whistler after a major ice storm had rolled through."

"I still haven't ever been out of the country."

"You have to experience it," she said. "Visiting other places changes your perspective. It helps you understand that no matter where you are, or what country you're in, people are pretty much the same everywhere."

Traffic began to slow as they exited the

West Side Highway, then slowed even more as they made their way east on the cross streets. Despite the cold, the sidewalks were jammed; she saw people carrying shopping bags and lining up near corner food vendors; others hurried home from work. Eventually they reached the point where they could see the lighted windows of Lincoln Center, which left them with the option of either sitting in an idling cab for another ten or fifteen minutes or getting out and walking.

They decided to walk and slowly made their way through a throng that extended beyond the front doors. Maggie kept her arms crossed and shifted from one foot to the other in hopes of staying warm, but thankfully the line moved quickly, and they entered the lobby after only a few minutes. Directed by the ushers, they found their seats in the first tier of the balcony of the David H. Koch Theater.

They continued to chat quietly before the show, taking in their surroundings and watching the seats fill with a mix of adults and children. In time, the lights dimmed, the music came up, and the audience was introduced to Christmas Eve at the Stahlbaum house.

As the tale unfolded, Maggie was transfixed by the dancers' grace and beauty, their soaring, delicate movements animating the dreamlike notes of Tchaikovsky's score. Occasionally Maggie peeked over at Mark, noting his rapt attention. He couldn't seem to tear his eyes from the stage, reminding her that he was a midwestern boy who'd probably never seen anything like it.

When the ballet was over, they joined the festive crowds as they poured onto Broadway. She was grateful that the Atlantic Grill was just across the street. Feeling cold and wobbly—maybe because of the pills, or because she'd eaten almost nothing all day— she looped her arm through Mark's as they approached the crosswalk. He slowed his pace, allowing her to use him for support.

It wasn't until they were seated at their table that she began to feel a bit better.

"Are you sure you'd rather not just call it a night?"

"I'll be okay," she said, not altogether convinced herself. "And I really need to eat."

When he didn't seem reassured, she went on. "I'm your boss. Think of this as a business dinner."

"It's not a business dinner."

"Personal business," she said. "I thought you wanted to hear more about my time in Ocracoke."

"I do," he said. "But only if you feel up to it."

"I really do have to eat. I'm not kidding about that."

Reluctantly, he nodded just as the waitress arrived and handed them the menus. Surprising herself, Maggie decided she would like a glass of wine, settling on a French burgundy. Mark ordered an iced tea.

As the waitress walked away, Mark took in the restaurant. "Have you ever been here before?"

"On a date, maybe five years ago? I couldn't believe they had a spot for us tonight, but I guess someone must have canceled."

"What was he like? The guy who brought you here?"

She tilted her head, trying to remember. "Tall, great salt-and-pepper hair, worked for Accenture as a management consultant.

Divorced, a couple of kids, and very smart. He wandered into the gallery one day. We had coffee and then ended up going out a few times."

"But it didn't work out?"

"Sometimes the chemistry just isn't there. With him, I figured it out when I went to Key Largo for a shoot and realized when I got back that I hadn't missed him at all. That's pretty much the story of my entire dating life, no matter who I dated."

"I'm afraid to ask what that means."

"In my twenties, when I first moved out here, I frequented the club scene for a few years...going out at midnight, staying out until almost dawn, even on weeknights. None of the guys I met there were the kind I could bring home to my family. Frankly, it probably wasn't a good idea to bring them back to my place."

"No?"

"Think...a lot of tattoos and dreams of being rappers or DJs. I definitely had a type back then."

He made a face, which made her laugh. The waitress returned with her glass of wine and she reached for it with a confidence she didn't quite feel. She took a small taste, waiting to see if her stomach rebelled, but it seemed okay. By then, they'd both decided on what they wanted—she ordered the Atlantic cod, he opted for the filet—and when the waitress asked if they wanted to start with appetizers or a salad, both of them declined.

When the waitress walked away, she leaned over the table. "You could have ordered more food," she chided. "Just because I can't eat much, you don't have to follow my lead."

"I had a couple of slices of pizza before you got to the gallery."

"Why would you do that?"

"I didn't want to run up the bill. Places like this are expensive."

"Are you serious? That's silly."

"That's what Abigail and I do."

"You're one of a kind, you know that?"

"I've been meaning to ask you...How did you start with travel photography?"

"Sheer persistence. And lunacy."

"That's all?"

She shrugged. "I also got lucky, since salaried gigs for magazines don't really exist anymore. The first photographer I worked for in Seattle already had a reputation as a travel photographer because he'd worked a lot for *National Geographic* back in the day. He had a pretty good list of contacts with magazines, tour companies, and ad agencies, and he'd sometimes bring me along to assist him. After a couple years, I went a bit crazy and ended up moving here. I roomed with some flight attendants, got discount flights and took pics in whatever place I could afford to visit. I also found work with a cutting-edge photographer here. He was an early adopter of digital photography and was always investing whatever fees he earned in more gear and software, which meant I had to as well. I started my own website, with tips and reviews and Photoshop lessons, and one of the photo editors at Condé Nast stumbled across it. He hired me to shoot in Monaco, and that led to a second job and then another. Meanwhile, my old boss in Seattle retired and he pretty much offered me his client list as well as a recommendation, so I took over a lot of the work he'd been doing."

"What allowed you to become fully independent?"

"My reputation grew to the point where I was able to book my own local gigs. My fee, which I purposely kept low for international work, always enticed editors. And the popularity of my website and blog, which led to my first online sales, made bills easier to pay. I was also an early user of Facebook, Instagram, and especially YouTube, which helped with name recognition. And then, of course, there was the gallery, which cemented things for me. For years, it was a scramble to get any paid travel work, and then, like a switch had been thrown, I suddenly had all the work I could handle."

"How old were you when you landed that shoot in Monaco?"

"Twenty-seven."

She could see the gleam in his eyes. "That's a great story."

"Like I said, I was lucky."

"Maybe at first. After that, it was all you."

Maggie took in the restaurant; like so many spots in New York, it was decorated for the holidays, featuring both an ornamented

Christmas tree and a glowing menorah in the bar area. There were, by her estimation, more than the average number of red dresses and red sweaters, and as she studied the patrons, she wondered what they would be doing on Christmas, or even what she would be doing.

She took another sip of her wine, already feeling its effects.

"Speaking of stories, do you want me to pick up where we left off now or wait until the food arrives?"

"If you're ready now, I'd love to hear it."

"Do you remember where I stopped?"

"You'd agreed to let Bryce tutor you and you'd just told your aunt Linda that you loved her."

She reached toward her glass, staring into its purplish depths.

"On Monday," she began, "the day after we bought the Christmas tree..."

BEGINNINGS

Ocracoke
1995

I woke to sunlight streaming through my window. I knew my aunt was long gone, though in my haze, I imagined I heard someone rummaging in the kitchen. Still groggy and dreading the *barf because it's morning* thing, I gently pulled the pillow over my head and kept my eyes closed until I felt like it was safe to move.

I waited for the nausea to take over while I slowly came back to life; by then, it was as predictable as the sunrise, but strangely, I continued to feel okay. I slowly sat up, waited another minute, and still nothing. Finally, putting my feet to the floor, I stood, certain that my stomach would start doing cartwheels any second, but still there was nothing.

Holy cow and hallelujah!

Because the house was chilly, I threw on a sweatshirt over my pajamas, then slid into some fuzzy slippers. In the kitchen, my aunt had thoughtfully stacked all my textbooks and various manila folders on the table, probably to get me kick-started first thing in the morning. I pointedly ignored the pile because I wasn't just *not sick*; I was actually hungry again. I fried an egg and reheated a biscuit for breakfast, yawning the whole time. I was more tired than usual because I'd stayed up late to finish the first draft of my paper on Thurgood Marshall. It was four and a half pages, not quite the five pages required but good enough, and feeling sort of proud of my diligence, I decided to reward myself by blowing off the rest of my homework until I felt more awake. Instead, I grabbed the Sylvia Plath book from my aunt's shelf, bundled up in a jacket, and took a seat on the porch to read for a while.

The thing is, though, I'd never really liked

reading for pleasure. That was Morgan's thing. I'd always preferred skimming bits here and there to get the general concept, and after opening the book to a random page, I saw a few lines that my aunt had underlined:

The silence depressed me. It wasn't the silence of silence. It was my own silence.

I frowned and read it again, trying to figure out what Plath had meant by that. I thought I understood the first part; I suspected she was talking about loneliness, albeit in a vague way. The second part wasn't so hard, either; to my mind, she was just making it clear that she was talking about loneliness specifically, not the fact that being in a quiet place is depressing. But the third sentence was trickier. I guessed she was referring to her own apathy, perhaps a product of her loneliness.

So why hadn't she just written, *Being lonely sucks*?

I wondered why some people had to make things so complicated. And, frankly, why was that insight even profound? Didn't everyone know that loneliness could be a bummer? I could have told them that and I was just a teenager. Hell, I'd been living it since I'd been marooned in Ocracoke.

Then again, maybe I'd misinterpreted the whole passage. I was no English scholar. The real question was why my aunt had underlined it. It obviously had meant something to her, but what? Was my aunt lonely? She didn't seem lonely and she spent a lot of time with Gwen, but then again, what did I really know about her? It wasn't as though we'd had any deeply personal conversations since I'd been here.

I was still thinking about it when I heard an engine and the sound of tires crunching gravel out front. After that, the thumping of a car door. Rising from my seat, I opened the slider and listened, waiting. Sure enough, I eventually heard someone knocking. I had no idea who it could possibly be. It was the first time I'd heard a knock at the door since I'd been there. Maybe I should have been nervous, but Ocracoke wasn't exactly a hotbed of criminal activity, and I doubted a criminal would knock in the first place. Without a care, I went to the front door and swung it open only to see Bryce standing before me, which pretty much made my brain freeze in confusion. I knew I'd agreed to let him tutor me, but somehow I'd thought I had a few days before we'd begin.

"Hi, Maggie," he said. "Your aunt said I should come by so we can get started."

"Huh?"

"Tutoring," he said.

"Uh…"

"She mentioned that you might need some help preparing for your tests. And maybe catching up on your homework."

I hadn't showered, hadn't brushed my hair, hadn't put on makeup. In my pajamas and slippers and jacket, I probably looked homeless. "I just got out of bed," I finally blurted out.

He tilted his head. "You sleep in your jacket?"

"It was cold last night." When he continued to stare, I went on. "I get cold easy."

"Oh," he said. "My mom does, too. But… are you ready? Your aunt said to be here at nine."

"Nine?"

"I talked to her this morning after I finished working out. She said she'd come back to the house and leave you a note."

I guess I *had* heard someone in the kitchen earlier. Oops. "Oh," I said, trying to buy time. There wasn't a chance I'd let him come in with the way I was looking now. "I thought the note said ten."

"Do you want me to come back at ten?"

"That might be better," I agreed, trying not to breathe on him. For his part, he looked...well, a lot like he had the day before. Hair slightly windblown, dimples flashing. He was wearing jeans and that cool olive jacket again.

"No problem," he said. "Until then, can you get me the stuff that your aunt Linda set out? She said it might help me get a handle on things."

"What stuff?"

"She told me it was on the kitchen table."

Oh yeah, I suddenly thought. *That thoughtful stack on the table, for the morning kick-start.*

"Hold on," I said. "Let me check."

I left him waiting on the porch and retreated to the kitchen. Sure enough, on top of the stack was a note from my aunt.

Good morning, Maggie,

I just spoke to Bryce and he'll be coming by at nine to get started with you. I also photocopied the list of assignments and homework, as well as quiz and test dates. I'm hopeful he'll be able to explain the subjects that I can't. Have a wonderful day and I'll see you this afternoon. Love you.

Blessings,
Aunt Linda

I reminded myself to keep my eye out for notes in the future. I was about to grab the stack when I remembered the paper I'd written. I went to the bedroom and retrieved it before scooping everything else into my arms and carrying it all to the front door, where I quickly realized my mistake.

"Bryce? Are you still here?"

"Yeah, I'm here."

"Can you open the door? My hands are full."

When the door swung open, I handed him the stack. "I think this is what she set out for you. I also wrote a paper last night, so I put that on top."

If he was surprised by the size of the pile, he didn't show it. "Great," he said, reaching for it. He took the stack, bobbling it slightly before rebalancing. "Do you mind if I figure this out here on the porch? Instead of going home and coming back?"

"Not at all," I said. I really, really wished I'd brushed my teeth. "I need a little time to get ready, okay?"

"Sounds good," he said. "I'll see you whenever. Take your time."

After closing the door, I went straight to my bedroom to find something to wear. Quickly undressing, I pulled out my favorite jeans from the pile in the closet, but when I buttoned the top, it dug into my skin and hurt. Same thing with my second-favorite pair. Which meant I'd probably have to wear the same baggy ones I'd worn on the ferry. I sorted through my tops, but thankfully they still fit. I picked something maroon with long sleeves. For shoes, though, I didn't have much. Sneakers, slippers, rubber boots, and Uggs. Uggs it would be.

With that decided, I showered, brushed my teeth, and dried my hair. After dabbing on some makeup, I slipped into the clothes I'd picked out. Because my aunt had been so insistent about the cleanliness thing, my room was all set, so all I really had to do was straighten the sheet, pull up the comforter, and prop Maggie-bear against the pillow. Not, of course, that I had any intention of showing him my bedroom, but if he needed to use the bathroom and peeked in, he might notice that I kept things tidy.

Not that it mattered.

I washed and dried the plate, glass, and utensils I'd used for breakfast, but other than that, the kitchen was all set. I pulled open the drapes, letting more light into the house, and taking a deep breath, went to the door.

Opening it, I saw him sitting on the front porch, legs perched on the steps.

"Oh, hey," he said, no doubt hearing me behind him. He realigned the pile and got to his feet, then suddenly froze. He stared as though seeing me for the first time. "Wow. You look really nice."

"Thanks," I answered, thinking that maybe I looked *all right*, even if I would never be as pretty as Morgan. But even so, I felt my cheeks redden slightly. "I just threw on whatever was lying around. You ready?"

"Let me grab this stuff."

He gathered up the stack and I stepped back so he could squeeze through the door. He stopped, no doubt wondering where to go.

"The kitchen table is fine," I said, motioning. "That's where I usually work."

In those rare instances I do work, I thought. And when I wasn't doing it in bed, which I wasn't about to tell him.

"Perfect," he said. In the kitchen, he set the stack on the table, pulled out the manila folder at the top, and settled in the chair I'd used for breakfast. Meanwhile, I was still thinking about what he'd said to me on the porch, and even though I'd invited him inside, the fact that he was actually at the kitchen table felt bizarre, like something you might see on television or at the movies but never expected to experience in real life.

I shook my head, thinking, *I need to get hold of myself.* Starting toward the kitchen, I veered to the cupboards near the sink. "Would you like some water? I'm going to get a glass."

"That would be great, thanks."

I filled two glasses and brought them to the table, then sat in the spot that was usually my aunt's. I was struck by the thought that the house looked entirely different from this angle, which made me wonder how it appeared to Bryce.

"Did you see the paper I wrote?"

"I read it," he said. "He's one of the most prominent justices ever to serve. Did you choose him, or did the teacher assign it?"

"The teacher picked it."

"You got lucky there because there's so much to write about." He folded his hands in front of him. "Let's start with this. How do you think you're doing in your classes?"

I hadn't expected the question and it took me a second to answer. "I'm doing okay, I guess. Especially considering that I'm supposed to learn all this on my own without having a teacher. I didn't do all that great on my recent quizzes or tests, but there's still time to get my grades up."

"Do you want to get your grades up?"

"What do you mean?"

"I grew up hearing my mom say 'There is no teaching, there is only learning' over and over. I must have heard it more than a hundred times, and for a long time, I didn't know what she meant. Because she was my teacher, right? Was she telling me that she wasn't a teacher? But as I got a little older, I finally understood that she was telling me that teaching is impossible unless a student wants to learn. I guess that's another way I could have phrased it. Do you want to learn? Really and truly? Or do you simply want to do enough to get by?"

Just like on the ferry, he came across as more mature than other people his age, but maybe because his tone was so nice, it made me reflect on what he was really asking.

"Well...I don't want to have to repeat my sophomore year."

"I get that. But it still doesn't really answer

my question. What grades would you like? What would make you happy?"

Straight A's without having to do the work, I knew, but I didn't think it would do me any good to say it out loud. The fact was, I was normally a B or C student, with more C's than B's. Sometimes I got an A in the easier classes like Music or Art, but I'd had a couple of D's, too. I knew I'd never compare with Morgan, but part of me still wanted to please my parents.

"I think that if I averaged B's I'd be happy with that."

"Okay," he said. He smiled again, dimples and all. "Now I know."

"That's it?"

"Not exactly. Where you are and where you would like to be aren't aligned right now. You're at least eight assignments behind in your math homework, and your test scores are pretty low. You're going to need to do outstanding work the rest of the semester to get a B in Geometry."

"Oh."

"You're way behind in Biology, too."

"Oh."

"Same situation in American History. And English and Spanish, too."

By then, I couldn't meet his eyes, knowing he probably thought I was an idiot. I understood enough to know that West Point was almost as hard to get into as Stanford.

"What did you think about my paper?" I asked, almost afraid of the answer.

His gaze flickered over it; it wasn't in the folder—he'd placed it on top of the stack of textbooks.

"I wanted to discuss that with you, too."

Because I'd never had a tutor before, I wasn't sure what to expect. Add in *the tutor is WAY cute* and I was even more clueless. I guess I imagined we'd work and then take a break and get to know each other, maybe even flirt a little, but the day was nothing like that, other than the first part.

We worked. I went to the bathroom. We worked some more. Yet another bathroom break. Repeat for hours.

Aside from going over my paper—he wanted me to make it more chronological as opposed to jumping back and forth in time—we spent most of the day on geometry, catching up on homework. There was no way I could get through everything, because he made me do every single problem by myself. Whenever I asked for help, he'd go through my textbook and find the section that explained the concept. He'd have me read through it and if I didn't understand, he'd try to break it down for me. When that still didn't help—which was most of the time—he'd examine the homework question that had me stumped and would then create an original question that was similar. After that, he'd patiently show me how to answer that sample question step by step. Only then would I go back to the original homework problem, which I had to do myself. All of which was seriously frustrating because it made the whole process slower while simultaneously increasing the amount of work I had to do.

My aunt came home just as Bryce was about to leave and they ended up speaking in the doorway. I have no idea what they discussed, but their voices sounded cheery; as for me, I hadn't moved from my chair and my forehead was on the table. Right before my aunt had walked in the door, and even after all I'd done, Bryce had given me *additional* homework, or rather, homework I was already supposed to have completed. In addition to reworking my paper, he wanted me to read chapters in both my biology and history textbooks. Though he'd smiled when he'd said it—as though his request were entirely reasonable after hours of brain-frying strain—his dimples meant absolutely nothing to me.

Except…

The thing is, he was really good at explaining things in a way that made intuitive sense, and he was patient the whole time. By the end, I kind of felt like I understood a bit more about what was going on and felt less intimidated by the sight of shapes and numbers and equals signs. But don't be misled: I hadn't suddenly turned into some sort of geometry whiz. I made big mistakes and little mistakes all day long, and by the end, I was pretty down on myself. Morgan, I knew, wouldn't have struggled at all.

As soon as he left, I took a nap. Dinner was ready when I finally woke, and after eating and cleaning the kitchen, I returned to my room and read from the textbooks. I still had more work to do on my paper, so I cranked up the Walkman and began scribbling. My aunt poked her head through my doorway a few minutes later and said something to me; I pretended I'd heard her, even though I hadn't. If it was important, I figured that she'd come back and tell me again later.

After I'd been writing for a while, I made the mistake of forgetting that I was pregnant. I shifted to a more comfortable position and all at once, nature called. *Again.* When I opened the door to the hallway, I was surprised to hear conversation drifting from the living room. Peeking around the corner to see who it was, I noticed Gwen placing a cardboard box full of ornaments and lights in front of the Christmas tree and vaguely remembered my aunt telling me that we were going to decorate it tonight after work.

What I hadn't expected was to see Bryce

chatting with my aunt as she tuned the radio, finally settling on a station that was playing Christmas music. I felt my stomach do a little flip at the sight of him, but at least I wasn't wearing pajamas and slippers and looking generally like I rode the rails, hobo style.

"There you are," Aunt Linda said. "I was about to come get you. Bryce just arrived."

"Hi, Maggie," Bryce said. He was still wearing the same jeans and T-shirt, and I couldn't help noticing the pleasing silhouette his shoulders and hips made. "Linda invited me over to help with the tree. I hope that's okay."

I was momentarily speechless, but I don't think any of them noticed. Aunt Linda was already slipping into her jacket on her way out the door. "Gwen and I are going to make a quick run to the store to get some eggnog," she said. "If you two want to get started on the lights, feel free. We'll be back in a few minutes."

I remained in the doorway before remembering with painful urgency why I'd left my room in the first place. I went to the bathroom and washed my hands afterward. Peering into the mirror above the sink, even I could tell I was tired, but there wasn't anything I could do about it. I ran a brush through my hair, took a breath, and went out, wondering why I suddenly felt nervous. Bryce and I had been alone in the house already for hours; why was this any different?

Because, a voice inside me whispered, *he's not here to tutor me. He's here because clearly Aunt Linda wanted him to come over, not for her, but because she thought I might like that.*

By the time I walked out of the bathroom, Aunt Linda and Gwen were gone and Bryce had pulled a strand of lights from the box. I watched him struggle to untangle them, and playing it cool, I fished out a different strand and started untangling, too.

"I finished my reading," I said. "Some of my paper, too." Without sunlight streaming through the windows, his hair and eyes seemed darker than usual.

"Good for you," he said. "I took Daisy for a walk on the beach and then my parents had me chop firewood. Thanks for having me over."

"Of course," I said, even though I'd had no say in the matter.

He finished with his strand and scanned the room. "I need to check to make sure the lights are working. Is there an outlet handy?"

I had no idea. I'd never needed to know where the outlets were, but I think he was mostly talking to himself, because he bent lower, peering under the table next to the couch. "There it is."

He squatted down, his movements fluid, and reached underneath to plug in the strand. I watched as the multicolored lights blinked on.

"I love decorating Christmas trees," he offered, heading to the box again. "It gets me into the spirit of things." He reached for another strand just as I finished untangling mine. I plugged it into the strand on the floor, watching as it blinked on as well, then reached for another strand.

"I've never decorated a tree."

"Really?"

"My mom usually does it," I said. "She likes it to look a certain way."

"Oh," he said, and I could tell he was

puzzled. "It's the opposite in our house. My mom sort of directs while the rest of us do it."

"She doesn't like to decorate?"

"She does, but you'd have to meet her to understand. The eggnog was my idea, by the way. That's part of our tradition and as soon as I mentioned it, your aunt Linda thought we should have some here, too. I was telling her how well I thought you did today. Especially at the end. I barely had to help you at all."

"I'm still pretty far behind."

"I'm not worried," he said. "If you keep going like you did today, you'll catch up in no time."

I wasn't so sure. He clearly had more confidence in me than I did. "Thanks for all your help. I'm not sure that I told you before you left. I was kind of out of it by then."

"No worries," he said. He took my strand and checked those lights as well. "How long have you lived in Seattle?"

"Since I was born," I said. "Same house. Same bedroom, in fact."

"I can't imagine what that would be like. Until we got here, I moved pretty much every other year. Idaho, Virginia, Germany, Italy, Georgia, even North Carolina. My dad was at Fort Bragg for a while."

"I don't know where that is."

"It's in Fayetteville. South of Raleigh, about three hours from the coast."

"Still doesn't help. My knowledge of North Carolina is pretty much limited to Ocracoke and Morehead City."

He smiled. "Tell me about your family. What do your mom and dad do?"

"My dad works on the line at Boeing. I think he does riveting, but I'm not really sure. He doesn't talk about it much, but I get the sense it's the same every day. My mom works part-time as a secretary at our church."

"And you have a sister, right?"

"Yeah." I nodded. "Morgan. She's two years older than me."

"Do you two look alike?"

"I wish," I said.

"I'm sure she says the same thing about you." His compliment caught me off guard, the same way it had in the morning when he'd told me I looked *really nice*. Meanwhile, Bryce retrieved an extension cord from the box. "I guess we're ready," he said. He plugged in the extension cord and attached the first strand of lights. "Do you want to lead or adjust?"

I wasn't sure what he was talking about. "Adjust, I guess."

"Okay," he said. Gripping the tree, he gently scooted it away from the front window, making more space. "It's easier to get around the tree this way. We can move it back when we're finished."

Making sure the cord had enough slack, he began stringing the lights at the back of the tree, then circled to the front. "Just make sure there are no gaps or places where the lights are too close together."

Adjusting. Got it.

I did as he asked; it wasn't long before the first strand was at an end, and he plugged in the next one. We repeated the process, working together.

He cleared his throat. "I've been meaning to ask what brought you to Ocracoke."

And there it was. *The question*. Actually, I was surprised it hadn't come up earlier, and I thought back to the conversation I'd had with my aunt and the impossibility of secrets in Ocracoke. And that, as she noted, it would be best if the answer came from me. I took a deep breath, feeling a flutter of fear.

"I'm pregnant."

He was still bent over as he glanced up to face me. "I know. I meant why are you here in Ocracoke and not with your family?"

I felt my mouth fall open. "You knew I was pregnant? Did my aunt tell you?"

"Linda didn't say anything. I just sort of put the pieces together."

"What pieces?"

"The fact that you're here but still enrolled in a school in Seattle? Because you're leaving in May? Because your aunt was vague about the reason for your sudden visit? Because she asked for an extra cushy seat on your bike? Because you used the bathroom a lot today? Pregnancy was the only explanation that made sense."

I wasn't sure whether I was more surprised by the idea that he'd figured it out so easily or the fact that there was no judgment in his tone or his expression as he said it.

"It was a mistake," I said in a rush. "I did

something stupid last August with a guy I barely knew, and now I'm here until I have the baby because my parents didn't want anyone to find out what happened to me. And I'd rather you not tell anyone, either."

He started wrapping the tree again. "I'm not going to say anything. But won't people learn what happened when they see you walking around with a baby?"

"I'm giving her up for adoption. My parents have it all figured out."

"It's a her?"

"I have no idea. My mom thinks it'll be a girl because she says my family only makes girls. I mean...my mom has four sisters, my dad has three sisters. I have twelve female cousins and no males. My parents had girls."

"That's cool," he offered. "Aside from my mom, it's all boys in our family. Can you hand me another strand?"

The change in subject threw me. "Wait... don't you have more questions?"

"Like what?"

"I don't know. How it happened or whatever?"

"I understand the mechanics," he said, his

tone neutral. "You already mentioned that it was a guy you barely knew and a mistake, and you're giving her up for adoption, so what else is there to say?"

My parents certainly had a lot more to say, but to his point, what did the details matter? In my confusion, I reached for another strand and handed it to him. "I'm not a bad person—"

"I never thought you were."

He started going around the tree again; by then, the lights were halfway to the top.

"Why doesn't any of this bother you?"

"Because," he answered, still placing the lights, "the same thing happened to my mom. She was a teenager when she became pregnant. I guess the only difference was that my dad married her, and I eventually came along."

"Your parents told you that?"

"They didn't have to. I know their anniversary, and I know my birthday. The math isn't hard."

Wow, I thought. I wondered if my aunt knew all this.

"How old was your mom?"

"Nineteen."

It didn't seem like a significant age difference but it was, even if he didn't say so. After all, at nineteen you're a legal adult and not in high school anymore. Instead, once he finished with the next strand, he said, "Let's step back and see how we're doing."

From a distance, it was easier to see the gaps and other places where the lights were too close together. At the tree, we both adjusted the strands, stepped back, then adjusted some more, the scent of pine filling the room as the branches moved. Strains of Bing Crosby played in the background as flickering light fell across Bryce's features. In the silence, I wondered what he was really thinking and whether he was as accepting as he seemed.

Once we finished, we strung the lights on the top half of the tree. Because he was taller, he did pretty much everything while I stood and watched. When he was done, we both stepped farther away again and studied our accomplishment.

"What do you think?"

"It's pretty," I answered, even though my mind was still a million miles away.

"Do you know if your aunt has a star or an angel for the top?"

"I have no idea. And...thanks."

"For what?"

"For not asking questions. For being so nice about the reason I'm in Ocracoke. For agreeing to tutor me."

"You don't have to thank me," he said. "Believe it or not, I'm glad you're here. Ocracoke can get kind of boring in the winter."

"You don't say."

He laughed. "I guess you've noticed that, huh?"

For the first time since he'd arrived, I smiled. "It's not all bad."

Aunt Linda and Gwen showed up about a minute later and oohed and aahed over the lights before pouring glasses of eggnog. The four of us sipped while adding tinsel to the tree along with the ornaments and the angel for the top, which had been stored in the hall closet. It didn't take long until the tree was finished. Bryce slid it back into place before adding more water to the base. Afterward, Aunt Linda plied us with cinnamon rolls she'd bought at the store, and though they weren't as fresh as her biscuits, we ate them with gusto at the table.

Even if it wasn't terribly late, it was probably time for Bryce to go, since Aunt Linda and Gwen had to wake up so early. Thankfully, he seemed to realize it and brought his plate to the sink, then said goodbye before we started toward the door.

"Thanks again for having me over," he said, reaching for the knob. "That was a lot of fun."

I wasn't sure if he meant decorating the tree or spending time with me was fun, but I felt a surge of relief that I'd told him the truth about myself. And that he'd been more than kind about all of it.

"I'm glad you came."

"I'll see you tomorrow," he said, his voice quiet, the words strangely sounding like both a promise and an opportunity.

"I told him," I said to Aunt Linda later, after Gwen had left. We were in the living room, moving the empty boxes to the hall closet.

"And?"

"He already knew. He'd figured it out."

"He's...very bright. The whole family is."

When I set the box on the floor, my jeans pinched my waist and I already knew my other pants were even tighter. "I think I'm going to need some bigger clothes."

"I was going to suggest that we do some shopping after church on Sunday for just that reason."

"You could tell?"

"No. But it's about that time. I brought a lot of young pregnant girls shopping when I was a nun."

"Is it possible to buy pants that don't make my situation so obvious? I mean, I know everyone's going to know, but..."

"It's fairly easy to hide in winter because sweaters and jackets can cover a lot. I doubt anyone will see your baby bump until March.

Maybe even April, and once it does show, you can always keep a lower profile then, if that's what you want."

"Do you think other people have figured it out? Like Bryce did? And that they're talking about me?"

My aunt seemed to choose her words carefully. "I think there's some curiosity about why you're here, but no one has asked me directly. If they do, I'll just tell them that it's personal. They'll know not to press."

I liked the way she was watching out for me. Gazing toward the open door of my room, I thought about what I'd read earlier in the Sylvia Plath book. "Can I ask you something?"

"Of course."

"Do you ever feel like you're all alone?"

She lowered her gaze, an odd expression on her face. "All the time," she said, her voice barely above a whisper.

I'm not going to bore you with the details of that first week, because they were pretty much the same, varying only by subject. I finished rewriting my paper and Bryce had me rewrite it a *second* time before he was finally satisfied. I slowly but steadily began to catch up on my homework, and on Thursday, we spent most of the day studying for Friday's geometry test. By then, I knew my brain would be too tired to take it after my aunt got back from work, so she came home from the shop to proctor the exam at eight the next morning, before Bryce arrived.

I was pretty nervous. As much as I'd studied, I was terrified of making stupid mistakes or seeing a problem that might as well have been written in Chinese. Right before my aunt handed me the test, I said a little prayer, even though I didn't think it would do any good.

Fortunately, I thought I understood what most of the questions were asking and then worked through them step by step the way Bryce had shown me. Even so, when I finally handed it over, I still felt like I swallowed a tennis ball. I'd scored in the fifties or sixties on the previous tests and quizzes and couldn't bear to watch my aunt as she graded it. I didn't want to see her using the red pencil to cross things out, so I pointedly stared out the window. When Aunt Linda eventually brought the test back to me, she was smiling, but I couldn't tell whether it was out of pity or because I'd done well. She put the test on the table in front of me, and after taking a deep breath, I finally had the courage to check.

I hadn't aced it. Didn't even get an A.

But the B I got was closer to an A than a C, and when I instinctively squealed with joy and disbelief, Aunt Linda held out her arms and I fell into them, the two of us hugging in the kitchen for a long time, and I realized how much I'd needed that.

When Bryce arrived, he reviewed the exam before handing it back to my aunt.

"I'll do better the next time," he said, even though I was the one who had taken it.

"I'm thrilled," I said. "And don't bother trying to feel bad, because I'm not going to accept it."

"Fair enough," he responded, but I could still see it was bothering him.

After Aunt Linda gathered up all my work—she shipped everything to my school on Fridays—and started toward the door, Bryce glanced at me, his expression uneasy.

"I wanted to ask you something," he said. "I know it's kind of last-minute and that I have to ask your aunt, too, but I didn't want to do that until I talked to you first. Because if you don't want to, then there's no reason to ask her, right? And, obviously, if she's not okay with the idea, then no worries."

"I have no idea what you're talking about."

"You know about the New Bern flotilla, right?"

"I've never heard of it."

"Oh," he said. "I should have guessed that. New Bern is a small town inland from More-head City, and every year, the town hosts a Christmas flotilla. It's basically a bunch of boats decorated in Christmas lights that float down the river like a parade. Afterwards, my family has dinner and then we visit this amazing decorated property in Vanceboro.

Anyway, it's an annual family tradition and it's all happening tomorrow."

"Why are you telling me this?"

"I was wondering if you'd like to come with us."

It took a couple of seconds before it dawned on me that he was asking me on something like a date. It wasn't a real date since his parents and younger brothers would be with us—it would be more of a *family outing*—but because of the bungling, circuitous way he'd broached the subject, I suspected it was the first time he'd ever asked a girl to join him in anything. It surprised me because he'd always seemed so much older than I was. In Seattle, boys would just ask, *Do you want to hang out?* and be done with it. J hadn't even done that much; he'd just sat down beside me on the porch and started talking.

But I kind of liked the bungling overcomplexity, even if I couldn't imagine anything romantic between us. Whether he was cute or not, the romance thing inside me had shriveled up like a raisin on a hot sidewalk, and I doubted whether I'd ever experience the feeling of desire again. Still, it was...*sweet.*

"If my aunt says it's okay, that sounds fun."

"There's something else you need to know first," he said. "We stay overnight in New Bern because the ferries don't run that late. My family rents a house, but you'd have your own room, of course."

"Maybe you'd better ask her before she leaves."

By then, my aunt was already out the door and heading down the steps. Bryce chased after her, and all I could think was that he'd just asked me on a date.

No...scratch that. A *family outing*.

I wondered what my aunt would say; it didn't take long before I heard Bryce coming back. He was grinning as he walked through the door. "She wants to talk to my parents and said she'd let us know this afternoon."

"Sounds good."

"I guess we should get started, then. With tutoring, I mean."

"I'm ready whenever you are."

"Great," he said, taking a seat at the table, his shoulders suddenly relaxing. "Let's start with Spanish today. You have a quiz on Tuesday."

And like a switch had been thrown, he went back to being my tutor, a role that clearly made him more comfortable.

Aunt Linda returned to the house a few minutes after three. Though I had the sense she was tired, she smiled as she walked in and shrugged off her jacket. It struck me that she always smiled when she walked in the door.

"Hi there," she said. "How did it go today?"

"It went well," Bryce answered as he gathered up his things. "How was it at the shop?"

"Busy," she said. She hung her coat on the rack. "I spoke to your parents and it's fine if Maggie wants to join you tomorrow. They said they'd meet us at the church on Sunday."

"Thank you for speaking with them. And for agreeing."

"My pleasure," she said. Then, to me, she added, "And after church on Sunday, we'll go shopping, okay?"

"Shopping?" Bryce asked automatically.

My aunt caught my eye for only a split second, but she knew what I was thinking. "Christmas gifts," she said.

And just like that, I had a date.

Kind of.

The following morning I slept late and for the sixth day in a row, my stomach felt fine. That was definitely a plus, which was followed by another surprise when I undressed before getting into the shower. My...*bust* was definitely larger. I'll admit I used the word *bust* instead of the one that had originally popped into my head, because of the crucifix hanging on the bathroom wall. It was, I figured, the word my aunt would have used.

I'd read that would happen, but not like this. Not overnight. Okay, maybe I hadn't been paying close attention and they'd been growing without my being aware of it, but as I stood in front of the mirror, I thought I suddenly looked like a miniature Dolly Parton.

On the downside, I noticed that my

once-small waist was already beginning to go the way of Atlantis. Examining myself from the side, I was both bigger and wider in the mirror. Though there was a scale in the bathroom, I couldn't work up the courage to check how much weight I'd gained.

For the first time since Bryce had started tutoring me, I had the house to myself for most of the day. I probably should have used the quiet to catch up on homework, but I decided to go to the beach instead.

After bundling up, I found the bike beneath the house. I was a little wobbly as I got going—it had been a while—but got the hang of it within a few minutes. I pedaled slowly in the cold wind and when I reached the sand, I propped the bike against a post that indicated a walking path through the dunes.

It was pretty at the beach, even if it was entirely different from the coast in Washington. Where I was used to rocks and cliffs and angry waves shooting plumes of water, there was nothing but gentle swells and sand and sawgrass. No people, no palm trees, no shuttered lifeguard stands or homes with oceanfront views. As I walked the empty stretch of shoreline, it was easy to imagine that I was the first to have ever been there.

Alone with my thoughts, I tried to picture what my parents were doing. Or would be doing later, because it was still early there. I wondered whether Morgan would be practicing the violin—she did that a lot on Saturdays—or whether she'd go shopping at the mall for gifts. I wondered if they'd gotten the tree yet or if that was something they would do later today or tomorrow or even next weekend. I wondered what Madison and Jodie were up to, whether either of them had met a new guy, what movies they'd gone to see lately, or where—if anywhere—they were going for the holidays.

Yet, for the first time since I'd left Seattle, the thoughts didn't make me ache with a sadness that felt overwhelming. Instead, I realized that it had been the right decision to come here. Don't get me wrong—I still wished none of this had ever happened—but somehow I knew that my aunt Linda was exactly what I needed at this time in my life. She seemed to understand me in a way that my parents never had.

Maybe because, just like me, she always felt alone.

After I returned to the house, I showered and stuffed the things I would need for church in one of the duffel bags I'd brought from Seattle, then spent the rest of the day reading various chapters in my textbooks, still trying to catch up and hoping that some of the information would stick in my head long enough for me to be able to complete the homework without having to do the extra problems that Bryce would no doubt concoct.

Aunt Linda returned at two—Saturdays were shorter days at the shop—and made sure that I'd packed everything else I needed but had forgotten, from toothpaste to shampoo. Afterward, I helped her set up the nativity scene on the fireplace mantel. As we worked, I noticed for the first time that her eyes were the same as my dad's.

"What are your plans tonight?" I asked. "Since you'll have the place to yourself?"

"Gwen and I are going to have dinner," she said. "We'll play gin rummy afterwards."

"That sounds relaxing."

"I'm sure you'll have a pleasant evening with Bryce and his family as well."

"It's no big deal."

"We'll see." The way she said it while also averting her eyes made my next question automatic.

"Do you not want me to go?"

"You two have spent a lot of time together already this week."

"Tutoring," I said. "Because you thought I needed it."

"I know," she said. "And while I agreed that you could go, I do have concerns."

"Why?"

She adjusted the figurines of Mary and Joseph before answering. "It's sometimes easy for young people to...lose themselves in feelings of the heart."

The words she'd used—both old-fashioned and nunlike—took me a few seconds to process, but I felt my eyes widen. "You think I'm going to fall for him?"

When she didn't answer, I almost laughed.

"You don't have to worry about that," I went on. "I'm pregnant, remember? I have no interest in him at all."

She sighed. "I wasn't worried about you."

Bryce showed up a few minutes after we'd finished decorating the mantel. Still a bit off-balance from my aunt's comment but kissing her on the cheek anyway, I stepped out the door with my duffel bag while he was still ascending the steps.

"Hey there," he said. Like me, he was dressed for a wintry night. The cool olive jacket had been replaced by a thick down coat like my own. "You ready? Can I take that for you?"

"It's not heavy, but sure."

After he grabbed the duffel, we waved goodbye to my aunt and made for his truck, the same one I'd seen on the ferry. Up close, it was bigger and taller than I remembered. He opened the passenger door for me, but it felt a bit like I was scaling a small mountain before I could finally crawl inside. He closed the door behind me and then got in from the other side, setting the duffel between us. Though the sky was clear, the temperature was already dropping. From the corner of my eye, I could see my aunt turn on the lights of the Christmas tree, which shone in the window, and for whatever reason, I suddenly thought back to the moment I'd first seen him and his dog on the ferry.

"I forgot to ask but is Daisy coming with us?"

Bryce shook his head. "No. I just dropped her off at my grandparents."

"They didn't want to come? Your grandparents, I mean?"

"They don't like leaving the island unless they have to." He smiled. "And by the way, my parents can't wait to meet you."

"Me too," I said, hoping they wouldn't ask *the question*, but I didn't have time to dwell on it. The ride only took a few minutes; their house was in the same general area as my aunt's shop, near the hotels and the ferry. Bryce pulled the truck into the drive, stopping next to a large white van, and I found myself peering at a home that initially struck me as the same as every other home in the village, except maybe a little larger and better maintained. As I was taking it in, the front door suddenly flew open and two young boys raced down the steps, jostling each other. I found my eyes flashing between them, thinking they were mirror images of each other.

"Richard and Robert, if you've forgotten," he said.

"I'll never be able to tell them apart."

"They're used to it. And they'll mess with you because of it."

"Mess with me how?"

"Robert's in the red jacket. Richard is in the blue jacket. For now, anyway. But they might switch, so be prepared. Just remember that Richard has a tiny mole below his left eye."

By then, the two of them had stopped near Bryce's truck and were staring at us. Bryce grabbed my duffel and opened his door before climbing down. I did the same, feeling like I was falling before my feet finally hit the gravel. We met at the front of the truck.

"Richard, Robert?" Bryce said. "This is Maggie."

"Hi, Maggie," they said in unison, their voices sounding both robotic and forced, machine-generated. Then, also in unison, they both tilted their heads to the left and when they went on, I knew it was an act. "It is a pleasure to meet you and to have the honor of your company this evening."

Playing along, I gave the *Star Trek* salute. "Live long and prosper."

They both giggled, and even though they were standing close and it was daytime, I couldn't detect the mole. But (blue jacket) Richard leaned into (red jacket) Robert, who pushed Richard, who then punched Robert, and after that, Robert was chasing Richard, finally vanishing behind the house.

From the corner of my eye, I saw movement to my right, at ground level beneath the house. When I turned, I saw a youngish-looking woman in a wheelchair emerge, followed by a tall man with a crew cut who I assumed was Bryce's father.

I'd seen people in wheelchairs, of course. There was a girl named Audrey in my third and fourth grade classes who was in a wheel-chair, and Mr. Petrie—like my dad, a deacon at the church—used one, too. But I hadn't expected his mom to be in one, if only because Bryce hadn't said anything about it. He could mention that she'd been a pregnant teen but forget to tell me this?

Somehow, I was able to keep my expression friendly but neutral. The two of them approached as his mom called out, "R and R...in the van! Or we'll leave without you!"

Seconds later, the brothers came roaring around the opposite side of the house from where I'd last seen them. Now (blue jacket) Richard was chasing (red jacket) Robert...

Or were they messing with me?

There was no way to tell.

"In the van!" Bryce's dad shouted, and circling it once, the twins opened the side door and jumped inside, the van bouncing slightly.

Smart or not, they definitely had energy.

By then, Bryce's parents had drawn closer and I could see the welcome on their faces. His mom's jacket was even puffier than mine, and her auburn hair was offset by green eyes.

His father, I noticed, stood ramrod straight, his black hair threaded with silver near his ears. Bryce's mom held out her hand.

"Hi, Maggie," she said with an easy grin. "I'm Janet Trickett, and this is my husband, Porter. I'm so glad you can join us."

"Hi, Mr. and Mrs. Trickett," I said. "Thanks for having me."

I shook Porter's hand as well. "Pleasure," he added. "It's nice to see a new face around here. I hear you're staying with your aunt Linda."

"For a few months," I said. Then, "Bryce has really been helpful with my studies."

"That's good to know," Porter said. "Are you both ready to go?"

"We are," Bryce said. "Is there anything still in the house that I need to grab?"

"I've already loaded the bags. We should probably head out, since you never know how crowded the ferry will be."

As I was about to head to the van, Bryce gently took hold of my arm, signaling for me to wait. I watched as his parents made their way to the side opposite the door his brothers had used. His father reached inside and

I heard the hum of hydraulics and watched a small platform extend from the van, then lower to the ground.

"I helped my dad and grandfather modify the van," he said, "so that my mom can drive it, too."

"Why didn't you just buy one?"

"They're expensive," he said. "And they didn't have a model that would work for us. My parents wanted one where either of them could drive, so the front seat had to be easily interchangeable. It basically slides from one side to the other, then locks down."

"The three of you figured that out?"

"My dad's pretty smart about those kinds of things."

"What did he do in the army?"

"Intelligence," he answered. "But he's also a genius with anything mechanical."

Why was I not surprised?

By then, Bryce's mom had vanished into the interior and the platform was rising again. Bryce took it as his cue to start walking. Opening the door on the opposite side, we got in, squeezing in beside the twins in the back seat.

After the van backed out, we started toward the ferry and I eyed the twin next to me. He was wearing a blue jacket, and peering closely, I thought I could see the mole. "You're Richard, right?"

"And you're Maggie."

"Are you the one into computers or aeronautical engineering?"

"Computers. Engineering is for geeks."

"Better than being a nerd," Robert added quickly. He leaned forward in his seat, turning his head to peer at me.

"What?" I finally asked him.

"You don't look sixteen," he said. "You look older."

I wasn't sure whether it was a compliment or not. "Thanks?" I offered.

His expression was steady on mine. "Why did you move here?"

"Personal reasons."

"Do you like ultralights?"

"Excuse me?"

"They're small, slow, very light planes that only need a short runway to land. I'm building one in the backyard. Like the Wright brothers did."

Richard cut in: "I make video games."

I turned toward him. "I'm not sure what you mean."

"A video game uses electronically manipulated images on a computer or other display device that allow a user to engage in quests, missions, or journeys, perform duties, or perform other tasks, either alone or with others as part of a competition or as a team."

"I know what a video game is. I didn't know what you meant by *make*."

"It means," Bryce said, "that he conceives games, writes the code, and then designs them. And I'm sure she'll want to hear all about it—and the plane—later, but how about the two of you let us ride to the ferry in peace?"

"Why?" Richard asked. "I'm just trying to talk to her."

"Richard! Let it be!" I heard Mr. Trickett call out.

"Your father's right," Mrs. Trickett added, glaring at them over her shoulder as well. "And you need to apologize."

"For what?"

"For being rude."

"How am I being rude?"

"I'm not debating with you," she said. "Apologize. Both of you."

Robert piped up. "Why do I have to apologize?"

"Because," his mom answered, "you were both showing off. And I'm not going to ask you again."

From the corner of my eye, I noticed both of them sink lower in their seats. "Sorry," they said in unison. Bryce leaned closer, his breath warm on my ear as he spoke. "I tried to warn you."

I stifled a giggle, thinking, *And I thought my family was weird.*

We waited in a longish line of cars for the ferry, but there was plenty of room on the deck, and we departed on schedule. Richard and Robert scrambled out of the van almost immediately, and we followed, watching as they raced toward the railing. Behind us, as I put on my hat and gloves, I heard the hydraulic lift. I gestured toward the upper enclosed seating area.

"Will your mom be able to go inside? I mean, is there an elevator?"

"Usually they spend most of the time in the van," Bryce answered. "But she enjoys the fresh air for a little while. Would you like to get a soda?"

I saw the crowd moving in that direction and shook my head. "Let's go up front for a while."

We walked toward the bow along with a few other people, but were able to find a place where we weren't sandwiched next to others. Despite the chilly air, the water was calm in all directions.

"Is Robert really building an airplane?" I asked.

"He's been working on it for almost a year now. My father helps, but it's his design."

"And your parents will let him fly it?"

"He'd need his pilot's license first. He's mainly doing it as an entry into some national student science competition, and knowing him, I'm sure it will fly. My dad will make sure it's safe, though."

"Your dad can fly, too?"

"He can do a lot of things."

"But your mom homeschools? Not your dad?"

"He always worked."

"How can your mom possibly teach any of you anything?"

"She's pretty smart, too." He shrugged. "She started at MIT when she was sixteen."

Then how did she become pregnant as a teenager? I wondered. *Oh, yeah. Sometimes it's just an oops.* But still...what a family. I'd never even heard of another one like it.

"How did your parents meet?"

"They were both interning in Washington, D.C., but I don't know much more than that. They don't really share those kinds of stories with us."

"Was your mom in a wheelchair then? I'm sorry, I know I probably shouldn't ask..."

"It's okay. I'm sure a lot of people wonder about it. She was in a car accident eight years ago. Two-lane highway, a car passing another car from the opposite direction. To avoid a head-on crash, my mom veered off the road, but she hit a telephone pole. She almost died;

it's actually kind of a wonder that she didn't. She spent almost two weeks in the ICU, had multiple surgeries and a ton of rehab. But her spinal cord was damaged. She was fully paralyzed from the waist down for over a year, but eventually she recovered some feeling in her legs. Now she can move them a little—enough to make dressing easier—but that's it. She can't stand."

"That's awful."

"It's sad. Before the accident, she was very active. Played tennis, jogged every day. But she doesn't complain."

"Why didn't you tell me about her?"

"I guess I didn't think about it. I know that sounds strange, but I don't really notice it anymore. She still teaches the twins, makes dinner, goes shopping, takes photographs, whatever. But you're right. I should have thought to mention it."

"Is that why your family moved to Ocracoke? So her parents could help out?"

"It's actually the opposite. Like I told you, after my dad retired from the military and started consulting, we could have gone anywhere, but my grandmother had had a stroke the year before. Not a bad one, but the doctor indicated that she might have more in the future. As for my grandfather, his arthritis is getting worse, which is another reason why my dad helps him whenever he's in town. The point is, my mom thought she could help her parents more than they could help her, so she wanted to live near them. Believe it or not, she's fairly independent."

"And she's the reason you're raising Daisy? To help someone like your mom who needs it?"

"That was part of it. My dad also thought I'd enjoy having a dog for a while since he travels so much."

"How much does he travel?"

"It varies, but it's usually four or five months a year. He'll be taking off again sometime after the holidays. But now it's your turn. We've been talking about me and my family and it feels like I don't know anything about you."

I could feel the wind in my hair, could taste the salt in the chilly air.

"I've told you about my parents and my sister."

"What about you, then? What else do you like to do? Do you have any hobbies?"

"I used to dance when I was little, and I played sports in middle school. But no real hobbies."

"What do you do after school or on the weekends?"

"Hang out with my friends, talk on the phone, watch TV." Even as I said it, I understood how lame that sounded and knew I needed to get off the subject of me as quickly as possible. "You forgot to bring your camera."

"For the flotilla, you mean? I thought about it, but I figured it would be a waste of time. I tried last year, and I couldn't get the photos to turn out right. The colored lights all came out white."

"Did you try using the automatic setting?"

"I tried everything, but I still couldn't make it work. At the time, I didn't realize I should have used a tripod and adjusted the ISO, but even then, the images probably wouldn't have come out. I think the boats were too far offshore, and obviously they were moving."

I had no idea what any of that meant. "Seems complicated."

"It is and it isn't. It's like learning anything in that it takes time and practice. And even if I think I know exactly what to do for a shot, I still find myself changing the aperture constantly. When I shoot in black and white—which I normally do—I also really have to watch the timer in the darkroom to get the shading just right. And now, with Photoshop, there's even more I can do in post."

"You have your own darkroom?"

"My dad built it for my mom, but I use it, too."

"You must be an expert."

"My mom's the expert, not me. When I have a problem with a print, either she helps or Richard does. Sometimes both of them."

"Richard?"

"With Photoshop, I mean. He automatically understands anything computer related, so if it's a Photoshop issue, he can figure it out. It's irritating."

I smiled. "I take it that your mom taught you photography, right?"

"She did. She's taken some incredible shots over the years."

"I'd like to see them. The darkroom, too."

"I'll be happy to show you."

"How did your mom get into photography?"

"She said she just picked up a camera one day in high school, took some photos, and got hooked. After I was born, neither my mom nor my dad wanted to put me in daycare, so she began to freelance with a local photographer on weekends, when my dad could stay with me. Then, whenever we moved, she'd find work assisting a new photographer. She did that up until the twins came along. By then, she'd started homeschooling me—and taking care of them—so photography became more of a hobby. But she still goes out with her camera whenever she can."

I thought about my own parents, trying to figure out their passions, but aside from work, family, and church, I couldn't come up with anything. My mom didn't play tennis or bridge or anything like that; my dad had never played poker or whatever it was guys did when they hung out together. They both worked; he took care of the yard and the garage and emptied the garbage, while she cooked, did laundry, and cleaned the house. Aside from going out to dinner every other Friday, my parents were pretty much homebodies. Which probably explained why I didn't do much, either. Then again, Morgan had the violin, so maybe I was just making excuses.

"Will you keep up the photography once you get to West Point?"

"I doubt I'll have the time. It's a fairly regimented schedule."

"What do you want to do in the army?"

"Maybe intelligence, like my dad? But part of me wonders what it would be like to go the special forces route and become a Green Beret or get selected for Delta."

"Like Rambo?" I asked, referring to the Sylvester Stallone character.

"Exactly, but hopefully without the PTSD afterward. And again, we're back to talking about me. I'd like to hear about you."

"There's not much to say."

"What's it been like? Moving to Ocracoke, I mean?"

I hesitated, wondering whether I wanted to

talk about it or how much I would tell him, but that feeling lasted only a few seconds and evolved to *Why not?* After that, the words just began to spill out. While I didn't tell him about J—what was there really to say, other than that I was stupid?—I told him about my mom finding me puking in the bathroom and picked up from there, talking about everything right up until the moment he'd shown up to tutor me. I thought it would be harder, but he didn't interrupt me often, allowing me the space I needed to tell the story.

By the time I finished, there was only half an hour left before the ferry was going to dock, and I was saying a silent prayer of thanks that I'd bundled up. It was freezing and we retreated to the van, where Bryce pulled out a thermos and poured two cups of hot chocolate. His parents were chatting up front and we said a quick hello before they went back to their conversation.

We sipped the hot chocolate as my face slowly returned to its normal color. Through it all, we continued to chat about regular teenage things—favorite movies and television shows, music, what kind of pizza we liked (thin crust with double cheese for me, sausage and pepperoni for him), and anything else that came to mind. Robert and Richard clambered back into the van just as Bryce's dad was starting the engine and the ferry was about to dock.

We drove along dark and quiet roads, past farmhouses and mobile homes decked out in Christmas lights. One small town gave way to the next. I could feel Bryce's leg pressed against my own, and when he laughed at something one of the twins had said, I thought about the easy way he seemed to relate to his family. His mom, probably thinking that I might be feeling left out, asked the kinds of questions that parents always asked, and even though I was happy to answer in a general way, I still wondered how much Bryce had told them about me beforehand.

When we reached New Bern, I was taken with how *quaint* it was. Historic homes fronted the river, the downtown area was lined with small shops, and lampposts at every intersection were decorated with illuminated wreaths. The sidewalks were crowded with people making their way to Union Point

Park, and after parking, we fell in alongside them.

By then, the temperature was even colder, my breath coming out in little puffs. At the park, more hot chocolate was proffered, along with peanut butter cookies. It wasn't until I took the first bite that I realized how hungry I was. Bryce's mom, seeming to read my mind, handed me another as soon as I finished the first, but when the twins asked for seconds, she told them they'd have to wait until after dinner. The conspiratorial wink she gave me immediately made me feel like I belonged.

While I was still nibbling, the flotilla began. Broadcasting live from beneath a tent, the local radio station announced via loudspeaker the owner and type of each boat as one by one they slowly floated past. For some reason I guess I was expecting yachts, but aside from a handful of sailboats, they were either similar in size or smaller than the fishing boats I saw in the docks at Ocracoke. Some were festooned with lights; some sported characters like Winnie the Pooh or the Grinch, and still others had simply placed decorated trees along the decking. The whole affair had a sort of Mayberry vibe to it, and though I thought it might arouse a feeling of homesickness, it didn't. Instead, I found myself focusing on how close Bryce was standing next to me, and watching his dad point and grin with the twins. His mom merely sipped the hot chocolate, her expression content. A short while later, when Bryce's dad leaned over and tenderly kissed his wife, I found myself trying to remember the last time I'd seen my father kiss my mother in the same way.

Afterward, we had dinner at the Chelsea, a restaurant not far from the park. We weren't the only ones who headed over there after the flotilla ended; the place was bustling. Nonetheless, the service was quick and the food satisfying. At the table, I found myself mainly listening while Richard and Robert debated their mom and dad on heady scientific topics. Bryce sat back, remaining as quiet as I was.

When dinner was over, we returned to the van and drove to what seemed like the middle of nowhere, eventually parking alongside the highway with our hazard lights flashing.

Climbing out, I could only stare in wonder as I tried to take it all in.

While houses decked out in Christmas lights were common in Seattle and the malls were decorated professionally, this was on an entirely different scale, with the holiday display spread over at least three acres. Off to my left sat a small house at the edge of the property with lights framing the windows and lining the roof; a Santa and sleigh perched near the chimney. But it was the remainder of the grounds that amazed me. Even from the highway, I could see scores of illuminated Christmas trees, a giant American flag glowing high in the treetops, tall teepee-like cones assembled only with lights, a "frozen" pond with a clear plastic surface lit from below by tiny brilliant bulbs, a decorated train, and synchronized lights making it appear as if reindeer were flying through the sky. In the middle of the property, a miniature glowing Ferris wheel rotated slowly, stuffed animals seated in the cars. Here and there, I could make out comic and cartoon characters painted on plywood, cut to exacting standards.

The twins ran off in one direction while Bryce's parents moved slowly in another, leaving Bryce and me alone. Winding among the decorations, I felt my gaze drifting here and there. Dew was moistening the toes of my shoes and I pushed my hands deeper in my pockets. All around us, families wandered the property, children racing from one display to the next.

"Who does all this?"

"The family who lives in the house," Bryce answered. "They set it up every year."

"They must really love Christmas."

"No doubt," he agreed. "I always find myself wondering how long it takes them to set all of this up. And how they pack it up, so they can do it again the following year."

"And they don't care that people are basically walking through their yard?"

"I guess not."

I cocked my head. "I'm not sure I'd like strangers traipsing through my yard all month. I think I'd always be wary of someone peeking in the windows."

"I think most people understand that's a no-no."

For the next half hour, we meandered among the decorations, chatting easily. In the background, I could hear Christmas music drifting from hidden loudspeakers, along with the joyful squealing of children. A lot of people were taking photographs, and for the first time, I found myself getting into the spirit of the season, something I couldn't have imagined before I'd met Bryce. He seemed to know what I was thinking, and when he caught my eye, I thought again about our recent conversations and how much I'd already shared with him. Bryce, I suddenly realized, probably knew the real me better than anyone else in my life.

That night we stayed in New Bern's historic district, not far from the park where we'd seen the flotilla. Grabbing my duffel bag, I followed the family inside the house, and Bryce's dad showed me to my room. After putting on my pajamas, I fell asleep within minutes.

In the morning, Bryce's dad made pancakes for breakfast. I sat beside Bryce, listening as the rest of them figured out their own shopping plans for the day. But the clock was ticking—no one wanted my aunt to have to wait in the church parking lot. After a quick shower, I repacked my things and we made the drive back to Morehead City while my hair was still air-drying.

Aunt Linda and Gwen were waiting, and after saying goodbye to the Tricketts—Bryce's mom offered a hug—we did the church thing. Lunch and the supply run followed, and while I knew I'd mentioned that I needed bigger clothes, my aunt casually reminded me of something I'd forgotten.

"You might want to pick up gifts for your parents and Morgan while we're out and about."

Oh yeah. And while I was at it, I figured I should probably get something for my aunt, too. Seeing as I was living with her, I mean.

We ventured to a nearby department store and split up. I bought a scarf for my mom, a sweatshirt for my dad, a bracelet for Morgan, and a pair of gloves for my aunt. On our way out, my aunt promised to box and ship out my family's gifts the following week.

We next visited a store that specialized in maternity clothing. How she knew about the place, I had no idea—it's not like she'd ever needed it—but I was able to find a couple of pairs of jeans with elastic waistbands, one for now and one for when I was watermelon-sized. In all honesty, I hadn't even known that such things existed.

I dreaded the idea of having to check out—I knew the cashier would give me that *look*—but thankfully, my aunt seemed to sense my concerns.

"If you want to head to the car and wait," she said casually, "I'll pay for these and Gwen and I will meet you there."

I felt my shoulders suddenly relax. "Thanks," I murmured, and as I pushed through the door, I was struck by the revelation that a nun—or former nun, whatever—was actually one of the coolest people I knew.

We met up with Bryce and his family on the ferry and saw that their van had a large Christmas tree strapped to the roof. Bryce and I hung out for most of the ride until my aunt strode over to let Bryce know that on Tuesday, she and I were going to take a "personal day," so Bryce wouldn't have to tutor. I had no idea what she meant but knew enough to stay quiet; Bryce took her comment in stride, and it wasn't until I was back at the house that I asked my aunt about it.

I had an appointment with the OB-GYN, Aunt Linda explained, and Gwen would be joining us.

But strangely, even though we'd bought the maternity jeans, it struck me that in the last couple of days, I hadn't thought about my pregnancy much at all.

Unlike Dr. Bobbi, my new OB-GYN, Dr. Chinowith, was male and older, with white hair and hands so huge he could have palmed a basketball twice the normal size. I was eighteen weeks along, and by his demeanor, I was pretty certain I wasn't the first teenage unwed mother-to-be he'd come across. It was also clear that he'd worked with Gwen numerous times in the past and they were comfortable with each other.

We did the whole checkup thing, he renewed the prescription for prenatal vitamins that Dr. Bobbi had originally written, and afterward, we spoke briefly about how I'd likely be feeling over the next few months. He told me that he usually saw his pregnant patients once a month, but because Gwen was an experienced midwife—and getting to appointments was an all-day, inconvenient thing—he was comfortable with seeing me less often unless there was an emergency and that I should speak to Gwen if I had any questions or concerns. He also reminded me that Gwen would be monitoring my health extra closely during the third trimester, so there was nothing to worry about on that end, either. Once Gwen and my aunt left the room, he mentioned the adoption and asked me whether I wanted to hold the baby after delivery. When I didn't answer right away, he asked me to think about it, assuring me that I still had time to figure it out. The whole time he was talking, I couldn't take my eyes from his hands, which actually frightened me.

When I was shown into an adjoining room for the ultrasound, the technician asked whether I wanted to know the sex of the baby. I shook my head. Later, though, as I was putting my jacket back on, I overheard her murmuring to my aunt, "It was hard to get a good angle, but I'm almost certain it's a girl," which confirmed my mom's earlier suspicion.

As the next days and weeks unfolded, my life settled into a regular routine. The December weather brought even chillier days; I completed homework assignments, reviewed chapters, wrote papers, and studied for exams. By the time I took the last round of tests before my winter break began, I felt like my brain was going to explode.

On the plus side, my grades were definitely improving, and when I spoke with my parents, I couldn't help bragging a little. While my scores weren't at Morgan's level—I'd never be at Morgan's level—they were a lot higher than they'd been when I left Seattle. Though my parents didn't say it, I could almost hear them wondering why studying suddenly seemed so important to me.

Even more surprising, I was slowly but surely getting used to life in Ocracoke. Yeah, it was small and boring and I still missed my family and wondered what my friends were up to, but the regular schedule made things easier. Sometimes, after I finished my studies, Bryce and I would walk the neighborhood; twice, he brought his camera and the light meter along. He'd take photos of random things—houses, trees, boats—from interesting angles, explaining what he was trying to achieve with each photo, his enthusiasm evident.

Three times, we ended the walk at Bryce's house. The kitchen featured a lowered prep area that Bryce's mom could easily access, their Christmas tree looked a lot like the one we'd decorated, and his home always smelled like cookies. His mom made a small batch almost every day, and as soon as we entered, she'd pour two glasses of milk and join us at the table. Through these snack-time chats, we gradually got to know each other. She told stories about growing up in Ocracoke—apparently it had been quieter back then than it was now, which I found almost impossible to believe—and when I asked how she'd been accepted to MIT at such a young age, she merely shrugged, saying that she'd always had a knack for science and math, as if that explained it all.

I knew there was a lot more to the story—there *had* to be—but because the topic seemed to bore her, we usually spoke about other things: what Bryce and the twins had been like when they were younger, what it was like to move every few years, life as a military wife, homeschooling, and even her struggles after the accident. She asked me lots of questions as well, but unlike my parents, she didn't ask what I intended to do with my life. I think she'd picked up on the fact that I had absolutely no idea. Nor did she ask why I'd come to Ocracoke in the first place, but I suspected that she already knew. Not because Bryce had said anything—it was more like a teen-pregnancy radar—but she always insisted that I have a seat while we chatted and never asked why I wore the same stretchy jeans and baggy sweatshirts.

We also spoke about photography. They showed me the darkroom, which kind of reminded me of my high school science lab. There was a machine called an enlarger and plastic tubs used for chemicals, along with a clothesline where prints were hung to dry. There was a sink and counters lining the walls, half of which were low enough for Bryce's mom to access, and a cool red light that made it seem like we'd traveled to Mars. Photos lined the walls of their home, and Mrs. Trickett sometimes mentioned the stories behind them. My favorite was one that Bryce had taken—an impossibly large full moon casting light over the Ocracoke lighthouse; even though it was in black and white, it looked almost like a painting.

"How did you get that shot?"

"I set up a tripod on the beach and used a special cable release because the exposure time had to be super long," he answered. "Obviously, my mom coached me a lot when it came to developing the print."

Because I was curious, Robert showed me

the ultralight he was building with his dad. Staring at it, I knew I wouldn't ride in the thing for a million dollars, even if it did fly. In turn, Richard showed me the video game he was creating, which was set in a world complete with dragons and knights in armor packing every weapon imaginable. The graphics weren't great—even he conceded that—but the game itself seemed interesting, which was saying something, since I'd never seen the appeal of parking myself in front of a computer for hours on end.

But hey, what did I know? Especially when compared to a kid—or a family—like that?

"Have you figured out what you want to get Bryce?" Aunt Linda asked. It was Friday evening, and Christmas was three days away. I was washing dishes at the sink and she was drying, even though she didn't have to.

"Not yet. I thought about getting him something for his camera, but I wouldn't know where to start. Do you think we could run by a store after church on Sunday? I know it'll be Christmas Eve, but it'll be my last chance. Maybe I can figure something out."

"Of course we can go," she said. "We'll have more than enough time. It'll be a long day."

"Sundays are always long."

She smiled. "Extra-long, then, because Christmas is on Monday. We have regular Sunday mass in the morning like always, and then midnight mass for the Christmas celebration. And a couple of other things in between, too. We'll stay overnight in Morehead City and catch the ferry back in the morning."

"Oh." If she heard the unhappiness in my tone, she ignored it. I washed and rinsed a plate and handed it to her, knowing it would be pointless to try to talk her out of it. "What did you get for Gwen?"

"A pair of sweaters and an antique music box. She collects those."

"Should I buy something for Gwen, too?"

"No," she said. "I added your name on the music box. It'll be from both of us."

"Thanks," I said. "What do you think I should get Bryce?"

"You know him better than I do. Have you asked his mom what he might want?"

"I forgot," I said. "I guess I could go over tomorrow and ask. I just hope it won't be too expensive. I have to get his family something, too, and I was thinking I'd get them a nice picture frame."

She put a plate into the cupboard. "Keep in mind that you don't have to buy Bryce anything. Sometimes the best gifts are free."

"Like what?"

"An experience, or maybe you can make something, or teach him something."

"I don't think there's anything I can teach him. Unless he's interested in makeup or painting his nails."

She rolled her eyes, but I could see the mirth in them. "I have faith you'll figure something out."

I thought about it while we finished up in the kitchen, but it wasn't until we moved to the living room that inspiration finally struck. The only problem was that I was going to need my aunt's help in more ways than one. She beamed as soon as I explained.

"I can do that," she said. "And I'm sure he's going to love it."

An hour later, the phone rang. I guessed it was probably my parents and was surprised when Aunt Linda handed me the phone, telling me that Bryce was on the other end. Which was, to my knowledge, the first time he'd called the house.

"Hi, Bryce," I said. "What's up?"

"I was wondering if it would be possible for me to stop by on Christmas Eve. I want to give you your gift."

"I'm not going to be here," I said. I explained about the double mass on Sunday. "I won't be back until Christmas Day."

"Oh," he said. "Okay. Well, my mom also wanted me to ask if you'd like to come by for our Christmas meal. It'll be around two."

His mom wanted me to come? Or did he want me to come?

Covering the receiver, I asked my aunt and

she agreed, but only if he would join us later for our Christmas dinner.

"Perfect," he said. "I've got something for your aunt Linda and Gwen, too, so we can do the gift thing then."

It was only after I hung up that the reality of the situation hit me. It was one thing to see the flotilla with his family or drop by his house after walking the beach, but spending time at both our houses on Christmas Day felt like something more, almost like we were taking a step in a direction I was pretty sure I didn't want to go. And yet…

I couldn't deny that I was happy about it.

Christmas Eve on Sunday was different than it was at my house in Seattle, and not just due to the ferry ride and two services. I guess I should have expected that for a pair of former nuns, it was important to find a way to honor the *true meaning* of the holiday, which is exactly what we did.

After church, we did our normal run to

Wal-Mart, where I found a pretty frame for Bryce's parents and a card for Bryce, but instead of the usual garage sale circuit, we visited a place called Hope Mission, where we spent a few hours prepping meals in the kitchen for the poor and homeless. My job was peeling potatoes, and though I wasn't that fast in the beginning, I felt like an expert by the end. On the way out, after Aunt Linda and Gwen had hugged at least ten people— I had the sense they volunteered there every now and then—I watched as my aunt surreptitiously slipped the shelter coordinator an envelope, no doubt a financial donation.

At sunset, we attended a living nativity program at one of the Protestant churches (my mom would have made the sign of the cross had she found out about that). We watched Joseph and Mary being turned away from the inn and ending up in the stable, the birth of Christ, and the appearance of the three wise men. It took place outside, chilly temperatures making the play seem more real somehow. When that part of the program ended, the choir began, and my aunt held my hand as we joined in on the carols.

Dinner came next, and then, because we still had hours until the midnight service, we went to the same motel we'd stayed at when I'd flown in from Seattle. I roomed with Aunt Linda, and after setting the alarm, we all took evening naps. At eleven, we were awake again, and if I was concerned about still being tired at the service, the priest used enough incense to keep anyone awake; my eyes couldn't stop watering. It was also kind of eerie, but in a spiritual way. There were candles glowing throughout the church, an organ adding depth and resonance to the solemn music. When I glanced at my aunt, I noticed her lips moving with silent prayers.

Then it was back to the motel, and onto the ferry first thing in the morning. It didn't feel much like Christmas at all, but my aunt tried to make up for it. In the seating area, she and Gwen shared stories of their favorite Christmases. Gwen, who'd grown up on a farm in Vermont, told us about the time she'd received an Australian shepherd puppy. She was nine years old, and she'd wanted a dog for as long as she could remember. In the morning, after unwrapping all of her packages, she'd been crestfallen, not realizing that her dad had slipped out the back door. He reappeared a minute later holding the puppy, who was wearing a red bow for a collar—and even almost half a century later, she could still recall the joy she'd felt when the puppy bounded over and began playing with her. On a quieter note, Aunt Linda recounted how she had baked cookies with her mother on Christmas Eve; it was the first time her mom had allowed her not only to help but to do most of the measuring and mixing. She remembered how proud she'd been when everyone in the family raved about the cookies, and in the morning, she received her own apron with her name stitched on it, as well as her own baking utensils. There were more stories like that—and as I sat with them, I remember thinking how *normal* the stories sounded. It had never occurred to me that future nuns had ordinary childhood experiences; I just assumed that they grew up praying all the time and finding Bibles and rosaries beneath the tree.

Back home, I chatted with my parents and Morgan on the phone, wrote the card for

Bryce, then started getting ready. I showered and did the hair-and-makeup thing. On went the stretchy jeans—God bless them, by the way—and a red sweater. Outside the window, darker clouds had filled the sky, so just in case, I put on my rubber boots. Evaluating myself in the mirror, except for my ever-expanding bust, I thought I barely looked pregnant.

Perfect.

Tucking the gift under my arm, I started toward the Trickett house. In the Pamlico Sound, I could see small whitecaps in the swells and the wind had picked up, playing havoc with my hair, which made me wonder why I'd bothered to style it in the first place.

Bryce opened the door as I was climbing the steps. In the distance, I heard a deep rumble echoing in the sky. The storm, I knew, would be coming soon.

"Hey there. Merry Christmas! You look amazing."

"Thanks. You too," I said, eyeing his dark wool slacks and button-up shirt, as well as his shiny loafers.

Inside, the house was a picture-perfect version of Christmas Day. The remains of wrapping paper had been crumpled up and packed into a cardboard box beneath the tree; the aromas of ham and apple pie and corn simmering in butter filled the air. The table was set, some side dishes already in place. Richard and Robert were on the couch in their pajamas and fuzzy slippers reading comic books, reminding me that as smart as they were, they were still kids. Daisy, who'd been nestled at their feet, rose and wandered toward me, tail wagging. In the meantime, Bryce introduced me to his grandparents. While they were perfectly friendly, I barely understood a word they said. I nodded and smiled, and after Bryce finally maneuvered me away, he whispered in my ear.

"Hoi Toider," he said. "It's an island brogue. There's maybe a few hundred people in the world who speak it. People on the islands didn't have much contact with the mainland for hundreds of years, so they developed their own dialect. But don't feel bad; half the time, I can't understand them, either."

Bryce's parents were in the kitchen and after

hugs and greetings, his mom handed him the mashed potatoes to bring to the table.

"Richard and Robert?" she called out. "Food's almost ready, so wash up and come find your seats."

Over dinner, I asked the twins what they'd received for Christmas and they asked me. When I explained that my aunt and I planned to open our gifts later, Robert or Richard— I still couldn't tell them apart—swiveled his gaze to his parents.

"I like opening the gifts on Christmas *morning*."

"Me too," the other one said.

"Why are you telling me this?" their mom asked.

"Because I don't want you to get any crazy ideas in the future."

He sounded so serious that his mom burst out laughing.

When everyone was finished eating, Bryce's mom opened the gift I'd brought, for which she and her husband thanked me graciously—and everyone pitched in to clean the kitchen. Leftovers went in Tupperware and then into the fridge, and when the table was cleared, Bryce's mom brought out a jigsaw puzzle. After dumping out the contents of the box, Bryce's parents, brothers, and even the grandparents began flipping the pieces, turning them right-side up.

"We always do a puzzle on Christmas," Bryce whispered to me. "Don't ask me why."

As I sat beside him, trying to find matching pieces along with the rest of the family, I wondered what my own family was doing. It was easy to imagine Morgan putting her new clothes away while my mom cooked in the kitchen and my dad caught a game on television. It occurred to me that after the morning frenzy of opening gifts, aside from the meal, everyone in my family did their own thing. I knew that families had their own holiday traditions, but ours seemed to keep us dispersed while Bryce's gathered them together.

Outside, it began to rain, then pour. As lightning flickered and thunder boomed, we worked steadily on the puzzle. There were a thousand pieces but the family were absolute puzzle wizards—especially Bryce's dad—and we finished it in about an hour. Had it been me putting it together alone, I was pretty sure I'd still be working on it until next Christmas. His family put on *Scrooge*— a musical version of Dickens's classic—and not long after it ended, it was time for Bryce and me to go. After fishing out a couple unopened gifts from under the tree, Bryce grabbed umbrellas and his truck keys while I hugged every member of his family goodbye.

It felt darker than usual as we drove the quiet roads. Heavy clouds blocked the starlight while the wipers pushed the rain aside. The storm had abated to a drizzle by the time we got to my aunt's, where we found her and Gwen in the kitchen. I savored another round of delicious aromas, even though I wasn't hungry in the slightest.

"Merry Christmas, Bryce," Gwen called out.

"Dinner should be ready in twenty minutes," Aunt Linda informed us.

Bryce put his gifts beneath the tree with the others and greeted both women with hugs. The house had been transformed in the hours I'd been gone. The tree was glowing, and candles flickered on the table, the mantel, and the end table near the sofa. Faint strains of holiday music drifted from the radio, reminding me of my childhood, when I'd be the first to sneak downstairs on Christmas morning. I'd wander to the tree and check out the gifts, noting which ones were for me and which ones were for Morgan before taking a seat on the steps. Sandy would usually join me and I'd stroke her head, letting the anticipation build until it was finally time to get everyone up.

As I recalled those mornings, I could feel Bryce's curious gaze on me.

"Good memories," I said simply.

"It must be hard being away from your family today."

I met his eyes, feeling warm in a way I hadn't expected. "Actually," I said, "I'm doing okay."

We took a seat on the couch and chatted in the glow of the lights from the Christmas tree until dinner was ready. My aunt had made turkey, and despite eating only small portions, I felt like I was going to pop when I finally put my fork down.

By the time we cleaned the kitchen and retreated to the living room, the storm had passed; though lightning still flickered on the horizon, the rain had stopped and a light fog had begun to roll in. Aunt Linda had poured herself and Gwen a glass of wine—it was the first time I'd ever seen either of them drink anything with alcohol—and we began opening gifts. My aunt loved the gloves; Gwen exclaimed over the music box, and I opened the gifts that my parents and Morgan had sent. I found a nice pair of shoes and some cute tops and sweaters that were one size larger than I usually wore, which I sup-posed made sense considering my situation. When it was Bryce's turn, I handed him the envelope.

I'd picked a fairly generic card, with room to write my own message. Because the light was so dim in the living room, he had to turn on the reading lamp to see what I'd written.

Merry Christmas, Bryce!

Thank you for all your help, and in the spirit of the holidays, I wanted to get you something I knew you would love, a gift that just might keep on giving for the rest of your life.

This card entitles you to the following:

1. My aunt's super-secret biscuit recipe; and

2. A baking lesson for the two of us, so that you can learn how to make them on your own.

Obviously, this gift is from both my aunt and me, but it was my idea.

Maggie
P.S. My aunt would like you to keep the recipe secret!

As he read the card, I stole a peek at Aunt Linda, whose eyes were glittering. When he finished, he turned first toward me, then toward her before finally breaking into a grin.

"This is great!" he declared. "Thank you! I can't believe you remembered."

"I wasn't sure what else to get you."

"It's the perfect gift," he said. Turning to my aunt, he said, "I don't want you to go to a lot of trouble, so if it's easier, we can go to your shop early and watch you prepare them like you always do."

"In the middle of the night?" I said, my eyes widening. "I don't think so."

Both Aunt Linda and Gwen laughed. "We'll figure it out," my aunt said.

Next were the gifts from Bryce. As my aunt carefully unwrapped the gift he'd given both of them, I caught a glimpse of the frame and knew immediately he'd given them a photograph. Curiously, my aunt and Gwen both stared at it without speaking, causing me to rise from my spot on the couch and peek over their shoulders. I suddenly understood why they couldn't stop staring.

It was a color image of the shop taken early in the morning, and from the angle, I suspected that Bryce had to lie in the road to take it. A customer—I guessed he fished for a living based on his attire—was leaving with a small bag in hand just as a woman was entering. Both were bundled up and you could actually see their breath frozen in space. In the window, I spotted the reflection of clouds, and beyond the glass, I could see my aunt's profile and Gwen placing a cup of coffee on the counter. Above the roof, the sky was slate gray, accentuating the faded painted siding and the weather-beaten eaves. Though I'd seen the shop countless times, I'd never seen it appear so arresting... beautiful, even.

"This... is incredible," Gwen managed to say. "I can't believe we didn't see you taking this."

"I was hiding. I actually went out there three mornings in a row to get just the shot I wanted. It took two rolls of film."

"Are you going to hang it in the living room?" I asked.

"Are you kidding?" my aunt replied. "This will be front and center at the shop. Everyone should see this."

Because my gift came in a box similar in shape and size, I knew that I'd been given a photograph as well. As I unwrapped it, I silently prayed that it wasn't a picture of me, something he'd sneakily taken when I hadn't been paying attention. As a general rule, I disliked photos of myself, let alone a photo taken while I was in baggy sweats or ugly pants with my hair being blown in every direction.

But it wasn't a photo of me; instead, it was the photograph I'd loved, the one of the lighthouse and the giant moon. Like me, Aunt Linda and Gwen were stunned by the image; they both agreed it should hang in my room where I could see it while lying in bed.

With the gifts opened, we visited for a little while, until Gwen announced that she wanted to go for a short walk. Aunt Linda joined her at the door and we watched while they bundled up.

"Are you sure you don't want to join us?" my aunt asked. "To help digest dinner before the rain comes back?"

"I'm okay," I said. "I think I'd just like to sit for a while, if that's all right."

She finished wrapping the scarf around her neck. "We won't be gone long."

After they left, I looked from the photograph to the glowing tree, to the candles, and then to Bryce. He was beside me on the couch, not wedged against me but close enough that if I leaned, our shoulders would brush against each other. Music continued to play on the radio and beneath that, barely detectable, was the sound of gentle swells lapping against the shoreline. Bryce was quiet; like me, he seemed content. I thought back to my first few weeks in Ocracoke— the fear and sadness and the ache of loneliness as I lay in my room, the notion that my friends would forget me, and the conviction that being away from home for the holidays was a wrong that could never be righted.

And yet as I sat beside Bryce with the photograph in my lap, I knew already that this had become a Christmas I would never forget. I thought about Aunt Linda and Gwen and Bryce's family and the ease and kindness I'd found here, but mostly I thought about Bryce. I wondered what he was thinking, and when his eyes suddenly flashed toward me, I wanted to tell him that he'd inspired me in ways he probably couldn't imagine.

"You're thinking about something," Bryce stated, and I felt my thoughts drift away like vapor, leaving only a single idea.

"Yeah," I said. "I was."

"Care to share?"

I glanced down at the photograph he'd given me before finally turning to meet his gaze.

"Do you think you could teach me photography?"

THE CHRISTMAS TREE

Manhattan
December 2019

When the waitress came by with the dessert menu and an offer of coffee, Maggie used the opportunity to catch her breath. She'd related her story throughout their meal, barely noticing as her mostly untouched plate was cleared. Mark ordered a decaf while Maggie declined, still nursing her original glass of wine. There were only a handful of occupied tables left and conversations had dropped to a low murmur.

"*Bryce* taught you how to take pictures?" Mark exclaimed.

Maggie nodded. "And he introduced me to the rudimentary basics of Photoshop, which was relatively new back then. His mom taught me a lot of darkroom technique—dodging and burning and cropping, the importance of timing in the development process... essentially, the now-lost art of making prints the old-fashioned way. Between the two of them, it was like a crash course. He also predicted that digital photography was going to replace film and that the internet was going to change the world—lessons I took to heart."

Mark raised an eyebrow. "Impressive."

"He was a smart guy."

"Did you start taking pictures right away?"

"No. Bryce being Bryce, he wanted me to learn the way he had, so he came by the day after Christmas with a photography book, a thirty-five-millimeter Leica camera, the manual, and a light meter," she said. "I was still technically on break, so I only had to finish the assignments I hadn't yet completed. In any case, by then, I had actually begun to pull ahead in my classes, which left more time to learn photography. He showed me how to load film, the way various settings altered the photo, and how to work the light meter. He walked me through the manual, and the book he brought touched on composition, framing, and what to think about when attempting to take a photograph. It was overwhelming, obviously, but he went through it all step by step. After which he'd quiz me, of course."

Mark smiled. "When did you take your first real photo?"

"Right before the new year. They were all black and white—it was much easier to develop negatives into contact sheets and make prints ourselves in Bryce's darkroom. We didn't need to send film to Raleigh for processing, which was good because I didn't have a ton of money. Just what my mom had given me at the airport."

"What did you shoot that first day?"

"Some images of the ocean, a few old fishing boats tied up at the dock. Bryce had me make adjustments to the aperture and shutter speed, and when I got the contact sheets back, I was..." She searched for the right word, remembering. "*Awestruck*. The differences in effect just floored me, and that was when I first and truly began to understand what Bryce meant when he said photography was all about capturing the light. After that, I was hooked."

"That fast?"

"You had to be there," she said. "And the funny thing is, the more I got into photography over the next few months, the easier my schoolwork became and the faster I completed it. Not because I was suddenly smarter, but because finishing early meant more time with the camera. I even started doing extra homework at night, and when he'd show up the next day, I'd hand over two or three assignments first thing. How crazy is that?"

"I don't think it's crazy at all. You'd found your passion. Sometimes I wonder if I'll ever find mine."

"You're going to be a pastor. If that doesn't require passion, I don't know what does."

"I suppose. It's definitely a calling, but it doesn't seem like the same feeling you had when you saw the contact sheet. There's never been a 'Eureka!' moment for me. The feeling has just always been there, simmering in my bones, ever since I was young."

"That doesn't make it less real. How does Abigail feel about it?"

"She's supportive. Of course, she also pointed out that it means she'll have to be the principal breadwinner in the family."

"What? No dreams of being a televangelist or building a megachurch?"

"I think we're all called in different ways. Neither of those appeals to me."

Maggie was pleased by his answer, convinced that many television preachers were hypocritical salesmen, more interested in their celebrity lifestyles than in helping others become closer to God. At the same time, she admitted, her knowledge of such people was limited to what she'd read in the newspapers. She'd never actually met a televangelist or a megachurch pastor.

The waitress came by with an offer to refill Mark's cup and he waved it off. When she left, he leaned over the table. "Can I pick up the dinner tab?"

"Not a chance," Maggie said. "I invited you. And besides, I know exactly how much you earn, Mr. Have a Slice of Pizza Before You Go to Dinner."

He laughed. "Thank you," he said. "This was fun. What a terrific evening, especially at this time of year."

She couldn't help flashing on her long-ago Christmas in Ocracoke, knowing there had been beauty in its simplicity, in spending time with people she cared about rather than being alone.

She didn't want to be alone on her last Christmas, and taking a few seconds to study Mark, she knew she suddenly didn't want him to be alone, either. The next words came almost automatically.

"I think we need more to get into the spirit of the season."

"What did you have in mind?"

"What the gallery needs this year is a Christmas tree, don't you think? How about I make arrangements to have a tree and decorations delivered? And then we'll trim it together after we close tomorrow?"

"That sounds like a fantastic idea."

The late dinner left Maggie feeling both exhilarated and exhausted, and she didn't wake until almost noon the next day. Her pain level was tolerable, but she swallowed the pills anyway, washing them down with a cup of tea. She forced herself to have a piece of toast, puzzled that even with butter and gobs of jelly, it still tasted salty.

She took a bath and dressed, then spent some time on the computer. She ordered a tree, paying triple for expedited delivery so it would arrive at the gallery by five. For the decorations, she went with a complete set called Winter Wonderland, which included white lights, silver silk strands, and white and silver ornaments. Again, to have it expedited cost a small fortune, but what did the cost really matter at this point? She wanted a memorable Christmas, and that was that. She then texted Mark, letting him know to take delivery and that she'd be there later.

Once that was done, she settled into the couch and wrapped herself in a blanket. She thought about calling her parents but decided to wait until tomorrow. On Sundays, she knew they'd both be around the house. She knew she should probably call Morgan, too, but she put that off as well. Morgan wasn't the easiest person to talk to lately; really, when Maggie was being honest with herself, aside from a few rare exceptions, talking to her sister had never been all that easy.

Why was that the case, though, she wondered again, even aside from their obvious differences? Maggie supposed that when she'd returned from Ocracoke, it had been even more evident that Morgan was the preferred daughter. She had maintained her 4.0 average, was homecoming queen, and eventually went off to Gonzaga University, where she joined just the right sorority. Their parents couldn't have been prouder and made sure Maggie always knew it. After graduating from college, Morgan began teaching music at a local school and dated guys who worked in banks or for insurance companies, the kind who wore suits to work every day. She eventually met Jim, who worked for Merrill Lynch, and after they'd dated for two years, he proposed. They'd had a smallish—but perfectly orchestrated—wedding, immediately moving into the house Jim and Morgan bought, complete with a grill in the backyard. A few years later, Morgan gave birth to Tia. Three years after that, Bella came along, giving rise to family photos so perfect they could have been used to sell frames.

Meanwhile, Maggie had abandoned the family and spent those years struggling to launch her career and living the wild life, which meant their relative positions as siblings hadn't changed. Both Maggie and Morgan knew their familiar roles—the star and the struggler—which informed their regular, if not frequent, phone conversations.

But then Maggie got her break and slowly earned a reputation that allowed her to regularly travel the world; after that her stewardship of the gallery. Over time even her social life stabilized. Morgan seemed discomfited by these developments, and there'd been times when Maggie had even sensed a bit of jealousy. It was never overt while Maggie was in her twenties; most often, it took the form of passive-aggressive digs. *I'm sure the new guy you're dating is a big step up from the last one*, or *Can you believe your luck?*, or *Have you seen the photographs in* National Geographic *this month? They're really incredible.*

The more successful Maggie became, the harder Morgan tried to keep the focus on herself. Usually, she'd describe one challenge after another—with the kids, with the house, with her job—before proceeding to explain how she'd solved the problems using both intelligence and perseverance. In those conversations, Morgan was simultaneously a victim and a hero, while Maggie was always just *lucky*.

For a long time, Maggie did her best to ignore those...*quirks*. Deep down, she knew Morgan loved her, and that having two young kids and taking care of a house while working a full-time job was stressful for anyone. Morgan's self-involvement wasn't unexpected, and besides, Maggie knew that, jealous or not, Morgan was proud of her.

It wasn't until Maggie got sick that she began to question her most basic assumptions. Not long after the initial diagnosis— back when Maggie still had hope—Morgan's marriage took a turn for the worse and those troubles became the focus of nearly every conversation. Instead of offering Maggie a chance to vent or express her worries about her cancer, Morgan would listen for only a short while before changing the subject. She'd complain that Jim seemed to regard her as a servant, or that Jim had closed down emotionally and wouldn't consider counseling because he'd said that Morgan was the one who needed counseling. Or she'd admit that they hadn't had sex in months, or that Jim had started working late at the office three or four days a week. It was one thing after another and whenever Maggie tried to clarify something Morgan had said, her sister would grow irritated and accuse Maggie of taking Jim's side. Even now, Maggie still wasn't sure exactly what had gone wrong in the marriage other than the old cliché that Morgan and Jim had simply drifted apart.

Because Morgan was so unhappy—the word *divorce* had begun creeping into the conversations—Maggie was caught off guard by Morgan's fury when Jim packed his bags and moved out. She was even more taken aback when the anger and bitterness intensified. While Maggie knew that going through a divorce was often a miserable experience, she couldn't understand why Morgan seemed intent on making things worse. Why couldn't they figure something out on their own, without adversarial attorneys throwing gasoline on the fire, all the while running up the bills and slowing the process to a crawl?

Maggie knew she was probably being naive. She'd never gone through a divorce, but even so, Morgan's sense of betrayal and absolute righteousness reflected her conviction that Jim deserved to be punished. For his part, Jim probably felt victimized as well, all of which meant a long and nasty divorce that took seventeen exhausting months to finally sort out.

But even that wasn't the end of it. Last summer, whenever they touched base, Morgan had still complained about Jim and his new, younger girlfriend, or she'd wax on about the fact that Jim wasn't measuring up as a parent. She would tell Maggie that Jim had been late to the parent-teacher conferences, or that he'd tried to take the kids hiking in the Cascades even though it was technically Morgan's weekend to have them. Or that Jim had forgotten to bring an EpiPen when he'd taken the girls to an apple farm, even though Bella was allergic to bees.

To all of those things, Maggie had wanted to add, *Chemotherapy sucks, by the way. My hair is falling out and I'm puking all the time. Thanks for asking.*

In all fairness, Morgan did ask how Maggie was feeling; Maggie simply had the sense that no matter how awful she felt, Morgan viewed her own situation as worse.

All of that meant fewer and fewer phone calls, especially in the last month and a half. Their last call had taken place on Maggie's birthday, before Halloween, and aside from a quick text and an equally quick response, they hadn't even touched base on Thanksgiving. She hadn't mentioned those things to Mark when talking about her reasons for wanting to stay quiet about her diagnosis for now. And it was also true that she didn't want to cast a pall over Morgan's Christmas, especially because of Tia and Bella. But for Christmas to remain peaceful, Maggie figured she'd be better off without her.

Maggie caught a cab to the gallery and arrived half an hour after closing. Despite the languid day and another dose of painkillers, she still felt thumped, like she'd been accidentally tossed into the dryer with the rest of the laundry. Her joints and muscles ached as though she'd exercised way too much, and her stomach was churning. When she caught sight of the Christmas tree just to the right of the door, however, her spirits lifted slightly. It was full and straight; since she hadn't chosen it, part of her had feared that she'd end up with the kind of tree Charlie Brown had picked in the old cartoon Christmas special. After unlocking the door, she stepped into the gallery just as Mark was emerging from the back offices.

"Hi," he said, his face brightening. "You made it. For a few minutes there, I wasn't sure you would."

"Time slipped away from me." It was more like not having enough steam to make the kettle whistle, but why start with the doom and gloom? "How was it today?"

"Moderately busy. There were a lot of groupies, but only a couple of photographs sold. We received a bunch of online orders, though."

"Anything for Trinity?"

"Just some online inquiries. I've already sent the information, so we'll see how that goes. There was also an email from a gallery in Newport Beach wondering if Trinity would be open to doing a show out there."

"He won't," Maggie said. "But I assume you passed the information along to his publicist?"

"I did. I also got all your online orders shipped."

"You've been busy. When did the tree arrive?"

"Around four or so? The decorations actually arrived earlier. I'm guessing they were really expensive."

"The tree is pretty, too. I'm sort of amazed they had a good one left. I would have thought they'd all be sold by now."

"Small miracles," he agreed. "I already added water in the base and I popped over to Duane Reade to get an extension cord in case we need it."

"Thanks." She sighed. Even standing, she realized, was taking more effort than she'd imagined it would. "Would you mind bringing my office chair out here? So I can sit?"

"Of course," he said. He turned and vanished into the back; a moment later, he was rolling the chair across the floor, finally adjusting it to face the tree. When Maggie sat, she winced and Mark frowned with concern.

"Are you feeling all right?"

"No, but I'm pretty sure I'm not supposed to be. What with the cancer eating my insides and all."

His gaze fell, making her regret that she hadn't come up with a gentler response, but cancer was anything but gentle.

"Can I get you anything else?"

"I'm all right for now," she said. "Thank you."

She studied the tree, thinking that it needed to be rotated slightly. Mark followed her eyes.

"You're not happy about the gap toward the bottom, right?"

"I didn't notice it when I saw the tree from outside."

He walked toward the tree. "Hmmm..." He gripped and lifted, rotating it half a turn. "Better?"

"Perfect," she said.

"I have a surprise," he added. "I hope you won't mind."

"I love surprises."

"Give me a minute, okay?"

He vanished into the back again, returning with a small portable speaker and candles tucked beneath his arm, along with two glasses filled with a creamy liquid. She assumed it was a smoothie, but as he drew near, she realized she was mistaken.

"Eggnog?"

"I thought it seemed appropriate."

He handed her a glass and she took a sip, hoping her stomach wouldn't sour. Thankfully, it didn't, nor was there much of an aftertaste. She took another drink, realizing how hungry she was.

"There's plenty in the back for refills," he said. He took a sip as well, then set his glass on a low wooden pedestal. He put the speaker next to the glass and pulled his phone from his pocket. A few seconds later, she was listening to Mariah Carey singing "All I Want for Christmas Is You," the volume low. He lit the candles, then went over and turned off most of the lights, leaving only the ones near the rear of the gallery illuminated.

He took a seat on the pedestal.

"My story really got to you, huh?" she asked.

"I told Abigail all about it when we FaceTimed last night. She suggested that if we were going to decorate the tree, I might as well try to re-create parts of your Ocracoke Christmas as well. She helped me with the playlist, and I picked up the eggnog and candles when I grabbed the extension cord."

Maggie smiled as she removed her gloves, but still chilled, she decided to keep her jacket and scarf on. "I'm not sure I'm going to have enough energy to help you with the tree," she confessed.

"That's fine. You can direct, like Bryce's mom did. Unless you'd like to try again tomorrow..."

"Not tomorrow. Let's do it now." She swallowed another mouthful of eggnog. "I wonder when people started putting up Christmas trees in the first place."

"I'm pretty sure it was the mid- to late sixteenth century in what's now Germany. For a long time, it was regarded as a Protestant custom. The first tree wasn't displayed at the Vatican until 1982."

"And you just happened to know that off the top of your head?"

"I did a report on it when I was in high school."

"I can't remember anything from the reports I did in high school."

"Even Thurgood Marshall?"

"Even him. And just so you know, even though my family was Catholic, we had Christmas trees growing up."

"Don't blame the messenger," he teased. "You ready to do some directing while I get to work?"

"Only if you're sure you don't mind."

"Are you kidding? This is great. I don't have a tree in my apartment, so this is the only chance I'll have this year."

He found the box, freed the lights from their plastic packaging, then plugged in the extension cord. Like Bryce long ago, he moved the tree out from the corner to string the lights, making adjustments as Maggie suggested. The silk ribbons came next, then finally a large matching bow, which he placed on top in lieu of a star. He finished by dispersing the ornaments throughout the tree, following Maggie's instructions. After scooting it back into place, he retreated to Maggie's side, the two of them evaluating it.

"Good?" he asked.

"It's perfect," she said.

Mark continued to stare at the tree before finally reaching for his phone. He took a series of pictures, then began tapping the screen.

"Abigail?"

She watched him actually blush. "She wanted to see the tree as soon as it was finished. I'm not sure she trusted me to do a good job. I'm sending it to my parents, too."

"Did you hear from your folks today?"

"They texted some photos from Nazareth and the Sea of Galilee. You've been to Israel, right?"

"It's an incredible country. When I visited, I kept thinking to myself that I might be following in Christ's footsteps. Literally, I mean."

"What were you photographing?"

"Tel Megiddo, the Qumran cliffs, and a few other archeology digs. I was there for about a week, and I've always wanted to go back but there were too many other places to see for the first time."

Mark leaned forward, his elbows on his knees as he stared up at her. "If I could visit one place in the world, what do you think that should be?" Light flickered in his eyes, making him appear almost childlike.

"A lot of people have asked me that question, but there's no single answer. It depends on where you are in life."

"I'm not sure I follow."

"If you've been stressed and working a zillion hours for months, maybe the best place to go would be a tropical beach somewhere. If you're in search of the meaning of life, maybe go hiking in Bhutan or visit Machu Picchu or attend mass in St. Peter's Basilica. Or maybe you just want to see animals, so you travel to Botswana or northern Canada. I can say that I see all those places differently—and I photographed them differently—based partly on my own life experiences at the time."

"I get that," he said. "Or at least I think I do."

"Where would you want to go? If you could only see one place?"

He reached for his eggnog and took a sip. "I like your Botswana idea. I'd love to go on safari, see the wild animals. I might even be convinced to bring a camera, though I'd stick with the automatic setting."

"I can give you a few photography pointers if you'd like. And who knows? Maybe you'll have your own gallery, too, one day."

He laughed. "Not a chance."

"Going on safari is a good choice. Maybe think about it for your honeymoon?"

"I hear it's kind of expensive. But I'm confident we'll get there one day. Where there's a will, there's a way and all that."

"Like your parents and their trip to Israel?"

"Exactly," he said.

She leaned back in her chair, finally beginning to feel closer to normal again. She wasn't yet warm enough to take off her jacket, but the bone-deep chill had passed. "I know your dad is a pastor, but I don't think I've ever asked about your mom."

"She's a child psychologist. She and my dad met when they were both getting their PhDs at Indiana."

"Does she teach or practice?"

"She's done a bit of both in the past, but now she mainly practices. She also assists the police when necessary. She's an on-call specialist if there's a child in trouble, and because she often serves as an expert witness, she testifies in court quite a bit."

"She sounds smart. And very busy."

"She is."

Though it took some effort, Maggie tucked her leg up, trying to get more comfortable. "I'm guessing that in your house, there wasn't a lot of shouting when emotions were high. Since your dad's a pastor and your mom is a psychologist?"

"Never," he agreed. "I don't think I've ever heard either of them raise their voice. Unless they were cheering for me in hockey or baseball, I mean. They prefer talking things out, which sounds great, but it can also be frustrating. It's no fun to be the only one shouting."

"I can't imagine that you ever shouted."

"I didn't do it much, but when I did, they'd ask me to lower the volume so we could have a reasonable discussion, or they'd tell me to go to my room until I calmed down, after which we'd have the reasonable discussion anyway. It didn't take long before I understood that shouting doesn't work."

"How long have your parents been married?"

"Thirty-one years," he said.

She did the mental calculation. "They're a little older, then, right? Since they met when they were getting their PhDs?"

"They'll both turn sixty next year. My mom and dad sometimes talk about retiring, but I'm not sure that day will ever come. They both love what they do too much."

She recalled her earlier reflections about Morgan. "Did you ever wish you had siblings?"

"Not until recently," he said. "Being an only child was all I knew. I think my parents wanted more kids, but it just didn't work out. And being an only child sometimes has its advantages. It's not like I had to make compromises when it came to what movie to see, or what to ride first at Disney World. But now that I'm with Abigail, and I see how close she is to her siblings, I sometimes wonder what it would have been like."

After Mark trailed off, neither of them said anything for a short spell. She had the sense that he wanted to hear more about her time in Ocracoke, but realized she wasn't quite ready to start just yet. Instead:

"What was it like growing up in Indiana?" she asked. "It's one of the states I've never visited."

"Do you know anything about Elkhart?"

"Not a single thing."

"It's in the northern part of the state, with a population of about fifty thousand, and like a lot of towns in the Midwest, it still has a small-town vibe. Most stores close at six, most of the restaurants are done serving at nine, and agriculture—in our case, dairy—plays a big part in the economy. I do think people there are genuinely kind. They'll help out a sick neighbor, and churches are central to the community. But when you're a kid, you don't really think about any of those things. What was important to me was that there were parks and fields to play on, baseball diamonds, basketball courts, a hockey rink. Growing up, as soon as I'd get home from school, I'd head straight back out to play with my friends. There was always a game going on somewhere. That's what I remember most about growing up there. Just . . . playing basketball or baseball or soccer or hockey every afternoon."

"And here I thought everyone in your generation was glued to their iPads," she said in mock wonder.

"My parents wouldn't let me have one. They didn't even allow me to get an iPhone until I was seventeen, and then they made me buy it. I had to work all summer to afford it."

"Were they anti-technology?"

"Not at all. I had a computer at home and they had cell phones. I think they wanted me to grow up the same way they had."

"Old-fashioned values?"

"I suppose."

"I'm beginning to like your parents more and more."

"They're good people. Sometimes I don't know how they do it."

"What do you mean?"

He stared into his eggnog, as though searching for words in the glass. "In her job, my mom can hear some pretty awful things, especially when she works with the police. Physical abuse, sexual abuse, emotional abuse, abandonment...And my dad...because he's a pastor, he does a lot of counseling, too. People come to him for guidance when they're having marital troubles, or struggling with addiction, or having problems on the job, or their kids are acting up, or even if they're having a crisis of faith. He also spends a lot of time at the hospital, as hardly a week goes by when someone in the church isn't sick, or in an accident, or needs comfort in their grief. It's draining for both of them. When I was growing up, there'd be times when one or the other of them would be really quiet while we were having dinner and I came to recognize the signs of a particularly hard day."

"But they still love it?"

"They do. And I think part of them feels a real sense of responsibility when it comes to helping others."

"It's obviously rubbed off on you. Here you are, staying late yet again."

"This is a pleasure," he said. "Not a sacrifice in the slightest."

She liked that. "I'd like to meet your parents one day. If they ever make it to New York, I mean."

"I'm sure they'd like to meet you, too. How about you? What are your parents like?"

"They're just parents."

"Have they ever come to New York?"

"Twice. Once in my twenties, and once when I was in my thirties." Then, as if realizing how that sounded, she added, "It's a long flight and they're not big fans of the city, so it was usually easier if I saw them in Seattle. Depending on where I was shooting, sometimes I would just route my return flight through Seattle and stay for a weekend. Until recently, that usually happened once or twice a year."

"Is your dad still working?"

She shook her head. "He retired a few years back. Now he plays with model trains."

"Seriously?"

"He had them when he was a kid, and after

he retired, he got back into it. He built a big layout in the garage—old western town, canyon, hills covered in trees—and he's continually adding new buildings or shrubbery or signs, or laying a new track. It's actually pretty impressive. The newspaper did an article on it last year, complete with pictures. And it keeps him busy and out of the house. Otherwise, I think my parents would drive each other crazy."

"And your mom?"

"She volunteers at the church a few mornings a week, but mainly she helps my sister, Morgan, with the kids. My mom picks them up from school, watches them during the summer, brings them to their events if Morgan is working late, whatever."

"What does Morgan do?"

"She's a music teacher, but she's also in charge of the drama club. There are always after-school rehearsals for concerts or shows."

"I'll bet your mom loves having the grandkids around."

"She does. And without her, I'm not sure what Morgan would do. She got divorced and it's been hard."

Mark nodded before lowering his eyes. Both of them were quiet for a moment before Mark finally motioned toward the tree. "I'm glad you decided to put up a tree in here. I'm sure the customers will appreciate it."

"The tree was for me, honestly."

"Can I ask you something?"

"Sure."

He turned to face her. "Was that Christmas in Ocracoke your favorite?"

In the background, she could still hear the music Mark had selected drifting from the speaker.

"In Ocracoke, as you know, I was in the middle of a very hard time. And of course all the childhood wonder about the holiday was gone. But...Christmas that year felt so *real* to me. The flotilla, decorating the tree with Bryce, volunteering on Christmas Eve, and going to midnight mass, and then, of course, Christmas itself. I loved it then, but over time, the memory has become even more special. It's the one Christmas I wish I could experience again."

Mark smiled. "I like that you have that memory."

"Me too. And I still have that print of the lighthouse, by the way. It's hanging on the wall of the bedroom I use as a studio."

"Did the two of you ever end up making the biscuits?"

"I suppose that's your way of asking what comes next in the story. Or am I wrong?"

"I'm dying to know what happened next."

"I suppose I could tell you a bit more. But only on one condition."

"What's that?"

"I'm going to need some more eggnog."

"You got it," he said. Grabbing both glasses, he went to the back, returning with the eggnog. Remarkably, the thick, sweet concoction was proving to be both easy on her stomach and strangely filling, something she hadn't felt in weeks. She took another swallow.

"Did I tell you about the storm?"

"You mean the one on Christmas? When it was raining?"

"No," she said. "A different storm. The one in January."

Mark shook his head. "You told me about the week after Christmas, when you powered through your schoolwork and Bryce began teaching you the basics of photography."

"Oh, yeah," she said. "That's right." She studied the ceiling as if scanning the exposed pipes for her lost memories. When she returned her gaze to Mark, she commented, "My grades were actually pretty good by the end of that first semester, by the way. For me, anyway. A couple of A's and the rest were B's. It ended up being my best semester in high school."

"Even better than the spring semester?"

"Yes," she said.

"Why? Because photography took over?"

"No," she said. "It wasn't that. I think..." She adjusted her scarf, buying time to figure out how best to pick up the thread where she'd left off.

"For Bryce and me, I think everything began to change right around the time that the nor'easter smashed into Ocracoke..."

THE SECOND TRIMESTER

Ocracoke
1996

The nor'easter arrived the second week of January, after three days in a row of higher-than-normal temperatures and sunny days that felt unfamiliar after the grayish gloom of December. I could never have predicted that a gigantic storm was in the offing.

Nor could I have seen the changes ahead in my relationship with Bryce. On New Year's Eve, I still considered him nothing more than a friend, even though he'd chosen to spend the evening at my house while the rest of his family went out of town. Gwen brought over her television and we tuned in to Dick Clark's show live from Times Square; as midnight approached, we counted down with the rest of America. When the ball dropped, Bryce set off a couple of bottle rockets from the porch that exploded over the water with loud bangs and tails of sparkles. The neighbors on their porches clanked pots with spoons as well, but within minutes, the town reverted to sleepy mode and lights in the nearby houses began to blink out. I called my parents to wish them a happy New Year, and they reminded me that they would be coming to visit me later in the month.

Despite the holiday, Bryce was back less than eight hours later, this time with Daisy, which was the first time he'd brought her over. He helped my aunt and me take down the tree—which was a definite fire hazard by then—and dragged it out to the road. After I repacked the decorations and swept up the needles, we took our places at the table for schoolwork. Daisy was sniffing around in the kitchen; when he called her over, she promptly lay down near his chair.

"Linda said it was okay to bring her when I asked her about it last night," he explained. "My mom says she still wanders too much."

I glanced at Daisy, who stared back at me with innocence and contentment, tail thumping.

"She seems fine to me. And look at her cute face."

Sure enough, Daisy seemed to know we were talking about her, and she sat up, poking her nose at Bryce's hand. When he ignored her, she moseyed toward the kitchen again. "See? This is exactly what I'm talking about," he said. "Daisy? Come."

Daisy pretended not to hear him. It wasn't until the second command that she finally returned to his side and lay down with a groan. Daisy, I noticed, was sometimes stubborn, and when she tried to wander off again, he ended up putting her on a leash and attaching it to the chair, a vantage point from which she watched us, looking glum.

That week or so was pretty similar to the previous week: schoolwork and photography. In addition to letting me take a lot of pictures, Bryce hauled over a file box filled with photos that he and his mother had taken over the years. On the back of every photo were notes on the technical aspects of the shot—time of day, lighting, aperture, film speed—and little by little, I began to anticipate how changing a single element could alter the image entirely. I also spent my first afternoon in the darkroom, watching Bryce and his mom develop twelve black-and-white photos I'd taken downtown. They walked me through the process of how to get the chemical baths just right—the developer, the stop bath, the fixer—and how to clean the negative. They showed me how to use the enlarger, and the way to create just the right balance of light and dark I wanted. Even though most of it went over my head, when I watched the ghostly images emerge, it seemed like magic.

What was interesting was that even though I was still a novice at taking pictures and developing prints, it turned out I was a bit of a natural when it came to Photoshop. Loading the images required a high-end scanner and a Mac computer, and Porter had purchased both for his wife a year earlier. Since then, Bryce's mom had edited a bunch of her favorite photographs, and for me, re-viewing her work was the perfect way to be introduced to the program because I could see both the before and after images...and then try to replicate them myself. Now, I'm not saying that I was the kind of computer wizard that Richard was, nor did I have the experience with the program that Bryce and his mom did, but once I learned one of the tools, it stuck with me. I also had a pretty good sense of what aspects of a photo needed editing in the first place, a sort of intuitive understanding that surprised them both.

The point is, between the holidays and tutoring and all things photography, Bryce and I were together from early in the morning until evening, pretty much every day from Christmas until the big storm hit. With Daisy our constant companion once January arrived—she loved nothing more than to follow us when we were practicing with the camera—my life began to feel almost abnormally normal, if that makes any sense. I had Bryce and a dog and a newfound passion; thoughts of home seemed far away, and I was actually excited to get out of bed in the mornings. It was a new feeling for me but also kind of scary in an *I hope it keeps going* kind of way.

I didn't think about what spending so much time with Bryce would mean for the two of us. In fact, I wasn't really thinking about him much at all. For most of that period, he was just *there*, like my aunt Linda or my family back home, or even the air I breathed. Once I'd picked up the camera or studied photographs or played around with Photoshop, I wasn't sure I even noticed his dimples anymore. I don't think I realized how important he'd become to me until shortly before the storm rolled in. He was standing on the porch after another long day together when he finally handed me his camera, the light meter, and a new roll of black-and-white film.

"What's this for?" I asked, taking it.

"In case you want to practice tomorrow."

"Without you? I still don't know what I'm doing."

"You know more than you think you do. You'll be fine. And I'm going to be pretty busy the next couple of days."

As soon as he said it, I felt an unexpected pang of sadness at the thought of not seeing him. "Where are you going?"

"I'll be here, but I have to help my dad get things ready for the nor'easter."

Although I'd heard my aunt mention it, I figured the storm wouldn't be much different from what we'd experienced on and off since I'd been in Ocracoke. "What's a nor'easter?"

"It's a storm on the East Coast. But sometimes—like it's supposed to do now—it collides with another weather system and it feels like an out-of-season hurricane."

As he explained, I was still trying to process my discomfort at the thought of not seeing him. Since we'd met, the longest time we'd spent apart was two days, which, I now realized, was also kind of strange. Aside from family, I hadn't spent that much time with *anyone*. If Madison and Jodie and I spent a weekend together, we were usually getting on each other's nerves by the end. But wanting to keep Bryce on the porch for just a little longer, I forced a smile. "What do you have to do with your dad?"

"Secure my granddad's boat, board up the windows at our house and my grandparents'. Others, too, around town, including your aunt's and Gwen's. It'll take a day to get everything set up and then the day after, we'll have to take everything back down."

Behind him were blue skies, and I was pretty sure that he and his father were over-reacting.

But they weren't.

The next day, I woke to an empty house after sleeping in later than usual, and my first thought was *No Bryce*.

To be honest, it left me feeling a bit out of sorts. I kept my pajamas on, ate toast in the kitchen, stood on the porch, wandered the house, listened to music, then ended up in bed again. But I couldn't sleep—I was more bored than tired—and after tossing and turning for a while, I finally summoned the energy to get dressed, only to think, *Now what?*

I suppose I could have studied for finals or continued working on the next semester's as-signments, but I wasn't in the mood for that, so I grabbed a jacket and the camera along with the light meter, loading all of it into the basket on my bicycle. I didn't really have an idea of where to go, so I pedaled around for a while, stopping now and then to practice taking the same kind of photos I'd been taking all along—street scenes, buildings and houses. Always, though, I ended up lowering the camera before pressing the shutter. In my mind's eye, I already knew that none would have been all that special—just more of the same—and I didn't want to waste the film.

It was around that time that I sensed that the mood of the village had shifted. It was no longer ghostlike and sleepy, but strangely busy. On practically every street, I heard the sounds of drills or hammers, and when I rode past the grocery store, I noticed that the parking lot was full, with additional cars lining the street out front. Trucks filled with lumber rolled past me, and at one of the businesses that sold tourist items like T-shirts and kites, I saw a man on the roof fastening a tarp. Boats at the docks were lashed with dozens of ropes while others had been anchored in the harbor. No doubt, people were getting ready for the nor'easter, and I suddenly realized that I had the opportunity to take a series of photos with an actual *theme*, something with a name like *People Before the Storm.*

I'm afraid I went a bit crazy with it, even though I only had twelve exposures. Because there was no joviality in the people I saw—just grim determination—I tried to be as circumspect with my camera as possible, all the while trying to remember everything that Bryce and his mom had taught me. The overall lighting, fortunately, was pretty good—thick clouds had rolled in, some grayish-black in color—and after checking the meter, I'd peer through the viewfinder and move around until finally achieving the perspective and composition that felt right. Thinking back on the photographs that I had studied with Bryce, I'd hold my breath, keeping the camera perfectly still while carefully pressing the shutter. I knew they weren't all going to be amazing, but I was hoping that one or two would be keepers. Notably, it was the first time I photographed people going about their daily lives...the fisherman securing his boat with a grimace; the woman carrying a baby while leaning into a wind; a lean and wrinkled man smoking in front of a boarded-up storefront.

I worked through lunch, only stopping at the shop for a biscuit sandwich as the weather began to perceptibly worsen. By the time I got back to my aunt's house, I had a single exposure left. My aunt had returned early from the shop—her car was in the drive—but I didn't see her, and I arrived just as Bryce's truck pulled in. When he waved, I crazily felt my heart speed up. His father was beside him, and I could see Richard and Robert in the bed of the truck. I grabbed the camera from the bike basket. After Bryce hopped out, he strolled toward me. He was wearing a T-shirt and faded jeans that accentuated his wide shoulders and angular hips, along with a leather tool belt that held a cordless drill and a pair of leather gloves. Smiling in that easy way of his, he waved.

"How did it go today?" he asked. "Anything good?"

I told him about my *People Before the Storm* idea and added, "I'm hoping that you or your mom will be able to develop them soon."

"I'm sure my mom will be happy to. The

darkroom is the happiest place in the house for her, the only place she can really be by herself. I can't wait to see them."

Behind him, at the truck, I saw his father unloading the ladder from the bed. "How was it on your end?"

"Nonstop, and we still have a few more places to go. We're heading to your aunt's shop next."

Up close, I noted the smudges of dirt on his shirt, which didn't detract from the way he looked in the slightest. "Aren't you cold? You probably need a jacket."

"I haven't had time to think about it," he said. Then, surprising me, "I missed you today."

Bryce glanced at the ground, then met my eyes again, his gaze holding steady, and for a split second I had the distinct sense that he wanted to kiss me. The feeling caught me off guard and I think he must have realized it, too, because he suddenly hooked a thumb over his shoulder, quickly becoming the Bryce I knew once more. "I should probably get going so we can finish before dark."

My throat felt dry. "Don't let me hold you up."

I stepped back, wondering if I'd been imagining things, as Bryce turned away. He fell in beside his father as they approached the storage area beneath the house.

Meanwhile, Richard and Robert lugged the ladder toward the porch. On instinct, I moved away from the house, unconsciously trying to figure out how best to frame a final shot with the single exposure I had left. Stopping when the angle seemed right, I adjusted the aperture and checked the light meter, making sure everything was ready to go.

Bryce and his father had vanished inside the storage room, but after a few seconds, I watched Bryce emerge with a piece of plywood. He leaned it against the wall, then returned for another; within minutes, there was a stack of them. Bryce and one of the twins carried one sheet to the front door, while Porter and the other twin did the same. They disappeared inside, my aunt holding the door open for them, only to reappear on the porch a few seconds later. I lifted the lens as they began putting up the plywood over the sliding glass door, but the shot wasn't worth taking because all of them had their backs to me. Bryce sank the first screw, the rest following in rapid succession. Up went the second piece of plywood with equal speed, and the four of them descended the ladder. Both times, I lowered the camera.

Two more pieces of plywood went over the front window just as quickly, and again I had a bad angle. I didn't get the shot I wanted until the ladder was moved to my aunt's bedroom.

Bryce went up the ladder first; the twins handed a smaller sheet of plywood to their father, who then passed it farther up to Bryce. I zeroed in on the focus and suddenly Bryce had to twist in my direction; as he gripped the plywood with both hands, I automatically pressed the shutter. Just as quickly, he twisted back, in position to secure the plywood, and I couldn't help but wonder if I'd missed it.

And just like that, the window was covered, making it obvious this wasn't their first rodeo. The twins carried the ladder back to the truck while Bryce and his father returned to the storage area. They emerged carrying something heavy that resembled a small engine. They set it next to the storage area, in a spot that would be sheltered from the wind and rain. With a pull of the cord, they started it, the sound akin to a lawn mower.

"Generator," Bryce called out, knowing I had no idea what I was seeing. "It's pretty much guaranteed the power will go out."

After shutting it off, they filled the tank from a large can of gasoline that had been in the bed of the truck, and Bryce ran a long power cord into the house. I absently began to rewind the film, hoping that I'd miraculously gotten the shot of Bryce that I'd wanted.

When the film clicked, I turned toward the water, which had already become a sea of whitecaps. Had he really wanted to kiss me? I continued to wonder as I saw him skip back down the steps. The others were already at the truck and after another exchange of waves, I watched him drive away.

Lost in my own thoughts, I debated heading inside before impulsively hopping on my bicycle again. I sped to Bryce's house, knowing they wouldn't be there yet, relieved when his mom opened the door.

"Maggie?" She stared at me, curious. "If you're here to see Bryce, he's working with his dad today."

"I know, but I have a big favor I wanted to ask. I know you might be busy getting ready for the storm and everything, but I was wondering if you wouldn't mind developing these for me." As with Bryce, I explained my theme, and I could see her studying me.

"You said you got one of Bryce, too?"

"I'm not sure. I hope so," I said. "It's the last photo on the roll."

She tilted her head, no doubt intuiting its importance to me before holding out her hand. "Let me see what I can do."

My aunt's house was dark and cave-like, no surprise since there wasn't a glint of light coming through the covered windows. In the kitchen, the refrigerator was pulled away from the wall, no doubt so it could be easily connected to the generator when the time came. My aunt was nowhere to be seen, and as I took a seat on the couch, I found myself replaying the moment when I thought Bryce might kiss me, still trying to figure it out.

Hoping to get my mind off it, I retrieved my textbooks and spent the next hour and a half studying and doing homework. My aunt eventually emerged from her room to start dinner, and as I was dicing tomatoes for the salad, I heard the unmistakable rumble of a vehicle on the gravel outside. My aunt heard it, too, and raised an eyebrow, no doubt wondering if I'd invited Bryce for dinner.

"He didn't mention that he would be coming over," I said with a shrug.

"Would you do me a favor and see who it is? I've got chicken in the pan."

I went to the door and recognized the Trickett family van in the driveway, Bryce's mom behind the wheel. The sky had grown increasingly dark and the wind was gusting hard enough to make me grip the railing hard. When I reached the van, his mom rolled down the driver's-side window and held out a manila envelope.

"I got the feeling you were in a hurry, so I started developing them as soon as you left. You took some wonderful shots. You caught a lot of character in some of the faces. I especially liked the one of the man smoking by the store."

"I'm sorry if you felt like you had to rush," I said, straining to be heard over the wind. "You didn't have to."

"I wanted to take care of it before we lost power," she said. "I'm sure you're on pins and needles. I remember the first roll I ever took by myself, too."

I swallowed. "Did the photo of Bryce come out?"

"It's my favorite," she said. "But of course, I'm biased."

"Are they back yet?"

"I'm guessing they'll be home any minute, so I should probably get going."

"Thank you again for doing this so fast."

"My pleasure. If I had my way, I'd spend every day in the darkroom."

I watched her back up, waved as the van started rolling forward, then scurried back into the house. In the living room, I turned on the lamp, wanting as much light as possible as I went through the photographs.

As I'd suspected, there were only a couple of good ones. Most were close, but not quite perfect. Either the focus was off, or the set-tings weren't ideal. My composition wasn't always great, either, but Bryce's mom was right in thinking the photo of the smoker was a definite keeper. It was the one of Bryce, however, that made me almost gasp.

The focus was sharp and the lighting dra-matic. I had caught him just as his upper body had turned in my direction; the muscles in his arms stood out as if etched in relief, and his expression reflected intense concentration. He looked very much like himself, unself-conscious and naturally graceful. I traced my fingertip lightly across his figure.

It dawned on me then that Bryce—just like my aunt—had come into my life at the time when I'd needed him most. More than that, he'd quickly become the closest friend I'd ever had, and I hadn't been wrong in reading his desire. Had we been alone, he might have even attempted a kiss, even if we both knew it was the last thing I wanted or needed. Like me, he had to know that there was no way a relationship between us could ever work. In a few short months, I'd leave Ocracoke behind and become someone new again, someone I didn't yet know. Our relationship was doomed to failure, but even as that knowledge weighed me down, I knew in my heart that—just like Bryce—I longed for something more between us.

My thoughts continued to tumble and flop like clothes in a dryer throughout dinner and even as the storm approached. It howled as darkness overtook us, growing in intensity with every passing hour. Rain and wind lashed the house, making it creak and shake. My aunt and I sat in the living room, neither one of us wanting to be alone. Just when I thought the storm couldn't get any worse, we'd be slammed by another gust, and rain would pound so hard it sounded like fire-crackers. The power, as predicted, went out and the living room went pitch black. We bundled up, knowing we had to get the generator started. As soon as Aunt Linda turned the knob, the door practically flew inward; the rain stung my face as we hurried down the steps, both of us gripping the railing so we wouldn't blow away.

Beneath the house, the wind kept me unsteady on my feet, but at least we were out of the downpour. I watched my aunt struggle to get the generator started; I took over and was finally able to get it going on the third attempt. We fought our way back into the house, where Aunt Linda lit a bunch of candles and plugged in the refrigerator. The tiny flickers did little to illuminate the room.

I finally fell asleep on the sofa sometime after midnight. The storm continued to rage until just after dawn. While it was still windy, the rain eventually diminished to a drizzle before finally stopping midmorning. Only then did we step outside to survey the damage.

A tree on the neighbor's property had toppled over, limbs scattered everywhere, and patches of shingles had been ripped from the roof. The road out front was under more than a foot of water. Neighboring docks had twisted or been torn away completely, the debris nearly reaching the house. The air was frigid, the wind positively arctic.

Bryce and his father showed up an hour before noon. By then, the wind was a whisper of what it had been. Aunt Linda brought out a bag of leftover biscuits while I started toward Bryce. As I walked, I tried to convince myself that my feelings from the day before were akin to a dream upon waking. They weren't real; they were nothing but flickers and sparks fated to vanish completely. But when I saw him reach for the ladder in the bed of the truck, I thought again about the way he'd paused before me and knew I was only kidding myself.

His smile was as ready as ever. He was wearing the sexy olive jacket again and a baseball hat along with his jeans and the tool belt. I kind of felt like I was floating but did my best to appear nonchalant, like it was just another day for us.

"What did you think about the storm?" he asked.

"That was crazy last night." It sounded like my words were coming from somewhere else. "How does the rest of the town look?"

He set the ladder on the ground. "There are a lot of toppled trees and there's no power anywhere. Utility crews will hopefully get here this afternoon, but who knows? One of the motels and a couple of other businesses flooded, and half of the downtown buildings have roof damage. I guess the big thing was that one of the boats broke free and washed onto the road near the hotel."

Because he seemed like his normal, casual self, I felt myself relaxing. "Was my aunt's shop damaged?"

"Not that I saw," he said. "We took down the plywood, but obviously we weren't able to go inside to check for leaks."

"And your house?"

"Just some downed limbs in the yard. Gwen and my grandparents were okay, too. But if you're planning to try for some pictures today, watch for downed power lines. Especially in flooded spots. They can kill."

I hadn't thought about that, and visions of getting electrocuted made me shiver. "I'm just going to hang with my aunt, maybe do a little studying. But I'd still like to see the damage and maybe take some pictures."

"How about I come by later and drive you around? I can grab some more film."

"Will you have time?"

"Taking the boards down goes a lot faster than putting them up, and my grandpa already took care of the boat."

When I agreed, he hoisted the ladder and carried it toward the porch. From there, Bryce and his father reversed the process from the day before; the only difference was that they used a caulk gun to fill in the screw holes. While they worked, my aunt and I began cleaning the debris from the yard, piling it near the street. We were still working when Bryce and his father backed down the drive.

With the yard done, Aunt Linda and I returned to the house, blinking at the light streaming through the windows. My aunt immediately went to the kitchen and started making peanut butter and jelly sandwiches.

"Bryce said the shop seemed okay," I commented.

"His dad said the same thing, but I need to head over there in a little while to make sure."

"I forgot to ask, but does the shop have a generator?"

She nodded. "It comes on automatically

when the power goes out. Or it's supposed to, anyway. That's another thing I want to check on. People will want biscuits and books tomorrow, since there won't be much in the way of cooking or anything to do until the power's restored. It'll be swamped until then."

I thought about volunteering to help, but because I hadn't had my biscuit-making lesson with Bryce yet, I figured I'd just slow her down. "Bryce is going to come by later," I said. "We're going to see what happened in the storm."

She put the sandwiches on plates and brought them to the table. "Be careful of downed power lines."

It seemed clear that everyone knew about this potential hazard but me. "We will."

"I'm sure you'll enjoy spending time with him."

"We're probably just going to take photographs."

I'm pretty sure Aunt Linda noticed my deflection, but she didn't press. Instead, she smiled.

"Then you'll probably become an excellent photographer one day."

After lunch I studied, or tried to, anyway. I kept getting interrupted by the sight of the manila envelope, which seemed to insist that I peek at Bryce's picture instead.

It was several hours before Bryce pulled up. As soon as I heard the truck idling in the driveway, I grabbed the camera and started down the steps, grinning at the sight of Daisy in the bed. She whined and wagged her tail as I approached, so I stopped to give her some love. Bryce, meanwhile, had hopped out and rounded the truck so he could open the door for me, and my heart did the crazy pitter-patter thing again. He offered an arm to help me up—he'd showered and I could see drops of water still dripping from his hair—and when he closed the door, a voice inside scolded me to get a grip.

We drove through town, chatting easily while stopping here and there to take photos. Near the hotel, where the boat was resting on its side in the middle of the road, I spent a lot of time trying to get just the right shot. In the end, I handed the camera to Bryce to let him try, and I found myself watching him walk away, noting again the fluid way he moved. I knew he was working out to get ready for West Point, but his natural grace and coordination made me think that he would have been good at any sport.

Then again, why should that surprise me? Bryce, as far as I could tell, seemed to be good at *everything*. He was the perfect son and older brother, smart and athletic, handsome and empathetic. Best of all, he made all of it seem effortless. Even his demeanor was like no one else's I'd known, especially when compared to the boys at my school. A lot of them seemed nice enough when I talked with them one-on-one, but when they hung out with their friends, they'd preen and act cool and say idiotic things and I'd end up wondering who they really were.

And yet, if Madison and Jodie found their attention flattering—and they definitely did—I wondered what they'd think of Bryce. Oh, they'd notice right off the bat that he was cute, but would they care about his intelligence or his patience or his interest in photography? Or that he was training an assistance dog to help someone in a wheel-chair? Or that he was the kind of teenager who helped his father board up homes for people like Aunt Linda and Gwen?

I wasn't sure, but I had the sense that for Madison and Jodie, the way he looked would have been more than enough, and the rest would be only mildly interesting. And, if J was any indication, I'd probably been the same way before I'd arrived here and met a guy who'd given me a reason to change my mind.

But why was that? I used to think I was mature for my age, but adulthood still seemed like a mirage, and I wondered if part of that had to do with high school in general. When I thought back, it seemed like I'd spent all my time trying to get people to like me, as opposed to figuring out whether I liked them. Bryce hadn't gone to school or had to deal with all those idiotic pressures, so maybe for him, that had never been an issue. He'd been free to be himself, and it made me wonder who I would have become had I not been so caught up in trying to be exactly like my friends.

It was too much to think about and I shook my head, trying to force the thoughts away. Bryce had climbed on top of a dumpster to get a better view of the boat in the road. Daisy, who'd tagged along with him, stared upward before finally remembering my presence. She trotted toward me, tail wagging, then curled around my legs. Her brown eyes were so friendly, I couldn't help but lean over. I cupped her jaw in my hands and kissed her on the nose. As I did, I heard the faint sound of a shutter clicking. When I glanced up, Bryce—still on the dumpster—wore a sheepish expression as he lowered the camera.

"I'm sorry," he called out. He jumped down, landing like a gymnast, and started toward me. "I know I should have asked, but I couldn't resist."

Though I'd never liked photos of myself, I shrugged. "It's okay. I took one of you yesterday."

"I know," he said. "I saw you."

"You did?"

He shrugged without answering. "What next? Anything else you want to see or do?"

At his questions, my thoughts began to race.

"Why don't we hang out at my aunt's house for a while?"

Aunt Linda had gone to the shop, leaving Bryce and me alone. We sat on the sofa, me on one end with my feet tucked up and Bryce on the opposite end. He was flipping through some of the photos I'd taken the day before, complimenting me even when I'd done something obviously wrong. Right before he got to the photograph of him, I suddenly felt the tiniest sensation in my tummy, like a butterfly flapping its wings. I automatically put my hands on my belly but otherwise stayed completely still. He must have asked a question, but concentrating hard, I missed it.

"What is it? Are you okay?"

Lost in what I was experiencing, I didn't answer; instead, I closed my eyes. Sure enough, I eventually felt the fluttering again, like ripples moving through a pond. Though I had no prior experience, I knew exactly what it was.

"I felt the baby move."

I waited for a bit but when nothing else happened, I settled into a more comfortable position. I knew from the book my mom had given me that in the not-too-distant future, those flickers would become kicks and my stomach would move on its own like that super-gross and scary scene in *Alien*. Bryce remained quiet but had paled a little, which seemed kind of funny, since he was ordinarily unflappable.

"You look like you've seen a ghost," I teased.

The sound of my voice seemed to snap him out of it. "I'm sorry," he responded. "I know you're pregnant, but I don't ever really think about it. You haven't even put on any weight."

I rewarded his lie with a grateful smile. I'd put on thirteen pounds. "I think your mom knows I'm pregnant."

"I didn't tell her anything—"

"You didn't have to. It's a mom thing."

Strangely, I realized that it was the first time my pregnancy had come up since we'd decorated the Christmas tree. I could tell he was curious but didn't know how to express it.

"It's okay to ask me questions about it," I said. "I don't mind."

He set the photos on the coffee table, his expression thoughtful. "I know you just felt the baby move, but what's it like to be pregnant? Do you feel any different?"

"I had morning sickness for a long time, so I definitely felt it then, but now it's mainly just small things. I'm more sensitive to smell, and sometimes I feel like I need a nap. And, of course, I pee a lot, but you already know that. Other than that, I haven't noticed much. I'm sure that will change once I start getting even bigger."

"When's the baby due?"

"May ninth."

"It's that exact?"

"According to the doctor. Pregnancies last two hundred and eighty days."

"I didn't know that."

"Why would you?"

He laughed under his breath before growing serious again. "Is it scary? The thought of giving up your baby for adoption?"

I deliberated over my answer. "Yes and no. I mean, I hope the baby will go to a wonderful couple, but you never really know. That part does kind of scare me when I think about it. At the same time, I know I'm not ready to be a mom yet. I'm still in high school, so there's no way I could support her. I don't even know how to drive."

"You don't have your driver's license?"

"I was supposed to start driver's training in November, but coming here sort of nixed that."

"I can teach you how to drive. If my parents say it's okay, I mean. And your aunt, of course."

"Really?"

"Why not? There's hardly ever any cars on the road to the far end of the island. It's where my dad taught me."

"Thanks."

"Can I ask another question about the baby?"

"Of course."

"Do you get to name her?"

"I don't think so. When I went to the doctor, the only thing he asked was whether I wanted to hold the baby after giving birth."

"What did you say?"

"I didn't answer, but I don't think I will. I'm afraid that if I do, it might be harder to give her up."

"Have you ever thought about names? If you could name her, I mean?"

"I've always liked the name Chloe. Or Sofia."

"Those are beautiful names. Maybe they should let you name her."

I liked that. "I have to admit, I'm not looking forward to labor. With first babies, sometimes it can last for more than a day. And I have no idea how an entire baby will…"

I didn't finish, but that was okay. I knew he understood when I saw him wince.

"If it makes you feel better, my mom has never mentioned how hard labor was. She does, however, remind us that none of us were good sleepers, and that we're still responsible for making up for her sleep-deprived years."

"That would be hard. I do like sleeping."

He brought his hands together and I saw the muscles in his forearm flex. "If you leave in May, will you go straight back to school?"

"I don't know," I answered. "I guess it

depends on whether I'm all caught up or even ahead. I might not need to be there except for finals, and I might be able to take them at home. I'm sure my parents will have an opinion on it, too." I ran a hand through my hair. "They're supposed to come visit me at the end of the month."

"I'm sure it will be nice for you to see them."

"Yeah," I agreed, but the truth was, I felt ambivalent about it. Unlike my aunt, they weren't the most relaxing people to be around.

"Do you have any crazy cravings?"

"I love my aunt's beef Stroganoff, mainly because it's the best ever. And right now, I'm kind of in the mood for a grilled cheese sandwich, but I don't know if that counts as a craving. I've always liked them."

"Do you want me to make you one?"

"That's sweet, but I'll be okay. My aunt will be making dinner soon."

He scanned the room, as if casting about for something else to ask. "How are your studies going?"

"Oh, don't ruin the conversation," I said. "I don't want to think about school right now."

"I will admit it's a relief to be finished with high school."

"When do you have to leave for West Point?"

"In July," he said.

"Are you excited?"

"It'll be different," he said. "It's not like being homeschooled. There's a lot of structure and I hope I'll be able to handle it. I just want to make my parents proud."

I almost laughed out loud at the absurdity of what he'd just said. I mean, what parent wouldn't be proud of him? It took me a moment before I suddenly realized he was serious.

"They are proud of you."

He reached for the camera, lifted it, then carefully set it back in the same position. "I know you've mentioned that your sister, Morgan, is the perfect one," he said, "but it's not easy having Richard and Robert as brothers, either." His voice was soft enough that I had to strain to hear him as he went on. "Did you know that they took the SAT last September? Remember, they're only twelve, and both of them got nearly perfect scores: 1570 and 1580, which were a lot higher than I scored. And who knows if Richard will even need to go to college? He could go straight into a career in coding. You know about the internet, right? It's going to change the world, trust me on that, and Richard is already making a name for himself in the field. He earns more than my grandfather does, working part-time and freelancing. He'll probably be a millionaire by the time he's my age. Robert will do the same. I think he's a bit jealous about the money, so for the last couple of months, he's been working with Richard on programming, in addition to building his plane. And of course, he finds it laughably easy. How can I compete with brothers like that?"

When he finished, I couldn't say anything. His insecurity made no sense at all...except that in his family, it kind of did. "I had no idea."

"Don't get me wrong. I'm proud of how smart they are, but it still makes me feel like I have to do something extraordinary, too. And West Point will be a challenge, even though

I'm under no illusions that I'll ever be able to replicate what my father did there."

"What did he do?"

"Every West Point graduate receives a final rating based on academics, merits, and demerits, which are influenced by character, leadership, honor, and things like that. My dad had the fourth-highest score in West Point history, right after Douglas MacArthur."

I'd never heard of Douglas MacArthur, but by the way Bryce said the name, I figured he'd been someone pretty important.

"And then, of course, there's my mom and MIT at sixteen..."

The more I thought about it, the more his insecurity began to seem justified, even if the standards in his family belonged in outer space.

"I'm sure you'll be a general by the time you graduate."

"Impossible." He laughed. "But thanks for the vote of confidence."

Outside, I heard my aunt's car pull onto the rutted drive and a loud squeak as the engine wound down.

Bryce must have heard it, too. "The drive belt makes that noise. It probably needs to be tightened. I can fix that for her."

I heard Aunt Linda coming up the steps before she pushed open the door. Her eyes went to the two of us and though she didn't say it, I was pretty sure she was happy about the fact that we were on opposite sides of the couch. "Hey there," she said.

"How'd it go?" I asked.

She took off her jacket. "No leaks and the generator is working fine."

"Oh, good. Bryce says he can fix your car."

"What's wrong with my car?"

"The drive belt needs to be tightened."

She seemed confused by the fact that I'd said it, not Bryce. When I glanced at him, I could tell he was still pondering his recent admissions. "Can Bryce stay for dinner?"

"Of course he can," she said. "But it's not going to be anything fancy."

"Grilled cheese sandwiches?"

"Is that what you'd like? Maybe with soup?"

"Perfect."

"Easy for me, too. How about in an hour?"

I felt my craving burst forth like popcorn cooking in the microwave. "I can't wait."

After dinner, I walked Bryce to the door. On the porch, he turned around.

"I'll see you tomorrow?" I asked.

"I'll be here at nine. Thanks for dinner."

"Thank my aunt, not me. I just do the dishes."

"I already thanked her." He tucked a hand into his pocket before going on. "I had a nice time today," he said. "Getting to know you better, I mean."

"I did, too. Even if you lied to me."

"When did I lie?"

"When you said I didn't look pregnant."

"You don't," he said. "Not at all."

"Yeah, well"—I gave a wry smile—"just wait a month."

The next week and a half was a blur of test prep for finals, getting a head start on next semester's assignments, and photography. I had a quick examination with Gwen, who said that both the baby and I were doing well. I also started paying for the film and photography paper I was using; Bryce's mom ordered in bulk so it was less expensive. Bryce was hesitant to take the money, but I was using so much film, it only seemed right. Best of all, with every roll I seemed to be getting a little bit better.

Bryce, for his part, almost always developed my film at night, when I did my extra schoolwork. We would review the contact sheets the next morning and decide together which images to print. He also helped me make flashcards when I thought I needed them, quizzed me on the chapters I needed to know in every subject, and pretty much had me ready for anything by the time my finals came around. I'm not going to say I aced them, but considering where my grades had been, I almost pulled a shoulder muscle patting myself on the back. Aside from that— and watching Bryce tighten the drive belt in my aunt's car—the only big thing left to do was have my aunt teach us how to make biscuits at the shop.

We went in on a Saturday, a few days before my parents were to arrive. My aunt had us wear aprons and went through each step with us.

As for the secrets, they really came down to this: It was important to use White Lily self-rising flour, not any other brand, and to sift the flour before measuring because it made the biscuits fluffier. Add Crisco, buttermilk, and a bit of (super-secret) confectioners' sugar, which some people in the South might consider blasphemous. After that, it was all about being careful not to overwork the dough when you mixed it together. Oh, and never twist the biscuit cutter; press it straight down after the dough has been rolled out. Then, when the biscuits are fresh and hot from the oven, coat both sides of them with melted butter.

Naturally, Bryce asked a zillion questions and took the lesson way more seriously than I did. When he took a bite, he practically moaned like a little kid. When my aunt said that he could share the recipe with his mother, he looked almost outraged.

"Not a chance. This was *my* gift."

Later that afternoon, Bryce finally showed me the photo he'd taken of me and Daisy when we'd been checking out the village after the storm.

"I printed one for you, too," he said, handing it to me. We were in his truck, parked near the lighthouse. I'd just taken a few sunset photos, and the sky was already beginning to darken. "In truth, my mom helped me print it, but you get the point."

I could see why he'd wanted one for himself. It really was an endearing photo, even if I happened to be in it. He'd cropped the image to capture only our faces in profile and he'd caught the instant when my lips touched Daisy's nose; my eyes were closed, but Daisy's were brimming with adoration. And best of all, my body wasn't shown, which made it easy to imagine the whole *oops!* thing had never happened at all.

"Thank you," I said, continuing to stare at the image. "I wish I could shoot as well as you do. Or your mom."

"You're a lot better than I was when I first started. And some of your shots are fantastic."

Maybe, I thought. *But maybe not.* "I've been meaning to ask you if you think it's okay that I'm in the darkroom. Being that I'm pregnant, I mean."

"I asked my mom about that," he said. "Don't worry—I didn't mention you—but she said she worked in the darkroom when she was pregnant. She said that as long as you use rubber gloves and aren't in there every day, it isn't dangerous."

"That's good," I said. "I love watching the images start to materialize on the paper. One second, there's nothing there...and then little by little, the picture comes to life."

"I totally get it. For me, it's an essential part of the experience," he added. "I wonder, though, what's going to happen when digital photography catches on. My guess is no one will develop pictures at all anymore."

"What's digital photography?"

"Instead of film, images are stored on a disk in the camera that you can then plug into a computer without having to use a scanner. They might even have cameras where you can see the pictures right away on a little screen in the back."

"That's a real thing?"

"It will be, I'm sure," he said. "The cameras are super expensive now, but just like computers, I'm sure the cost will keep dropping. In time, I think most people will want to use those kinds of cameras instead. Including me."

"That's kind of sad," I said. "It takes some of the magic away."

"It's the future," he said. "And nothing lasts forever."

I couldn't help wondering whether he might also be referring to the two of us.

As my parents' visit drew near, I began to feel antsy, a low-level nervousness that hummed beneath the surface. They were flying to New Bern on Wednesday and would take the early ferry to Ocracoke on Thursday morning. They weren't staying long—only through Sunday afternoon—and the plan was for all of us to go to church and say our goodbyes in the parking lot right after the service.

On Thursday morning, I woke earlier than usual to shower and get ready, but even when Bryce showed up, I still had trouble concentrating on my studies. Not that there was much of anything to do—with finals behind me, I was plowing through second-semester work at a pace that would have made even Morgan proud. Bryce could tell I was anxious and I'm pretty sure Daisy picked up on it, too. At least twice an hour she'd come to my side and nuzzle at my hand before whining, the sound coming from deep within her throat. Despite her efforts to put me at ease, when Aunt Linda showed up to drive me over to the ferry so I could meet my parents, my legs were wobbly as I stood from the chair.

"It's going to be all right," Bryce said. He

was stacking my work into neat little piles on the kitchen table.

"I hope so," I said. As distracted as I'd been, I hardly noticed how cute he was or how much I'd come to depend on him lately.

"Are you sure you still want me to come over tomorrow?"

"My parents said they wanted to meet you."

I didn't mention that the thought of being alone in the house with my parents while Aunt Linda was at the shop kind of terrified me.

By then, my aunt had poked her head inside the front door.

"You ready? The ferry should be here in ten minutes."

"Almost," I told her. "We were just cleaning up."

I dropped off my schoolwork in my bedroom, and after grabbing my jacket, Bryce followed me down the stairs. He offered a quick wink as he hopped into his truck, which gave me the encouragement I needed to crawl into my aunt's car, despite my nerves.

It was cold and gray as we drove to the docks. My parents' rental car was the second vehicle to roll off the ferry. When they saw us, my dad pulled the car to a stop and we walked over to join them.

Hugs and kisses, a couple of *good to see you*s, no comments about my size, probably because they wanted to pretend I wasn't pregnant at all, and then I was back in the car with my aunt. My eyes occasionally flashed to the side mirror while my parents followed us home, and after parking beside us, they got out of the car and stared at the house. In the gloom, it struck me as shabbier than usual.

"So this is it, huh?" my mom asked, pulling her coat tighter against the chill. "I understand why we had to book a room at the hotel. It seems kind of small."

"It's comfortable and has a great view of the water," I offered.

"The ferry seemed to take forever. Is it always that slow?"

"I guess so," I said. "But after a while, you get used to it."

"Hmm," she said. My dad, meanwhile, remained quiet, and my mom added nothing more.

"How about some lunch?" my aunt chimed in with forced cheer. "I made chicken salad earlier and thought we could do sandwiches."

"I'm allergic to mayonnaise," my mom said.

Aunt Linda recovered quickly. "I think I still have meatloaf leftovers, and I could make you a sandwich with that."

My mom nodded; my dad remained silent. The four of us started up toward the front door, the pit in my stomach growing larger with every step.

Somehow, we made it through lunch, but the conversation was just as stilted. Whenever an uncomfortable silence settled over the table, Aunt Linda reverted to talking about the shop, chattering away as though their visit was nothing out of the ordinary. Afterward, we all piled into my aunt's car for a quick tour of the village. She pretty much repeated the same things she'd told me when she'd first shown me around, and I'm pretty sure my parents were as unimpressed as I had been. In the back seat, my mom appeared almost shell-shocked.

They seemed to like the shop, though. Gwen was there and even though they'd eaten, she insisted on giving them dessert biscuits, which were essentially biscuits made with blueberries and topped with a sugary glaze. Gwen immediately picked up on the awkward vibe with my family and kept the conversation light. In the book area, she pointed out some of her favorites, in case either of my parents was interested. They weren't—my parents weren't readers—but they nodded anyway, making me feel like we were participating in a play where all of the characters wanted to be somewhere else.

Back at the house, Aunt Linda and my dad began chatting about family—their other sisters and my cousins—so after a while, my mom cleared her throat.

"How about we take a walk on the beach?" she suggested to me.

She made it sound like I didn't have much of a choice, and the two of us drove to the beach, parking the rental car near the dune.

"I thought the beach would be closer," she said.

"The village is on the sound side."

"How do you get here?" she asked.

"I ride my bike."

"You have a bike?"

"Aunt Linda picked it up at a garage sale before I arrived."

"Oh," she said. Back at home, she knew, my bike was in the garage, with tires cracking and low on air from disuse, the seat covered in dust. "At least you're getting outside now and then. You're too pale."

I shrugged without answering. We got out of the car and I zipped my jacket up all the way before stuffing my hands in my pockets. Starting for the water's edge, we skirted the dune, our feet sinking and sliding with every step. It wasn't until we'd started up the beach that my mom spoke again.

"Morgan said to tell you that she wished she could come. But she's the lead in the school play and there were rehearsals. She's also trying for a scholarship with the Rotary, even though she's already earned enough in scholarships to cover most of her tuition."

"I'm sure she'll get it," I mumbled. Which was true, and though I felt the familiar pang of insecurity, I realized it didn't make me feel as bad about myself as it had in the past.

We walked a few more steps before I heard my mom's voice again. "She says that the two of you haven't spoken in the last couple of weeks."

I wondered if Aunt Linda had mentioned that she took the phone cord with her to work. "I've been really busy with school. I'll call her next week."

"Why did you fall so far behind in the first place? Your aunt was really worried about you, and so were your teachers."

I felt my shoulders sag a little. "I guess it just took me a while to adjust to being here."

"You're not missing anything back home."

I wasn't sure what to say to that. "Have you heard from Madison or Jodie?"

"They haven't called the house, if that's what you're asking."

"Do you know what they've been up to?"

"I have no idea. I suppose I could ask Morgan when I get home."

"That's okay," I said, knowing my mom

wouldn't. To her mind, the less people were talking or wondering about me, the better.

"If you want to write them letters," she went on, "I suppose I can have them delivered for you. Of course, you can't be too specific or hint at what's really going on."

"Maybe," I said. I didn't want to lie to them, and since I couldn't tell the truth, either, I wouldn't have anything to say.

She adjusted her jacket collar to cover her neck. "What did you think about the doctor Linda found? I know Gwen could probably deliver the baby, but I told Linda that I'd be more comfortable if you were in a hospital."

As soon as she asked, I immediately visualized Dr. Chinowith's giant hands. "He's older, but he seems nice and Gwen has worked with him a lot. I'm having a girl, by the way."

"The doctor's a man?"

"Is that a problem?"

She didn't seem to want to answer and simply shook her head. "Anyway, you'll be home and back to normal in just a few more months."

At a loss, I asked, "How's Dad doing?"

"He's had to work overtime because there's a big order for the new planes. But other than that, he's the same."

I thought about Bryce's parents and the tender way they treated each other, which was so different from mine. "Are you still going out to dinner twice a month?"

"Not lately," she said. "There was a plumbing leak and between getting that repaired, Christmas, and coming out here to see you, we've been on a tight budget."

Even though she probably hadn't meant to, that made me feel bad. In fact, the whole walk was making me feel more depressed than I'd been before they arrived. But it got me to wondering...

"I guess the tutoring is expensive, too."

"That's being taken care of."

"By Aunt Linda?"

"No," she said. She seemed to debate before explaining and finally sighed. "Some of your expenses are being taken care of by the prospective parents, through the agency. Your school, the part of your doctor's bills that our insurance won't cover, your flights out here and back. Even a little spending money for you."

Which explained the envelope of cash she'd given me in the airport. "Have you met the parents? I mean, are they nice people?"

"I haven't met them. But I'm sure they'll be loving parents."

"How do you know for sure if you haven't met them?"

"Your aunt and her friend Gwen have worked with this particular agency before and they know the woman in charge, so she screened the candidates personally. She's very experienced, and I'm sure she's evaluated the prospective parents thoroughly. That's really all I know, and you shouldn't want to know more than that, either. The less you worry, the easier it will be in the end."

I suspected she was right. Even though the baby was moving regularly now, my pregnancy still didn't always seem real. My mom knew better than to harp on the subject, so she let it pass. "It's been quiet in the house since you've been gone."

"It's quiet here, too."

"Seems like it. I guess I thought the town would be bigger. It's so remote. I mean...what do people do here?"

"They fish and cater to tourists. In the off season, they fix their boats and equipment and hunker down for the winter," I answered. "Or they own or work for small businesses that keep the town up and running, like Aunt Linda does. It's not an easy life. People have to work hard to get by."

"I don't think I could live here."

But it was okay for me, right? And yet... "It's not all bad."

"Because of Bryce?"

"He's my tutor."

"And he's teaching you photography, too?"

"His mom got him into it. It's been a lot of fun and I think I might keep it up when I get back home."

"Do you ever go to his house?"

I was still wondering why she didn't seem interested in my new passion. "Sometimes."

"Are his parents home when you visit?"

With that, I suddenly understood where all this was coming from. "His mom is always there. His brothers are usually there, too."

"Oh," she said, but in that single syllable, I could hear her relief.

"Would you like to see some of the photos I've taken?"

She walked a few steps without saying anything. "It's great you found a hobby, but don't you think you should be concentrating on school instead? Maybe use your free time to study on your own?"

"I do study on my own," I said, hearing the defensiveness in my tone. "You saw my grades, and I'm already way ahead this semester, too." From the corner of my eye, I could see the waves rolling steadily toward the shore, as though trying to erase our footprints.

"I'm just wondering if you're spending too much time with Bryce, instead of working on yourself."

"What do you mean by working on myself? I'm doing okay in school, I've found a cool hobby, I've even made friends…"

"Friends? Or friend?"

"In case you haven't noticed, there aren't a lot of people here my age."

"I'm just worried about you, Margaret."

"Maggie," I reminded her, knowing my

mom only used *Margaret* when she was upset. "And you don't have to worry about me."

"Have you forgotten why you're here?"

Her comment stung, reminding me that no matter what I did, I would always be the daughter who let her down. "I know why I'm here."

She nodded, saying nothing, her eyes darting downward. "You're barely showing."

My hands went automatically to my belly. "The sweater you bought hides a lot."

"Are those maternity pants?"

"I had to get them last month."

She smiled, but it couldn't hide her sadness. "We miss you, you know."

"I miss you, too." And in that moment, I did, even if she sometimes made it very hard to do.

My interactions with my father were just as awkward. He spent nearly all of Thursday afternoon with my aunt, the two of them either sitting at the kitchen table or standing out back, near the water's edge. Even at dinner, he didn't say much to me other than "Can you pass the corn?" Tired from their trip, or maybe just stressed out of their minds, my parents left for their hotel not long after dinner was over.

When they returned the following morning, they saw Bryce and me working at the table. After a quick introduction—Bryce was his normal charming self while my parents studied him with reserved expressions—they sat in the living room, speaking quietly while we went back to work. Even though I was ahead in my assignments, their presence while I was studying made me nervous anyway. To say the whole thing felt weird was an understatement.

Bryce picked up on the tension, so we both agreed to make it an early day and finished by lunch. Aside from my aunt's shop, there were only a few places to eat, and my parents and I ended up at the Pony Island Restaurant. I'd never been there, and though it served only breakfast food, my parents didn't seem to mind. I had French toast, as did my mom, while my dad had eggs and bacon. Afterward, they poked around my aunt's shop while I went back to the house to nap. By the time I got up, my mom was talking to Aunt Linda, who'd already returned to the house. My dad was drinking coffee on the porch and I went out to join him, sitting in the other rocker. My first thought was that he looked as low as I'd ever seen him.

"How are you doing, Dad?" I asked, pretending I hadn't noticed.

"I'm okay," he said. "How about you?"

"I'm kind of tired, but that's normal. According to the book, anyway."

His eyes flashed to my stomach, then up again. I adjusted myself in the chair, trying to get more comfortable. "How's work? Mom says you've had a lot of overtime lately."

"There are a lot of orders for the new 777-300," he said, as though everyone shared his expertise in Boeing aircraft.

"That's good, right?"

"It's a living," he grunted. He took a sip of his coffee. I shifted in my seat again, wondering if my bladder would start screaming at me, giving me an excuse to go back into the house. It didn't.

"I've enjoyed learning photography," I ventured.

"Oh," he said. "Good."

"Would you like to see some of my photographs?"

It took him a few seconds to answer. "I wouldn't know what I was seeing." In the silence after his answer, I could see the steam rising from his coffee before quickly vanishing, a temporary mirage. Then, as if knowing it was his turn to move the conversation forward, he sighed. "Linda says you've been a big help around the house."

"I try," I said. "She gives me chores, but that's okay. I like your sister."

"She's a good lady." He seemed to be trying hard to avoid looking in my direction. "I still don't know why she moved here."

"Have you asked her?"

"She said that once she and Gwen left the order, they wanted to live a quiet life. I thought convents were quiet."

"Were you close growing up?"

"She's eleven years older than me, so she took care of me and our sisters after school when I was little. But she moved away when she was nineteen and I didn't see her again for a long time. She'd write me letters, though. I always liked her letters. And after your mom and I were married, she came out to visit a couple of times."

It was as much as my dad ever said in one go, which kind of startled me.

"I only remember her visiting us once, when I was little."

"It wasn't easy for her to get away. And after she moved to Ocracoke, she couldn't."

I stared at him. "Are you really doing okay, Dad?"

It took him a long time to answer. "I'm just sad is all. Sad for you, sad for our family."

I knew he was being honest, but just like the things my mom had said, his words made me ache.

"I'm sorry, and I'm doing my best to make it right."

"I know you are."

I swallowed. "Do you still love me?"

For the first time, he faced me, and his surprise was evident. "I'll always love you. You'll always be my baby girl."

Peering over my shoulder, I could see my mom and my aunt at the table. "I think Mom is worried about me."

He turned away again. "Neither of us wanted this for you."

After that, we sat without speaking until my dad finally rose from his seat and went back inside for another cup of coffee, leaving me alone with my thoughts.

Later that evening, after my parents had gone back to the hotel, I sat in the living room with my aunt. Dinner had been awkward, with comments about the weather interspersed with long silences. Aunt Linda was sipping tea in the rocker while I lounged on the couch, my toes tucked under the pillow.

"It's like they aren't even happy to see me."

"They're happy," she said. "It's just that seeing you is harder for them than they thought it would be."

"Why?"

"Because you're not the same girl who left them in November."

"Of course I am," I said, but as soon as the words came out, I knew they weren't true. "They didn't want to see my photographs," I added.

Aunt Linda set her tea off to the side. "Did I tell you that when I worked with young women like you, we had a painting room set aside? With watercolors? There was a big window that overlooked the garden and nearly all the girls gave painting a try while they were there. Some of them even grew to love it, and when their parents visited, many wanted to show off their work. More often than not the parents said no."

"Why?"

"Because they were afraid they'd see the artist's reflection, instead of their own."

She didn't explain further, and later that night, while cuddling with Maggie-bear in bed, I thought about what she'd said. I imagined pregnant girls in a bright, airy room in the convent with wildflowers blooming outside. I thought about how they felt as they lifted a brush, adding color and wonder to a blank canvas and feeling—if only for a brief moment—that they were like other girls their age, unburdened by past mistakes. And I knew that they felt the same way I did when I stared through the lens, that finding and creating beauty could illuminate even the darkest periods.

I understood then what my aunt had been trying to tell me, just as I knew my parents still loved me. I knew they wanted the best for me, now and in the future. But they wanted to see their own feelings in the photos, not mine. They wanted me to see myself in the same way they did.

My parents, I knew, wanted to see disappointment.

My epiphany didn't lift my spirits, even if it helped me understand where my parents were coming from. Frankly, I was disappointed in me, too, but I'd tried to lock that feeling away into some unused corner of my brain because I didn't have time to beat myself up in the way I once had. Nor did I want to. For my parents, almost everything I was doing had its roots in my mistake. And every time there was an empty seat at the table, every time they passed by my unused room, every time they received copies of grades that I earned across the country, they were reminded of the fact that I'd temporarily broken up the family while shattering the illusion that—as my dad had put it—I was still their baby girl.

Nor did their visit improve. Saturday was pretty much the same as the day before except that Bryce didn't come by. We explored the village again, which left them about as bored as I expected. I took a nap, and though I could feel the baby kicking whenever I lay down, I made sure not to tell them. I read and did homework assignments in my room with the door closed. I also wore my baggiest sweat-shirts and a jacket, doing my best to pretend that I looked the same as I always had.

My aunt, thank God, carried the conver-sation whenever tension began to creep in. Gwen too. She joined us for dinner on Satur-day night, and between the two of them, I barely had to speak at all. They also avoided any mention of Bryce or photography; instead, Aunt Linda kept the focus on family, and it was interesting to discover that my aunt knew even more about my other aunts and cousins than my parents. As she did with my father, she wrote to all of them regularly, which was yet another thing I didn't know about her. I guessed that she probably wrote the letters when she was at the shop, since I'd never seen her put pen to paper.

My dad and Aunt Linda also shared stories about growing up in Seattle when the city still had plenty of undeveloped land. Once in a while, Gwen talked about her life in Vermont, and I learned that her family had six prized cows that produced a rich butter used in some upscale restaurants in Boston.

I appreciated what Aunt Linda and Gwen were doing, yet even as I listened, I found my thoughts wandering to Bryce. The sun was going down and had my parents not been here, he and I would have begun playing around with the camera, trying to capture the perfect light of the golden hour. In those moments, I realized, my world shrank to nothing but the task at hand while expanding exponentially at the same time.

I wanted more than anything for my parents to share in my interest; I wanted them to be proud of me. I wanted to tell them that I'd begun to imagine a career as a photographer. But then the subject turned to Morgan. My parents talked about her grades and her popularity and the violin and the scholarships she'd received to Gonzaga University. When I saw the way their eyes lit up, my gaze dropped, and I wondered whether my parents would ever glow with pride in the same way when talking about me.

On Sunday, they finally left. They were flying out in the afternoon, but we all caught the morning ferry, went to mass, and had lunch before we said our goodbyes in the parking lot. My mom and dad hugged me but neither of them shed a tear, even as I felt my own forming. After pulling back, I wiped my cheeks, and for the first time since they'd arrived, I felt something resembling sympathy from both of my parents.

"You'll be home before you know it," my mom assured me, and though all my dad did was nod, at least he looked at me. His expression was mournful as usual, but more than that, I detected helplessness.

"I'll be okay," I said, continuing to swipe at my eyes, and though I meant it, I'm not sure either of them believed me.

Bryce appeared at the door later that evening. I'd asked him to come over, and though it was chilly, we sat on the porch, in the same spot that my dad and I had a couple of days earlier.

I poured out the story of my parents' visit, leaving nothing out, and Bryce didn't interrupt. By the end, I was crying and he scooted his chair closer to mine.

"I'm sorry it wasn't the visit you wanted it to be," he murmured.

"Thanks."

"Is there anything I can do to help you feel better?"

"No."

"I could drop Daisy off and you could snuggle with her tonight."

"I thought Daisy wasn't supposed to get on the furniture."

"She's not. So how about I make you some hot chocolate instead?"

"That's okay."

For the first time since I'd known him, he reached over and placed his hand on mine. He gave it a squeeze, his touch electric.

"It might not mean anything, but I think you're amazing," he said. "You're smart and you have a great sense of humor and obviously, you already know how beautiful you are."

I felt myself blush at his words, thankful for the darkness. I could still feel his hand on mine, radiating warmth up my arm. He seemed in no rush to let go.

"You know what I was thinking about?" I asked. "Right before you got here?"

"I have no idea."

"I was thinking that even though my parents

were here for only three days, it seemed like an entire month."

He chuckled before meeting my eyes again. I felt his thumb teasing the back of my hand, featherlight.

"Do you want me to come by tomorrow to tutor? Because if you need a day to unwind, I completely understand."

Avoiding Bryce, I knew, would make me feel even worse. "I want to keep going on my reading and my assignments," I said, surprising even myself. "I'll be okay after I get some sleep."

His expression was gentle. "You know they love you, right? Your parents, I mean. Even if they aren't too good at showing it?"

"I know," I answered, but strangely, I found myself suddenly wondering whether he was talking about them, or about himself.

As we eased into February, Bryce and I fell back into our regular routine. It wasn't quite the same as before, though. For starters, something deeper had taken root when I'd sensed he wanted to kiss me and had grown even stronger when he'd taken my hand. Though he didn't touch me again—and certainly didn't attempt a kiss—there was a new charge between us, a low-level and insistent hum that was almost impossible to ignore. I'd be doing a geometry problem and I'd catch him staring at me in a way that seemed unfamiliar, or he'd hand me the camera and hold it for an instant too long, making me pull, and I felt like he was trying to keep his emotions in check.

Meanwhile, I was sorting through my own feelings, especially right before drifting off to sleep. I'd get to the point of no return—that brief and hazy period where consciousness blends with the unconscious and things get swimmy—when all of a sudden, I'd picture him on the ladder or remember the way his touch had set my nerves on fire, and I'd immediately wake up.

My aunt, too, seemed to notice that my relationship with Bryce had...*evolved.* He was still having dinner with us two or three times a week, but instead of leaving immediately afterward, Bryce would sit with us in the living room for a while. Despite the lack of privacy—or maybe because of it—he and I began to develop our own secret nonverbal communication. He'd gently raise an eyebrow and I'd know that he was thinking the same thing that I was, or when I impatiently ran a hand through my hair, Bryce knew I wanted to change the subject. I thought we were pretty subtle about the whole thing, but Aunt Linda wasn't easily fooled. After he'd finally gone home, she'd say something that would make me reflect on what she was really trying to tell me.

"I'm going to miss having you around here once you leave," she'd say casually, or "How are you sleeping? Pregnancy can have all kinds of effects on hormones."

I'm pretty sure it was her way of reminding me that falling for Bryce wasn't in my best interest, even if she wouldn't say it directly. The net effect was that I would reflect on her comments after acknowledging their underlying truth: my hormones *were* running wild and I *was* going to be leaving soon.

And yet, the heart is a funny thing, because

even though I knew there was no future for Bryce and me, I would lie awake at night listening to the gentle lapping of sea against the shoreline, knowing that a big part of me simply didn't care.

If I could point to a single notable change in my habits since I'd arrived in Ocracoke, it was my diligence when it came to school-work. By the second week of February, I was completing March assignments and I'd done well on all of my quizzes and exams. Simultaneously, I continued to grow more confident with the camera, and my proficiency was steadily improving. Chalk it up to our narrow focus on schoolwork and photography, but Valentine's Day was just...*okay.*

I'm not saying that Bryce forgot about it. He showed up that morning with flowers, and though I was momentarily touched, I quickly noticed he'd brought two bouquets, one for me and one for my aunt, which sort of diminished their impact. I later confirmed that he'd gotten his mother flowers as well. All of which left me wondering whether everything that was happening between us was simply a hormone-induced fantasy.

Two nights later, however, he made up for it. It was Friday evening—we'd been together twelve hours by then—and my aunt was in the living room while we were on the porch. It was a warmer-than-usual night compared to what it had been, so we left the slider open slightly. I figured my aunt could hear us, and even though she had a book open in her lap, I suspected she was sneaking the occasional peek at us as well. Meanwhile, Bryce squirmed in his chair and shuffled his feet like the nervous teenager he was.

"I know you have to be up early on Sunday morning, but I was hoping you might be free tomorrow night."

"What's happening tomorrow night?"

"I've been building something with Robert and my dad," he said. "I want to show it to you."

"What is it?"

"A surprise," he answered. Then, as though he was in danger of promising too much, he went on, the words coming quickly. "It's not a big deal. And it has nothing to do with photography, but I was checking the weather and I think the conditions will be perfect. I guess I could show you during the day, but it will be a lot better at night."

I had no idea what he was talking about; the only thing I knew for sure was that he was acting the same way he had before inviting me to the New Bern Christmas flotilla with his family. The *sort-of* date. He really was unbearably cute when he was nervous.

"I'll have to check with my aunt."

"Of course," he said.

I waited and when he added nothing else, I asked the obvious. "Can you give me a little more information?"

"Oh yeah. Right. I was hoping to take you to dinner at Howard's Pub, and then after that, the surprise. I can probably have you home by ten."

Inwardly, I smiled, thinking that if a boy asked my parents whether I could stay out until ten, even *they* would have agreed. Well…in the past they would have, but maybe not now. But still, this sounded like a *date* date, not a *sort-of* date, and even though my heart suddenly boomed in my chest, I rotated in my rocker, trying to look calm and hoping to catch my aunt's eye.

"Ten o'clock is fine," she said, still gazing toward her book. "But no later."

I faced Bryce again. "All good."

He nodded. Shuffled his feet. Nodded again.

"So...what time?" I asked.

"What do you mean?"

"I mean what time do I have to be ready tomorrow?"

"How about nine?"

Though I knew exactly what he meant, I pretended not to, just to be funny. "You'll pick me up at nine, we'll have dinner at Howard's Pub, see the surprise, and you'll have me home by ten?"

His eyes widened. "Nine in the morning," he said. "For photos, I mean, and maybe a little Photoshop practice. There's also this place on the island I want to show you. Only the locals know about it."

"What place?"

"You'll see," he said. "I know I'm not making much sense, but..." He trailed off and

I suppressed a thrill at the thought that he'd actually asked me out on a *date* date. Which sort of scared me but kind of excited me, too. "See you tomorrow?" he finally added.

"I can't wait."

And truth be told, I couldn't.

My aunt was quiet after I closed the door. Oh, she hid it well—what with the open book and all—and she didn't offer any remarks brewing with hidden meanings, but I sensed her concern, even though I felt like I was floating.

I slept well, better than I had in weeks, and woke feeling refreshed. I had breakfast with my aunt, and in the morning, Bryce and I shot some pictures near his house. Afterward, we worked with his mom at the computer. Bryce sat close to me, radiating heat, making it harder than usual to concentrate.

We had lunch at his house, then climbed in his truck. I thought he was taking me back to my aunt's, but he turned onto a street I'd ridden down dozens of times but never really noticed.

"Where are we going?" I asked.

"We're taking a quick detour to Great Britain."

I blinked. "You mean England? Like the country?"

"Exactly," he answered with a wink. "You'll see."

We passed a small cemetery on the left, then another on the right before he finally pulled the truck over. When we got out, he brought me to a granite memorial located near four neat rectangular graves surrounded by pine bark and bouquets of flowers, all encircled by a picket fence.

"Welcome to Great Britain," he said.

"You've lost me completely."

"In 1942, HMT *Bedfordshire* was torpedoed by a German submarine just off the coast and four bodies washed ashore in Ocracoke. They were able to identify two of the men, but the other two were unknown. They're buried here, and this spot has been leased to the British Commonwealth in perpetuity."

There was more information on the

memorial, including the names of everyone who'd been on the trawler. It seemed impossible that German submarines had patrolled here, in the waters of these desolate islands. Wasn't there someplace else they should have been? Though World War II was a topic in my history books, my views of the war had been shaped by Hollywood movies more than books, and I found myself visualizing how horrible it must have been to be on board as an explosion ripped through the hull. That only four bodies were recovered out of the thirty-seven on board struck me as terrible and I wondered what had happened to the rest of the crew. Had they gone down with the ship, entombed in the hull? Or washed ashore elsewhere, or perhaps floated farther out to sea?

The whole thing gave me shivers, but then I'd never been really comfortable in cemeteries. When my grandparents had died—all four of them before I was ten—my parents would bring Morgan and me to their graves, where we'd leave flowers. All I could ever think about was the fact that I was surrounded by dead people. I know death is pretty much unavoidable, but it still wasn't something I liked to think about.

"Who put the flowers here? The families?"

"Probably the coast guard. They're the ones who take care of the plots, even though it's British territory."

"Why were there German submarines here in the first place?"

"Our merchant fleet would pick up supplies in South America or the Caribbean or wherever, and then follow the Gulf Stream north, then over to Europe. But early on, the merchant ships were slow and unprotected, so they were easy targets for the submarines. Scores of merchant ships were sunk just offshore. That's why the *Bedfordshire* was here. To help protect them."

As I studied the neatly manicured graves, I realized many of the sailors on board the ship probably hadn't been much older than I was and that the four people buried here were an ocean away from the relatives they'd left behind. I wondered if their parents had ever made the trip to Ocracoke to see how they'd been laid to rest, and how heartbreaking it was, no matter what the answer might be.

"It makes me sad," I finally said, knowing why Bryce hadn't suggested that we bring the camera. It was a place better remembered in person.

"Me too," he offered.

"Thank you for bringing me here."

He brought his lips together and after a while, we walked back to the truck, moving more slowly than usual.

After he dropped me off, I took a long nap and then called Morgan. I'd done that a couple of times since my mom and dad had visited, and we chatted for fifteen minutes. Or more accurately, Morgan did pretty much all the talking and all I had to do was listen. After hanging up, I started getting ready for my date. Clothing-wise, I was limited to the stretchy jeans and the new sweater I'd received for Christmas. Thankfully, my acne had receded, so I didn't need a lot of foundation or powder. Nor did I go overboard with blush or eye shadow, but I did put on lip gloss.

For the first time, I could really tell I was pregnant. My face was rounder and I was just...*bigger*, especially my bust. I definitely needed larger bras. I'd have to get them after church, which didn't quite seem appropriate somehow, but it wasn't like I had another option.

Aunt Linda was at the stove; she was planning on making beef Stroganoff and I knew Gwen would be joining her. The aroma of her cooking made my stomach rumble and she must have heard it. "Do you want some fruit? To tide you over until dinner?"

"I'll be okay," I said. I took a seat at the table.

Despite my answer, she dried her hands and grabbed an apple. "How was today?"

I told her about Photoshopping and the trip to the cemetery. She nodded. "Every year on May eleventh, the anniversary of the sinking, Gwen and I go there to leave flowers and pray for their souls."

Figures. "I'm glad you do. Have you ever been to Howard's Pub?"

"Many times. It's the only restaurant here that's open year-round."

"Except for yours."

"We're not a real restaurant. You look pretty."

She quickly sliced the apple into wedges and brought them to the table.

"I look pregnant."

"No one will be able to tell."

She went back to cleaning mushrooms while I nibbled on one of the apple slices, which was exactly what my stomach needed. But it made me think...

"How bad is labor?" I asked. "I mean, I've heard so many horror stories."

"That's hard for me to answer. I've never given birth so I can't speak from experience. And with the girls who stayed with us, I was only in the hospital room with a few of them. Gwen could probably give you a better answer since she's a midwife, but from what I know, contractions aren't pleasant. And yet, it's not so terrible that women refuse to go through it again."

That made sense, even if it didn't really answer my question.

"Do you think I should hold the baby after I give birth?"

She took a few seconds to answer. "I can't answer that, either."

"What would you do?"

"I honestly don't know."

I picked up another wedge, nibbling on it, thinking, but was interrupted when I saw headlights flash through the windows and across the ceiling. *Bryce's truck*, I thought with an unexpected burst of nervousness. Which was silly. I'd already spent half the day with him.

"Do you know where Bryce is taking me after dinner?"

"He told me today before you went to his house."

"And?"

"Make sure you bring a jacket."

I waited, but she added nothing else. "Are you mad at me for going out with him?"

"No."

"But you don't think it's a good idea."

"The real question is whether *you* think it's a good idea."

"We're just friends," I responded.

She said nothing, but then again, she didn't have to. Because like me, I realized, she was nervous.

Confession time: This was my first real dinner date. Oh, I'd met a boy and some friends at a pizza parlor once, and the same boy had taken me to get ice cream, but other than that, I was pretty much a novice when it came to how to act or what I was supposed to say.

Fortunately, it took me all of two seconds to realize that Bryce hadn't ever been on a dinner date, either, since he was acting even more nervous than I was, at least until we got to the restaurant. He'd splashed on an earthy-smelling cologne and he wore a button-up shirt, rolling the sleeves to his elbows, and—maybe because he knew my clothing options were limited—he was wearing jeans just like I was. The difference was that he could have strolled out of a magazine photo shoot, while I resembled a puffer version of the girl I wanted to be.

As for Howard's Pub, it was pretty much as I expected, with wooden plank floors and walls decorated with pennants and license plates, and fronted by a crowded, boisterous bar. At the table, we picked up the menus, and less than a minute later, a waitress came by to take our drink orders. We both ordered sweet tea, probably making us the only two who hadn't come for the *pub* part in the restaurant's name.

"My mom says the crab cakes are good here," Bryce remarked.

"Is that what you're getting?"

"I'll probably go with the ribs," he said. "It's what I always get."

"Does your family come here often?"

"Once or twice a year. My parents come more often, whenever they need a break from us kids. Supposedly there are times when we can be a bit overwhelming."

I smiled. "I've been thinking about that cemetery," I commented. "I'm glad we didn't take pictures."

"I never do, mostly because of my grandfather. He was one of those merchant marines that the *Bedfordshire* was trying to protect."

"Has he ever talked about the war?"

"Not much, other than to say it was the scariest time of his life. Not only because of the submarines, but also because of the storms in the North Atlantic. He's been through hurricanes, but the waves in the North Atlantic were beyond terrifying. Of course, before the war, he'd never even set foot on the mainland, so pretty much everything was new to him."

I tried and failed to imagine a life like that. In the silence, I felt the baby move—that watery pressure again—and my hand automatically went to my stomach.

"The baby?" he asked.

"She's getting very active," I said.

He set his menu aside. "I know it's not my decision or even my business, but I'm glad you decided to put the baby up for adoption and not have an abortion."

"My parents wouldn't have let me. I suppose I could have gone to Planned Parenthood or whatever on my own, but the thought never crossed my mind. It's a Catholic thing."

"I meant that if you had, you never would have come to Ocracoke and I wouldn't have had the chance to meet you."

"You wouldn't have missed much."

"I'm pretty sure that I would have missed everything."

I felt a sudden heat at the back of my neck,

but thankfully the waitress arrived with our drinks, rescuing me. We placed our orders— crab cakes for me, ribs for him—and while we sipped our tea, the conversation drifted toward easier, less blush-inducing topics. He described the many places around the United States and Europe he had lived; I related the conversation I'd had with Morgan—which mostly revolved around the stress *she* was under—and shared stories about Madison and Jodie and some of our girlhood adventures, which really centered around slumber parties and occasional makeup fiascoes. Strangely, I hadn't thought about Madison or Jodie since the conversation with my mom when we'd walked on the beach. Had anyone suggested before I'd arrived here that they would slip my mind for even a day or two, I wouldn't have believed them. Who, I wondered, was I becoming?

Our salads arrived, then our meals, as Bryce discussed the grueling application process to West Point. He'd received recommendations from both of North Carolina's U.S. senators, which sort of amazed me— but he said that even if he hadn't gotten in, he would have gone to another university, then entered the army as an officer after graduation.

"And then the Green Beret thing?"

"Or Delta, which is another step up. If I qualify, I mean."

"Aren't you afraid of getting killed?" I asked.

"No."

"How can you not be afraid?"

"I don't think about it."

I knew I'd think about it all the time. "What about after the military? Have you ever thought about what you want to do then? Would you want to be a consultant like your dad?"

"Not a chance. If it was possible, I'd follow in my mom's footsteps and try to do some travel photography. I think it would be cool to go to remote places and tell stories with my pictures."

"How do you even get a job doing that?"

"I have no idea."

"You could always go into dog training. Daisy's doing much better lately at not wandering off."

"It would be too hard to give the dogs away over and over. I get too attached."

I realized that I'd be sad, too. "I'm glad you're bringing her to the house, then. So you can see her as much as possible before she leaves."

He rotated his glass of tea. "Would you mind if I stopped to pick her up tonight?"

"What? For the surprise?"

"I think she'd have fun."

"What are we doing? Can you at least give me a hint?"

He thought about it. "Don't order dessert."

"That doesn't help."

I saw the slightest of twinkles in his eyes. "Good."

After dinner, we drove to Bryce's house, where we found his parents and the twins watching a documentary on the Manhattan Project, which didn't surprise me in the slightest. After loading an excited Daisy into the bed, we were back on the road and it didn't take long before I knew where we were going. The road led to only one place.

"The beach?"

When he nodded, I peered at him. "We're not going in the water, right? Like that opening scene in *Jaws*, where the lady goes out swimming and gets eaten by a shark? Because if that's your plan, you can turn around now."

"The water's too cold to go swimming."

Instead of stopping in the parking area, he made for a gap in the dunes, then turned onto the sand and began driving down the beach.

"Is this legal?"

"Of course," he said. "But it's not legal to run over anyone."

"Thanks," I said, rolling my eyes. "I wouldn't have guessed that."

He laughed as we bounced through the sand, my hand gripping the handle above the door. It was dark—really, really dark—because the moon was just a tiny sliver, and even through the windshield, I could see stars spreading across the sky.

Bryce remained quiet while I strained to make out a shadowy outline ahead. Even with the headlights, I couldn't tell what it was, but Bryce turned the wheel as we drew near and eventually brought the truck to a halt.

"We're here," he said. "But close your eyes and wait in the truck until I get things ready. And don't peek, okay?"

I closed my eyes—why not?—and listened as he got out and closed the door behind him. Even so, I could vaguely hear him occasionally reminding Daisy not to run off while he made a few trips back and forth between the truck and wherever he was going.

After what was probably a few minutes but seemed longer, I finally heard his voice through my window.

"Keep your eyes closed," he called through the glass. "I'm going to open the door and help you down and walk you to where I want you to go. Then you can open them, okay?"

"Don't let me fall," I cautioned.

I heard the door open, felt his hand when I reached for it. Lowering myself carefully, I stretched out my toe until it finally reached the ground. After that, it was easy, Bryce guiding me across the cool sand, the strong wind whipping my hair about.

"There's nothing in front of you," he assured me. "Just walk."

After a few steps I felt a surge of heat and there seemed to be light pushing its way through my eyelids. He gently pulled me to a stop.

"You can open your eyes now."

The shadowy outline I had spotted earlier was a pile of sand forming a semicircular wall around a flat-bottomed pit about two feet deep. On the ocean side of the hole was a pyramid of wood already glowing with dancing flames, and he'd set up two small lawn chairs facing it, with a blanket draped over each. In between the chairs was a small cooler and behind that was something mounted on a tripod. In the realm of romantic movie gestures, it might not have counted for much, but to me it was absolutely perfect.

"Wow," I finally said, my voice quiet. I was so overwhelmed that nothing else leaped to mind.

"I'm glad you like it."

"How did you get the fire going so fast?"

"Charcoal briquettes and lighter fluid."

"And what's that thing?" I asked, pointing toward the tripod.

"A telescope," he said. "My dad let me borrow it. It's his, but the whole family uses it."

"Am I going to see Halley's Comet or something like that?"

"No," he said. "That came in 1986. The next time it's visible will be 2061."

"And you just happen to know that?"

"I think everyone with a telescope knows it."

Of course he thinks that. "What will we see, then?"

"Venus and Mars. Sirius, which is also called the Dog Star. Lepus. Cassiopeia. Orion. A few other constellations. And the moon and Jupiter are almost in conjunction."

"And the cooler?"

"S'mores," he said. "They're fun to cook over campfires."

He swept an arm toward the chairs and I sauntered over, choosing the one farthest away. I leaned forward, freeing the blanket, but as I spread it across my lap, I realized that the wind was now practically nonexistent because of the pit and the sand wall behind me. Daisy wandered up and lay beside Bryce. With the campfire, it felt downright toasty.

"When did you do all this?"

"I dug the hole and set up the wood and charcoal after I dropped you off."

While I was napping. Which explained the difference between him and me—he did, while I slept. "It's...incredible. Thank you for doing all this."

"I also got you something for Valentine's Day."

"You already brought me flowers."

"I wanted to give you something that will remind you of Ocracoke."

I already had a feeling I'd remember this place—and this night—forever, but I watched in fascination as he reached into the pocket of his jacket, removed a small box wrapped in red-and-green paper, and handed it to me. It weighed next to nothing.

"Sorry. There was only Christmas wrapping paper in the house."

"It's fine," I said. "Should I open it now?"

"Please."

"I didn't get you anything."

"You let me take you to dinner, which is more than enough."

At his words, my heart did that funny racing thing again, which had been happening all too often lately. I lowered my gaze and began picking at the wrapping before finally pulling it free. Inside was a box for a staple remover.

"There were no gift boxes, either," he apologized.

When I opened it and tilted the box, a thin gold chain fell into my palm. I gently shook the chain, freeing up a small gold pendant in the shape of a scallop shell. I held it up to the flickering light of the fire, too heart-struck to say anything. It was the first time a boy had ever bought me jewelry of any kind.

"Read the back," he said.

I turned it over and leaned closer to the firelight. It was hard to read, but not impossible.

Ocracoke
Memories

I continued to stare at the pendant, unable to turn my gaze away. "It's beautiful," I whispered past the lump in my throat.

"I've never seen you wear a necklace, so I wasn't sure you'd like it."

"It's perfect," I said, finally turning to him. "But now I feel bad about not getting you anything."

"But you did," he said, the firelight flickering in his dark eyes. "You gave me the memories."

I could almost believe the two of us were alone in the world, and I longed to tell him how much he meant to me. I searched for the right words, but they wouldn't seem to come. In the end, I let my gaze slip away.

Beyond the firelight, it was impossible to see the waves, but I could hear them rolling onto the shore, muffling the sound of the crackling fire. I smelled smoke and salt and noticed that even more stars had emerged overhead. Daisy had curled into a ball at my feet. Feeling Bryce's eyes on me, I suddenly knew that he had fallen in love with me. He didn't care that I was carrying someone else's child or that I would be leaving soon. It didn't matter to him that I wasn't as smart as he was, or as talented, or that even on my best day, I would never be pretty enough for a boy like him.

"Will you help me put it on?" I was finally able to ask, my voice sounding alien to me.

"Of course," he murmured.

I turned and lifted my hair, feeling his fingers brush the nape of my neck. When it was hooked, I touched the pendant, thinking it felt as warm as I did, and slipped it inside my sweater.

I sat back again, dizzy at the realization that he loved me, and wondering how and when it had happened. My mind flashed through a library of memories—meeting Bryce on the ferry, and the morning he'd shown up at my door; his simple response when I'd told him that I was pregnant. I thought about standing beside him at the Christmas flotilla and the sight of Bryce striding among the decorations at the farm in Vanceboro. I remembered his expression when I'd gifted him the biscuit recipe and the anticipation in his eyes when he'd first handed me his camera. Lastly, I pictured him standing on the ladder as he boarded up windows, the image I knew I would own forever.

When he asked if I wanted to gaze through the telescope, I rose from my chair in a dreamlike state and put my eye to the eyepiece, listening as Bryce described what I was seeing. He rotated and adjusted the lens several times before launching into an introduction to planets and constellations and distant stars. He referenced legends and mythology, but distracted by his closeness and my newfound realizations, I barely registered anything he said.

I was still under a kind of spell when Bryce showed me how to make the s'mores. Loading marshmallows onto wooden stakes, he showed me how high above the flames to hold them so they wouldn't catch on fire. Assembling the graham crackers and Hershey bars, we each put together our s'mores, savoring the sweet and gooey delight. I watched as a strand of marshmallow trailed from his lips on his first bite, making him lean forward and fumble with the s'more. He sat up quickly, bobbling the sticky concoction, somehow getting the strand into his mouth. He laughed, reminding me that as good as he was at practically everything, he never seemed to take himself too seriously.

A few minutes later he stood from his chair and walked back to his truck. Daisy trailed behind as Bryce pulled something large and bulky from the bed; I couldn't tell what it was. He carried it past our spot and finally stopped at the hard-packed sand near the water's edge. Only when he launched the kite did I recognize what he was holding, and I watched it rise higher, until it vanished in the darkness.

He waved at me with childlike glee, and I rose from my spot to join him.

"A kite?"

"Robert and my dad helped me build it," he explained.

"But I can't see it."

"Can you hold this for a second?"

Though I hadn't flown a kite since I was a child, this one seemed glued to the sky. From his back pocket, Bryce pulled out what appeared to be a remote control, similar to a television's. He pressed a button and the kite suddenly materialized against the dark sky, lit by what I guessed were red Christmas

lights. The lights ran along the wood framing, etching a large triangle and series of
boxes in the sky.

"Surprise," he said.

I took in his excited face, then turned
back to the kite again. It bobbed a little
and I moved my arm, watching the kite respond. I let out some more string, watching
as the kite rose higher, almost hypnotized
by the sight. Bryce was staring up at it,
too.

"Christmas lights?" I said in wonder.

"Yes, along with batteries and a receiver. I
can make the lights blink if you'd like."

"Let's leave it the way it is," I said.

Bryce and I stood close enough that I
sensed his warmth despite the wind. When
I concentrated, I could feel the seashell
pendant pressing against my skin; I thought
about dinner and the fire and the s'mores and
the telescope. Staring up at the kite, I thought
about who I'd been when I'd first arrived in
Ocracoke and marveled at the new person I'd
become.

I sensed Bryce turn toward me and I
mirrored him, watching as he took a hesitant

step closer. He reached out, placing a hand on my hip, and all at once, I knew what was coming. I felt as he tugged me ever so slightly, his head beginning to tilt. He leaned toward me, his lips drawing ever closer, until they finally touched my own.

It was a gentle kiss, soft and sweet, and part of me wanted to stop him. I wanted to remind him that I was pregnant and a visitor who would soon be leaving; I should have told him there was no future for us as a couple.

But I didn't say anything. Instead, feeling his arms slide around me and his body press against mine, I suddenly knew I wanted this. His mouth slowly opened and when our tongues came together, I lost myself in a world where spending time with him was the only thing that mattered. Where holding him and kissing him were all I ever wanted.

It wasn't my first kiss, or even my first French kiss, but it was the first kiss that felt perfect and right in every way, and when we finally separated, I heard him sigh.

"You don't know how long I've wanted to do that," he whispered. "I love you, Maggie."

Instead of answering, I leaned back into

him, allowing him to hold me, feeling as his fingertips gently traced my spine. I imagined his heart beating in unison with my own, even as his breath seemed steadier than mine.

My body was shaky, and yet I'd never felt more comfortable, more complete.

"Oh, Bryce," I murmured, the words coming naturally. "I love you, too."

HOLIDAY SPIRIT AND

CHRISTMAS EVE

Manhattan
December 2019

In the glow of the gallery's Christmas tree lights, the memory of that kiss remained vivid in Maggie's mind. Her throat was dry, and she wondered how long she'd been speaking. As usual, Mark had stayed quiet as she'd recounted the events of that period of her life. He was leaning forward, forearms on his thighs, his hands clasped together.

"Wow," he finally said. "The perfect kiss?"

"Yeah," she agreed. "I know how it sounds. But…that's what it was. To this day, it's the kiss that all others have been compared to."

He smiled. "I'm happy you had the chance

to experience that, but I admit it leaves me feeling a little intimidated."

"Why?"

"Because when Abigail hears about it, she may ask herself whether she's missing out— she might go off in search of her own perfect kiss."

Laughing, Maggie tried to recall how long it had been since she'd sat with a friend for hours and simply... *talked*. Without self-consciousness or worries, where she felt like she could really be herself? Too long...

"I'm sure Abigail melts whenever you kiss her," she teased.

Mark blushed to his hairline. Then, suddenly serious, he said, "You meant it. When you said you loved him."

"I'm not sure I ever stopped loving him."

"And?"

"And you'll have to wait to hear the rest. I don't have the energy to keep going tonight."

"Fair enough," he said. "It can hold. But I hope you don't make me wait too long."

She stared at the tree, inspecting its shape, the glittering and artfully draped ribbons.

"It's hard for me to believe this will be my last Christmas," she mused. "Thank you for helping me make it even more special."

"You don't have to thank me. I'm honored you've chosen to spend part of it with me."

"You know what I've never done? Even though I've lived in New York City all these years?"

"Seen *The Nutcracker*?"

She shook her head. "I've never gone ice skating at Rockefeller Center under the giant tree. In fact, I haven't even seen the tree except on TV since my early years here."

"Then we should go! The gallery is closed tomorrow, so why not?"

"I don't know how to ice skate," she said with a wistful expression. *And I'm not sure I'd have the energy, even if I did.*

"I do," he said. "I played hockey, remember? I can help you."

She eyed him uncertainly. "Don't you have something better to do on your day off? You shouldn't feel like it's your responsibility to indulge your boss's crazy whims."

"Believe me, it sounds a lot more fun than what I usually do on Sundays."

"Which is what, exactly?"

"Laundry. Grocery shopping. A little video gaming. Are we on?"

"I'm going to need to sleep late. I wouldn't be ready until midafternoon."

"Why don't we meet at the gallery at two or so? We can catch an Uber uptown together."

Despite her reservations, she agreed. "Okay."

"And afterwards, depending on how you feel, maybe you can fill me in on what happened next between you and Bryce."

"Perhaps," she said. "Let's see how I feel."

Back in her apartment, Maggie felt a profound exhaustion overtake her, pulling her down like an undertow. She removed her jacket and lay down in bed, wanting to rest her eyes for a minute before changing into her pajamas.

She woke at half-past noon the following day, still dressed in the clothes she'd worn the day before.

It was Sunday, December 22, three days before Christmas.

Even if she trusted Mark, Maggie was nervous about the thought of falling on ice. Though she'd slept heavily overnight—she doubted she'd even rolled over—she felt weaker than normal, even for her. The pain was back, too, simmering just below a boil, making even the thought of eating impossible.

Her mom had called earlier that morning and left a short message, just checking in on her, hoping she was doing well—the usual—but even in the message, Maggie could hear the strains of worry. Worrying, Maggie had long ago decided, was the way her mom showed Maggie how much she loved her.

But it was also wearying. Worrying, after all, had its roots in disapproval—as though Maggie's life would have been better if only she'd listened to her mom all along—and over time it had become her mom's default position.

While Maggie had wanted to wait until Christmas, she knew she had to call back. If she didn't, she'd likely receive another, even more frantic message. She sat on the edge of the bed and, after glancing at the clock, realized there was a chance her parents would be at church, which would be ideal. She could leave a message, say that she had a busy day ahead, and avoid the potential for any unnecessary stress. But no such luck. Her mom picked up on the second ring.

They spoke for twenty minutes. Maggie asked about her father and Morgan and her nieces, and her mom dutifully filled her in. She asked Maggie how she was feeling, and Maggie replied that she was doing as well as could be expected. Thankfully, it stopped there and Maggie breathed a sigh of relief, knowing she'd be able to hide the truth until after the holiday. Toward the end of the conversation, Maggie's father got on the line, and he was his normal laconic self. They spoke about the weather in Seattle and New York, he updated her on the season the Seahawks were having—he loved football— and mentioned that he'd purchased a set of binoculars for Christmas. When Maggie asked why, she was told that her mom had joined a bird-watching club. Maggie wondered how long the interest in the club would last and assumed it would go the same way as other clubs her mom had joined over the years. Initially there would be a lot of enthusiasm and Maggie would listen to raves about how fascinating the members were; after a few months, her mom would note that there were a few people in the club she didn't get along with; and later, she'd announce to Maggie that she'd quit because most of the people were just awful. In her mom's world, someone else was always the problem.

Her dad said nothing else, and after hanging up the phone, Maggie wished again that she had a different relationship with her parents, especially with her mom. A relationship characterized more by laughter than by sighs. Most of her friends had good relationships with their moms. Even Trinity got along with his mom, and he was temperamental when compared to other artists. Why was it so hard for Maggie?

Because, Maggie silently acknowledged,

her mom made it hard, and she'd done so for as long as Maggie could remember. To her, Maggie was more of a shadow than a real person, someone whose hopes and dreams felt incomprehensibly alien. Even if they shared the same opinion on a particular subject, her mom wasn't likely to find comfort in such a thing. Instead she'd focus her attention on a related area of disagreement, with worry and disapproval as her primary weapons.

Maggie knew her mom couldn't help it; she'd probably been the same way as a child. And it was childlike in a way, now that Maggie thought about it. *Do what I want, or else.* For Maggie's mom, tantrums were sublimated into other, more insidious means of control.

The years after returning from Ocracoke, before she'd moved to New York, had been particularly trying. Her mom had believed that pursuing a career in photography was both silly and risky, that Maggie should have followed Morgan to Gonzaga, that she should try to meet the right kind of man and settle down. When Maggie had finally moved away, she'd dreaded speaking to her mom at all.

The sad thing was that her mom wasn't a terrible person. She wasn't necessarily even a bad mom. Thinking back, she'd made the right decision to send Maggie to Ocracoke, and she wasn't the only parent who cared about grades, or worried that her daughter was dating the wrong kind of guys, or believed that marriage and having children were more important than a career. And, of course, some of her other values *had* stuck with Maggie. Like her parents, Maggie drank infrequently, avoided recreational drugs, paid her bills, valued honesty, and was law-abiding. She didn't, however, attend church any longer; that had ended in her early twenties when she'd had a crisis of faith. Well, a crisis of pretty much everything, in fact, which led to her spontaneous move to New York and a series of awful relationships, assuming they could be called relationships at all.

As for her dad...

Maggie sometimes wondered whether she had ever really known him. If pressed, she would say that he was a product of another era, a time when men worked and provided for their family and went to church and understood that complaining seldom offered solutions. His general quietude, however, had given way to something else since he'd retired, a near reticence to speak at all. He spent hours alone in the garage even when Maggie visited, and was content to let his wife speak for him during dinners.

But the call was completed, at least until Christmas, and it made her realize how much she was dreading the next one. No doubt, her mom would demand that Maggie return to Seattle, and she'd use every guilt-based weapon at her disposal to try to get her way. It wasn't going to be pretty.

Pushing that thought away, she tried to focus on the present. She noted that the pain was getting worse and wondered whether she should text Mark and cancel. With a grimace, she made her way to the bathroom and retrieved the bottle of pain pills, remembering Dr. Brodigan telling her that they were addictive if used inappropriately. What a silly thing to say. What did it really matter if Maggie became addicted at this point? And how much was inappropriate? Her insides felt like a pincushion and even touching the back of her hand triggered little flashes of white in the corners of Maggie's eyes.

She swallowed two pills, debated, and then took a third, just in case. She decided to see how she felt in half an hour before making a final decision about today and went to sit on the couch while they took effect. Though she'd wondered whether the pills would work as usual, like magic, the pain began to fade. When it was finally time to go, she was floating on a wave of well-being and optimism. She could always watch Mark skate, if it came down to it, and it was probably a good idea to get some fresh air, wasn't it?

She caught a cab to the gallery and spotted Mark standing outside the doors. He was holding a to-go cup, no doubt her favorite smoothie, and when he saw her, he hailed her with a wide grin. Despite her condition, she was certain she'd made the right call.

"Do you think we'll be able to skate?" Maggie asked when they arrived at Rockefeller Center and saw the crowds overflowing the rink. "I didn't even consider the idea we might need reservations."

"I called this morning," Mark assured her. "It's all set up."

Mark found a place for her to sit while he went to wait in line and Maggie sipped her smoothie, thinking the third pill had done the trick. She felt a bit loopy but not as ebullient as earlier; in any case, the pain had diminished to an almost tolerable level. Moreover, she actually felt warm for the first time in what seemed like forever. Though she could see her breath, she wasn't shivering and her fingers didn't ache, for a change.

The smoothie was going down easily as well, which was a relief. She knew she needed every calorie, and wasn't that ironic? After a lifetime of watching what she ate and groaning every time the scale ticked a pound upward, now that she actually needed calories, they were almost impossible to ingest. Lately, she was afraid to get on the scale because she was terrified to see how much weight she'd lost. Beneath her clothes, she was turning into a skeleton.

But enough of the doom and gloom. Mesmerized by the mass of moving bodies on the ice, she only vaguely heard her phone ding. Reaching into her pocket, she saw that Mark had texted, saying that he was on his way back so he could escort her to the rink and help her with her skates.

In the past, his offer of assistance would have humiliated her. But the fact was, she doubted she'd be able to put on the skates without his help. When he reached her, he offered his arm and the two of them walked slowly down the steps to the changing area, where they'd don their skates.

Even though he was supporting her, she felt like the wind would topple her over.

"Do you want me to keep holding you?" Mark asked. "Or do you think you have the hang of it?"

"Don't even think of letting go," she replied through gritted teeth.

Adrenaline, amplified by fear, had a way of

clearing the mind, and she decided that ice skating was much better as a concept than in practice. Trying to stay upright on two thin blades over a slippery sheet of ice while in her condition hadn't been the brightest of ideas. In fact, a pretty strong case could be made that it was idiotic.

And yet…

Mark made it as easy and safe as possible. He was skating backward in front of her, both hands firmly on her hips. They were near the outer edge of the rink and moving slowly; inside, pretty much everyone from little old ladies to toddlers was zipping past, looking carefree and joyous. But with Mark's help, at least, Maggie was gliding. There were a few people who, like Maggie, clearly had never donned ice skates before, and they gripped the outer wall with every slow shuffle, their legs occasionally shooting out in unpredictable directions.

Ahead of them, Maggie witnessed just such an incident.

"I really don't want to fall."

"You're not going to fall," Mark said, his eyes fixed on her skates. "I've got you."

"You can't see where you're going," she protested.

"I'm using my peripheral vision," he explained. "Just let me know if someone takes a tumble right in front of us."

"How long do we have?"

"Thirty minutes," he said.

"I don't think I'll be able to last that long."

"We'll stop whenever you want."

"I forgot to give you my credit card. Did you pay for this?"

"It was my treat. Now stop talking and try to enjoy yourself."

"Almost falling every second isn't enjoyable."

"You're not going to fall," he said again. "I've got you."

"That was fun!" Maggie exclaimed. In the changing area, Mark had just helped her remove her skates. Though she hadn't asked, he'd also helped her put her shoes back on. In all, they'd circled the rink four times, which had taken thirteen minutes.

"I'm glad you enjoyed it."

"Now I can say I actually did the big New York tourist thing."

"Yes, you can."

"Did you have a chance to see the tree? Or were you too busy keeping me from breaking my neck?"

"I saw it," he said. "But barely."

"You should go skate. You still have a few minutes."

To her surprise, he actually seemed to consider it. "Would you mind?"

"Not at all."

After helping her up—and offering his arm—he walked her to the side of the rink and made sure she could support herself before letting go. "You okay?"

"Go ahead. Let's see how you do without a sick old woman slowing you down."

"You're not old." He winked, and duck-walking over to the ice, he took three or four quick steps, speeding into the turn. He jumped, rotating in the air, and started skating backward while accelerating even faster, flying beneath the tree on the far side of the rink. He spun again, speeding forward into the next curve, one hand nearly at the ice, then flew past her. Almost automatically, she retrieved her iPhone from her pocket. She waited until he was beneath the tree and snapped off a couple of photos; on the next lap, she shot video.

A few minutes later, after the session ended and Mark was in the changing area, she took a peek at the photos and found herself thinking about the shot she'd taken of Bryce on the ladder. Just as she'd done back then, she'd seemed to capture the essence of the young man she'd come to know. Like Bryce, Mark had also become strangely important to her in a relatively short period. And yet, as she'd had to with Bryce, she knew she'd eventually have to say goodbye to Mark as well, which suddenly made her ache in a way that eclipsed the physical pain lurking in her bones.

Once they were back on solid ground, she texted the pictures and video to Mark and they had a stranger snap an additional shot of the two of them with the tree in the background. Mark immediately began fiddling with the phone, no doubt forwarding the images.

"Abigail?" Maggie asked.

"And my parents."

"I'm sure they're missing you this Christmas."

"I think they're having the time of their lives."

She pointed to the restaurant adjacent to the rink. "Is it okay with you if we swing by the Sea Grill? I think I'd like a hot tea at the bar."

"Whatever you'd like."

She hooked her arm through Mark's and walked slowly to the glass-enclosed restaurant. She told the bartender what she wanted and Mark ordered the same thing. When the teapot was placed before her, she poured some of the tea into her cup.

"You're an excellent skater."

"Thanks. Abigail and I go sometimes."

"Did she like the photo you texted?"

"She replied with three heart emojis, which I take as a yes. But I've been wondering…"

When he paused, she finished for him. "About the story?"

"Do you still have the necklace that Bryce gave you?"

Instead of answering, Maggie reached behind her neck and unhooked the clasp before sliding the necklace off. She handed it to him, watching as he carefully took it. He stared at the front before flipping it over and examining the engraving on the back.

"It's so delicate."

"I can't think of a day I haven't worn it."

"And the chain never broke?"

"I'm pretty careful with it. I don't sleep with it on or shower with it. But other than that, it's part of my everyday ensemble."

"And whenever you put it on, you remember that night?"

"I remember that night all the time. Bryce wasn't just my first love. He's the only man I've ever loved."

"The kite was pretty cool," Mark conceded. "I've done the campfire-and-s'mores thing with Abigail—at the lake, not at the ocean—but I've never heard of a kite strung with Christmas lights. I wonder if I could build one."

"These days, you can probably Google it, or maybe even order one."

Mark appeared contemplative as he stared into his own cup of tea. "I'm glad you had a night like that with Bryce," he said. "I think everyone deserves at least one perfect evening."

"I think so, too."

"But you do understand you were falling for him all along, right? It didn't start when the storm rolled in. It started on the ferry, when you first saw him in that olive-green jacket."

"Why do you say that?"

"Because you didn't walk away and you clearly could have. And when your aunt asked if Bryce could be your tutor, you agreed pretty quickly."

"I needed help in school!"

"If you say so," he said with a grin.

"Now it's your turn," she said, changing the subject. "You took me skating, but is there anything you really want to do now that we're here in Midtown?"

He swished the tea around in his cup. "You'll probably think it's silly. Since you've been living here so long, I mean."

"What is it?"

"I want to see some of the department stores' window displays on Fifth Avenue— the ones that are all decorated for Christmas? Abigail told me it was something I have to do. And in an hour and a half, there will be a choir performing outside St. Patrick's Cathedral."

The choir she could understand, but window displays? And why did it not seem out of character that he'd want to do something like that?

"Let's do it," she agreed, forcing herself not to roll her eyes. "I'm not sure how much I'll be able to walk, though. I feel a little wobbly."

"Great," he said, beaming. "And we'll travel by cab or Uber whenever we have to, okay?"

"One question," she said. "How do you know a choir will be performing today?"

"I did some research this morning."

"Why do I get the sense you're trying to make this Christmas special for me?"

When his eyes flickered with sadness, she knew he didn't have to explain.

After finishing their teas, they stepped outside into the chilly air and Maggie felt a sharp pain deep in her chest, one that continued to flare with every heartbeat. It was blinding white—knives, not needles—worse than ever. She froze, closing her eyes and pressing hard with a fist, right below her breast. With her free hand, she gripped Mark's arm and his eyes went wide.

"Are you okay?"

She tried to breathe steadily, the pain continuing to flash and burn. She felt Mark's arm wrap around her. "It hurts," she rasped out.

"Do you need to go back inside and sit? Or should I take you home?"

With clenched teeth, she shook her head. The thought of moving at all seemed impossible and she concentrated on her breathing. She didn't know if that would do any good, but it was what Gwen had told her to do when she was suffering through the agony of labor. After the longest minute of her life, the pain finally began to fade, a flare slowly dying out as it sank to the horizon.

"I'm okay," she finally croaked, even though her vision seemed to be swimming.

"You don't seem okay," he countered. "You're shaking."

"Pac-Man," she muttered. She took a few more breaths before finally lowering her hand. Moving slowly, she reached into her bag and pulled out her prescription bottle. She tapped another pill free and dry-swallowed it. She squeezed her eyes shut until she was able to breathe normally again, the pain finally receding to a bearable level.

"Does this happen a lot?"

"More than it used to. It's becoming more frequent."

"I thought you were going to pass out."

"Impossible," she said. "That would be too easy, since then I wouldn't feel the pain."

"You shouldn't make jokes," he chided. "I was just about to call for an ambulance."

Hearing his tone, she forced a smile. "Really. I'm okay now."

A lie, she thought, *but who's counting?*

"Maybe I should take you home."

"I want to see the windows and listen to the carols."

Which, oddly, was the truth, even if it was kind of silly. If she didn't go now, she knew she never would. Mark seemed to be trying to read her.

"Okay," he finally said. "But if it happens again, I'm bringing you home."

She nodded, knowing he might need to.

They rode first to Bloomingdale's, then over to Barneys, then to Fifth Avenue, where every store seemed to be trying to outdo the next with its window decorations. She saw Santa and his elves, polar bears and penguins with holiday-themed collars, artificial snow in rainbow colors, elaborate installations highlighting selected apparel or items that probably cost a fortune.

By Fifth Avenue, she'd begun to feel better, even a little floaty. No wonder people got addicted to the pills; they actually *worked*. She clung to Mark's arm as people swarmed past them in both directions, carrying bags bearing the labels of every brand on the planet. Many of the stores had long lines of people waiting to enter, last-minute shoppers hoping for the perfect gift, none of whom appeared happy in the slightest to be standing in the cold.

Tourists, she thought, shaking her head. People who wanted to go home and say things like *You wouldn't believe how crowded it was* or *I had to wait an hour just to go inside the store*, like it was a badge of honor or act of courage. No doubt they would tell that same story for years to come.

And yet she found the stroll curiously pleasant, maybe because of the floatiness, but mostly because Mark was so clearly gobsmacked. Though he kept a firm grip on her hand, he was constantly straining to see over the shoulders of the crowds, eyes widening at the sight of Santa crafting a Piaget watch, or smiling in delight at oversize reindeer decked out in Chanel harnesses, all of them wearing Dolce & Gabbana sunglasses. She was used to grimacing at the crass commercialization of the holiday, but observing Mark's sense of wonder made her regard the stores' creativity with new appreciation.

They finally reached St. Patrick's Cathedral, arriving with pretty much everyone else in the vicinity who'd come for the same reason. The crowd was so large that they were stranded halfway down the block, and though Maggie couldn't see the singers, she could hear them thanks to the large speakers they had set up. Mark, though, was disappointed, and she realized she should have warned him this would happen. She'd learned upon moving to New York that *attending* an event in the city and really *seeing* the event were often two entirely different things. In her first year here she'd ventured out to see the Macy's Thanksgiving Day Parade. She'd found herself wedged against a building, surrounded by hundreds, and stuck in place for hours, her primary view the backs of people's heads. She'd had to crane her neck to see the famous balloons and had awakened the following morning so sore that she'd had to visit a chiropractor.

Ah, the joys of city living, right?

The choir, even if unseen, sounded rapturous

to her ears, and as she listened, Maggie found herself reflecting back on the last few days with a light sense of wonder. She'd seen *The Nutcracker*, decorated a tree, shipped gifts to her family, skated at Rockefeller Center, seen the window displays on Fifth Avenue, and now this. She was checking off once-in-a-lifetime experiences with someone she'd come to care about, and sharing the story of her past had lifted her spirits.

But as the floatiness started to fade, she felt fatigue setting in, and she knew it was time to go. She squeezed Mark's arm, signaling that she was ready. They'd listened to four carols by then, and turning, he began leading her back through the crowd that had formed behind them. When they finally had breathing space, he stopped.

"How about some dinner?" he asked. "I'd love to hear the rest of the story."

"I think I need to lie down for a while."

He knew enough not to argue with her. "I can ride with you."

"I'll be okay," she said.

"Do you think you'll make it to the gallery tomorrow?"

"I'll probably stay home. Just in case."

"Will I see you Christmas Eve? I want to give you your gift."

"You didn't have to get me anything."

"Of course I did. It's Christmas."

She thought about it, finally deciding *Why not?* "Okay," she offered.

"Do you want to meet at work? Or have dinner? Whatever is easiest for you."

"I tell you what—why don't I have dinner delivered to the gallery? We can eat under the tree."

"Can I hear the rest of your story?"

"I'm not sure you'll want to. It's not really a holiday story. It gets very sad."

He turned, raising his hand to hail her an oncoming cab. As the taxi pulled over, he glanced at her without pity. "I know," he said simply.

For the second night in a row, Maggie slept in the clothes she'd been wearing.

The last time she'd peeked at the clock, it

was a few minutes before six. Dinner hour in much of America; still-at-the-office hour in much of NYC. She woke more than eighteen hours later feeling weak and dehydrated, but thankfully pain-free.

Not willing to risk a relapse, she took a single pain pill before wobbling her way to the kitchen, where she forced down a banana, along with a piece of toast, which made her feel slightly better.

After taking a bath, she stood in front of the mirror, barely recognizing herself. Her arms were stick thin, her collarbones bulged beneath her skin like tent supports, and her torso sported numerous bruises, some of them deep purple. In her skeletal face, her eyes resembled an alien's, bright and bewildered.

What she'd read about melanoma—and it felt like she'd read just about everything on the subject—suggested that there was no way to predict her final months. Some people had significant pain, requiring morphine via an IV drip; for others, it wasn't debilitating. Some patients had worsening neurological symptoms while others were clear-headed up until the end. The location of the pain was as varied as the patients, which she supposed made sense. Once cancer metastasizes, it can go anywhere in the body, but Maggie had been hoping for the more pleasant version of dying. She could handle the loss of appetite and excessive sleep, but the prospect of excruciating pain frightened her. Once she moved to IV morphine, she knew she might never get out of bed again.

But the actually-being-dead part didn't frighten her. Right now, she was too busy being inconvenienced for death to be anything but hypothetical. And who knew what it was actually like? Would she see the bright light at the end of a tunnel, or hear harps as she entered the pearly gates, or would she simply fade away? When she thought of it at all, she imagined it as akin to going to sleep without dreaming, except she'd never wake up. And, obviously, she wouldn't care about not waking up because ... well, because death made caring—or not caring—impossible.

But yesterday's last-ditch holiday celebrations drove home the fact that she was one seriously sick woman. She didn't want more pain, and she didn't want to sleep eighteen hours a day. There wasn't enough time for those things. More than anything, she wanted to live normally up until the very end, but she had a growing suspicion that it wasn't going to be possible.

In the bathroom, she slipped her necklace back on. She pulled a sweater over a set of thermal underwear, and thought about putting on jeans, but what was the point? Pajama bottoms were more comfortable, so she stuck with those. Finally, she donned warm fuzzy slippers and a knit hat. The thermostat was set in the midseventies, but still a little chilly, she plugged in a space heater. There was no reason to care about the electricity bill; it wasn't as though she had to save for retirement.

She heated a cup of water in the microwave, then wandered to the living room. She sipped at it, thinking about where she'd left off in her story with Mark. Reaching for her phone, she texted him, knowing he would already be at work.

Let's meet at the gallery at six tomorrow, ok? I'll tell you the rest of my story and then we can have dinner.

Almost immediately, she saw the dots indicating that he was responding to the text, and his reply popped up in bubble form.

Can't wait! Take care of yourself. Looking forward to it. All good at work. Busy today.

She waited, seeing if he would add anything else, but he didn't. Finishing the hot water, she reflected on how her body was choosing to defy her. Sometimes it was easy to imagine that the melanoma was speaking to her in a haunted, creepy voice. *I shall take you in the end, but first? I shall make your insides burn and force you to waste away. I'll take your beauty and steal your hair and deprive you of conscious hours, until there's nothing left but a skeletal shell…*

Maggie gave a morbid chuckle at the thought of that imagined voice. Well, it would be silenced soon enough. Which raised the question…what was she going to do about her funeral?

She'd been thinking about it on and off since her last meeting with Dr. Brodigan. Not frequently, just every now and then when the thought suddenly surfaced, often in the most unexpected moments. Like right now. She'd done her best to ignore it—death still being hypothetical and all—but yesterday's pain made that impossible.

What *was* she going to do? She supposed she really didn't have to do anything. Her parents or Morgan would no doubt take care of it, but she didn't want them to have to assume that burden. And since it was her funeral, she certainly deserved some say in the matter. But what was it that she wanted?

Not the typical funeral, she knew that much. She had no desire for an open casket, or sappy songs like "Wind Beneath My Wings," and definitely no long eulogy from a priest who didn't even know her. That wasn't her style. But even if it had been—where would the funeral take place? Her parents would want her to be buried in Seattle, not New York, but New York was her home now. She couldn't imagine forcing her mom and dad to find a local funeral home and cemetery, or to arrange for a Catholic service in a strange city. Nor was she sure her parents could even handle such a thing, and while Morgan was more capable, she was already overwhelmed with young children at home. All of which left only one option.

Maggie had to arrange everything in advance.

Rising from the couch, Maggie found a pad of paper in the kitchen drawer. She made some notes about the kind of service she wanted. It was less depressing than she'd imagined, likely because she rejected outright all the somber stuff. She reviewed what she'd written, and while it wouldn't make sense to her parents, she was glad she'd thought to express her dying wishes. She made a note to herself to contact her attorney in the new year so it could all be finalized.

Which left only one more thing to do.

She needed to get Mark something for Christmas.

Though she'd given him a bonus earlier in December, just as she'd done for Luanne, she felt like something more was warranted, especially after these past few days. But what to get him? Like most young people, especially those who intended to go to graduate school, he'd probably appreciate an additional gift of money more than anything else. Lord knows, when she was in her twenties, that's what she would have wanted. It would also be easy—all she had to do was write a check—but it didn't feel right to her. She sensed that his gift for her was something personal, which made her think she should reciprocate in a similar vein.

She asked herself what Mark enjoyed, but even that didn't lead to many answers. He loved Abigail and his parents, he intended to lead a religious life, he was interested in contemporary art, and he grew up in Indiana and played hockey. What else did she know about him?

She flashed back to their first interview, remembering how prepared he'd been, and the answer finally presented itself. Mark admired the photographs she'd taken; more than that, he thought of them as her legacy. So why not give Mark a gift that reflected Maggie's passion?

In the drawers of her desk, she found several flash drives; she'd always kept plenty on hand. For the next few hours, she began to transfer photographs onto the drives, choosing her favorites. Some of them hung on the walls of the gallery, and though the photographs wouldn't be part of the limited-edition runs—and thus without monetary value—she knew that Mark wouldn't care about that. He wouldn't want the photographs for financial reasons; he'd want them because she'd taken them, and because they'd meant something to her.

When she was finished, she dutifully consumed some food. Salty cardboard, as disgusting as ever. Throwing caution to the wind, she also poured herself a glass of wine. She found a station playing Christmas music on the radio, and she sipped her wine until she became drowsy. She traded her sweater for a sweatshirt, put on socks in place of the slippers, and crawled into bed.

She woke at noon on Christmas Eve, feeling rested and, miracle of miracles, completely pain-free.

But just in case, she took her pills, washing them down with half a cup of tea.

Knowing that it would most likely be a late night, she lounged most of the day. She called her favorite neighborhood Italian restaurant, where until recently she had been a regular, and learned that a delivery for two shouldn't be a problem despite the large crowd expected for dinner that evening. The manager, whom she knew well and who she guessed knew of her illness due to her appearance, was particularly solicitous. He anticipated what she might enjoy, remembering the dishes she frequently ordered and suggesting a few specials as well as their famous tiramisu. She thanked him warmly after reading him her credit card number and scheduling the delivery for eight p.m. *And who said New Yorkers were callous?* she thought with a smile as she hung up.

She ordered a smoothie, drank it while taking her bath, and then reviewed the flash drives she'd created for Mark. As always, when revisiting her past work, her mind re-created the particulars of every shot.

Losing herself in the memories of so many exhilarating trips and experiences made the hours pass quickly. At four, she took a nap, even though she was still feeling pretty good; after she woke, she slowly got ready. As she had in Ocracoke so long ago, she chose a red sweater, albeit with more layers underneath. Black wool slacks over tights, and a black beret. No jewelry except for the necklace, but enough makeup so she wouldn't frighten the cabdriver. She added a cashmere scarf to hide her gangly neck, and then put her pills in her bag, just in case. She hadn't had time to wrap Mark's gift, so she emptied a tin of Altoids and used the container for the drives. She wished she had a bow but figured Mark wouldn't care. Finally, with a sense of dread, she retrieved one of the letters her aunt Linda had written, which she kept in her jewelry box.

Outside, the weather was bone-chilling and

damp, the sky promising snow. In the short cab ride to the gallery, she passed a Santa Claus ringing a bell, soliciting donations for the Salvation Army. She saw a menorah in an apartment window. On the radio, the cab-driver was listening to music that sounded Indian or Pakistani. Christmas in Manhattan.

The door to the gallery was locked, and after entering, she locked it again behind her. Mark was nowhere to be seen, but the tree was glowing, and she smiled when she saw that he had set up a small fold-out table flanked by two fold-out chairs in front of the tree and covered it with a red paper table-cloth. On the table was a gift-wrapped box and a vase with a red carnation, along with two glasses of eggnog.

He must have heard her enter because he emerged from the back as she was admir-ing the table. When she turned, she noticed that he, too, wore a red sweater and black slacks.

"I'd say you look fantastic, but I think that might come across as self-serving," she observed as she removed her jacket.

"If I didn't know better, I'd think you came

by earlier to see what I'd be wearing," he countered.

She motioned toward the table. "You've been busy."

"I figured we'd need a place to eat."

"You do understand that if I have the eggnog, I won't be able to eat at all."

"Then just think of it as table decoration. Can I take your jacket?"

She handed it over and he disappeared into the back again while Maggie continued to survey the scene. In no small way, it reminded her of the Christmas she'd spent in Ocracoke, which had no doubt been his intention.

She took a seat at the table, feeling content, as Mark emerged from the back with a coffee cup in hand. He set it before her.

"It's just hot water," he explained, "but I brought a tea bag if you'd like a little flavor."

"Thank you." Because tea sounded good, and the caffeine even better, she added the bag to her water, letting it steep. "Where did you get all this?" She swept her arm over the scene.

"The chairs and table are from my

apartment—it's actually my temporary dining set. The cheap tablecloth came from Duane Reade. More importantly, how are you doing? I've been worried about you since I saw you last."

"I've slept a lot. I feel better."

"You look good."

"I'm a walking cadaver. But thank you anyway."

"Can I ask you a question?"

"Haven't we moved beyond that yet? Where you have to ask permission to ask me something?"

He stared into his cup of eggnog, his brow creased by a slight frown. "After we finished skating, you know, when...you started feeling bad. You said something like...Pac-Man? Or Packmin? Or..."

"Pac-Man," she said.

"What does that mean?"

"Have you never heard of *Pac-Man*? The video game?"

"No."

Dear God, he really is young. Or I'm getting old. She pulled out her phone, went to YouTube, selected a quick video, and handed the phone to him. He started the video and began watching.

"So Pac-Man moves through a maze eating dots along the way?"

"Exactly."

"What did that have to do with the way you were feeling?"

"Because that's sometimes how I think about cancer. That it's like Pac-Man, moving through the maze of my body, eating all my healthy cells."

As she answered, his eyes went wide. "Oh…wow. I'm so sorry I brought this up. I shouldn't have asked…"

She waved a hand at him. "It's not a big deal. Let's just forget about it, okay? Are you hungry? I hope you don't mind, but I went ahead and ordered from my favorite Italian restaurant. The food should arrive by eight." Even if she couldn't eat more than a few bites, she was hoping to enjoy the smell.

"Sounds great. Thanks for that. And before I forget, Abigail told me to wish you a merry Christmas. She said she wishes she could be here with us and that she can't wait to meet you when she comes to New York in a few days."

"Likewise," Maggie said. She gestured at the gift. "Should I open it now, since the food won't be here for a while?"

"Why don't we wait until after dinner?"

"And until then, let me guess... You want to hear the rest of my story."

"I've been thinking about it ever since you left off."

"It's still better if we end with the perfect kiss."

"I'd rather hear it all, if you don't mind."

She took a swallow of tea, letting it warm the back of her throat while the years rolled in reverse. She closed her eyes, wishing she could forget, but knowing she never would.

"Later that night, after Bryce brought me home, I barely slept at all..."

THE THIRD TRIMESTER

Ocracoke
1996

Part of my insomnia had to do with my aunt. When I got home, she was still on the couch, the same book open in her lap, but when she lifted her eyes in my direction, one look was all it took. No doubt I was radiating moonbeams, because her eyebrows twitched slightly, and I finally heard her sigh. It was an *I knew this was going to happen* kind of sigh, if you know what I mean.

"How was it?" she asked, underplaying the obvious. Not for the first time, I found myself wondering how someone who spent decades squirreled away in a convent could be so worldly.

"It was fun." I shrugged, trying to play it cool, even though we both knew it was pointless. "We had dinner and went to the beach. He built a kite with Christmas lights on it, but you probably already knew that. Thanks again for letting me go."

"I'm not sure there was anything I could have done to stop it."

"You could have said no."

"Hmm" was all she said, and I suddenly understood that there'd been an inevitability to Bryce and me all along. As I stood before my aunt, I inexplicably found myself back on the beach again with Bryce in my arms. I felt an undeniable surge of heat up my neck and began to remove my jacket in the hope she wouldn't notice.

"Don't forget that we have church in the morning."

"I remember," I confirmed. I stole a peek at her as I walked past her toward my bedroom, noticing that she'd returned to reading her book.

"Good night, Aunt Linda."

"Good night, Maggie."

Lying in bed with Maggie-bear, I was too wired to sleep. I kept replaying the evening and thinking about the way Bryce had gazed at me over dinner or how his dark eyes had caught the firelight. Mostly I remembered the taste of his lips, only to realize that I was smiling in the darkness like a crazy person. And yet, as the hours ticked by, my giddiness gradually gave way to confusion, which also kept me awake. While I knew deep down that Bryce loved me, it still made no sense. Didn't he know how extraordinary he was? Had he forgotten I was pregnant? He could have any girl he wanted, while I was nothing but ordinary in all the ways that mattered and a definite screwup in one of the biggest ways of all. I wondered if his feelings for me had more to do with simple proximity than with anything particularly unique and wonderful about me. I fretted that I wasn't smart or pretty enough, and even momentarily questioned whether I'd made the whole thing up. And while I tossed and turned, it dawned on me that love was the most powerful emotion of all, because it made you vulnerable to the possibility of losing everything that really mattered.

Despite the emotional whiplash, or maybe because of it, exhaustion finally won out. In the morning, I woke to a stranger in the mirror. There were bags under my eyes, the skin on my face felt like it was sagging, and my hair seemed stringier than usual. A shower and makeup allowed me to be somewhat presentable before I emerged from my room. My aunt, because she seemed to know me better than I knew myself, made pancakes for breakfast and avoided any doublespeak. Instead, she casually steered the conversation to the date itself and I walked her through most of it, leaving out only the important things, although my enraptured expression probably made the remainder unnecessary.

But the easy conversation was exactly what I needed to feel better, and the trepidation I'd experienced overnight gave way to a warm sense of contentment. On the ferry, as we sat upstairs at the table with Gwen, I gazed out the window and watched the water, lost again in the memories of the previous evening. I thought about Bryce while I was at church and again when we picked up supplies; at one of the garage sales, I found a kite for sale and wondered if it would fly if I added Christmas lights to it. The only time I didn't think about him was when it came time to shop for larger bras; it was all I could do to hide my embarrassment, especially when the owner of the shop—a stern-looking brunette with flashing black eyes—gave me the once-over, pausing at my stomach, while leading me to the fitting room.

When we finally got back to the house, the lack of sleep had caught up to me. Even though it was already dark, I took a quick catnap and woke just as dinner was about to be served. After eating and cleaning up the kitchen, I went back to bed, still feeling like a zombie. I closed my eyes, wondering how Bryce had spent his day, and whether being in love would change things between us. But mostly I thought about kissing him again, and right before I finally dozed off, I realized that for me, the moment couldn't come soon enough.

The dreamy feeling persisted when I awoke; in fact, it permeated every waking hour for the next week and a half, even when I had my next sit-down with Gwen concerning my pregnancy. Bryce loved me and I loved him, and my world pretty much revolved around that thrilling idea, no matter what the two of us were doing.

Not that our day-to-day routines changed much. Bryce was nothing if not responsible. He still came over to tutor me with Daisy in tow, and he did his best to keep me focused even when I sometimes squeezed his knee before giggling at his suddenly flustered expression. Despite my frequent attempts at flirting when I was supposed to be working, I nonetheless continued to forge ahead in my studies. On the exams, I extended my pretty-darn-good streak, even though Bryce remained disappointed in his abilities as a tutor. My photography lessons didn't change that much, either, except that he also began teaching me how to take indoor shots using a flash and other lighting, as well as the occasional nighttime shot. Those we usually did at his house, because the equipment was right there. For evening shots of the star-filled sky, we used a tripod and a remote, since the camera had to be absolutely stable. Those shots required a super-slow shutter speed— sometimes as long as thirty seconds—and on a particularly clear night when there was no moon in the sky, we caught part of the Milky Way, which looked like a glowing cloud in a darkened sky illuminated by fireflies.

We also continued to eat dinner together three or four times a week. Half of those were with my aunt, the other half with his family, often including his grandparents. His dad had left town on the Monday after our date on a two-month consulting gig. Bryce didn't know exactly where he'd gone or what he'd be doing, except that it was for the DOD, but he didn't seem particularly interested; he just missed having him around.

Really, about the only thing that changed for Bryce and me was the times when we were taking a break from my studies or when we set the camera aside. In those moments, we talked more deeply about our families and friends, even recent events in the news, though Bryce had to carry those latter conversations. With no television or newspaper, I was pretty clueless about the state of the world—or the U.S., or Seattle, or even North Carolina— and honestly didn't care all that much. But I liked hearing him talk and he occasionally posed serious questions about serious issues. After pretending to think about it, I'd say something like "That's difficult to answer. What do you think?" and he'd start explaining his thoughts on the matter. I suppose it was also possible I learned something, but lost in my feelings for him, I didn't remember much. Every now and then, I'd again find myself wondering what he saw in me and I'd feel a sudden pang of insecurity, but as though reading my mind, he would reach for my hand, and the feeling would pass.

We also kissed a lot. Never when my aunt or his family could see us, but pretty much every other moment was up for grabs. I'd be writing an essay and take a second to collect my thoughts, then notice the way he was watching me, and I'd lean over to kiss him.

Or after examining one of the photographs from the file box, Bryce would lean in and kiss me. We kissed on the porch at the end of an evening or as soon as he stepped into my aunt's house to tutor me. We kissed at the beach and in town, near his house and outside my aunt's, which sometimes meant ducking behind the dune or around the corner. Sometimes he'd wrap a strand of my hair around his finger; other times, he'd simply hold me. But always, he'd tell me again that he loved me, and every single time it happened, my heart would start beating funny in my chest, and I'd feel as though my life was as perfect as it would ever be.

In early March, I had to see Dr. Huge Hands again. It was to be my last appointment with him before the delivery, since Gwen would continue to supervise my care for the rest of the term. Right on schedule, I'd begun having the occasional Braxton Hicks contraction, and when I told the doctor I wasn't a fan, he reminded me that it was my body's way of getting ready for labor. I did the ultrasound, avoided even a glimpse at the monitor, but let out an automatic breath of relief when the technician said that the baby (*Sofia? Chloe?*) was doing just fine. Although I was trying hard not to think of the baby as a person who belonged to me, I still wanted to know she was going to be okay. The technician added that *mama* was doing fine, too—which meant *me*, but it was still weird to hear her say it— and when I finally sat down with the doctor, he went over a bunch of things that I might experience in the last stage of my pregnancy. I pretty much stopped listening once he said the word *hemorrhoids*—it had come up during the pregnant teen meeting at the Portland YMCA, but I'd forgotten all about it—and by the time he finished, I was downright depressed. It took me a second to understand that he was asking me a question.

"Maggie? Did you hear me?"

"Sorry. I was still thinking about hemorrhoids," I said.

"I asked whether you were exercising," he said.

"I walk when I'm taking pictures."

"That's great," he said. "Just remember that exercise is good for both you and the baby, and it will shorten the time your body needs to recover after delivery. Nothing too intense, though. Light yoga, walking, things like that."

"How about riding a bike?"

He brought a giant finger to his chin. "As long as it's comfortable and doesn't hurt, that's probably okay for the next few weeks. After that, your center of gravity will begin to shift, making balance more difficult, and falling would be bad for both you and the baby."

In other words, I'd be getting even fatter, which I knew was coming, but it was still as depressing as the idea of hemorrhoids. I did like the notion that my body might get back to normal faster, though, so the next time I saw Bryce, I asked if I could bike along with him on his morning runs.

"For sure," he said. "It'll be great to have company."

The following morning, after waking up way too early, I put on my jacket and rode to Bryce's house. He was stretching out front and he jogged toward me, Daisy at his side. As he leaned in to kiss me, I suddenly realized I hadn't brushed my teeth, but I kissed him anyway and he didn't seem to mind.

"You ready?"

I thought it would be easy since he was running and I was on a bike, but I was wrong. I did okay for the first couple of miles, but after that, my thighs started to burn. Even worse, Bryce kept trying to have a conversation, which wasn't easy since I was huffing and puffing. Just when I thought I couldn't go any farther, he stopped near a gravel road that led toward the canals and said that he had to do sprints.

I rested on my bike seat, one foot on the ground, and watched as he sprinted away from me. Even Daisy had trouble keeping up, and I watched his image grow smaller in the distance. He stopped, rested for a short bit, then sprinted toward me again. He went up and back five times, and even though he was breathing a lot harder than I'd been and Daisy's tongue almost reached her legs, he immediately started jogging again after he'd finished, this time in the direction of his house. I thought we were done, but I was wrong again. Bryce did push-ups, sit-ups, and then jumped up and down from the picnic table in his yard before finally doing multiple sets of pull-ups using a pipe hung beneath his house, his muscles flexing against his shirt. Daisy, meanwhile, lay in place, panting. When I checked my watch after he'd finished, he'd been going nonstop for almost ninety minutes. Despite the cool morning air, his face was shiny with sweat and there were wet circles on his T-shirt as he approached.

"You do this every morning?"

"Six days a week," he said. "But I vary it. Sometimes the run is shorter and I do more sprints or whatever. I want to be ready for West Point."

"So every time you arrive to tutor me, you've already done all of this?"

"Pretty much."

"I'm impressed," I said, and not just because I'd enjoyed the sight of his muscles. It *was* impressive, and it made me wish that I could be more like him.

Despite the addition of regular morning exercise, the pounds kept coming and my tummy kept growing. Gwen continually reminded me that was normal—she began dropping by the house regularly to check my blood pressure and listen to the baby with a stethoscope—but it still didn't make me feel better. By the middle of March, I was up twenty-two pounds. By the end of the month, I was up twenty-four, and it was pretty much impossible to hide the bulge no matter how baggy the sweatshirt. I began to resemble a character from a Dr. Seuss book: small head and skinny legs with a bulging torso, but without the cute look of Cindy-Lou Who.

Not that Bryce seemed to mind. We still kissed, he still held my hand, and he always told me I was beautiful, but as the month wore on, I began to feel pregnant almost all the time. I had to balance just right when I sat down to keep from plopping into the seat, and getting up from the sofa required momentary planning and concentration. I still went to the bathroom practically every hour, and once, when I sneezed on the ferry, my bladder actually seemed to *spit*, which was absolutely mortifying and left me feeling wet and gross until we got back to Ocracoke. I felt the baby moving a lot more, especially whenever I lay down—I could also *watch* it moving, which was really trippy—and I had to start sleeping on my back, which wasn't comfortable at all. My Braxton Hicks contractions were coming more regularly, and like Dr. Huge Hands, Gwen said it was a good thing. I, on the other hand, still thought it was a bad thing because my whole stomach tightened and I felt all crampy, but Gwen ignored my complaint. About the only terrible things that hadn't happened were hemorrhoids or a sudden starburst of acne on my face. I still had the occasional extra pimple or two, but my makeup skills kept it from being all that noticeable and Bryce never said a word about it.

I also did pretty well on my midterms, not that either of my parents seemed all that impressed. My aunt, though, was pleased, and it was around that time that I began to notice that she kept her own counsel when it came to my relationship with Bryce. When I'd mentioned that I was going to start exercising in the mornings, all she'd said was "Please be careful." On those nights Bryce stayed for dinner, she and he chatted as amiably as ever. If I told her that I would be taking photographs on Saturday, she would simply ask what time I thought I would be back, so she would know what time to have dinner ready. At night, when it was just Aunt Linda and me, we talked about my parents or Gwen or what was going on with my studies or at the shop before she'd pick up a novel while I perused books on photography. And yet, I couldn't shake the sense that something had grown up between us, some kind of *distance*.

Early on, I hadn't minded it so much. The fact that my aunt and I rarely spoke about Bryce made the relationship feel a little secretive, vaguely illicit and therefore more exciting. And while not encouraging, Aunt Linda at least seemed accepting of the idea that her niece was in love with a young man who met her approval. At night, when it was time for me to walk Bryce to the door, more often than not, she would rise from her spot on the sofa and head to the kitchen, giving us a bit of privacy, enough for a quick kiss goodbye. I think she intuitively knew that Bryce and I wouldn't go overboard. We hadn't even gone on an official second date; really, since we saw each other pretty much all day every day, there wasn't a reason to. Nor had we ever considered sneaking out at night to see each other or going somewhere without telling my aunt in advance. With my body beginning to shape-shift, sex was absolutely the last thing on my mind.

And yet, after a while, the distance began to bother me. Aunt Linda was the first person I'd known who was completely on my side. She accepted me for who I was, faults and all, and I wanted to think I could talk to her about anything. It all sort of came to a head as we were sitting in the living room near the end of March. We'd had dinner, Bryce had gone home, and it was coming up on the time she usually went to bed. I cleared my throat awkwardly, and my aunt glanced up from her book.

"I'm glad you let me live here," I said.

"I don't know if I've told you enough how thankful I am."

She frowned. "What brought that on?"

"I don't know. I guess I've been so busy lately that we haven't had the chance to be alone so I could tell you how much I appreciate everything you've done for me."

Her expression softened and she set the book aside. "You're welcome. You're family, of course, and that's the reason I was initially willing to help. But once you got here, I began to realize how much I enjoyed having you around. I never had children of my own, and in some ways, I feel like you've become like the daughter I never had. I know it's not my place to say such things, but I've learned that it's okay at my age to pretend every once in a while."

I moved my hand over the bulge of my stomach, thinking of everything I'd put her through. "I was a pretty terrible guest in the beginning."

"You were fine."

"I was moody and messy and zero fun to be around."

"You were scared," she said. "I knew that. Frankly, I was frightened, too."

That, I hadn't expected. "Why?"

"I worried that I wouldn't be what you needed. And if that happened, I worried that you might have to go back to Seattle. Like your parents, I just wanted what was best for you."

I fiddled with a few strands of my hair. "I still don't know what I'm going to say to my friends when I get back. For all I know, some people already suspect the truth and they're talking about me, or they'll spread rumors that I was in rehab or something."

Her expression remained calm. "A lot of the girls I worked with at the convent were afraid of the same thing. And the reality is, those things might happen, and it's terrible when they do. And yet, you might be surprised. People tend to focus on their own lives, not someone else's. As soon as you're back, doing normal things with your friends, they'll forget the fact that you were gone for a while."

"Do you think so?"

"Every year, when school finishes, kids

scatter to all sorts of different places all summer long, and while they might see some friends, they don't see others. But as soon as they're all back together, it's like they were never apart."

Though it was true, I also knew some who loved nothing better than juicy gossip, people who made themselves feel better by putting others down. I turned toward the window, noting the darkness beyond the glass, and wondered again why she hadn't seemed to want to talk about my feelings for Bryce and their implications. In the end, I just came out with it.

"I'm in love with Bryce," I said, my voice barely above a whisper.

"I know. I see the way you look at him."

"He's in love with me, too."

"I know. I see the way he looks at you."

"Do you think I'm too young to be in love?"

"That's not for me to say. Do you think you're too young?"

I suppose I should have expected her to turn the question around on me. "Part of me knows I love him, but there's this other voice in my head whispering that I can't possibly know, since I've never been in love before."

"First love is different for everyone. But I think people know it when they feel it."

"Have you ever been in love?" When she nodded, I was pretty certain she was referring to Gwen, but she didn't elaborate so I went on. "How do you know for sure it's love?"

For the first time, she laughed, not at me, but almost for herself. "Poets and musicians and writers and even scientists have been trying to answer that question since Adam and Eve. And keep in mind that for a long time, I was a nun. But if you're asking me my opinion—and I lean toward the practical, less romantic side—I think it comes down to the past, the present, and the future."

"I'm not sure what you mean," I said, tilting my head.

"What attracted you to the other person in the past, how did that person treat you in the past, how compatible were you in the past? It's the same questions in the present, except that a physical longing for the other person is added. The desire to touch and hold and kiss. And if all of the answers make you feel like you never want to be with anyone else, then it's probably love."

"My parents are going to be furious when they find out."

"Are you going to tell them?"

I almost answered on instinct, but when I noticed my aunt had raised her eyebrow, my words caught in my throat. Was I actually going to tell them? Until that moment, I'd just assumed that I would, but even if I did, what did that mean for Bryce and me? In reality? Would we even be able to see each other? In the flurry of those thoughts, I remembered my aunt saying that love came down to the past, present, and...

"What does the future have to do with love?" I asked.

As soon as I asked, I realized that I already knew the answer. My aunt, however, kept her tone almost light.

"Can you see yourself being with the person in the future, for all the reasons you love them now, through all the inevitable challenges that will come to pass?"

"Oh" was all I could muster.

Aunt Linda absently tugged at her ear.

"Have you ever heard of Sister Thérèse of Lisieux?"

"I can't say that I have."

"She was a French nun who lived in the 1800s. She was very holy, one of my heroes, really, and she probably wouldn't have appreciated my reference about love also coming down to the future. She said, 'When one loves, one does not calculate.' She was a lot wiser than I can ever hope to be."

My aunt Linda really was the best. But despite her comforting words that night, I was troubled and gripped Maggie-bear hard. It was a long time before I fell asleep.

As a highly skilled procrastinator—which I learned in school, as a result of being required to do boring school stuff—I managed not to think about the conversation with my aunt just yet. Instead, when thoughts of leaving Ocracoke and Bryce surfaced, I tried to remind myself of the *when one loves, one does not calculate* thing, and usually it worked. In all fairness, my ability to avoid thinking about the subject might have had to do with the fact that Bryce was so irresistibly good-looking and it was pretty easy for me to get lost in the moment.

Whenever Bryce and I were together, my brain kept me in gaga mode, probably because we continued to sneak kisses whenever possible. But in the evenings when I was alone in my room, I could practically hear the clock ticking toward my departure, especially whenever the baby moved. The reckoning was definitely coming, whether I wanted it or not.

The beginning of April found us taking photographs of the lighthouse, where I watched as Bryce changed lenses on the camera under a rainbow sky. Daisy trotted here and there, sniffing the ground and occasionally wandering over to check on him. The weather had warmed and Bryce was wearing a T-shirt. I caught myself staring at the starkly defined muscles in his arms as though they were a hypnotist's pendulum. I was almost thirty-five weeks pregnant, and I'd had to put the brakes on bicycle riding with Bryce in the mornings, figuratively speaking anyway. I was also becoming more self-conscious about being seen in public. I didn't want people on the island to assume that Bryce had knocked me up; Ocracoke was, after all, his home.

"Hey, Bryce?" I finally asked.

"Yes?"

"You know I have to go back to Seattle, right? Once I deliver the baby?"

Lifting his eyes from the camera, he gawked at me as though I were wearing a snow cone as a hat. "Really? You're pregnant and leaving?"

"I'm being serious," I said.

He lowered the camera. "Yeah," he said. "I know."

"Have you ever thought about what that might mean for us?"

"I've thought about it. But can I ask you a question?" When I indicated he could, he went on. "Do you love me?"

"Of course I do," I said.

"Then we'll find a way to make it work."

"I'll be three thousand miles away. I won't be able to see you."

"We can talk on the phone..."

"Long-distance calls are expensive. And even if I can figure out a way to pay for them myself, I'm not sure how often my parents will even let me call. And you're going to be busy."

"Then we'll write to each other, okay?" For the first time, I heard anxiety creeping into his voice. "We're not the first couple in history that had to figure out the long-distance thing, my parents included. My dad was deployed overseas for months at a time, twice for almost a year. And he travels all the time now."

But they were married and had children together. "You're going off to college while I still have two years of high school left."

"So?"

You might meet someone better. She'll be smarter and prettier and the two of you will have more in common than we do. I heard the voices in my head but said nothing, and Bryce approached. He touched my cheek, tracing it gently, then leaned in to kiss me, the feeling as light as the air itself. He held me then, neither of us saying anything until I finally heard him sigh.

"I'm not going to lose you," he whispered, and while I closed my eyes and wanted to believe him, I still wasn't sure how it would be possible.

In the days that followed, it seemed like both of us were trying to pretend that the conversation had never happened. And for the first time, there were moments when we were awkward in each other's presence. I would catch him staring off into the distance and when I asked what he was thinking about, he'd shake his head and force a quick smile, or I'd cross my arms and suddenly sigh and realize that he knew exactly what I was thinking.

Though we didn't talk, our need to touch became even more pronounced. He reached for my hand more frequently and I moved in for a hug whenever fears of the future intruded. When we kissed, his arms held me even tighter, as though clinging to an impossible hope.

We stayed in more due to the advanced state of my pregnancy. There were no more bike rides and instead of taking photos, I studied the ones in the file box. Even though it was probably safe, I nonetheless stayed out of the darkroom.

Just as I'd done throughout March, I worked extra hard on my readings and assignments, mainly as a distraction from the inevitable. I wrote an analysis of *Romeo and Juliet*, which wouldn't have been possible without Bryce and was also my last big paper of the year in any class. As I'd read the play, I'd wondered at times whether I was even reading English; he'd had to translate virtually every passage. But by contrast, when I played around with Photoshop, I trusted my instincts and continued to surprise both Bryce and his mom.

Still, Daisy seemed to sense the cloud hanging over Bryce and me; she frequently nuzzled one of my hands while Bryce held the other. One Thursday after dinner, I walked Bryce to the porch while my aunt simultaneously found a reason to check something in the kitchen. Daisy followed us out and sat beside me, gazing up at Bryce as he kissed me. I felt his tongue meet my own, and afterward, he leaned his forehead gently against mine while we held each other.

"What are you doing Saturday?" he finally asked.

I assumed he was asking me to go on another date. "Saturday night, you mean?"

"No," he said with a shake of his head. "During the day. I have to bring Daisy to Goldsboro. I know you've been trying to keep a low profile, but I was hoping you'd come with me. I don't want to be alone on the drive back and my mom has to stay with the twins. Otherwise they might accidentally blow up the house."

Though I'd known it was coming, the idea that Daisy was leaving made a lump form in my throat. I automatically reached for her, my fingers finding her ears.

"Yeah...Okay."

"Do you need to ask your aunt? Since it's the day before Easter?"

"I'm sure she'll let me go. I'll talk to her later and if anything changes, I'll let you know."

His lips were pursed as he nodded. I

stared down at Daisy, feeling my eyes well with tears.

"I'm going to miss her."

Daisy whined at the sound of my voice. When I looked at Bryce, I realized his eyes were glistening as well.

On Saturday, we caught the early ferry from Ocracoke and made the long drive from the coast to Goldsboro, an hour past New Bern. Daisy rode in the front of the truck, sandwiched between us on the seat, both of us running our fingers through her fur. Content to soak up the affection, she barely moved at all.

Eventually, we pulled into a Wal-Mart parking lot, and Bryce spotted the people he'd come to meet. They were standing near a pickup truck with a plastic kennel in the bed. Bryce angled the truck toward them, slowing gradually. Daisy sat up to see what was happening and stared through the windshield, excited about a new adventure but clueless as to what was really happening.

Because the lot was crowded with Saturday shoppers, Bryce hooked the leash to Daisy's collar before opening the door. He got out first and Daisy jumped down, her nose going to the ground so she could sniff her new surroundings. Meanwhile, I crawled down from my side, which was becoming a serious challenge by that point, and I joined Bryce. He offered me the leash.

"Can you hold this for a minute? I need to get her paperwork from the truck."

"Of course."

I bent lower, petting Daisy again. By then, the visitors had started toward us, both coming across as far more relaxed than I felt. One was a woman in her forties who wore her long red hair in a ponytail; the man appeared to be about ten years older and was dressed in a polo and chinos. Their familiar demeanor made it clear they knew Bryce well.

Bryce shook both their hands before handing over the folder. They introduced themselves to me as Jess and Toby, and I said hello. I watched their eyes flash momentarily to my tummy and I crossed my arms, more self-conscious than usual. They were kind enough not to stare, and after a minute of small talk about the drive and what he'd been up to lately, Bryce began to fill them in on Daisy's training. Even so, I knew they were trying to figure out whether Bryce was the father of the baby, and I focused on Daisy again. I barely paid attention to the conversation. When Daisy licked my fingers, I knew I'd never see her again and felt tears beginning to form.

Jess and Toby clearly knew the drill and that prolonging the goodbye would only make things harder for Bryce. They brought the conversation to a close and Bryce squatted lower. He took Daisy's face in his hands, the two of them staring at each other.

"You're the best dog I've ever had," he said, his voice choking slightly. "I know you're going to make me proud and that your new owner is going to love you as much as I do."

Daisy seemed to absorb every word, and when Bryce kissed the top of her head, her eyes closed. He handed the leash to Toby and turned away, his expression grim, walking toward the truck without another word. I, too, kissed Daisy one last time and followed. Peeking over my shoulder, I saw Daisy sitting patiently, watching Bryce. Her head was tilted to the side as though she was wondering where he was going, a sight that nearly broke my heart. Bryce opened my door and helped me up into the truck, remaining silent.

He got in beside me. In the side mirror, I spotted Daisy again. She continued to watch us as Bryce started the engine. The truck moved forward slowly, passing one parked car after another. Bryce focused directly ahead of him, and we rolled through the parking lot, toward the exit.

There was a stop sign but no traffic. Bryce turned onto the access road, the trip back to Ocracoke already underway. I peered over my shoulder one last time. Daisy remained seated, her head still tilted, no doubt watching the truck grow smaller in the distance. I wondered if she was confused or frightened or sad, but she was too far away to tell. I watched Toby finally tug the leash, and Daisy followed slowly to the rear of his truck. He lowered the tailgate and Daisy hopped up; then we passed another building, blocking them entirely from view, and suddenly she was gone. Forever.

Bryce remained quiet. I knew he was hurting and knew how much he'd miss the dog he'd raised since she was a puppy. I swiped at my tears, unsure what to say. To voice the obvious meant little when the wound was so fresh.

Up ahead was the on-ramp for the highway, but Bryce began to slow the truck. For an instant, I thought he was going to return to the parking lot, so he could really say goodbye to Daisy. But he didn't. He turned the truck into a gas station, coming to a stop near the edge of the property, where he shut off the ignition.

After swallowing hard, he lowered his face into his hands. His shoulders began to quake and when I heard the sound of him crying, it was impossible to keep my own tears in check. I sobbed and he sobbed and though we were together, we were alone in our sadness, both of us already missing our beloved Daisy.

When we reached Ocracoke, Bryce dropped me off at my aunt's. I knew he wanted to be alone and I was exhausted and needed a nap. When I woke, Aunt Linda made grilled cheese sandwiches and tomato soup. While I sat, I involuntarily kept reaching for Daisy under the table.

"Would you like to go to church tomorrow?" my aunt asked. "I know it's Easter, but if you'd rather stay home, I understand."

"I'll be okay."

"I know you will. I was asking for another reason."

Because you're clearly looking pregnant, she meant.

"I'd like to go tomorrow, but after that, I think I'll take a break."

"Okay, honey," she said. "Starting next Sunday, Gwen will be around if you need anything."

"She won't go to church, either?"

"It's probably not a good idea. She needs to be here, just in case."

In case you go into labor, she meant, and when I reached for my sandwich, I was struck by yet more changes, signaling that my time here was coming to a close, more quickly than I wanted.

On Monday, two days later, my first thought upon waking was that I only had about a month to go. Leaving Daisy behind had made the reality of saying goodbye that much more concrete somehow, not just for me but for Bryce, too. He was subdued during our tutoring session, and afterward, instead of photography, he suggested that we start driving lessons. He mentioned he'd spoken to both my aunt and his mom about it, and they'd both approved.

I knew that he'd grown used to having Daisy with us during our shoots, and that he wanted to do something to take his mind off it. After I agreed, he drove to the road that led to the far end of the island and we traded places. It wasn't until I was behind the wheel that I realized the truck had a standard, not automatic, transmission. Don't ask me why I hadn't noticed before, but it was probably because Bryce made driving seem effortless.

"I don't think I'm going to be able to do this."

"It's good to learn with a standard, in case you ever have to drive one."

"That's never going to happen."

"How do you know?"

"Because most people are smart enough to have cars that do all the shifting automatically."

"Can we get started now? If you're finished complaining?"

It was the first time that day that Bryce sounded like his old self, and I felt my shoulders relax. I hadn't realized how tense they'd been. I listened as he described the process of using the clutch.

I'd imagined it would be easy, but it wasn't. Releasing the clutch in the same instant the accelerator caught was a lot harder than Bryce made it seem, and the first hour of my driving lesson was essentially a long series of quick, lurching bucks of the truck followed by the engine stalling. After my first series of attempts, Bryce had to fasten his seat belt.

Eventually, once I got the truck going, he had me accelerate, shifting into second and third gear before starting the process all over again.

By the middle of the week, I seldom stalled the truck any longer; by Thursday, I was good enough to test the village streets, which was far less dangerous for all involved than it sounded, since there was seldom any traffic there, either. I oversteered and understeered when making turns, which meant spending most of that day practicing my navigation. By Friday, fortunately, I was no longer embarrassing myself behind the wheel as long as I was careful in the turns, and at the end of the lesson, Bryce wrapped his arms around me and told me again that he loved me.

As he held me, my mind couldn't help flashing to the fact that the baby was due in twenty-seven days.

I didn't see Bryce that Saturday, as he'd let me know after I'd finished my driving lesson the day before that because his father was still out of town, he would be spending the weekend fishing with his grandfather. Instead, I went to the shop and spent some time alphabetizing the books and arranging the videocassettes by category. Afterward Gwen and I discussed my Braxton Hicks contractions again, which had recently started up after a period of relative quiet. She reminded me that it was a normal phenomenon, and also walked me through what I should expect once I went into labor.

That night, I played gin rummy with my aunt and Gwen. I thought I'd hold my own, but it turns out that these two former nuns were pretty much card sharks and after finally putting the deck away, I wondered what exactly went on in convents after the lights were out. I had visions of a casino-like atmosphere with nuns wearing gold bracelets and sunglasses as they sat at felt-lined tables.

Sunday, however, was different. Gwen came by with her blood pressure monitor and the stethoscope and asked the same questions

Dr. Huge Hands normally did, but as soon as she left, I felt out of sorts. Not only wasn't I in church, but aside from studying for tests, I was pretty much done with school, as I'd finished all of my assignments for the semester. Nor had Bryce left me with his camera, so photography was out as well. The batteries in my Walkman were dead— my aunt had told me she'd pick some up later—leaving me with nothing whatsoever to do. Though I suppose I could have gone for a walk, I didn't want to leave the house. It was too bright, people were out and about, and my pregnancy was so noticeable that stepping outside was equivalent to having two giant neon arrows pointing toward my tummy, letting everyone know why I'd come to Ocracoke in the first place.

In the end, I finally called my parents. I'd had to wait until midmorning because of the time difference and though I don't know what I was hoping to hear, my mom and dad didn't make me feel much better. They didn't ask about Bryce or my photography, and when I mentioned how far ahead I was in school, my mom barely waited a beat before telling me that Morgan had won yet another scholar-ship, this time from the Knights of Columbus. When they put my sister on the phone, she seemed tired, which left her quieter than usual. For the first time in a long time, it felt like an actual back-and-forth conversation, and unable to help myself, I told her a little about Bryce and my newfound love of the camera. She sounded almost dumbfounded and then asked when I was coming home, which left me reeling. How could she not have known anything about Bryce or that I'd been taking pictures, or that the baby was due on May 9? As I hung up the phone, I wondered whether my parents and Morgan ever spoke about me at all.

With nothing better to do, I also cleaned the house. Not just the kitchen and my room and my own laundry, but everything. I made the bathroom sparkle, I vacuumed and dusted, and I even scrubbed the oven, though that ended up making my back ache, so I prob-ably didn't do the greatest job on it. Still, because the house was small, I had hours remaining to kill before my aunt got home, so I went to sit on the porch.

The day was gorgeous, spring making its arrival felt. The sky was cloudless and the water shimmered like a tray of blue diamonds, but I didn't really pay much attention. Instead, all I could think was that the day kind of felt like a waste, and I didn't have enough days left in Ocracoke to ever waste one again.

Tutoring with Bryce now merely consisted of prepping for next week's exams, the last big round before finals. Because I could do only so much studying, our sessions grew shorter; because we'd gone through pretty much every photograph in the file box, we worked our way through one photography book after another. I realized over time that while almost anyone could learn to frame and compose a photo if they practiced enough, at its best photography truly was an art. An excellent photographer somehow put their *soul* into their work, conveying a distinct sensibility and personal viewpoint through the picture. Two photographers shooting the same thing at the same time could produce startlingly different images, and I began to understand that the first step in taking an excellent photograph was the simple act of knowing oneself.

Despite the weekend fishing, or maybe because of it, our time together didn't feel quite the same. Oh, we kissed and Bryce told me that he loved me, he still held my hand when we sat on the couch, but he wasn't as... *open* as he'd seemed to be in the past, if that makes any sense. Occasionally I got the feeling that he was thinking of something else, something he didn't want to share; there were even moments when he seemed to forget I was there at all. It didn't happen often, and whenever he caught himself, he would apologize for his distraction, although he never explained what was preoccupying him. Yet after dinner, when we were on the porch saying goodbye, his demeanor was clingy, as though he was reluctant to let me go.

Despite my general aversion to leaving the house, we went for a walk on the beach on Friday afternoon. We were the only ones out, and we held hands as we strolled near the water's edge. Waves rolled lazily toward the shore, pelicans skimmed the breakers, and though we brought the camera with us, we hadn't yet taken any pictures. It made me realize that I wanted a photo of the two of us together, since we didn't have a single one. But no one was around to take it, so I remained quiet and eventually we turned back toward the truck.

"What do you want to do this weekend?" I asked.

He took a few steps before answering.

"I'm not going to be around. I have to go fishing with my grandfather again."

I felt my shoulders sink. Was he already pulling away from me, so things would be easier when the time came to say good-bye? But if that was the case, why did he continue to tell me that he loved me? Why were his embraces so prolonged? In my confusion, I was able to force out only a single syllable.

"Oh."

Hearing my disappointment, he gently stopped me. "I'm sorry. It's just something I have to do."

I stared at him. "Is there something you're not telling me?"

"No," he said. "There's nothing at all."

For the first time since we were together, I didn't believe him.

On Saturday, bored again, I tried to study for my tests, thinking the better I did, the more protection I would have in case I bombed the finals. But because I'd done all the reading and assignments and I'd already studied all week, it felt like overkill. I knew I wasn't going to have any problems and eventually drifted to the porch.

Feeling fully prepared with all my school-work behind me was an odd sensation, but it also made me realize why Bryce was so much farther ahead academically than I was. It wasn't simply because he was intelligent; homeschooling meant cutting out all the nonacademic activities. At my school, there were breaks between classes, minutes for students to settle down at the beginning of every class, school announcements, club sign-ups, fire drills, and longish lunch breaks that were akin to social hours. In class, teachers often had to slow their lessons for the benefit of students who struggled even more than I did, and all those things added up to hours of wasted time.

Even so, I still preferred going to school. I liked seeing my friends, and frankly, the thought of spending day after day with my mom gave me the chills. Besides, social skills were important, too, and even through Bryce seemed perfectly normal, some people—like me, for instance—benefited from mixing with others. Or that's what I wanted to believe, anyway.

I was pondering all of this while I waited on the porch for my aunt to get back from the shop. My mind wandered to Bryce and I tried to imagine what he was doing on the boat. Was he helping to drag in the net or did they have a machine for that? Or was there no net at all? Was he gutting fish or did they do that at the dock, or was someone else responsible? It was hard to picture, mainly because I'd never been fishing, never been on the boat, and had no idea what they were trying to catch.

It was around that time that I heard crunching in the gravel drive. It was still too early for my aunt to be home, so I had no idea who it could be. To my surprise, I saw the Trickett family van and I heard the sound of the hydraulics being engaged. Grasping the rail, I slowly descended the steps, reaching the bottom when I saw Bryce's mom rolling toward me.

"Mrs. Trickett?" I asked.

"Hi, Maggie. Am I catching you at a bad time?"

"Not at all," I said. "Bryce is out fishing with his grandfather."

"I know."

"Is he all right? He didn't fall off the boat or something like that?" I frowned, feeling a surge of anxiety.

"I doubt he fell overboard," she assured me. "I'm expecting him back around five."

"Am I in trouble?"

"Don't be silly," she said, coming to a stop at the foot of the steps. "I went by your aunt's shop a little earlier and she said it would be all right if I came by. I wanted to speak with you."

Because it felt funny towering over her, I took a seat on the steps. Up close, she was as pretty as ever, the sunlight illuminating her eyes like emerald prisms.

"What can I do for you?"

"Well...first off, I wanted to tell you that I'm really impressed with your camera work. You have wonderful instincts. It's extraordinary how far you've come in such a short time. It took me years to get to where you are."

"Thank you. I've had good teachers." She moved her hands to her lap and I sensed her unease. I knew she hadn't driven here to talk to me about photography. Clearing my throat, I went on. "When is your husband coming home?"

"Soon, I think. I'm not sure of the exact date, but it'll be good to have him back. It's not always easy raising three boys alone."

"I'm sure it isn't. At the same time, your kids are pretty extraordinary. You've done an incredible job."

She glanced away before clearing her

throat. "Did I ever tell you about Bryce after my accident?"

"No."

"Obviously, it was a very hard time, but thankfully the army allowed Porter to work from home for the first six months, so he could take care of me and the kids while we got the house retrofitted for wheelchair access. Eventually, though, he had to go back to work. I was still in a lot of pain and I wasn't moving nearly as well as I do now. Richard and Robert were four at the time, and they were a real handful. Tons of energy, picky eaters, messy. Bryce pretty much had to become the man of the house while his dad was at work, even though he was only nine years old. In addition to having to look after his brothers, he had to help take care of me, too. He read to them, entertained them, cooked for them, got them in the tub, put them to bed. All of it. But because of me, he also had to do things that a kid should never have to do, like helping me in the bathroom or even getting me dressed. He didn't complain, but I still feel bad about that. Because he had to grow up more quickly than other kids his age." When she sighed, I noticed her face seemed to be creased with lines of regret. "After that, he was never a kid again. I don't know whether that's been a good thing or a bad thing."

I tried and failed to come up with an adequate response. Finally: "Bryce is one of the most extraordinary people I've ever met."

She turned toward the water, but I had the sense she wasn't really seeing it.

"Bryce has always believed that both of his brothers are...better than he is. And while they're both brilliant, they're not Bryce. You've met them. As smart as they are, they're still kids. When Bryce was their age, he was already an adult. By the time he was six, he'd announced his intent to attend West Point. Even though we're a military family, even though it's Porter's alma mater, we had nothing to do with that decision. If it were up to Porter and me, we'd send him to Harvard. He was accepted there, too. Did he ever tell you that?"

Still trying to process what she'd told me about Bryce, I shook my head.

"He said he didn't want us to have to

pay anything. It was a point of pride for him to be able to go to college without our assistance."

"That sounds like him," I admitted.

"Let me ask you something," she said, finally turning toward me again. "Do you know why Bryce has been fishing with his grandfather these past couple of weekends?"

"Because his grandfather needed his help, I guess. Because his dad isn't back yet."

Mrs. Trickett's mouth formed a sad smile. "My dad *doesn't* need Bryce's help. Usually he doesn't need Porter's help, either. Porter mainly helps with equipment and engine repairs, but on the water, my dad doesn't need anyone aside from the deckhand who's worked for him for decades. My dad's been a fisherman for over sixty years. Porter goes out with them because he likes to keep busy and enjoys being outside, and because he and my dad get along very well. The point is, I don't know why Bryce went out with him, but my dad mentioned that Bryce had brought up some things that concerned him."

"Like what?"

Her eyes were steady on mine. "Among

other things, that he's rethinking his decision to go to West Point."

At her words, I blinked. "But...that... doesn't make any sense," I finally stammered.

"It didn't make any sense to my dad, either. Or to me. I haven't mentioned it to Porter yet, but I doubt he'll know what to make of it."

"Of course he's going to West Point," I babbled. "We've talked about it plenty of times. And look at the way he's been exercising, trying to get ready."

"That's another thing," she said. "He stopped working out."

I hadn't expected that, either. "Is it because of Harvard? Because he wants to go there instead?"

"I don't know. If he does, he probably has to get the paperwork in soon. For all I know, the deadline might have passed." She lifted her eyes to the sky before bringing them back to me. "But my dad said he also asked a lot of questions about the fishing business, the cost of the boat, repair bills, things like that. He's been pestering my dad relentlessly for details."

All I could do was shake my head. "I'm sure it's nothing. He hasn't said anything to me about it. And you know how curious he is about everything."

"How has he been lately? How has he been acting?"

"He's been a little off ever since he gave away Daisy. I thought it was because he missed her." I didn't mention the moments when he'd seemed clingy; it felt too personal, somehow.

She scanned the water again, so blue today it almost hurt the eyes. "I don't think this has to do with Daisy," she concluded. Before I could dwell on what she'd just said, she put her hands on the wheels of her chair, clearly about to depart. "I just wanted to see if he'd mentioned anything to you, so thanks for talking to me. I'd better get home. Richard and Robert were doing some sort of science experiment and Lord only knows what might happen."

"Of course," I said.

She turned the wheelchair around, then stopped to face me again. "When is the baby due?"

"May ninth."

"Will you come to the house to say good-bye?"

"Maybe. I'm kind of trying to keep a low profile. But I want to thank all of you for being so kind and welcoming to me."

She nodded as though she'd expected the answer, but her expression remained troubled.

"Do you want me to try to talk to him?" I called out as she wheeled toward the van.

She merely waved and answered over her shoulder, "I have the sense that he's going to be talking to you."

I was still sitting on the steps when Aunt Linda returned from the shop an hour later. I watched her pull up, saw her studying me before finally getting out of the car.

"Are you okay?" she asked, coming to a stop before me.

When I shook my head, she helped me stand up. Back inside, she led me to the kitchen table and sat across from me. In time, she reached for my hand.

"Do you want to tell me what happened?"

Taking a deep breath, I went through it all, and when I finished, her expression was soft.

"I could tell she was concerned about Bryce when I saw her earlier."

"What should I say to him? Should I talk to him? Should I tell him that he has to go to West Point? Or at least tell him to speak to his parents about what he's thinking?"

"Are you supposed to know any of it?"

I shook my head. Then, "I don't know what's going on with him."

"I think you probably do."

You, she meant. "But he knows I'm leaving," I protested. "He's known all along. We've talked about it lots of times."

She seemed to consider her response. "Maybe," she said, her voice soft, "he didn't like what you said."

I didn't sleep well that night and on Sunday, I found myself wishing I could have done the twelve-hour church-marathon thing as a distraction from the churn of my thoughts. When Gwen came over to check on me, I could barely concentrate, and after she left, I felt even worse. No matter where I went in the house, my concerns followed, raising one question after another. Even the occasional Braxton Hicks contraction didn't divert me for long, as inured as I was becoming to the spasms. I was exhausted with worry.

It was April 21. The baby was due in eighteen days.

When Bryce came to the house on Monday morning, he said little about his weekend. I asked him about it in a conversational way and he mentioned that they'd had to go farther offshore than they'd originally planned, but the season for yellowfin tuna had heated up, and on both days, they'd had a decent haul. He said nothing about his reasons for vanishing the previous two weekends, nor about his college plans, and unsure whether to go on, I let the topic pass.

Instead, it was business as usual, almost like nothing was amiss. More studying, even more photography. By then, I understood the camera like the back of my hand and could make adjustments blindfolded; I'd practically memorized the technical aspects of every photo in the file box and understood the mistakes I'd made when taking my own photos. When my aunt got home, she asked if Bryce had a few minutes to help her install more shelves for the book section of the shop. He willingly agreed, though I stayed behind.

"How did it go?" I asked when she returned alone.

"He's like his father. He can do anything," she marveled.

"How was he?"

"No strange questions or comments, if that's what you're asking."

"He seemed okay with me today, too."

"That's good, right?"

"I guess."

"I forgot to mention it earlier, but I spoke to

the headmaster and your parents today about school."

"Why?"

She explained, and although I was in accordance, she must have seen something in my expression. "Are you doing okay?"

"I don't know," I admitted. And even though Bryce had acted as if everything was normal, I think he was unsure as well.

The rest of the week was much the same, except that Bryce ate dinner with my aunt and me on both Tuesday and Wednesday. On Thursday, after I'd taken three exams and my aunt had returned to the shop, he asked me on a second date for the following evening—another dinner—but I quickly declined.

"I really don't want to be gawked at in public," I said.

"Then why don't I make dinner here? We can watch a movie afterwards."

"We don't have a TV."

"I can bring mine over, along with the

VCR. We could watch *Dirty Dancing* or whatever."

"*Dirty Dancing?*"

"My mom loved it. I haven't seen it."

"How can you not have seen *Dirty Dancing?*"

"In case you haven't noticed, there are no movie theaters in Ocracoke."

"It came out when I was a little kid."

"I've been busy."

I laughed. "I'm going to have to check with my aunt to make sure it's okay."

"I know."

As soon as he said it, my mind suddenly flashed to his mom's visit the previous weekend. "Does it have to be an early night? If you're going fishing on Saturday again?"

"I'll be here this weekend. There's something I want to show you."

"Another cemetery?"

"No. But I think you'll like it."

After I completed my exams on Friday morning with satisfying results, Aunt Linda not only agreed to the second date but added that she'd be happy to spend the evening at Gwen's. "It's not much of a date if I'm sitting there with you. What time do you need me to be out of here?"

"Is five o'clock okay?" Bryce asked. "So I have time to make dinner?"

"That's fine," she said, "but I'll likely be home by nine."

After she left to head back to the shop, Bryce mentioned that his dad would be returning home the following week. "I'm not sure exactly when, but I know my mom is happy about it."

"Aren't you?"

"Of course," he affirmed. "Things are easier at the house when he's around. The twins aren't so wild."

"Your mom seems to have it under control."

"She does. But she doesn't like always having to be the bad guy."

"I can't imagine your mom being the bad guy."

"Don't let her fool you," he said. "She's pretty tough when she needs to be."

Bryce left in midafternoon to take care of a few chores. Waking from a late-afternoon nap, I found myself staring in the mirror. Even my stretchy jeans—the bigger ones—were getting tight, and the larger tops my mom had bought for me at Christmas merely stretched across the bulge.

With no possibility of looking dazzling in an outfit, I went a little bolder with makeup than usual, primarily using my Hollywood-quality eyeliner skills; aside from Photoshop, applying eyeliner was the only thing I'd ever been naturally good at. When I stepped out of the bathroom, even Aunt Linda did a quick double take.

"Too much?" I asked.

"I'm not the proper judge of such things," she said. "I don't wear makeup, but I think you look striking."

"I'm tired of being pregnant," I whined.

"At thirty-eight weeks, all women are tired of being pregnant," she said. "Some of the girls I worked with would start doing pelvic tilts in the hopes of inducing labor."

"Did it work?"

"Hard to say. One poor girl went more than two weeks past her expected due date and did pelvic tilts for hours, crying in frustration. It was miserable for her."

"Why didn't the doctor induce labor?"

"The physician we worked with back then was pretty conservative. He liked pregnancies to run their natural course. Unless, of course, the woman's life was in danger."

"In danger?"

"Sure," she said. "Pre-eclampsia can be very dangerous, for instance. It makes the blood pressure skyrocket. But there are other issues, too."

I'd been avoiding thinking about such things, skipping over any frightening chapters in the book my mom had given me. "Am I going to be okay?"

"Of course you are," she said, squeezing my shoulder. "You're young and healthy. Anyway, Gwen has been keeping a close eye on you, and she says you're doing great."

Though I nodded, I couldn't help noting

that the other girls she'd been talking about had been young and healthy, too.

Bryce arrived promptly, carrying a grocery bag. He visited with my aunt briefly before she left and then returned to his truck to get the television and VCR. He spent a little while setting it all up in the living room, making sure the system worked, then got down to business in the kitchen.

With my feet hurting and feeling the discomfort of yet another Braxton Hicks contraction coming on, I took a seat at the kitchen table. After the contraction passed and I could breathe normally again, I asked, "Do you need my help?"

I didn't bother to hide the tepid nature of my offer, and clearly Bryce picked up on it.

"I guess you could go outside and chop wood for the fire."

"Ha, ha."

"No worries. I've got it. It's not too hard."

"What are you making?"

"Beef Stroganoff and a salad. You mentioned it was one of your favorites and Linda
gave me the recipe."

Because he'd been at the house so many
times, he didn't need my help to find knives
or the chopping block. I watched him dice
lettuce, cucumbers, and tomatoes for the
salad, then onions, mushrooms, and the steak
for the entrée. He got a pot boiling on the
stove for the egg noodles, dusted the steak
in flour and spices, then browned it in butter
and olive oil. He sautéed the onions and
mushrooms in the same pan as the steak,
added the steak back in with beef broth and
cream of mushroom soup. The sour cream,
I knew, would be added at the end; I'd seen
Aunt Linda make it more than once.

As he cooked, we chatted about my pregnancy and how I was feeling. When I asked
him again about the fishing trips, he said
nothing about the things that had concerned
his mother. Instead, he described the early-
morning outings, a hint of reverence in his
tone.

"My grandfather just knows where the fish
will be," he said. "We left the docks with four

other boats, and they each went in a different direction. We pulled in more than anyone else every time."

"He's had a lot of experience."

"So have the others," he said. "Some of them have been fishing nearly as long as he has."

"He seems like an interesting man," I observed. "Even if I still can't understand a word he says."

"Did I mention that Richard and Robert have been learning the dialect? Which is kind of hard to do, since there's no book on it. They've been having my mom make recordings and then they memorize them."

"But not you?"

"I've been too busy tutoring this girl from Seattle. It takes a lot of time."

"The brilliant, beautiful one, right?"

"How did you know?" he responded with a grin.

When dinner was ready, I summoned the energy to set the table; the salad went into a bowl on the side. He'd also brought over powdered lemonade, which I mixed in a pitcher before we sat down to eat.

Dinner was delicious and I reminded myself to get the recipe before I left. For most of the meal, we reminisced about our childhoods, a memory of his sparking a memory of mine and vice versa. Despite my massive tummy—or maybe because of it—I couldn't eat very much, but Bryce had a second helping and we didn't settle into the living room until half past six.

I leaned into him as we watched the movie, his arm around my shoulders. He seemed to enjoy it and I did, too, even though I'd seen it five or six times. Along with *Pretty Woman*, it was one of my favorites. When the film reached the climax—when Johnny lifted Baby on the dance floor in front of her parents—I had tears in my eyes, like always. As the credits rolled, Bryce looked over, amazed.

"Really? You're crying?"

"I'm pregnant and hormonal. Of course I'm crying."

"But they danced well. It's not like one of them got hurt or she messed up."

I knew he was just teasing me and I rose from my spot on the couch to retrieve a box of tissues. I blew my nose—so much for trying to be glamorous, but with my tummy, I knew glamour was a long way off. Meanwhile, Bryce seemed inordinately pleased with himself and when I returned to the couch, he put his arm around me again.

"I don't think I'm going to go back to school," I said.

"Ever?"

I rolled my eyes. "I mean when I get home. My aunt talked with my parents and the headmaster, and they're going to let me take my finals at home. I'll start up again next fall."

"Is that what you want to do?"

"I think it would be weird to show up right before school lets out for the summer."

"How are things with your parents? Do you still talk to them once a week?"

"Yeah," I said. "We usually don't talk long."

"Do they tell you that they miss you?"

"Sometimes. Not always." I shifted slightly, leaning into his warmth. "They're not the touchy-feely types."

"With Morgan they are."

"Not really. They're proud of her and brag

about her, but that's different. And deep down, I know that they love us both. For my parents, sending me here is a sign of how much they love me."

"Even if it was hard for you?"

"It's been hard for them, too. And I think my situation would be hard for most parents."

"How about your friends? Any word about them?"

"Morgan said that she saw Jodie at the prom. I guess some senior brought her, but I don't know who it was."

"Isn't it a little early for prom?"

"My school hosts the proms in April. Don't ask me why. I've never thought about it."

"Have you ever wanted to go to a prom?"

"I haven't thought about that, either," I said. "I guess I would if someone asked, depending on who they were or whatever. But who knows if my parents would let me go, even if I did get asked?"

"Are you nervous about how things will be with your parents when you get back?"

"A little," I conceded. "For all I know, they're not going to let me out of the house again until I'm eighteen."

"And college? Have you changed your mind about that? I think you'd do well in college."

"Maybe if I had a full-time tutor."

"So...let me get this straight. You might be stuck in the house until you're eighteen, your friends might have forgotten you, and your parents haven't told you lately that they missed you. Did I get all that right?"

I smiled, knowing I'd verged on melodrama, even if it did feel more than a little true. "Sorry for being such a downer."

"You're not," he said.

I lifted my head and when we kissed, I could feel his hands in my hair. I wanted to tell him that I was going to miss him but knew the words would make me start crying again.

"This has been a perfect night," I whispered instead.

He kissed me again before his eyes lingered on mine. "Every night with you is perfect."

Bryce came over the following day—the last Saturday in April—and again, he seemed his normal self. His mom had ordered a new photography book from a store in Raleigh, and we spent a couple of hours looking through it. After a lunch of leftovers, we went for another walk on the beach. As we strolled through the sand, I wondered if this was the spot he'd wanted to bring me to, the one he'd mentioned on Thursday. But when he said nothing, I gradually accepted the idea that he'd just wanted to get me out of the house for a while. It was strange to think that Bryce's mom had come to see me just a week ago.

"How are the workouts going?" I finally asked.

"I haven't done much in the last couple of weeks."

"Why not?"

"I needed a break."

It wasn't much of an answer...or then again, maybe it was, and his mom had been reading too much into it.

"Well," I began, "you were working out hard for a long time. You're going to run circles around your entire class."

"We'll see."

Another nonanswer. Bryce could sometimes employ doublespeak as well as my aunt. Before I could clarify, he changed the subject. "Do you still wear the necklace I gave you?"

"Every day," I answered. "I love it."

"When I was having it engraved, I wondered whether to add my name, so you would remember who bought it for you."

"I won't forget. Besides, I like what you wrote."

"It was my dad's idea."

"I'll bet it will be good to see him, huh?"

"Yeah," he said. "There's something I need to speak with him about."

"What?"

Instead of answering, he simply squeezed my hand, and I felt a sudden flutter of fear at the idea that as normal as he seemed on the surface, I had no idea what was going on with him at all.

On Sunday morning, Gwen came by to check on me and let me know that I was "almost there," something the mirror had made pretty obvious.

"How are your Braxton Hicks?"

"Irritating," I answered.

She ignored my comment. "You might start thinking about getting a bag ready for the hospital."

"I still have time, don't you think?"

"Toward the end, it's impossible to predict. Some women go into labor early; some take a little longer than expected."

"How many babies have you delivered? I don't think I've ever asked."

"I can't remember exactly. Maybe a hundred?"

My eyes widened. "You've delivered a hundred babies?"

"Something like that. There are two other pregnant women on the island right now. I'll probably do their deliveries."

"Are you upset that I wanted to go to the hospital instead?"

"Not in the slightest."

"I also want to thank you. For staying here on Sundays and checking on me, I mean."

"It wouldn't be right to leave you alone. You're still young."

I nodded, though part of me wondered if I would ever feel young again.

Bryce showed up soon after, wearing khakis and a polo along with loafers, looking older and more serious than usual.

"Why are you dressed up?" I asked.

"There's something I want to show you. The thing I mentioned the other day."

"The not-another-cemetery thing?"

"That's the one," he said. "But no worries. I swung by right before coming here, and there's no one around." Reaching out, he took my hand and kissed the back of it. "You ready?"

All at once, I knew he'd planned something big, and I took a small step backward. "Let me brush my hair first."

I'd already brushed my hair, but I retreated to my bedroom, wishing there were a way to rewind the last couple of minutes and just start over. While Recent Bryce had occasionally seemed off, today's version was entirely new, and all I could think was that I wished Old Bryce had shown up instead. I wanted to see him in jeans and his olive jacket, with a file box of photos beneath his arm. I wanted him at the table, helping me learn equations or quizzing me on Spanish vocabulary; I wanted Bryce to hold me like he had on the beach that night with the kite, when all felt right with the world.

But New Bryce—all dressed up and who'd kissed my hand—was waiting for me, and as we started down the steps, I had another Braxton Hicks contraction. I had to grip the rail while Bryce looked on in concern.

"It's getting close, isn't it?"

"Eleven days, give or take," I answered, wincing. When the feeling finally passed and I knew I could safely move again, I waddled the rest of the way down. From the bed of the truck, Bryce grabbed a small step stool so I could climb in, just like he'd done before we'd gone to the beach.

The drive took only a few minutes and it wasn't until he'd turned off the engine at the end of a dirt road that I even realized we were there. Beyond the windshield, I stared at a small cottage. Unlike at my aunt's place, the nearest neighbors were barely visible through the trees and there was no water in sight. As for the dwelling itself, it was smaller than my aunt's, set lower to the ground, and even more dilapidated. The wooden planking was faded and peeling, the railings on the front porch appeared to be rotting away, and I noted clumps of moss on the shingles. It wasn't until I spotted the FOR RENT sign that I felt a sudden sense of dread, my breath catching in my throat as the pieces came together.

Lost in my daze, I hadn't heard Bryce get out of the truck, and by then he had reached my side. The door swung open, the step stool already in place. He reached for my arm and helped me down and my brain started repeating the word *no*...

"I know that what I'm about to say might sound crazy at first, but I've given it a lot of thought over the last few weeks. Trust me when I tell you it's the only solution that makes any sense."

I closed my eyes. "Please," I whispered. "Don't."

He went on, as though he hadn't heard me. Or maybe, I thought, I hadn't said the words aloud, only thought them, because none of this felt real. It had to be a dream...

"From the first moment we met, I've known how special you are," Bryce began. His voice sounded close and distant at the same time. "And the more time we spent together, the more I realized that I'd never meet anyone like you again. You're beautiful and smart and kind, you have a great sense of humor, and all of that makes me love you in a way that I know I'm never going to be able to love anyone else."

I opened my mouth to speak, but nothing came out. Bryce kept going, his words coming even faster.

"I know you're going to have the baby and that you're supposed to leave right afterwards, but even you admit that going home will be a challenge. You don't have a great relationship with your parents, you don't know what will happen with your friends, and you deserve more than that. We both deserve more, and that's why I brought you here. That's why I went fishing with my grandfather."

No, no, no, no...

"We can stay here," he said. "You and me. I don't have to go to West Point, and you don't have to go back to Seattle. You can homeschool like I did, and I'm sure we could get everything done so you can graduate next year, even if you decide to keep the baby. And after that, maybe I go to college, or maybe we both go. We'll figure it out like my parents did."

"Keep the baby? I'm only sixteen..." I finally croaked out.

"In North Carolina, if there's a birth of a child, we can petition the courts and they'd allow you to stay. If we live here together, you could be emancipated. It's a little complicated, but I know I can find a way to make it work."

"Please stop," I whispered, knowing I'd somehow been expecting this since the moment he'd kissed my hand.

He suddenly seemed to recognize how overwhelmed I felt. "I know it's a lot to take in right now, but I don't want to lose you."

He drew in a deep breath. "The point is, I've found a way that we can be together. I have enough money in the bank to afford to rent this house for almost a year, and I know I can earn enough working with my grandfather to pay the rest of the bills without you having to work at all. I'm willing to tutor you in school, and I want nothing more than to be the father of your baby. I promise to love and adore her and treat her like my own daughter, even adopt her, if you're willing to let me do that." He reached for my hand, taking it, before lowering himself to one knee. "I love you, Maggie. Do you love me?"

Even though I knew where all of this was going, I couldn't lie to him. "Yes, I love you."

He looked up at me, eyes beseeching. "Will you marry me?"

Hours later, I sat on the couch, waiting for my aunt to return in what can only be likened to shell shock. Even my bladder seemed stunned into submission. As soon as Aunt Linda got home, she must have noted my expression and she immediately sat beside me. When she asked what had happened, I told her everything, but it wasn't until I finished that she finally asked the obvious.

"What did you say?"

"I couldn't say anything. The world was spinning, like I'd been caught in a whirlpool, and when I didn't speak, Bryce finally said that I didn't have to answer right away. But he asked me to think about it."

"I was afraid this might happen."

"You knew?"

"I know Bryce. Not as well as you know him, obviously, but enough not to be completely blindsided. I think his mom was worried about something like this as well."

No doubt about it, and I wondered why I alone hadn't seen it coming. "As much as I love him, I can't marry him. I'm not ready to be a mom or a wife or even to be a grown-up yet. I came here just wanting to put all of this behind me so I could go back to my normal life, even if it is kind of boring. And he's right—things could be better back home with my parents or my sister or whatever, but they're still my family."

Even as I said the words, my eyes filled with tears and I began to cry. I couldn't help it. I hated myself for that, even as I knew I was telling the truth.

Aunt Linda reached over and squeezed my hand. "You're wiser and more mature than you think you are."

"What am I going to do?"

"You're going to need to speak with him."

"What should I say?"

"You need to tell him the truth. He deserves that much."

"He's going to hate me."

"I doubt that," she said, her voice quiet. "What about Bryce? Do you think he really thought this through? That he's really ready to be a husband and father? To live in Ocracoke as a fisherman, or doing odd jobs? To give up West Point?"

"He said that's what he wanted."

"What do you want for him?"

"I want..." What did I want? For him to be happy? To be a success? To chase his dreams? To become an older version of the young man I'd learned to love? To stay with me forever?

"I just don't want to hold him back," I finally said.

Her smile couldn't hide the sadness in her expression. "Do you think you would?"

The stress I was feeling made restful sleep impossible, and—maybe because I'd been in shock earlier—the Braxton Hicks contractions returned, with a vengeance, making their presence known all night long. Almost every time I was about ready to doze off, another would strike and I'd have to squeeze Maggie-bear hard just to get through it. I woke up Monday morning exhausted, and even then, they kept going.

Bryce didn't show up at the house at his usual time, and I wasn't in any mood to study. Instead, I spent most of the morning on the porch, thinking about Bryce. My mind flitted through dozens of imaginary conversations, none of them good, even as I reminded myself that I'd known all along that falling in love made a painful and terrible goodbye inevitable. I'd just never expected it to be like this.

I knew he'd come, though. As the morning sun gradually warmed the air, I could almost sense his spirit. I imagined him lying on his bed, his hands clasped behind his head, his eyes focused on the ceiling. Every now and then, he'd likely glance at the clock, wondering whether I needed more time before I was ready to give him an answer. I knew he'd want me to say yes, but what did he think would happen even if I did? Did he expect the two of us to march over to his house and tell his mom and that she'd be happy about it? Did he hope to listen on the phone while I called my parents and told them? Didn't he know they'd fight the idea of emancipation? And what if his parents stopped speaking to him? And all of that ignored the fact that I was only sixteen and in no way ready for the kind of life he'd proposed.

As Aunt Linda had implied, it didn't seem like he'd really thought through the ramifications. He seemed to view the answer through a lens that focused only on the two of us seeing each other, as though no one else would be affected. As romantic as that sounded, it wasn't reality, and it ignored my feelings as well.

I think that's what was bothering me most. I knew Bryce well enough to assume that the reasons made sense to him, and all I could think was that he, like me, suspected that a long-distance relationship wouldn't work for us. We might be able to write and call— though calls would be expensive—but when would we be able to see each other again? If I doubted whether my parents were going to let me date, there wasn't a chance they'd let me go to the East Coast to see him. Not until I graduated, and even then, if I was still living at home, they might not agree. Which meant at least two years, maybe more. And what about him? Could he fly out to Seattle in the summers? Or did West Point have mandatory leadership programs when school wasn't in session? Part of me thought they probably did, and even if not, Bryce was the type of person who'd ordinarily line up an internship at the Pentagon or whatever. And, as close as he was to his family, he'd have to spend time with them as well.

Could you continue to love and be with someone if you never spent any time with them?

For Bryce, I began to understand, the answer was no. Something within him needed to see me, hold me, touch me. Kiss me. He knew that if I returned to Seattle and he went to West Point, not only were these things impossible, but we wouldn't even have the kind of simple moments that led to us falling in love in the first place. We wouldn't study at the table or walk the beach; we wouldn't spend afternoons taking photographs or developing prints in the darkroom. No lunches or dinners or watching movies while sitting on the couch. He'd live his life and I'd live mine, we'd grow and change, and distance would take its inevitable toll, like drops of water wearing down a stone. He'd meet someone or I would, and eventually, our relationship would come to an end, leaving nothing but Ocracoke memories in its wake.

For Bryce, either we could be together or we couldn't; there were no shades of gray, because all those shades reached the same inevitable conclusion. And, I admitted, he was probably right. But because I loved him, and though it was going to break my heart, I suddenly knew exactly what I had to do.

The realization, I'm pretty sure, caused another Braxton Hicks, this one the strongest yet. It lasted what seemed like forever but finally passed only minutes before Bryce finally showed up. Unlike the day before, he was in jeans and a T-shirt, and though he smiled, there was something tentative about it. Because the day was pleasant, I gestured for him to lead the way back down the stairs. We took a seat in the same spot I'd been when his mother had come by.

"I can't marry you," I said straight-out, and watched as he suddenly lowered his gaze. He clasped his hands together, the sight of it making me ache. "It's not because I don't love you, because I do. It has to do with me and who I am. And who you are, too."

For the first time he glanced over.

"I'm too young to be a mother and a wife. And you're too young to be a husband and father, especially since the child wouldn't even be yours. But I think you already know those things. Which means you wanted me to say yes for all the wrong reasons."

"What are you talking about?"

"You don't want to lose me," I said. "That's not the same thing as wanting to be with me."

"They mean exactly the same thing," he protested.

"No, they don't. Wanting to be with someone is a positive thing. It's about love and respect and desire. But not wanting to lose someone isn't about those things. It's about fear."

"I do love you, though. And respect you—"

I reached for his hand to stop him. "I know. And I think you're the most incredible, intelligent, kind, and handsome guy I've ever met. It scares me to think that I met the love of my life at sixteen, but maybe I have. And maybe I'm making the biggest mistake of my life by saying what I am. But I'm not right for you, Bryce. You don't even really know me."

"Of course I know you."

"You fell in love with the marooned, six-teen-year-old pregnant and lonely version of me, who also happened to be just about the only girl in Ocracoke even close to your age. I barely know who I am these days and it's hard for me to remember who I was before I got here. Which also means that I have no idea who I'm going to be when I'm a year older and I'm not pregnant. You don't know, either."

"That's silly."

I forced myself to keep my voice steady. "Do you know what I've been thinking about ever since we met? I've been trying to picture who you'll be when you're an adult. Because I look at you and see someone who could probably be the president, if that's what you set your mind to. Or fly helicopters or earn a million dollars or be the next Rambo or become an astronaut or anything else, be-cause your future is unlimited. You have a potential that others can only dream about, simply because you're you. And I could never ask you to give up those kinds of opportunities."

"I told you that I could go to college next year—"

"I know you could," I said. "Just as I know you'd always take me into account when you made that decision, too. But even that's a limit and I couldn't live with myself if I thought my presence in your life would ever take anything away from you."

"How about if we wait a few years, then? Until I graduate?"

I raised an eyebrow. "A long engagement?"

"It doesn't have to be an engagement. We can date."

"How? We won't be able to see each other."

When he closed his eyes, I knew my earlier thoughts had been correct. There was something in him that didn't only want but also needed me.

"Maybe I could go to school in Washington," he muttered.

I could tell he was grasping, making it hard to go on. But I had no other choice. "And give up your dream? I know how much you've always wanted to go to West Point, and I want that for you, too. It would break my heart to think you gave up even one of your dreams for me. I want nothing more than for you to know I loved you enough to never take something like that away from you."

"Then what are we going to do? Just walk away as though you and I never happened?"

I felt my own sadness expanding through me like an inflating balloon. "We can pretend it was a beautiful dream, one that we remember forever. Because we both loved each other enough to allow the other to grow."

"That's not good enough. I can't imagine knowing that I'm never going to see you again."

"Then let's not say that. Let's give it a few years. Meanwhile, you make decisions that are best for your future, and I'll do the same. We go to school, we get jobs, we figure out who we are. And then, if we both think we want to give it another try, we can find each other and see what happens."

"How long are you thinking?"

I swallowed, feeling the pressure behind my eyes begin to build. "My mom met my dad when she was twenty-four."

"More than seven years from now? That's crazy." In his eyes, I thought I saw something like fear.

"Maybe. But if it works then, we'll know it's right."

"Do we talk until then? Or write letters?"

That would be too hard for me, I knew. If I received regular letters, I'd never stop thinking about him, nor would he stop thinking about me. "How about a single Christmas card every year?"

"Are you going to date other people?"

"I don't have anyone in mind, if that's what you're asking."

"But you're not saying that you won't."

The tears began to fall. "I don't want to fight with you. I've known all along that saying goodbye would be hard, and this is all I can think to do. If we're meant to be, we can't just love each other as teenagers. We have to love each other as adults. Don't you get that?"

"I'm not trying to fight. It's just such a long time..." His voice cracked.

"It is for me, too. And I hate that I'm saying this to you. But I'm not good enough for you, Bryce. Not yet, anyway. Please give me a chance to be, okay?"

He said nothing. Instead, he gently brushed the moisture from my cheeks. "Ocracoke," he finally whispered.

"What?"

"On your twenty-fourth birthday, let's plan to meet at the beach. Where we had our date, okay?"

I nodded, wondering if it would even be possible, and when he kissed me, I thought I could almost taste his sadness. Instead of staying with me, he helped me to my feet and put his arms around me. I could smell him, clean and fresh, like the island where we'd met.

"I can't help thinking I'm running out of days to hold you. Can I see you tomorrow?"

"I'd like that," I whispered, feeling his body against my own, already knowing that the next goodbye would be even worse and wondering how I would ever get through it.

What I didn't know then was that I would never get the chance.

MERRY CHRISTMAS

Manhattan
December 2019

Seated at the table with the remnants of dinner in front of them, Maggie noted Mark's rapt attention. Though the food had arrived about half an hour later than expected, they'd finished eating somewhere around the point in the story when she'd told him that she'd ridden with Bryce to drop off Daisy. Or rather, Mark had finished; Maggie had only picked at her food. Now it was coming up on eleven and Christmas Day was only an hour away. Remarkably, Maggie wasn't exhausted or uncomfortable, especially compared to how she'd been feeling earlier. Reliving the past had revived her in a way she hadn't expected.

"What do you mean you never got the chance?"

"Those Braxton Hicks I'd been having that Monday weren't Braxton Hicks. They were actual labor contractions."

"And you didn't know?"

"Not at first. It wasn't until Bryce left and the next one hit that the thought even crossed my mind. Because that one was a doozy. But I was still so emotional about Bryce, and because my due date wasn't until the following week, I somehow tucked the thought away until my aunt got home. By then, of course, I'd had even more contractions."

"What happened?"

"As soon as I mentioned that they'd been coming more frequently and were a lot stronger, she called Gwen. By then, it was at least a quarter past three, maybe half past. When Gwen arrived, it took her less than a minute to make the decision to go to the hospital, because she didn't think I'd make it until the morning ferry. My aunt tossed a bunch of things in my duffel bag—the only thing I really cared about was Maggie-bear—then called my parents and the doctor and we were out the door. Thank God the ferry wasn't crowded and we were able to get on. I think that by then, the contractions were coming every ten to fifteen minutes apart. Usually, you wait until they're five minutes apart before you go to the hospital, but the ferry and drive to the hospital was three and a half hours. A long three and a half hours, I might add. By the time the ferry docked, the contractions were coming four to five minutes apart. I'm amazed I didn't squeeze the stuffing out of Maggie-bear."

"But you made it."

"I did. But what I remember most was how calm my aunt and Gwen were the whole time. No matter how many crazy noises I made when the contractions hit, they just kept chatting away like nothing unusual was going on at all. I guess they'd driven lots of pregnant mothers to the hospital."

"Did the contractions hurt?"

"It was like a baby dinosaur chomping through my uterus."

He laughed. "And?"

"We got to the hospital, and I was checked into a room on the maternity floor. The doctor came by, and both my aunt and Gwen stayed with me for the next six hours until I was finally dilated. Gwen had me concentrate on my breathing, my aunt brought me ice chips—all the usual things, I guess. Sometime around one a.m. or so, I was ready to deliver. The next thing I knew, nurses were getting things ready and the doctor came in. And three or four pushes later, it was over."

"That doesn't sound so bad."

"You forgot the munching baby dinosaur. Every single contraction was agonizing."

It had been, even if she could no longer remember the exact sensation. In the dim light, Mark seemed transfixed.

"And Gwen was right. It was a good thing you caught the afternoon ferry."

"I'm pretty sure Gwen could have handled the birth, since there weren't any complications. But I did feel better about being in a hospital instead of giving birth on my bed or whatever."

He stared at the tree before coming back to her again. Sometimes, she thought, he seemed so familiar to her, it was scary.

"What happened after that?"

"Lots of commotion, of course. The doctor made sure I was okay, checked the afterbirth while the pediatrician examined the baby. Weight, Apgar, measurements, and immediately afterwards, the nurse whisked the baby to the nursery. And just like that, it was all suddenly behind me. Even now, it sometimes seems surreal, more like a dream than reality. But after the doctor and nurses cleared out, I grabbed Maggie-bear and started to cry and I couldn't stop for a long time. I remember that my aunt was on one side of me and Gwen was on the other, both of them consoling me."

"It had to have been very emotional."

"It was," she said. "But I'd known all along that it would be. And of course, by the time my tears stopped falling, it was the middle of the night. My aunt and Gwen had been up nearly twenty-four hours straight and I was even more tired than they were. We all eventually fell asleep. They'd brought in an extra chair for my aunt—Gwen used the other one—so I can't speak to how much rest they actually got. But I was out like a light.

I know the doctor came in sometime during the morning to make sure I was doing okay, but I barely remember that. I went right back to sleep and didn't wake again until almost eleven. I remember thinking how strange it was to wake up in the hospital bed alone, because neither my aunt nor Gwen was there. I was starved, too, but my breakfast was still on the tray. I had to eat it cold, but I couldn't have cared less."

"Where were your aunt and Gwen?"

"In the cafeteria." When he tilted his head slightly, Maggie changed the subject. "Is there still any eggnog in the back?"

"There is. Would you like me to get you a glass?"

"If you wouldn't mind."

Maggie watched as Mark rose from the table and headed toward the back. As he vanished from sight, she felt her mind drift back to the moment Aunt Linda had entered the room, the past becoming real again.

*Carteret General Hospital, Morehead City
1996*

Aunt Linda approached the bed before pulling up a chair. Reaching over, she brushed the hair from my eyes.

"How are you feeling? You slept a long time."

"I think I needed it," I said. "Did the doctor come in earlier?"

"He did," she said. "He said you were doing very well. You should be out of the hospital tomorrow morning."

"I have to stay another night?"

"They like to monitor you for at least twenty-four hours."

The sunlight from the window behind her seemed to frame her in a golden halo.

"How's the baby?"

"Perfect," she said. "The staff is excellent and it was a quiet night. I think yours is the only one in the nursery right now."

I absorbed what she'd said, imagining the scene, and the next words came automatically. "Do you think you could do something for me?"

"Of course."

"Can you bring Maggie-bear to the nursery? And let the nurses know that I'd like the baby to have her? And maybe they could tell the parents, too?"

My aunt knew how much Maggie-bear meant to me. "Are you sure?"

"I think the baby needs her more than I do right now."

My aunt offered a tender smile. "I think that's a wonderful and generous gift."

I handed her the teddy bear, watching as she cradled it before reaching for my hand. "Now that you're awake, can we talk about the adoption?" When I nodded, she went on. "You know you're going to have to formally give the baby up, which means paperwork, of course. I've reviewed it, so has Gwen, and as I mentioned to your parents, we've worked for years with the woman who set up the adoption. You can trust me that everything is in order, or if you wish, I could arrange for you to have an attorney."

"I trust you," I said. And I did. I think I trusted my aunt Linda more than anyone.

"The important thing you should know is

that this is a closed adoption. You remember what that means, right?"

"That I don't know who the parents are, right? And they won't know me?"

"That's correct. I want to make sure that's still what you'd like to do."

"It is," I said. The thought of knowing anything would drive me crazy. "Are the new parents here yet?"

"I heard that they arrived this morning, so we'll take care of the paperwork in a little bit. But there's something else you should probably know."

"What is it?"

She took a deep breath. "Your mom is here now, and she's arranged for you to fly home tomorrow. The doctor wasn't thrilled by that because of the possibility of blood clots, but your mom was fairly insistent about it."

I blinked. "How did she get here so fast?"

"She found a flight yesterday right after I called. She actually arrived in New Bern late last night, before you delivered. She came by this morning to see you but you were still asleep. She hadn't eaten, so Gwen and I took her to the cafeteria to get her something."

Preoccupied with thoughts about my mom, I realized that I'd almost tuned out the other thing she'd told me. "Wait. Did you say I'm leaving tomorrow?"

"Yes."

"You mean I'm not going back to Ocracoke?"

"I'm afraid not."

"What about the rest of my things? And the picture Bryce gave me for Christmas?"

"I'll ship everything to you. You don't have to worry about that."

But...

"What about Bryce? I didn't even get a chance to say goodbye. I didn't say goodbye to his mom or his family, either."

"I know," she murmured. "But I don't think there's anything you can do. Your mom made the arrangements, and that's why I wanted to come up here to tell you right away. So you wouldn't be surprised."

I could feel the tears again, different tears than the previous night's, filled with a different kind of fear and pain.

"I want to see him again!" I cried. "I can't just leave like this."

"I know," she said, compassion weighting every word.

"We had a fight," I said. I could feel my lip beginning to quiver. "I mean, sort of a fight. I told him I couldn't marry him."

"I know," she whispered.

"You don't understand," I said. "I have to see him! Can't you try to talk to my mom?"

"I did," she said. "Your parents want you to come home."

"But I don't want to leave," I said. The thought of living with my parents again, not my aunt, wasn't something I could face right now.

"Your parents love you," she promised me, squeezing my hand. "Just like I love you."

But I feel it with you more than I do with them. I wanted to say that to her, but my throat locked up and this time, I simply gave in to the sobbing. And, just as I knew she would, my sweet and wonderful aunt Linda held me tight for a long time, even after my mom finally entered the room.

Manhattan
2019

"Are you okay? You look troubled."

Maggie watched as Mark set the eggnog in front of her. "I was remembering the next morning at the hospital," Maggie said. She reached for the glass while he took his seat again. When he was settled, she told him what had happened, noting his dismay.

"And that was it? You didn't return to Ocracoke?"

"I couldn't."

"Did Bryce make it to the hospital? Couldn't he have caught the ferry?"

"I'm sure he thought I'd be coming back to Ocracoke. But even if he had figured it out and made it to the hospital, I can't imagine what it would have been like with my mom there. After my aunt and Gwen left, I was devastated. My mom couldn't understand why I kept crying. She thought I was questioning the decision to give up the baby for adoption, and even though I'd already signed the papers, I think she was afraid that I was going to change my mind. She kept telling me that I was doing the right thing."

"Your aunt and Gwen left?"

"They needed to catch the afternoon ferry back to Ocracoke. I was a wreck after saying goodbye to them. Eventually my mom got tired of it. She kept going downstairs to get coffee, and after I had dinner, she ended up returning to the hotel."

"Leaving you alone? Even though you were so upset?"

"It was better than having her there and I think both of us knew it. Anyway, I eventually fell asleep and the next thing I really remember is the nurse wheeling me out of the hospital while my mom pulled up the rental car. My mom and I didn't have much to say to each other in the car or the airport, and once I got on the plane, I remember staring out the window and feeling the same sense of dread that I'd felt when I'd left Seattle to come to North Carolina. I didn't want to go. In my head, I kept trying to process everything that had happened. Even when I got home, I couldn't stop thinking about Bryce and Ocracoke. For a while, the only thing that made me feel better was Sandy. She knew I was struggling, and she wouldn't leave my side. She'd come into my room or follow me around the house, but of course every time I saw her, I was reminded of Daisy."

"And you didn't go back to school?"

"No," she said. "That was actually a good decision by my parents and the headmaster. When I think back, it's clear I was depressed. I slept all the time, had zero appetite, and wandered around feeling like a stranger in my own house. I wouldn't have been able to handle school. I couldn't concentrate at all, so I ended up bombing every single final. But because I'd done well until then, my overall grades still ended up okay. The only upside to my depression was that I dropped all the baby weight by the time summer started. After a while, I finally felt up to seeing Madison and Jodie, and little by little, I began to inch my way back into my old life."

"Did you talk or write to Bryce?"

"No. And he didn't call or write, either. I wanted to, every single day. But we had our plan, and whenever I thought about contacting him, I reminded myself that he was better off without me. That he needed to concentrate on him, just like I needed to focus on me. My aunt wrote to me regularly, though, and she'd offer the occasional nugget about Bryce. She informed me that he became an Eagle Scout, went off to college on schedule, and a couple of months after that, she mentioned that Bryce's mom had come by the shop to let her know that Bryce was doing exceptionally well."

"How were you doing?"

"Despite my renewed contact with my friends, I still felt strangely disconnected. I remember that after getting my driver's license, I'd sometimes borrow the car after church and visit garage sales. I was probably the only teenager in Seattle scouring the newspaper for used bonanzas."

"Did you ever find anything?"

"I did, actually," she said. "I found a Leica thirty-five-millimeter camera, older than the one Bryce used but still perfectly functional. I rushed home and begged my dad to buy it for me, promising to pay him back. To my surprise, he did. I think he understood more than my mom how desperate and displaced

I felt. After that, I started taking pictures, and that centered me. When school started, I joined the yearbook staff as a photographer so I could take photos in school, too. Madison and Jodie thought it was silly, but I couldn't have cared less. I'd spend hours at the public library, flipping through photography magazines and books, just like I did in Ocracoke. I'm pretty sure my dad thought the phase would pass, but at least he humored me when I showed him the photos I'd taken. My mom, on the other hand, was still doing her best to turn me into Morgan."

"How did that go?"

"It didn't. Compared to what they'd been in Ocracoke, my grades were terrible in my last two years of high school. Even though Bryce had taught me how to study, I couldn't make myself care enough to try all that hard. Which, of course, is one of the reasons I ended up at community college."

"There was another reason?"

"The community college actually had some classes that interested me. I didn't want to go to college and spend my first two years doing gen-ed and studying the same things I had in high school. The community college offered a class on Photoshop, and others on indoor and sports photography—they were taught by a local photographer—as well as a few classes in web design. I never forgot what Bryce had told me about the internet becoming the next big thing, so I figured that was something I needed to learn. Once I finished all those, I started working."

"Did you live at home the whole time you were in Seattle? With your parents?"

Maggie nodded. "The job didn't pay much, so I didn't have a choice. But it wasn't bad, if only because I didn't spend much time there. I was either at the studio or the lab or on location shooting, and the less I was around, the better my mom and I seemed to get along. Even if she still made it a point to let me know she thought I was wasting my life."

"How was your relationship with Morgan?"

"To my amazement, she was actually interested in what had happened to me while I'd been in Ocracoke. After making her swear not to tell our parents, I ended up spilling pretty much the whole story, and by the end of that first summer, we were closer than we had ever been. But once she started at Gonzaga, we drifted apart again because she was rarely at home. She took summer classes after her first year, worked at music camps the summers after that. And, of course, the older she got and the more she settled into college life, the more it became clear to both of us that we really didn't have anything in common. She didn't understand my lack of interest in college, couldn't relate to my passion for photography. In her mind, it was as if I had quit school to become a musician."

Mark leaned back in his chair and raised an eyebrow. "Did anyone ever figure it out? The real reason you'd gone to Ocracoke?"

"Believe it or not, they didn't. Madison and Jodie didn't suspect a thing. They had questions, of course, but I was vague in my answers, and soon enough, it was back to the usual. People saw us together and none of them really cared enough to probe in detail why I'd left. Like Aunt Linda had predicted, they were preoccupied with their own lives, not mine. When school started again in the fall, I was nervous on the first day, but everything was completely normal. People treated me exactly the same, and I never got wind of any rumors. Of course, I wandered the halls that entire year feeling like I had little in common with any of my classmates, even while I was taking pictures of them for the yearbook."

"How about your senior year?"

"It was strange," she mused. "Because no one ever mentioned it, by that point, my stay in Ocracoke began to feel like a dream. Aunt Linda and Bryce seemed as real as ever, but there were moments when I could convince myself that I'd never had a baby. As the years went on, that became even easier. One time, maybe ten years ago, a guy I'd met for coffee asked me if I had kids, and I told him no. Not because I wanted to lie to him but because in that instant, I truly didn't remember. Of course, almost immediately, I did remember, but there was no reason to correct myself. I had no desire to explain that chapter of my life."

"How about Bryce? Did you send him a Christmas card? You haven't mentioned him."

Maggie didn't answer right away. Instead,

she swirled the thick liquid in her glass before meeting Mark's eyes.

"Yes. I sent him a card that first Christmas after I returned home. Actually, I sent it to my aunt and asked her to deliver it to his house, because I couldn't remember Bryce's address. Aunt Linda was the one who put it in his mailbox. Part of me wondered whether he'd forgotten all about me, even though he'd promised that he wouldn't."

"Was the card...personal?" Mark inquired, his tone delicate.

"I wrote a message, just kind of updating him on what had gone on since I'd last seen him. I told him about the delivery, apologized for not saying goodbye. I told him that I'd gone back to school and bought a camera. But because I wasn't sure how he felt about me, it wasn't until the very end that I admitted that I still thought about him, and that the time we had together meant the world to me. I also told him that I loved him. I can still remember writing those words and being absolutely terrified of what he might think. What if he didn't bother to send a card? What if he'd moved on and met someone new? What if he'd eventually come to regret our time together? What if he was angry with me? I didn't have any idea what he was thinking or how he would respond."

"And?"

"He sent a card, too. It arrived only a day after I sent mine, so I knew he couldn't have read what I'd written, but he followed the same script I had. He told me he was happy at West Point, that he'd done well in his classes and had made a number of good friends. He mentioned that he'd seen his parents on Thanksgiving and that his brothers had already started exploring various colleges they might want to attend. And, just like I'd done, in the last paragraph, he told me that he missed me and he still loved me. He also reminded me of our plan to meet on my twenty-fourth birthday in Ocracoke."

Mark smiled. "That sounds just like him."

Maggie took another sip of her eggnog, still enjoying the taste. She made a note to keep it stocked in her refrigerator, assuming she'd be able to find it after the holidays. "It took a few more years of Christmas cards for me to believe that he was really committed to our plan. To us, I mean. Every year, I'd think to myself that this was the year the card wouldn't come or that he'd tell me it was over. But I was wrong. In every Christmas card that arrived, he counted down the years until we could see each other again."

"He never met anyone else?"

"I don't think he was interested. And I really didn't date much, either. In my last years of high school and community college, I was asked out here and there and occasionally I went, but I never had romantic interest in any of them. No one measured up to Bryce."

"And he graduated from West Point?"

"In 2000," she said. "Afterwards, like his dad, he went to work in military intelligence in Washington, D.C. I'd graduated from high school and finished taking classes at community college as well. Sometimes I think we should have followed his suggestion and reunited right after he graduated, instead of waiting until I was twenty-four. It all feels so arbitrary now," she said, a melancholy look coming over her. "Things would have turned out differently for us."

"What happened?"

"We both did what I'd recommended and became young adults. He worked at his job and I worked at mine. Photography was my whole world early on, not just because I was passionate about it but also because I wanted to be someone worthy of Bryce, not just someone he loved. Meanwhile, Bryce was making adult decisions about his life, too. Do you know that old army commercial? Where the song goes, 'Be all that you can be…in the army'?"

"Vaguely."

"Bryce had never given up on the idea of becoming a Green Beret, so he applied to SFAS. Aunt Linda wrote and told me about it. I guess Bryce's parents had mentioned it to her and she knew I'd want to know."

"What's SFAS?"

"Special Forces Assessment and Selection. It's at Fort Bragg, back in North Carolina. Long story short, Bryce was assessed with flying colors, eventually went through the training, and ended up being selected. All of that happened by the spring of 2002. Of course, by then, the military had made special forces a priority and wanted the highest-quality people they could find, so I'm not surprised Bryce made it."

"Why was it a priority?"

"Nine Eleven. You're probably too young to remember what a cataclysmic event that was, a turning point in America's history. In Bryce's Christmas card in 2002, he said that he couldn't tell me where he was—which even to me was a tip-off that he was someplace dangerous—but that he was doing okay. He also said that he might not be able to make it to Ocracoke the following October, when I was to turn twenty-four. He said that if he wasn't there, not to read anything into it— he'd find a way to let me know if he was still deployed and would arrange for an alternate time and place for us to finally meet."

She fell silent, remembering. Then: "Strangely, I wasn't all that disappointed. More than anything, I was amazed that after all those years, both of us still wanted to be together. Even now, it still seems implausible that our plan worked. I was proud of him and proud of myself, too. And of course, I was incredibly excited to see him again, no matter when that would be. But once again, it wasn't in the cards. Fate had something else in store for us."

Mark said nothing, waiting. Instead of speaking, Maggie faced the Christmas tree again, forcing herself not to dwell on what had happened next, a skill she'd mastered over the years. Instead, she stared at the lights, noting the shadows and tracking the movement of traffic outside the gallery door. When she was finally confident the memory had been fully locked away, she reached for her handbag to retrieve the envelope she'd stashed inside earlier, right before she'd left her apartment. Without a word, she handed it to Mark.

She didn't watch as he no doubt studied the return address and realized he was holding a letter from her aunt Linda; nor did she watch as he lifted the seal on the envelope. Though she'd read the letter only once, she knew with utter clarity what Mark would see on the page.

Dear Maggie,

It's late at night, rain is falling, and though I should have been asleep hours ago, I find myself at the table wondering whether I have the strength to tell you what I must. Part of me believes that I should talk to you in person, that maybe I should fly to Seattle and sit down with you at your parents' house, but I'm afraid you'll find out from other sources before I've had the chance to let you know what happened. Some of the information is already on the news, and that's why I overnighted this letter. I want you to know that I've been praying for hours, both for you and for me.

There is, after all, no easy way to tell you. There is nothing easy about any of this, nor is there any way to diminish the overwhelming grief I feel at the news that I received today. Please know that even now, I ache for you even more deeply, and as I write, I can barely see the page through the tears in my eyes. Know that I wish I could be there to hold you, and that I will forever pray for you.

Bryce was killed in Afghanistan last week.

I don't know the specifics. His father

didn't know much, either, but he believes that Bryce was caught in a firefight that somehow went wrong. They don't know when or where or how it happened, because information is scant. Perhaps in time, they'll know more, but for me, the details don't matter. For you, I doubt they matter, either. In times like this, it's hard even for me to understand the plan that God has for all of us, and it is a struggle to hold on to my faith. Right now, I am shattered.

I'm so sorry for you, Maggie. I know how much you loved him. I know how hard you've been working, and I know how much you wanted to see him again. You have my deepest and sincerest condolences. I am hopeful that God will grant you the strength you'll need to somehow get through this. I will regularly pray that you eventually find peace, no matter how long that takes. You are always in my heart.

I'm so very sorry for your loss. I love you.

Aunt Linda

Mark sat in stunned silence. As for Maggie, she kept her unseeing eyes fixed on the tree, trying to steer her memories down other paths—any path besides the one that led to her memories of what had happened to Bryce. She'd faced it once, had fully experienced the horror, and had vowed not to relive it. Despite her rigid self-control, she felt a tear slip down her cheek and swiped at it, knowing that another would likely follow.

"I know you probably have questions," she finally whispered. "But I don't have the answers. I never tried to find out exactly what happened to Bryce. Like my aunt said in the letter, the details didn't matter to me. All I knew was that Bryce was gone, and afterwards, something broke inside me. I went crazy. I wanted to run away from everything I knew, so I quit my job, left my family, and moved to New York. I stopped going to church, stayed out every night, and dated one bum after another for a long time, until that wound finally began to close. The only thing that kept me from going completely off the deep end was photography. Even when my life felt out of control, I tried to keep learning and improving. Because I knew that's what Bryce would have wanted me to do. And it was a way of hanging on to something we had shared."

"I'm...so sorry, Maggie." Mark seemed to struggle to control his voice. He swallowed. "I don't know what to say."

"There's nothing to say except that it was the darkest period of my life." She focused on steadying her breath, her ears half-tuned to the sound of Christmas Eve revelers in the street. When she spoke, her voice was subdued. "It wasn't until the gallery opened that a day passed when I didn't think about it. When I wasn't angry or sad about what had happened. I mean, why Bryce? Of anyone in the entire world, why him?"

"I don't know."

She barely heard him. "I spent years trying not to wonder what would have happened had he just stayed in intelligence, or had I moved to Washington, D.C., after he graduated. I tried not to imagine what our lives might have been like, or where we would have lived, or how many kids we would have had, or the vacations we would have taken. I think that's another reason why I jumped at every travel gig I could get. It was an attempt to leave those obsessive thoughts behind, but I should have known that never works. Because we always bring ourselves with us wherever we go. It's one of the universal truths of life."

Mark lowered his gaze to the table. "I'm sorry I asked you to finish the story. I should have listened and let you end it with the kiss on the beach."

"I know," she said. "That's how I've always wanted to end it, too."

As the clock continued its countdown to Christmas, their conversation gently drifted from one topic to the next. Maggie was thankful that Mark hadn't pressed further about Bryce; he seemed to recognize how painful the topic was for her. As she described the years that followed Bryce's death, she marveled that the strands that informed so many of her decisions always stretched back to Ocracoke.

She described the estrangement from her family that occurred when she moved away; her parents had never given much credence to her love for Bryce, nor did they grasp the impact of his loss. She confessed that she hadn't trusted the man Morgan had chosen to marry, because she'd never seen him gaze at Morgan the way Bryce had gazed at her. She talked about the growing resentment she felt toward her mother and her judgmental pronouncements; often, she found herself reflecting on the differences between her mom and Aunt Linda. She also spoke about the dread she felt on the ferry to Ocracoke when she finally worked up the courage to visit her aunt again. By that time, Bryce's grandparents had passed away and his family had moved from the island to somewhere in Pennsylvania. During her stay, Maggie had visited all the places that had once meant so much to her. She'd gone to the beach and the cemetery and the lighthouse and stood outside the house where Bryce once had lived, wondering if the darkroom had been converted into a space more suitable to the new owners. She was rocked by waves of déjà vu, as though the years had rolled backward, and there were moments when she almost believed that Bryce might suddenly round the corner, only to realize it was an illusion, which reminded her again that nothing turned out the way it was supposed to.

At some point in her thirties, having consumed too many glasses of wine, she'd Googled Bryce's brothers to see how they'd turned out. Both had graduated from MIT at seventeen and were working in the tech world—Richard in Silicon Valley, Robert in Boston. Both were married with children; to Maggie, though their photographs showed them to be grown men, they would always remain twelve years old.

As the clock's hands inched toward midnight, Maggie could feel the exhaustion overtaking her, like a storm front rapidly approaching. Mark must have seen it in her face because he reached over to touch her arm.

"Don't worry," he said. "I won't keep you up much longer."

"You couldn't even if you tried," she said weakly. "There comes a time now when I just shut down."

"You know what I was thinking? Ever since you started telling me the story?"

"What?"

He scratched at his ear. "When I think back on my life—and granted, I'm not all that old—I can't help thinking that while I've had different phases, I've always just become a slightly older version of me. Elementary school led to middle school and high school and college, youth hockey led to junior hockey and then high school hockey. There were no periods of major reinvention. But with you, it's been just the opposite. You were an ordinary girl, then you became the pregnant you, which altered the course of your life. You became someone else once you returned to Seattle, then cast that person aside when you moved to New York. And then transformed yourself again, becoming a professional in the art world. You've become someone entirely new, over and over."

"Don't forget the cancer version of me."

"I'm serious," he said. "And I hope you're

not taking it the wrong way. I find your journey to be fascinating and inspiring."

"I'm not that special. And it's not as though I planned it. I've spent most of my life reacting to things that happened to me."

"It's more than that. You have a courage that I don't think I have."

"It's not courage as much as survival instincts. And hopefully learning some things along the way."

He leaned over the table. "You want to know something?"

Maggie gave a tired nod.

"This is the most memorable Christmas I've ever had," he stated. "Not just tonight; the entire week. Of course, I also had the chance to listen to the most amazing story I've ever heard. It's been a gift and I want to thank you for that."

She smiled. "Speaking of gifts, I got something for you." From her handbag, she pulled out the Altoids tin and slid it across the table. Mark scrutinized it.

"Did I have too much garlic?"

"Don't be silly. I didn't have the time or energy to wrap it."

Mark lifted the lid. "Flash drives?"

"They have my photographs on them," she said. "All of my favorites."

His eyes widened. "Even the ones in the gallery?"

"Of course. They're not officially numbered, but if there are any that you particularly like, you can have them printed up."

"Are the photos from Mongolia there?"

"Some of them."

"And *Rush*?"

"That one, too."

"Wow..." he said, gently lifting one of the drives from the box. "Thank you." He put the first drive down, lifted the second reverently, and put it back. Touched the third and fourth ones, as though making sure his eyes weren't deceiving him.

"I can't tell you how much this means to me," he said solemnly.

"Before you think it's too special, I'll probably do the same thing for Luanne in the next month or so. Trinity too."

"I'm sure she'll love it as much as I do. I'd rather have this than one of Trinity's pieces."

"You should take the Trinity piece if he

offers it. Maybe sell it and buy yourself a nice-sized house."

"Yeah," he agreed, but it was clear his mind was still on the gift. He peered at the photos displayed on the walls around him before shaking his head in what looked like wonder. "I can't think of anything else to say except thank you again."

"Merry Christmas, Mark. And thank you for making this week very special for me, too. I don't know what I would have done had you not been so willing to humor my whims. And, of course, I'm looking forward to meeting Abigail, too. I think you said she's coming out on the twenty-eighth?"

"Saturday," he said. "I'll make sure she comes to the gallery on a day when you're here."

"I don't know if I'm going to be able to give you the whole time off while she's here. I can't promise anything."

"She understands," Mark assured her. "We also have a full Sunday planned and we have New Year's Day, too."

"Why don't we close the gallery on the thirty-first? I'm sure Trinity won't mind."

"That would be great."

"I'll make it happen. As a boss who understands the importance of spending time with the people you love, I mean."

"Okay," he agreed. He closed the lid of the Altoids tin before looking up at her again. "If you could have anything you'd like for Christmas, what would that be?"

The question caught her off guard. "I don't know," she finally offered. "I guess I'd say that I'd like to turn back the clock and move to Washington, D.C., right after Bryce graduated. And I'd beg him not to join the special forces."

"What if you couldn't turn back the clock? What if it's something in the here and now? Something that was actually possible?"

She considered it. "It's not really a Christmas wish, or even a New Year's resolution. But there are certain…closures that I'd like while I still have time. I want to tell my mom and dad that I understand they always did what they thought was best for me and how much I appreciate all their sacrifices. I know that deep down, my parents have always loved me and been there for me, and I want to thank them for that. Morgan too."

"Morgan?"

"We may not have had much in common, but she's my only sister. She's also an amazing mother to her daughters, and I want her to know that in a lot of ways, she's been an inspiration."

"Anyone else?"

"Trinity, for all he's done for me. Luanne for the same reason. You. Lately, it's become very clear to me with whom I want to spend my remaining time."

"How about a last trip somewhere? To the Amazon or something like that?"

"I think my traveling days are behind me. But that's okay. I don't have regrets on that end. I've traveled enough for ten lives."

"How about one last feast at a Michelin-starred restaurant?"

"Food tastes bad to me now, remember? I'm pretty much living on smoothies and eggnog."

"I keep trying to think of something else..."

"I'm fine, Mark. Right now, the apartment and the gallery are more than enough."

He stared at the floor, head bowed. "I can't help wishing that your aunt Linda were here for you."

"You and me both," she agreed. "At the same time, I wouldn't want her to have to see me like this, to have to support me in the difficult days ahead. She already did that once for me, back when I needed it most."

He nodded in silent acknowledgment before glancing at the box on the table. "I guess it's my turn to give you your gift, but after wrapping it earlier, I wasn't sure whether I should give it to you."

"Why?"

"I don't know how you'll feel about it."

She raised an eyebrow. "Now you've got me curious."

"Even so, I'm still hesitant to offer it."

"What's it going to take?"

"Could I ask you something first? About your story? Not about Bryce. But you left out something."

"What did I leave out?"

"Did you end up holding the baby?"

Maggie didn't answer right away. Instead, she remembered those frenzied couple of minutes after birth—the relief and exhaustion she suddenly felt, the sound of the baby crying, the doctors and nurses hovering over both of them, everyone knowing exactly what to do. Hazy images, nothing more.

"No," she finally answered. "The doctor asked if I wanted to, but I couldn't do it. I was afraid that if I did, I would never let go."

"Did you know then that you were going to give away your teddy bear?"

"I'm not sure," she said, trying and failing to re-create her thought processes. "At the time it felt like a spur-of-the-moment thing, but now I wonder if I'd known all along that I would do it."

"Were the parents okay about it?"

"I don't know. I remember signing the papers and saying goodbye to Aunt Linda and Gwen and then suddenly being alone in the room with my mom. Everything is pretty hazy after that." Though it was the truth, talking about the baby triggered a thought she'd kept locked away over the years, and now it came rushing back. "You asked me what I wanted for Christmas," she finally went on. "I guess I'd like to know whether all of it had been worth it. And whether I'd made the right decision."

"You mean about the baby?"

She nodded. "Putting a baby up for adoption is scary, even if it's the right thing to do. You never know how it's going to turn out. You wonder if the parents raised the child right, or if the child was happy. And you wonder about the little things, too—favorite foods or hobbies, whether they inherited your physical tics or temperament. There are a thousand different questions and no matter how you try to suppress them, they still sometimes rise to the surface. Like when you see a child holding his parent's hand, or you spot a family eating at the table next to you. All I could do was hope and wonder."

"Did you ever try to find the answers?"

"No," she said. "A few years ago, I toyed with the idea of putting my name on one of those adoption registries, but then I got melanoma and I wondered whether anything good could come of it, given my prognosis. In all candor, cancer kind of takes over your life. Though it would be gratifying to know how it all turned out. And if he wanted to meet me, then I definitely would have wanted to meet him."

"Him?"

"I had a boy, believe it or not," she said

with a chuckle. "Surprise, surprise. The technician was mistaken."

"Not to mention a mother's instincts—you were so sure." He slid the package toward her. "Why don't you go ahead and open it. I think you might need this more than I do."

Intrigued, Maggie stared at Mark curiously before finally reaching for the ribbon. It came free with a single tug and the loosely taped paper came off easily as well. It was a shoe box, and when she finally freed the lid, all she could do was stare. Her breath locked in her throat as time slowed, warping the very air around her.

The coffee-colored fur was matted and pilled; a second Frankenstein stitch had been added to one of the legs, but the original stitch was still there, as was the sewn-on button eye. Her name in Sharpie ink was almost impossible to make out in the dim light, but she recognized her childhood scrawl, and all at once, a wave of memories washed over her of sleeping with it as a child; holding it tight as she lay in her bed in Ocracoke; clutching it as she groaned through labor on the way to the hospital.

It was Maggie-bear—not a replica, not a replacement—and as she gently lifted it from the box, she caught the familiar scent, one strangely unchanged by the passage of time. She couldn't believe it—Maggie-bear couldn't be here; there was no possible way...

She raised her eyes to Mark, her face slack with shock. A thousand different questions flooded her mind, then slowly began to resolve as she grasped the full meaning of the gift he'd given her. He'd turned twenty-three earlier in the year, meaning he'd been born in 1996...Aunt Linda's convent had been somewhere in the Midwest, where Mark had been raised...He'd struck her as strangely familiar...And now she was holding the teddy bear she'd given to her baby in the hospital...

It couldn't be.

And yet it was, and when Mark began to smile, she felt a tremulous smile form in response. He stretched his hand across the table, taking her fingers in his own, his expression tender.

"Merry Christmas, Mom."

MARK

Ocracoke
Early March 2020

On the ferry to Ocracoke, I tried to imagine the fear Maggie felt when she first arrived on the island so long ago. Even for me, there was a sense of trepidation, that I was being drawn into the unknown. Maggie had described the drive from Morehead City to Cedar Island, where the ferry launched, but her description didn't quite capture the remoteness I felt as I passed the occasional lonely farmhouse or isolated mobile home. Nor was the landscape anything like Indiana's. Though misty, the world was lush and green, clumps of Spanish moss hanging from branches that had twisted and gnarled in the unceasing coastal winds. It was cold, the early-morning sky white across the horizon, and the gray waters of the Pamlico Sound seemed to begrudge the passage of any boat attempting the crossing. Even with Abigail beside me, it was easy to understand Maggie's use of the word *marooned*. As I watched the village of Ocracoke grow larger on the horizon, it felt like a mirage that might evaporate. Before my trip here, I'd read that Hurricane Dorian had ravaged the town back in September and caused catastrophic flooding; when I'd seen the news photographs, I wondered how long it would take to rebuild or repair. Of course, I was reminded of Maggie and the storm she'd experienced, but then lately, most of my thoughts had been preoccupied with her.

On my eighth birthday, my parents told me that I was adopted. They explained that God had somehow found a way for us to become a family, and they wanted me to know they loved me so much that their hearts sometimes felt like bursting. I was old enough to understand what adoption meant but too young to really question them about the details. Nor did it really matter to me; they were my parents and I was their son. Unlike some children, I didn't have much curiosity about my biological parents; except in rare instances, I hardly ever thought about being adopted at all.

At fourteen, though, I was in an accident. I was goofing around with a friend in a barn—his family owned a farm—and I cut myself on a scythe that I probably shouldn't have touched in the first place. I happened to nick an artery so there was a lot of blood and by the time I reached the hospital, my face was almost gray. The artery was stitched and I was given blood; it turned out that I was AB-negative, and obviously, neither of my parents had the same blood type. The good news is that I was out of the hospital by the following morning and pretty much back to normal soon after. But for the first time, I began to wonder about my birth parents. Because my blood type was relatively rare, I occasionally wondered if my mother's and father's were rare as well. I also wondered if there were any other genetic issues of which I should be aware.

Another four years passed before I brought

up the subject of my adoption with my parents. I was afraid of hurting their feelings; only in retrospect did I realize they had been expecting the conversation ever since they'd sat me down on my birthday so long ago. They explained to me that the adoption had been closed, that court orders were probably necessary to open the files, and it was unclear whether I would prevail if I went that route. I might, for instance, be able to learn necessary health information, but nothing more unless the birth mother was willing to allow the records to be unsealed. Some states have a registry for just such a thing—those who are adopted and those who offered a child for adoption can both agree that they'd like the records to be unsealed—but I couldn't find evidence of such an option in North Carolina, nor did I know if my birth mother had sought one out. I assumed I was at a dead end, but my parents were able to provide enough information to help me with the search.

They'd learned several facts from the agency: that the girl was Catholic and the family didn't believe in abortion, that she was healthy and under a physician's care, that she was doing her schoolwork remotely, and that she was sixteen when she delivered. They also knew she was from Seattle. Because I was born in Morehead City, the adoption had been more complex than I'd realized. To adopt me, my parents had to move to North Carolina in the months preceding my birth in order to establish state residency. That knowledge wasn't important to learning Maggie's identity, but it underscored how desperate they'd been to have a child and how much they—like Maggie—had been willing to sacrifice in order to give me a wonderful home.

They shouldn't have known Maggie's name, but they did, partly by circumstance, partly by Maggie's design. In the hospital, one had to pass through the maternity ward to reach the nursery, and it had been a quiet night at the hospital when I was born. When my parents arrived, only two of the maternity rooms were occupied, and one of those hosted a Black family with four other children. The other room, however, bore the name *M. Dawes* on a small placard near the door. In the nursery, they were also given the teddy bear, which had the name *Maggie* scrawled on the bottom of its foot, and all at once, they pieced together the name of the mother. It was something neither of my parents would ever forget, although they claimed never to have discussed it again, until they finally had the conversation with me.

My first thought was the same as probably everyone my age: Google. I typed in *Maggie Dawes* and *Seattle* and up popped a biography of a well-known photographer. Obviously, I couldn't be certain then that she was my mother, and I scoured the rest of her photography website without luck. There were no references to North Carolina, no references to marriage or children, and it was clear that she now lived in New York. In her photograph, she looked too young to be my mother, but I had no idea when the portrait had been taken. As long as she hadn't been married—and taken her husband's name—I couldn't rule her out.

There were links on her website that connected to her YouTube channels and I ended up watching a number of her videos, a habit I continued even while in college. Though most of the technical information in her videos was incomprehensible to me, there was something captivating about her. I eventually uncovered another clue. In the background of the work studio in her apartment hung a photograph of a lighthouse. In one of her videos, she even referenced it, noting that it was the photograph that first inspired her interest in the profession back when she was a teenager. I froze the video and took a picture, then Googled images of North Carolina lighthouses. It took less than a minute to figure out that the one on Maggie's wall was located in Ocracoke. The nearest hospital, I also learned, was in Morehead City.

Though my heart skipped a beat, I knew it still wasn't enough to be absolutely certain. It wasn't until three and a half years ago, when Maggie first posted that she had cancer, that I became convinced. In that video, she noted that she was thirty-six, which also meant that she'd been sixteen years old in 1996.

The name and age were right. She was from Seattle and had been in North Carolina as a teenager, and Ocracoke seemed to fit as well. And, when I looked hard enough, I thought I even noted a resemblance between us, though I admit that might have been just my imagination.

But here was the thing: while I thought I wanted to meet her, I didn't know if she wanted to meet me. I wasn't sure what to do and I prayed for guidance. I also began to watch her videos obsessively—all of them—especially the ones about her illness. Oddly, when discussing cancer on camera, she radiated a kind of offbeat charisma; she was honest and brave and frightened, optimistic and darkly funny, and like a lot of people, I felt compelled to keep watching. And the more I watched, the surer I was that I wanted to meet her. In no small way, it felt as though she'd become something akin to a friend. I also knew, based on her videos and my own research, that remission was unlikely, which meant I was running out of time.

By then, I'd graduated from college and had begun working at my dad's church; I'd also made the decision to further my education, which meant taking the GRE and applying to graduate schools. I was fortunate enough to be accepted at three terrific institutions, but because of Abigail, the University of Chicago was the obvious choice. My intention was to enroll in September of 2019, like Abigail, but a visit to my parents changed all that. While I was there, they asked me to move some boxes into storage; after hauling them to the attic, I came across another box. It was labeled MARK'S ROOM, and curious, I lifted the lid. There I found some trophies and a baseball mitt, folders filled with old school-work, hockey gloves, and numerous other keepsakes that my mom hadn't had the heart to throw out. In that box, alongside those items, was Maggie-bear, the stuffed animal that shared my bed until I was nine or ten years old.

The sight of the bear, and Maggie's name, made me realize again that it was time to make a decision about what I really wanted to do.

I could do nothing, obviously. Another option was to surprise her in New York with the information, perhaps have lunch together, and then return to Indiana. That's what I assume many people might have done, but it struck me as unfair to her, given what she was already living through, since I still had no idea whether she even wanted to meet the son she'd long ago given up for adoption. Over time, I began to consider a third option: perhaps I could fly to New York to meet her, without informing her who I was.

In the end, after much prayer, I chose the third option. I initially visited the gallery in early February, tagging along with a group from out of state. Maggie wasn't there, and Luanne—trying to distinguish between buyers and tourists—barely noticed me. When I stopped by the gallery again the following day, the crowds were even larger; Luanne looked harried and barely able to keep up. Maggie was absent again, but it slowly began to dawn on me that beyond having a chance to meet Maggie, I might be able to help her at the gallery. The more I thought about it, the more the idea took hold. I told myself that if I eventually had the sense that she wanted to know who I was, I would reveal the truth.

It was a complicated matter, though. If I received a job offer—and I didn't even know whether a job was available at that time—

I would have to defer graduate school for a year, and though I assumed Abigail would accept my decision, she likely wouldn't be happy about it. More importantly, I needed my parents to understand. I didn't want them to think that I was somehow trying to replace them or didn't appreciate all they had done for me. I needed them to know that I would always consider them my parents. When I returned home, I told them what I'd been considering. I also showed them a number of Maggie's videos about her battle with cancer, and in the end, I think that's what did it. They, like me, knew I was running out of time. As for Abigail, she was more understanding than I expected, despite the wrench it threw in our longstanding plans. I packed my bags and returned to New York, unsure how long I would stay and wondering whether it would work out. I learned everything I could about Trinity's and Maggie's work, and eventually brought my résumé to the gallery.

Sitting across from Maggie during my interview was the most surreal moment of my life.

Once I was hired, I found a permanent place to live and deferred graduate school, but I'll admit there were times when I wondered whether I'd made a mistake. In my first few months, I barely saw Maggie, and when we did cross paths, our interaction was limited. In the autumn we began to spend more time together, but Luanne was often with us. Strangely, though I'd wanted to work in the gallery for personal reasons, I discovered that I had an aptitude for the job and eventually came to enjoy it. As for my parents, my dad chose to refer to my work as "a noble service"; my mom simply said she was proud of me. I think they anticipated that I wouldn't be home for Christmas, which was why my dad arranged the trip to the Holy Land with members of the church. While it had always been a dream of theirs to go, I think there was a part of them that didn't want to be at home during the holidays if their only child wasn't around. I tried to remind them frequently of my love for them, and how much I'd always cherish them as the only parents I ever knew or wanted.

After Maggie opened her gift, she asked me countless questions—how I'd found her, details about my life and my parents. She also asked me whether I wanted to meet my biological father. She might, she speculated, be able to offer enough information to get me started on a search, if that's what I wanted. Though my curiosity had originally been piqued because of my rare-ish blood type, I realized that finding J didn't interest me in the slightest. Meeting and getting to know Maggie had been more than enough, but I was nonetheless touched by her offer.

In time, Maggie grew so exhausted that I accompanied her on her cab ride home. After helping her inside, I didn't hear from her again until midafternoon. We spent the rest of Christmas Day together at her apartment, and I finally got to see the photo of the lighthouse firsthand.

"This photo changed both our lives," she mused out loud. I could only agree.

But in the days and weeks after Christmas, I realized that Maggie didn't really know how to be my mother and I didn't know how to be her son, so for the most part we simply became closer friends. Though I'd called her Mom when I gave her the teddy bear, I reverted to Maggie after that, which felt more comfortable to both of us. She was nonetheless thrilled about meeting Abigail, and the three of us had dinner together twice while she was in town. They got along well, but when Abigail enveloped Maggie in a goodbye hug, I noted that Maggie was growing smaller with each passing day, the cancer stealing away her substance and heft.

Right before the new year, Maggie posted the video that updated her prognosis, and then contacted her family. As she'd anticipated, her mom pleaded with Maggie to return to Seattle, but Maggie was unequivocal about her intentions.

Once Luanne returned from Maui, Maggie filled her in regarding both her prognosis and my identity. Luanne, who insisted she'd known something was up all along, informed Maggie that we needed to spend as much time together as possible, so she promptly scheduled my vacation. As the new manager—both Maggie and Trinity agreed she was the obvious choice—it was her decision, and it allowed Maggie and me the time we needed to fill in any blanks we hadn't yet shared about our lives.

My parents came to New York in the third week of January. Maggie wasn't bedridden yet, and she asked to speak to the two of them privately as she sat on the couch in her living room. Afterward, I asked my parents what they'd discussed.

"She wanted to thank us for adopting you," my mom said with barely restrained emotion. "She said that she felt blessed." My mom, toughened by the confessions associated with her profession, seldom cried, but in that instant she was overcome, her eyes brimming with tears. "She wanted to tell us that we were wonderful parents, and that she thought our son was extraordinary."

When my mom leaned in to hug me, I knew what had touched her most was that Maggie had referred to me as *their* son. For my parents, my decision to come to New York had been more difficult than I'd realized, and I wondered how much secret turmoil I'd caused them.

"I'm glad you were able to meet her," my mom murmured, still holding me tight.

"Me too, Mom."

After my parents' visit, Maggie never made it to the gallery again, nor was she able to leave her apartment. Her pain medication had been increased, administered by a nurse who came by three times a day. She sometimes slept up to twenty hours at a stretch. I sat with her during many of those hours, holding her hand. She lost even more weight and her breathing was ragged, a wheeze that was painful to listen to. By the first week of February she was no longer able to rise from her bed, but in the moments she was awake, she still found a way to smile. Usually, I did most of the talking—it was too much effort on her part—but every now and then, she would tell me something I didn't know about her.

"Do you remember when I told you that I wanted a different ending to the story of Bryce and me?"

"Of course," I said.

She gazed up at me, the ghost of a smile playing on her lips. "With you, I got the ending that I wanted."

Maggie's parents came to stay in February, settling in at a boutique hotel not far from Maggie's apartment. Like me, her mom and dad simply wanted to be close to her. Her dad remained quiet, deferring to his wife; most of the time, he sat in the living room with the television tuned to ESPN. Maggie's mom occupied the chair near the bed and wrung her hands compulsively; whenever the nurse arrived, she demanded explanations for every adjustment to Maggie's pain medicine, as well as other aspects of her care. When Maggie was awake, her mom's constant refrain was that what was happening wasn't fair, and she repeatedly reminded Maggie to pray. She insisted the oncologists in Seattle might have been able to do more and that Maggie should have listened to her; she knew someone who knew someone who knew someone else who also had stage IV melanoma but was still in remission after six years. She sometimes lamented the fact that Maggie was alone and had never gotten married. Maggie, for her part, endured her mother's anxious nattering patiently; it was nothing she hadn't heard her entire life. When Maggie also thanked her parents and told them that she loved them, her mom seemed nonplussed that Maggie felt she'd needed to say those words at all. *Of course you love me!* I could picture her thinking. *Look at all I've done for you, despite the choices you made in your life!* It was easy to understand why Maggie found her parents draining.

Her parents' relationship with me was more complicated. For nearly a quarter of a century, they'd been able to pretend that Maggie had never been pregnant at all. They treated me warily, like a dog that might bite, and kept both physical and emotional distance. They asked me little about my life but overheard quite a bit when Maggie and I were talking, since her mom tended to hover whenever Maggie was awake. When Maggie asked to speak to me alone, Mrs. Dawes always left the room in a huff, which only made Maggie roll her eyes.

Because her children were young, it was harder for Morgan to visit, but she made it out on two separate weekends. On her second visit in February, Maggie and Morgan spoke for twenty minutes. After Morgan left, Maggie briefed me on their conversation, cracking a wry smile despite her now-constant pain.

"She said that she'd always been jealous of the freedom and excitement of my life." Maggie gave a weak laugh. "Can you believe that?"

"Absolutely."

"She even claimed that she often wished we could trade places."

"I'm glad the two of you were able to talk," I said, squeezing her birdlike hand.

"You know what's craziest, though?"

I raised an eyebrow.

"She said it was hard for her growing up because our parents always favored me!"

I had to laugh. "She doesn't really believe that, does she?"

"I think she does."

"How could she?"

"Because," Maggie said, "she's more like my mom than she realizes."

Other friends and acquaintances visited Maggie in the final weeks of her life. Luanne and Trinity came by regularly, and she gave them both the same gift she'd given me. Four different photo editors also swung by, along with her printer and someone from the lab, and during these visits I heard more stories about her adventures. Her first boss in New York and two former assistants made appearances, along with Maggie's accountant and even her landlord. For me, though, all of those visits were painful to watch. I could see her friends' sadness as they entered the room, could sense their fear of saying the wrong thing as they approached the bed. Maggie had a way of making all of them feel welcome, and she went out of her way to tell them how much they'd meant to her. To each of them, she introduced me as her son.

Somehow, in the few periods I wasn't around her apartment, she also made arrangements for a gift for Abigail and me. Abigail had flown out again in the middle of February, and as we sat on the bed, Maggie said that she'd prepaid for a safari to Botswana, Zimbabwe, and Kenya for Abigail and me, a trip that would last more than three weeks. Both of us insisted it was too much, but she waved off our concerns.

"It's the very least I can do."

We both hugged and kissed and thanked her, and she squeezed Abigail's hand. When we asked her what we might expect to see, she regaled us with stories of exotic animals and camps located in the wilderness, and as she spoke, there were moments when she seemed exactly like her old self.

Still, as the month wore on, there were times when her illness was unbearable for me, and

I'd need to leave the apartment and go for a walk to clear my head. As grateful as I was to get to know her, part of me felt greedy for more. I wanted to show her around my hometown in Indiana; I wanted to dance with her at my wedding to Abigail. I wanted a photograph of her holding my son or daughter, joy shining in her eyes. I hadn't known her long, but at some level I felt as though I knew her as intimately as I knew Abigail or my parents. I wanted more time with her, more years, and in the stretches when she slept, I sometimes broke down and wept.

Maggie must have sensed my grief. When she woke, she offered a tender smile.

"This is hard for you," she croaked out.

"It's the hardest thing I've ever had to go through," I admitted. "I don't want to lose you."

"Do you remember what I said to Bryce about that? Not wanting to lose someone has its roots in fear."

I knew she was right, but I wasn't willing to lie to her. "I am afraid."

"I know you are." She reached for my hand; hers was covered in bruises. "But never forget that love is always stronger than fear. Love saved me, and I know it will save you, too."

They were her very last words.

Maggie passed away later that night, near the end of February. For her parents' sake, she'd arranged for a service to be held at a nearby Catholic church, even though she'd insisted on being cremated. She met the priest only once before she passed, and per her instructions, he kept the service brief. I delivered a short eulogy, though my legs seemed so weak that I felt like I would topple over. For the music, she chose "(I've Had) The Time of My Life," from the movie *Dirty Dancing*. Her parents didn't understand the choice, but I did, and as the song played, I tried to picture Bryce and Maggie sitting on the couch together on one of her final nights in Ocracoke.

I knew what Bryce looked like, just as I knew how Maggie had looked as a teenager.

Before she passed, she'd given me the photographs that had been taken so long ago. I saw Bryce holding the plywood as he was about to board up a window; I saw Maggie kissing Daisy's nose. She wanted me to have them because she thought that I, more than anyone, would appreciate how precious they were to her.

Strangely, they were almost as precious to me.

Abigail and I arrived in Ocracoke on the morning ferry, and after getting directions, we rented a golf cart and visited some of the places Maggie had described in her story. We saw the lighthouse and the British Cemetery; we drove past fishing boats in the harbor and the school that neither Maggie nor Bryce had attended. After asking around, I even found the site of the shop where Linda and Gwen once made biscuits; it now sold tourist trinkets. I didn't know where either Linda or Bryce had lived, but I drove every street and knew I must have passed by both of their houses at least once.

Abigail and I had lunch at Howard's Pub, then eventually made our way to the beach. In my arms, I carried an urn containing some of Maggie's ashes; in my pocket was a letter that Maggie had written to me. Most of her remains, in another urn, were with her parents in Seattle. Before she'd passed away, Maggie had asked me if I would be willing to do her a favor, and there was no way I could say no.

Abigail and I walked down the length of the beach; I thought of the many times Maggie and Bryce had been there together. Her description had been accurate; it was austere and undeveloped, a stretch of shore untouched by modernity. Abigail held my hand, and after a while, I brought us to a halt. Though there was no way to be certain, I wanted to pick a place where Bryce and Maggie might have had their first date, a place that somehow felt right to me.

I handed the urn to Abigail and pulled the letter from my pocket. I had no idea when she'd written it; all I knew for sure was that it was on the small table beside her bed when she'd passed away. On the outside of the envelope she had scrawled instructions, asking me to read it when I was in Ocracoke.

Opening the flap, I pulled out the letter. It wasn't long, though the writing was scratchy and sometimes difficult to decipher, a consequence of medication and weakness. I felt something else fall out as well, catching it in my hand just in time—yet another gift to me. I took a deep breath and began to read.

Dear Mark,

First, I want to thank you for finding me, for becoming my wish somehow made true.

I want you to know how special you are to me, how proud I am of you, and that I love you. I've told you all of these things before, but you must know that you've given me one of the most beautiful gifts I've ever received. Please thank your parents and Abigail for me again, for allowing you the time we needed to get to know, and love, each other. They, like you, are extraordinary.

These ashes represent what's left of my heart. Symbolically, anyway. For reasons I don't have to explain to you, I want them spread in Ocracoke. My heart, after all, has always remained there. And, I've come to believe, Ocracoke is an enchanted place, where the impossible sometimes becomes real.

There's something more I've been longing to tell you, though I know it will seem crazy at first. (Maybe I am crazy at the present time; cancer and drugs wreak havoc on my thoughts.) Yet I do believe what I'm about to tell you, no matter how far-fetched it sounds, because it's the only thing that seems intuitively true right now.

You remind me of Bryce in more ways than you know. In your nature and your gentleness, in your empathy and charm. You look a little like him, and—perhaps because you were both athletes—you also move with the same fluid grace. Like Bryce, you are mature beyond your years, *and as our relationship has deepened, these similarities have become even more apparent to me.*

This, then, is what I've chosen to believe: somehow, through me, Bryce became part of you. When he took me in his arms, you absorbed a piece of him; when we spent our sweetest days together in Ocracoke, you somehow inherited his unique qualities. You are a child, then, of both of us. I know such a thing is impossible, but I choose to believe that the love Bryce and I felt for each other somehow played a role in producing the remarkable young man I've come to know and love. To my mind, there's no other explanation.

Thank you for finding me, my son. I love you.
Maggie

After finishing the letter, I slipped it back into the envelope and eyed the necklace she had enclosed. She'd shown it to me before, and on the back of the seashell pendant I noted the words *Ocracoke Memories*. The pendant felt strangely heavy, as though it held their entire relationship, a lifetime of love condensed into a few short months.

When I was ready, I put the pendant and letter back into my pocket and gently took the urn from Abigail. The tide was going out and moving in the same direction as the wind. I stepped into damp sand, my feet beginning to sink, and thought about Maggie on the ferry, meeting Bryce for the first time. The waves were steady and rhythmic, and the ocean stretched toward the horizon. Its vastness felt incomprehensible, even as I imagined lighted kites floating in the night-time sky. Above me, the sun was at half-mast and I knew that darkness was coming early. In the distance, a lone truck was parked on the sand. A pelican skimmed the breakers. I closed my eyes and saw Maggie standing in a darkroom next to Bryce or studying at a battered kitchen table. I imagined a kiss when, at least for a moment, everything in Maggie's world seemed perfect.

Now Bryce and Maggie were both gone, and I felt an overwhelming sadness wash through me. I twisted the lid, opening the urn, and tipped it, allowing the ashes to scatter in the outgoing tide. I stood in place, recalling flashes of *The Nutcracker* and ice skating and decorating a Christmas tree before suddenly swiping at unbidden tears. I remembered her rapt expression when she had lifted Maggie-bear from the box and knew I would always believe that love was stronger than fear.

Taking a long breath, I finally turned, walking slowly toward Abigail. I kissed her gently, clasping her hand in mine, and the two of us walked in silence back up the beach together.